A RAMPAGE OF PASSIONS AS DANGER BECAME THE CATALYST FOR COURAGE AND DESIRE

Kit Carson—Legendary frontiersman, now Colonel of the First New Mexico Volunteers and commander of the Indian campaign. He held a Springfield carbine and a nation's future in his hands.

Ted Henderson—Heroic cavalry scout and commander of Fort Laramie. Family and honor demanded his first loyalty . . . and he would compromise neither, though death and disgrace be his fate.

Judy Hubbard—Stunningly beautiful blond wife of Colonel Abel Hubbard. She would become a fallen woman to trap a Confederate spy.

Long Walker—The fierce blue-eyed half-breed warrior. He had dreams of glory that could only be won with the white man's blood.

Emery Church—Army officer and archenemy of Ted Henderson. He was obsessed with two things: his hatred for Indians and his vow to break Ted Henderson.

Wind Flower—Lovely Navajo princess. She would follow the rough-riding Irishman she loved into the white man's world—even if it meant heartbreak.

Bantam books by Donald Clayton Porter

WINNING THE WEST Book I: RIO GRANDE

WINNING THE WEST
Book II

FORT
LARAMIE

Donald Clayton Porter

 Created by the producers of
Wagons West, White Indian, and
Stagecoach.

Book Creations, Inc., Lyle Kenyon Engel, Founder

BANTAM BOOKS
TORONTO • NEW YORK • LONDON • SYDNEY • AUCKLAND

FORT LARAMIE
A Bantam Book / July 1987

Produced by Book Creations, Inc.
Lyle Kenyon Engel, founder

ISBN 0-553-26463-X

Published simultaneously in the United States and Canada

Bantam Books are published by Bantam Books, Inc. Its trademark,
consisting of the words "Bantam Books" and the portrayal of a
rooster, is registered in U.S. Patent and Trademark Office and in
other countries. Marca Registrada. Bantam Books, Inc., 666 Fifth
Avenue, New York, New York 10103.

PRINTED IN THE UNITED STATES OF AMERICA

O   0 9 8 7 6 5 4 3 2 1

FORT LARAMIE

Territory
Yellowstone R.
FORT BERTHOLD
Minn.

Dakota
Belle Fourche River
BLACK HILLS
Cheyenne River
FORT SULLY
Territory
Missouri River
Iowa

Wyoming Country
North Platte River
FORT LARAMIE
2
Niobrara River
4
Nebraska Territory
Platte River
OMAHA

JULESBURG
Platte R.
3
South Platte
DENVER
FORT KEARNY
Republican R.
FORT LEAVENWORTH
FORT RILEY

MOUNTAIN

Colorado Territory
Kansas
WICHITA
FORT SCOTT

FORT GARLAND
Rio Grande
TAOS
GLORIETTA PASS
SANTA FE
ALBUQUERQUE
LLANO ESTACADO
Canadian R.
Indian Territory
Red River

New Mexico Territory
FORT SUMNER
BOSQUE REDONDO
Colorado River
EL PASO
Texas

RAMIE

BOOK CREATIONS INC. 1986

One

Colonel Kit Carson eased his lathered horse to a stop just below the crown of the hill overlooking the Colorado River. His weary sigh tinged with dread, he twisted in the saddle to study the twenty-man cavalry patrol of First New Mexico Volunteers.

Carson noted with pride that not a single trooper slumped in his saddle, despite the constant pounding of the southwest wind, the stinging sand, and the blast-furnace heat of the West Texas summer. Instead, as the patrol halted, the sunburned men automatically reached for the stocks of well-used Springfield carbines.

The slightly built colonel nodded to himself. *Not a recruit in the bunch*, he thought. *They know as well as I do what we can expect over that ridge*. Carson's alert eyes swept the rolling grasslands, the occasional patch of brush. Nothing seemed to move in the broad expanse of wind-whipped prairie. But Kit Carson was not in the least assured. He turned to the grizzled sergeant at his right stirrup.

"What do you make of it, Sergeant Rollins?"

The soldier rolled a quarter-sized wad of tobacco to the other unshaven cheek and spat a stream of amber liquid onto the parched grass. "Don't look good, Colonel Carson," the non-com said. "Them Kiowas we been trackin' made for this spot like the crow flies. Was I a bettin' man, sir, I'd say them folks at the stage station up ahead seen their last sunup."

Carson nodded grimly. "Call for carbines at the ready, skirmish line, Sergeant. Not that I think we're going to be seeing any action down below. But soldiers don't pass age fifty by not being ready, especially where the Kiowa are concerned."

1

Touching his knees to his mount, Carson led the line of soldiers to the top of the ridge. Below, the remnants of the stage station lay in ashes. A coach, gutted by flames, sagged against one charred wall that still stood. Scattered amid the wreckage were the bodies of the victims. Carson swallowed against the bile in his throat as he surveyed the scene for several moments. He dreaded the necessity of inspection and burial. *You never get used to it,* he thought sadly. *No matter how many times you see it, it never gets easy.*

As the column approached the carnage, more than one veteran soldier turned his face away, his stomach churning.

Carson heard the quiet, angry curses of his troops as he knelt to finger a pile of ashes. They were cool.

"How long ago, Colonel?" Sergeant Rollins asked.

Carson let the ashes trickle through his fingers. "A day and a half at least," he said. "Victims?"

"Seven men killed, sir. Tracks say a woman and child taken. No way to identify the dead. Butchered and burned too bad. Burial detail is already at work, Colonel."

The former frontiersman nodded. "We'll move out as soon as the graves are filled."

"Any chance of catchin' them red devils, Colonel?"

Carson shook his head, the hot wind rippling his gray-streaked blond hair, which fell below his sweat-stained hat. "Practically none, Sergeant. But we have to try. Half-rations for the men until further notice."

Rollins moved away, leaving his commander to his own thoughts. The Kiowa were showing all the signs of working up to full-scale warfare, Carson reflected. Before, their targets had been small and isolated ranches, farms, and an occasional wood or water detail of soldiers. But now the Indians were raising their sights toward bigger game. Their war parties were getting larger, too. Carson figured up to a hundred warriors were in the group that had hit this stage station. With the captured guns, as well as horses and mules from the station, the Kiowa war party would be even more formidable.

Reluctantly Carson joined the burial detail, which was finishing its grim task.

Most of the cavalrymen in the patrol had been with him during the Confederate invasion attempt that had been turned back at Glorieta Pass. They had also ridden with him through the Apache campaign and then to subdue the Navajo in the climactic Canyon de Chelly invasion. Three different types of

wars, and now a return to the most difficult of all. The troopers
on this patrol understood the Plains Indian better than most of
the soldiers now in the field. They knew that from birth, the
Plains Indian was trained as a warrior. Fighting was his only
way of life, and fame and wealth came to the bravest of
warriors.

The mutilation of an enemy was not merely a wanton act
of savagery. Though it was an outrage in the white man's
culture, to the Indian it simply made certain that an enemy did
not enter the otherworld as a whole man, perhaps to return
again to take up the lance against his old foes. The Plains
warrior expected no quarter, and he gave none. In his culture
an act of mercy was a display of cowardice. Indeed, the
supreme salute from a war party was the nonmutilation of a
fallen foe who had displayed great courage in battle.

At last there was the signal that the grisly job had been
done.

"Call the patrol to horse, Sergeant Rollins," Carson said.
"Let's see how far we can chase these Kiowa. It looks to me like
the Plains tribes are about to kick the lid off the stove from top
to bottom on the map. It's our job to see that not too many
people get singed."

Carson swung into his own saddle as the soldiers hurried
to their mounts. For a moment the veteran Indian fighter felt a
pang of disappointment at the turn of events. After the Navajo
campaign, he had been promised the post of Indian agent, a
job in which he could work with, instead of against, the
Indians. It would also have had the advantage of being near his
beloved wife, Josefa, and his children at the ranch near Taos.
But it was not to be. The Indians had taken advantage of the
war between the Union and the Confederacy to launch more
and more raids. His services had been needed desperately.
There were too few men available with the experience and the
knowledge to deal with Indian uprisings, and as the war
ground on, there were fewer veteran soldiers to lead.

"Someday," he said to himself, "I'm going to have to learn
to say no and make it stick."

He waved the column toward the north at a walk. The
Kiowa band, apparently flushed with success at the raid on the
stage station, had made no effort to conceal their trail.
According to frontier legend, Carson could read a man's mind
from a bent blade of grass; so he only had to glance at the earth

from time to time to make sure the band had not begun to split up.

Despite the cold trail and the lack of any ambush spot for miles around, Kit Carson remained alert and vigilant. A Kiowa, he well knew, was unpredictable and a master of guerrilla tactics. He recalled the saying among the plainsmen with whom he had ridden so many miles ago, "You frets when you sees 'em, and you frets most when you don't."

Now, he realized, was a time for some heavy fretting. The Kiowa and their cousins, the Kiowa-Apache, had joined forces already. There were signs the Comanche, who alone had spread fear and ashes for years from north of the Red River deep into Mexico, were about to ally with the Kiowa. While none of the three tribes individually could field a significant number of warriors, together they could cast a dark shadow over the southern Plains.

The former frontiersman gazed for a long moment toward the northwest, letting the memories of the cool, high country in the Rocky Mountains wash the West Texas heat from his mind.

Idly he wondered how his friends and former comrades-in-arms to the north were faring. Since the bloody outbreak of the Santee Sioux in Minnesota a couple of years earlier, troubles had been building in the northern Plains.

If any man could keep the lid on the stewpot, Carson told himself, it would be his former second in command in the Navajo campaign, Ted Henderson, now a colonel in the regular army. Henderson had been the man who led a column of the U.S. Cavalry Third Regiment on that impossible winter march from Wyoming to New Mexico to bolster the staggering Union forces in the showdown at Glorieta Pass. There, after destroying an enemy supply train, Henderson and the Third had been the reinforcements necessary to turn the tide in the Union's favor, beating back the Confederates and Texans in their bold bid to cut the Union in half and turn the immense wealth of California to the Rebel cause. Carson readily admitted to himself he would very much like to have the quiet, confident, and competent Henderson at his side during this patrol. But Ted now was in command at Fort Laramie.

Thirty miles northwest of the burned-out stage station, Carson called his saddle-weary patrol to a halt. He dismounted, feeling the stiffness in his knees.

"What's up, Colonel?" Sergeant Rollins asked, swinging

down from his mount to carefully eye the trail. "Looks to me like the sign's getting mighty fresh."

Carson nodded while glancing toward the lowering sun. He knelt, scrutinizing a couple of near-invisible marks in the grass.

"Every Kiowa travels in a certain way," Carson said. "I know the warrior leading this party. His name is Lone Tree. I know where and when he's going to camp—and we have an excellent chance of recovering the captives. Lone Tree is one of the finest warriors I've ever faced, but he has the typical Kiowa trait of carelessness. In all these miles, he's traveled slowly, and he has not set one brave to study the back trail. My guess is he's sure there is no pursuit."

Carson stood. "We'll rest the horses and men here until three o'clock in the morning. Then we'll see if we can't take Lone Tree down a peg or two."

When the horses had been picketed, Carson called his patrol together and outlined his plan. "Be sure of your targets," he cautioned in conclusion. "And keep a sharp eye out. There are no Kiowa women in this party, only warriors. We don't want the captive woman and child shot by our soldiers. The Kiowa will attempt to kill the captives if they have time, so we must hit them hard and fast."

Kit Carson dismissed the cavalrymen to get whatever rest they could. He caught only brief naps himself, watching the stars and listening to the night sounds of the prairie. A sliver of moon overhead and Carson's excellent night vision revealed only the expanse of short grass barely moving as the wind died. The occasional mournful howl of a coyote or whir of a nighthawk's wings reached his ears.

By the time the first pale light streaked the eastern sky, the New Mexico Volunteers were in position. The colonel nodded to himself in satisfaction. As he had suspected, Lone Tree was camped in the shallow depression around Sweetwater Spring near the headwaters of the Colorado River. The confident Kiowa had posted no sentries. No shelters had been erected; each sleeping brave was only a huddled shape.

The slow brightening of the sky brought some stirring to the sleepy encampment below. Carson had little difficulty spotting the woman and child bound at the edge of the camp. The rope with which they were tied was looped around the wrist of a single warrior. Carson knew it would be that brave's duty to make sure the captives did not escape—and to kill them if necessary.

The colonel slipped from his horse, rifle in hand, and knelt. The Kiowa guarding the prisoners stirred and began to rise to his feet. Carson squeezed the trigger.

The slam of the rifle shattered the dawn. Through the flash of flame and smoke from his carbine, Carson saw the brave spin and fall heavily to the earth. At Carson's shot, the remaining troopers, handguns cocked, charged over the hill, yelling.

The camp below erupted. Braves scrambled for their horses and weapons as the cavalrymen swept through the Kiowa, revolvers blazing. As the troopers charged past the Indians, Carson saw one blue-clad figure reach down and slash the rope binding the captives to the dead Kiowa. The trooper swept the pair onto his army mount with him and, according to the plan, continued to ride hard to the south. The remainder of the Volunteers pivoted their horses for a second sweep through the encampment.

Calmly and with a practiced eye, Carson kept up a deadly fire from above. Three Indians went down before his rifle fire, one as he was about to release an arrow into a trooper's back.

Suddenly a soldier's horse stumbled and fell. Its rider expertly kicked free of the stirrups and landed on his feet, firing a revolver almost point-blank into a warrior. Sergeant Rollins checked his own mount and went to the side of the downed soldier, who swung aboard behind Rollins's saddle. In moments the last of the Volunteers had cleared the camp and were beyond the protective ridge.

The horsemen spurred their mounts in a circle to place themselves between any pursuing Indians and the rescued captives. Carson saw one warrior carrying a rifle and running toward the southern edge of the camp. The colonel dropped the Indian with a single shot. Off to his left, the young trooper who had been sent to stampede the Kiowa pony herd emerged safely, chasing after the Indian ponies. Only the few mounts tethered in the camp proper remained for the Indians.

Kit vaulted onto his own big gray gelding, wheeled the horse to the east, and circled the camp at a dead run.

The company had already begun to form again when its commander arrived. A quick count of his men brought a smile to Carson's face. Every trooper was accounted for.

He kneed his gray toward the woman who was seated on a spare army mount, holding her child.

"Are you all right, ma'am?" Carson's voice showed genuine concern.

The dazed woman slowly nodded. "You—you're—American soldiers?"

"Yes, ma'am. First New Mexico Volunteers, Colonel Christopher Carson at your service. If there is anything you need, anything at all, just ask."

"Colonel Carson," the woman said, "my child and I are forever indebted to you. I—couldn't have faced more of what we—I—went through last night. . . ."

Carson touched his hat brim in salute. "Just doing our job, ma'am. Now if you'll excuse me, I wish to check on my men. We'll talk later."

Sergeant Rollins materialized at Carson's side. "Sir, there's a number of Kiowa headed north. Should we follow?"

"No. We've accomplished our objective—to rescue the prisoners and punish the Kiowa. Our horses are almost done in. Any idea about casualties?"

"Rode back for one quick look. 'Bout a dozen Kiowa killed or wounded, near as I can tell. Murphy got grazed by a lance. Nothin' serious. Only injury to our group, sir."

"Excellent, Rollins. My compliments to the men on a superb job. We've turned Lone Tree's triumph into a sad occasion for the Kiowa. There will be much wailing in the camp when he gets back home. Speaking of which, we have a long ride ahead of us. Let's move out. As soon as we're clear of any Kiowa with ideas of glory, we'll call a halt for rest and a hot meal."

Carson turned toward the northwest and looked toward the distant but distinct row of steep hills that marked the beginning of the vast, inhospitable Llano Estacado—the Staked Plains.

The Texas Panhandle and South Plains region was a land where the Indian thrived while the white man struggled against thirst, hunger, cold, and heat. It was said that everything in the Llano Estacado either stuck, stank, or stung, Carson thought, and that assessment was not far from wrong. He knew that even with fresh horses, four times as many men as he now had, and adequate supplies, there would be no catching the Kiowa once they reached the distant hills known as the Cap Rock.

He waved the patrol forward, toward Fort Sumner on the Bosque Redondo Indian Reservation. It was not exactly home, but it was the better of the alternatives.

Many miles to the north, in the Wyoming country, Colonel Ted Henderson pulled his spare Colt Dragoon from a saddlebag, carefully checked the loads in the heavy pistol, then thrust the weapon into his belt.

The sporadic rifle shots seemed so near he could almost feel the balls whiz by. In their own grim way, those rifle shots did spell a measure of hope, Ted thought. At least some members of the besieged wagon train just beyond the low ridge ahead had survived to put up a defense; the soldiers from the Third Regiment had not been entirely too late.

Ted, his face rugged and tan, glanced at the line of blue and buckskin-clad figures of the patrol from Fort Laramie. Ordinarily so few men would not be enough. But these were not ordinary men. All was ready now, and each second's delay meant increased danger for the wagon train survivors. Ted's rangy bay gelding seemed to have shaken off the fatigue of the long, forced march. The lean muscles along the horse's shoulders and neck trembled eagerly. The animal knew the battle was near.

Along the skirmish line, every third man had dismounted, tethered his horse, and was crawling toward the crest of the low ridge. Each of the dismounted men carried a Spencer .56 repeating rifle. Their job was to keep the attacking Indians pinned down until the mounted cavalry could break through and reach the wagon train. The Indians would then be trapped in a deadly cross fire.

Although Ted Henderson had not yet seen the wagon train, he was aware of the situation ahead. Scout Carl Keller's report had been complete—almost down to the last Indian's rifle pit or boulder. Henderson waited a few more seconds until the five-man detail of crack rifle shots had settled into position on the far right flank, where they would have a clear field of fire.

Satisfied that all was in readiness, Ted slammed his spurs into the lean bay. The animal responded by hitting his top speed within four strides.

The blast of the Spencers from the top of the ridge joined the rising thunder of hooves as the Third's skirmish line burst over the top of the ridge and into the midst of the surprised

Indians. Riding low over the neck of his lunging horse, Ted snapped a shot toward a war-painted Indian. The impact of the .45-caliber ball slammed the brave onto his back. The heavy blasts of the Spencers fused with the lighter crack of handguns as the mounted troopers slashed into the Indian positions.

Ted let the battle-wise bay have its head, trusting the animal to make the right moves at the right time. Feeling a tug at his sleeve, he knew a rifle slug had punched through his shirt. He fired at a dodging Indian but saw the dust kick up just beyond the brave's head. Then the Indian staggered and sank to his knees as a round from another cavalryman found its mark.

The bay suddenly swerved, narrowly avoiding a collision with a war-painted body. Ted slashed downward with the heavy pistol, feeling the solid *thump* of the butt strap against bone. To his right he saw a soldier suddenly stiffen in the saddle and grasp his shoulder. But the soldier did not stop; he shifted his revolver to his left hand and put a slug into a brave some twenty yards away.

Then the troopers broke through the ranks of the Indians. Ted brought his mount to a sliding stop by one of the wagons, pulled his carbine from its scabbard, jumped off his horse, and crabbed his way beneath the wagon. Spinning on his belly, he drew a careful bead on a warrior and squeezed the trigger. The running Indian pitched forward. Before the brave had hit the ground, Ted had levered another round into the Spencer.

Only then did he become aware of the teenager beside him. The youth, nearly half Ted's age, had a bloody bandage wrapped around his upper chest.

"God, Colonel, are we glad to see you!" the boy yelled above the din of gunshots.

Other carbines began to crackle from the line of wagons. Caught in the withering cross fire, the Indians broke and ran. Ted and the other soldiers continued to fire at the fleeing Indians, killing several more.

As suddenly as it had begun, the fight came to an end.

Ted turned to the injured youth at his side. "How many dead and wounded do you have, boy?"

"Don't know, sir," the lad answered, "but there's a bunch. And if you'd been an hour later, we'd all be dead. I just loaded my last ball."

A dust-and-smoke pall settled over the battle scene, now quiet except for an occasional shot as a soldier put an end to the suffering of a badly wounded brave. Even the big guns of the long-range riflemen had fallen silent.

Ted squirmed from beneath the wagon and surveyed the scene. The civilians and the Indians had both paid a high price for the attack.

He yelled to a buckskin-clad figure nearby. "Get the dead and wounded aboard any wagons that still work, Carl! We don't want to get caught here if they come back." The scout waved a hand and immediately set to work.

The young man with the bandaged chest struggled from beneath the wagon. He held a knife in one hand.

"Gonna get me an Injun scalp," he said eagerly.

Ted abruptly grabbed the boy's arm and spun him about. "You'll do no such thing! I'll have no member of my party mutilate an enemy, and as of now I am in command of this wagon train! Am I understood?"

The youngster nodded sullenly.

"I know how you feel, boy," Ted said. "But we simply don't do that in the Third. Besides, I need your help in getting what's left of this train rolling again, in a hurry. How bad are you hit? Let me take a look."

"Not too bad, Colonel. It'll keep."

With no surgeon along on the patrol, it was up to the cavalrymen to treat the injured as best they could. Despite the boy's protest, Ted stripped the bandage from the boy's chest and did a bit of emergency patching.

"It'll hurt some on the way, but it isn't likely to kill you. We'll get you proper treatment when we reach Fort Laramie."

Almost two hours went by before Carl Keller signaled that the wagon train was ready to move. The groans of the wounded and the soft crying of those who had lost friends and family in the ambush continued as Ted raised an arm and started the battered train toward Laramie.

Ted, on his tired but game horse, took the position of point scout himself, alert for signs of a returning Indian raiding party. For the moment all was clear. But a long ride lay ahead.

Finally the protective walls of Fort Laramie came into view, and for the first time in almost twenty-four hours, Ted was able to relax. He slumped just a bit in the saddle, watching the escort column of infantry from the fort draw near his own thin line of cavalry and the battered survivors of the wagon train. The North Platte Road ambush would forever remain a nightmare to a lot of people.

The thirty soldiers in blue and a sprinkling of frontiers-men known as Henderson's Scouts flanked each side of the wagon train. Ted was thankful the crack troopers had been available for the rescue mission. They were all seasoned veterans, specially trained and equipped, and although they drew the toughest assignments, the competition for a spot in the elite R Company was fierce among the regulars at Fort Laramie.

It was a constant battle to convince the War Department that experienced soldiers were needed as desperately in the West as they were in the battlefields of the East. So far, Ted's efforts had been successful. He fervently hoped his luck would hold.

Hearing hoofbeats alongside him, Ted glanced at the sweaty, dust-covered ebony giant who had ridden up.

"Colonel Henderson, I never thought I'd be so glad to see home," Sergeant Major Albert Jonas said, swatting a huge hand through a swarm of gnats buzzing about him. "I've had a itch between mah shoulders ever since we rode out."

Ted nodded. "I know the feeling, Sergeant Jonas. A Sioux arrow can spoil a man's whole day. How's Private Edwards doing?"

"Restin' easy, Colonel. Takes more'n a musket ball to stop old Edwards's cussin'. I had to order him into the wagon. He wanted to come in on horseback, just like he left." Jonas shifted his position, flashing a quick grin at his commanding officer. "Don't understand why he was so all-fired determined to come in on horseback. If mah backside wasn't black, it'd sure as heck be blue by now."

Ted smiled. He had lived in the saddle for most of his adult life, first as a mountain man and rancher, then as the most celebrated rider in the entire Pony Express operation. His acclaimed ride with the Third Regiment to the relief of the Union forces had helped turn back the Confederate invasion of the West, and subsequent Indian campaigns with Kit Carson had further toughened him to the saddle. Ted knew that if he himself was tired, even the toughest of the Third must be in almost physical pain. And Ted Henderson was not too proud to admit he was tired.

Despite their exhaustion after a long ride and the brief but hard fight, the soldiers still were alert, rifles at the ready, even in the shadow of the fort gates. No one, red man or white thief, was going to get a shot at the survivors of the ill-fated wagon train.

The lieutenant leading the infantry relief column waved his men into position alongside the wagons, then greeted Ted with a salute.

"Tough time, sir?"

"Bad enough, Lieutenant. We have a lot of wounded civilians, some hurt seriously. Are the surgeons at their post?"

The lieutenant nodded. "Yes, sir. Your wife saw to that, soon as the wagon train was in sight. She's also taken over the refugee center, getting it ready and making some room."

Ted smiled at the mental image of his wife scurrying about, issuing instructions in that soft but persuasive voice—and barking an order when necessary—as the Laramie Women's Relief Unit mobilized to receive the survivors. Part soldier, part nurse, part mother, and all woman; add all that together and you still did not have the complete picture of his Wilma, he decided.

"If I might add, sir," the lieutenant said, "she's a remarkable woman."

At Ted's side the black sergeant threw back his head in a hearty laugh. "Lieutenant," Albert Jonas remarked, "you just said it all. The colonel here's a mighty lucky man, if a mere non-com won't get busted for sayin' so."

Ted clapped the black man's shoulder. Some desk general probably would go into a fit at the lack of decorum between Ted and his men. But desk generals with their stiff necks did not depend on the men next to them, regardless of rank, to keep some Sioux or Arapaho from lifting their well-trimmed hair.

"Sergeant Jonas," Ted said, "would you please pass along my compliments to the men? I plan to do so in person later, but there's still a lot of work to do today. I want them to know that lesser men could not have done what they accomplished."

Leaving the details of the homecoming to the young infantry lieutenant and the veteran sergeant, Ted kneed his mount into a slow trot toward the gates of the fort. Laramie, the major outpost protecting the central Plains, and the keystone to Western travel and supply routes, was rapidly changing from a frontier outpost into a fair-sized town. Only a day had gone by since the patrol had hurried through the gates, yet it seemed the settlement had grown still more.

Makeshift shelters stood alongside the houses built by early arrivals to Laramie. Many of the older settlers had opened their homes to the increasing flow of survivors fleeing the Indian raids, helping ease the pressure somewhat on the refugee camp.

Ted guided his horse through the dusty streets, ignoring the curious crowd that had gathered to watch the ill-fated wagon train rumble in. He skirted the front bastion of the fort and rounded the corner to where the makeshift refugee center already buzzed with activity.

Reining his horse to a stop, he watched in silent admiration as his wife leaned her weight into a rope to help raise a tent—a temporary haven for the refugees.

Wilma glanced up and saw Ted still astride his horse. Even from a distance Ted could see the relief and love in her eyes. He swung down from the saddle, his knees almost buckling at the unaccustomed contact with earth. Slowly he flexed his aching muscles.

Wilma reached him in a half-dozen long, fluid strides and threw herself into his arms. He could feel the moisture on her cheek as she held him close.

"Welcome home, Ted," she said, her voice trembling. "Thank the Lord you're safe."

"It's good to be back, honey." He glanced over her shoulder. "Is everything ready? I'm afraid we've brought you a considerable amount of work this time."

"Work is something to welcome," she said, snuggling for a moment against his shoulder, "especially when you consider the alternative."

"How is little William Ted?"

Wilma's face brightened even more. "Fit as a young colt, our son is. He's staying with the Kellers, probably playing with little Ellen right now. I'll swear, if adults could get along as well as our little white boy and the adopted Arapaho daughter of your scout, we wouldn't have these troubles." Abruptly she released Ted. "But they don't, so we do, and I've got to get back to work. You do, too, Colonel." The sparkle in her eyes belied her scolding tone. "You, sir, will receive your welcome home later—after you're rested up."

Ted, his heart feeling much lighter despite the tension and strain of the past twenty-four hours, swung back onto his horse.

He saluted the officer of the guard at the gate opening onto the Fort Laramie parade ground and tossed the reins to a waiting trooper, who would care for his horse. Then he made his way to the post commander's office. He had neither sought nor asked for command. But when the fates called a man's name, he had to do the assigned job as best he could.

He stepped inside, welcoming the relative cool of the interior, and saluted the officer of the day.

"Afternoon, Major Webber. Is Lieutenant Colonel Hubbard nearby?"

The major shook his head. "No, sir. He's gone on patrol along the Sweetwater River. We've had reports of a growing number of Indians in the area. Colonel Hubbard decided to check it out personally, since he knows the leaders of many tribes in the vicinity."

"I see. Any problems around here?"

"No, sir. Just the usual run-of-the-mill squabbles and petty thefts. Oh—there are a couple of letters for you, sir. Came in by courier yesterday. They are on your desk," Major Webber reported.

"Thank you. When Abel Hubbard returns, will you please ask him to report to me immediately?"

"Yes, Colonel."

A knock on the door made Ted glance up. A young assistant surgeon poked his head head into the office.

"Miss Wilma—uh—Mrs. Henderson—asked me to see if there were some more ointments available at the commissary, sir. A few of the wagon train survivors have bad burns. May I check?"

"Certainly," Ted said. "And do me a favor, will you, please? Would you ask the quartermaster to report to me as soon as possible on our long-range supply situation? Tell him we may need to make plans for a major stores buildup soon."

The assistant surgeon nodded and saluted, then went about his business.

"Colonel Henderson?" Webber cleared his throat.

"Yes, Major?"

"If I may be so bold as to ask, sir—why should we contemplate a heavier-than-usual stockpile of supplies?"

"Of course you may ask, Major. Your scalp could be involved, too." Ted sighed heavily. "The fact is that if Abel Hubbard and I are unable to negotiate a just peace with the tribes of the northern Plains, I fear every fort, ranch house, farm, and wagon train between here and Saint Louis may find itself under a state of siege!"

* * *

Wilma Henderson had to blink rapidly to clear the mist from her eyes as she finished wrapping the bandage around the head of a seven-year-old girl. The child's whimpers of pain gradually subsided as Wilma rocked the girl in her arms.

The surgeon's tunic Wilma wore was spattered with blood, and the stench of burned flesh lay heavily in the air. She paused for a moment and watched as the skilled surgeons repaired what they could among the last of the wounded.

At her right, a young woman sat on a campstool and moaned softly. Wilma studied her for a long moment: The woman was staring blankly into space, her eyes fixed on some point in the distant horizon. She had not spoken since her arrival on the wagon train from the North Platte.

An aged woman, wrinkles deep around blue eyes filled with pain and despair, approached and placed an arm over the moaning woman's shoulders. She glanced up at Wilma.

"My daughter-in-law," the older woman said. "She seen her husband—my son—shot full of arrows not forty feet from our wagon." Tears trickled down her creased cheeks. "Has the good Lord done left us? All we wanted was a fresh start. Lost our farm in Virginny, burnt to the ground, 'cause of some fool war we didn't want no part of. Never owned no niggers, didn't plan to own none, but it didn't make no never mind to them sojers. They shot my man down when he put up a fight to save the farm."

Her thin shoulders, drooped by years of toil and heartbreak, sagged still more. "And now this pore girl," the old woman said. "It just don't seem fair. My boy gone—ever' cent we had tied up in this here wagon train. Man in Saint Louie said they weren't no danger of Injuns." The blue eyes turned sharp and bitter.

"How's come these here sojers didn't show up when they was needed? They coulda whupped them red savages easy. But they's Union, so I reckon they don't care none what happens to us pore Virginny folk!"

Wilma checked a sharp retort. After what the woman had been through, it would serve no purpose to argue. "They came as soon as they could, ma'am," Wilma said, keeping her voice calm. "My husband was one of them. They were in the saddle within minutes after learning of your plight." She placed the now-sleeping child on a makeshift pallet. "Believe me, you have my deepest sympathies for your loss." She stood, studying the younger woman's vacant face. Then she glanced over the compound, caught the eye of a strikingly beautiful young woman helping a family settle in at their relief tent, and beckoned.

She met Judy Hubbard, the wife of Ted's second in command, Abel, a few steps from the two grieving women. "I have no right to ask," Wilma said, keeping her voice low, "but there is a young woman here who needs your help. She's—suffering from the same condition you went through."

Judy glanced toward the woman on the campstool; her body grew rigid as if she were bracing herself for a trying ordeal. After a long moment she nodded.

"Wilma, I have finally come to terms with what I did a couple of years ago. Because of my stupidity and impulsiveness, I caused my father's death and almost lost my husband—and my mind—afterward. I remember vaguely what I looked like in those weeks when my head was too filled with pain and guilt to be truly rational. The same expression is in those eyes." Judy sighed in sympathy. "I'll see what I can do. Perhaps someone who has been through it all can reach past that curtain of grief," she said, her words tight with memory.

Wilma watched Judy walk slowly toward the young woman and her mother-in-law. Judy knelt before the young woman and began to talk softly.

Wilma felt a lump return to her throat and swallowed hard. "Lord," she said in a soft whisper, "I know I ask a lot from You, especially considering my own past. But, please, give Judy the strength and the words to go with her newfound courage. Work through her to reach that unfortunate girl."

Then she turned and slowly began to make her way to the Kellers' to pick up her son, leaving Judy to face her own personal demons once more in the hopes of helping a stranger.

Wilma swept a sweat-sticky strand of dark hair from her forehead. Impulsively she glanced back over her shoulder before going out the door. The young woman was speaking with Judy. And as Wilma watched, the refugee collapsed into Judy's arms. Wilma's spirits soared. At least one battle had been won today! Now she knew for sure that the spoiled, impulsive, and flirtatious young girl Judy Hubbard had been was no more. In her place stood the woman Judy Hubbard—mature, courageous, still beautiful, and finally at peace with herself and the tragedy of the past.

Making her way down the street, Wilma wondered if she

herself would have such strength. To her left, blacksmiths and wheelwrights worked on the scorched wagons from the ill-fated wagon train, pirating parts from those beyond repair to fix those that could be returned to service.

Her mind occupied with the details of preparing dinner for little William Ted and easing the fatigue of her husband, Wilma was unaware of the whispered conversation between two women behind her.

"Is that her? The woman who used to run the bawdy-house?" The speaker, a thin, waspish woman who was new to Laramie, spoke with the sting of censure.

The matron at her side turned quickly. "Don't you *ever* refer to Wilma Henderson that way again," she warned ominously. "You newcomers don't know her. I was here when Wilma opened her— business. At the time us early settlers thought like you do. But believe me, that woman has proved herself, and I'll tolerate no snippy remarks about her. Is that understood?"

The thin woman flushed in anger, spun on a heel, and strode off. The older woman stood for a moment, watching Wilma stride away. She had not bothered to explain, for the newcomer would hear the story soon enough, how Wilma had pulled Ted Henderson from drink-sodden grief after his first wife and daughter had been butchered by Confederate agents; how she had abandoned her oath never to have anything to do with men personally, sold her brothel, and married the former Pony Express rider; how she had fought off Indians at her new husband's side; and how she had picked up a shotgun and almost single-handedly saved young Judy Hubbard from a band of Arapaho Indians barely a mile from Fort Laramie. Also, she faced with dignity the most difficult task of a soldier's wife—watching him ride off to battle, not knowing when or if he would return.

The older woman shook her head in silent admiration. Along the frontier, Wilma Henderson's exploits were becoming almost as legendary as those of her husband. "Gossipy Johnny-come-latelies," the woman snorted. "Can't get it through their giggly heads just how important that woman is to this country, and her past be damned."

Lieutenant Colonel Abel Hubbard slumped in a straight-backed chair alongside Ted Henderson's cluttered desk in the commanding officer's quarters. The feeble rays of the setting sun filtering through a window emphasized the lines in his youthful face.

Ted studied his second in command and knew that Abel's frown was not one of exhaustion. Though he was Ted's junior by several years, in his midtwenties, the one-time prospector and Pony Express rider could match Ted's own tolerance for saddle fatigue. Besides, Abel's patrol had been brief in terms of normal Fort Laramie patrols, only two days, and the horses were still as fresh as the group of soldiers who had returned only moments ago.

"You look worried, Abel," Ted said. "Something afoot out there?"

Abel nodded. "I'm afraid so. I know you've been without rest for over twenty-four hours, so I'll keep this as brief as possible. I'll fill in the details later.

"Right now the Plains Indians are walking a narrow trail between peace and all-out war. As you well know, the Santee Sioux who escaped Sibley's roundup after the outbreak in Minnesota two years ago have been talking warpath with all the other Sioux tribes in the territory from here to the north. From the increasing number of attacks lately, it's obvious they're meeting with some success."

Abel stood, walked to a window, and inhaled the cool air. "Now, talk of war has spread to some of the Cheyenne, Arapaho, even the Ute camps. The southern Plains tribes already have gone on a rampage."

Ted wiped a hand across his eyes, feeling the fatigue and sleeplessness there like small grains of sand that would not go away. Despite his physical exhaustion, he immediately grasped the ominous meaning behind Abel's brief report.

"If all those tribes quit squabbling among themselves and decide to go after the whites, we're going to be in the middle of a prairie fire," Ted said.

The young man turned from the window and fixed his gaze on Ted. "From what I hear from the camps in this area, some outside force is working toward just that end."

"Confederate sympathizers?" Ted asked sharply.

"So it would appear. I thought after we had hit the Confederate supply ring so hard at the raid on the Belle Fourche a few months back, we would have seen the end of them," Abel said. "But I suppose that was just wishful thinking on my part. As long as the Confederacy stays alive, they have everything to gain, and little to lose, by stirring up Indian trouble on this frontier." Abel sighed. "At any rate, we did cut off the trade in guns and ammunition long enough to bring a sort of uneasy peace here around Laramie."

Ted absently fingered a pen lying amid the clutter on his desk. "I'm afraid you may be right, Abel," he said. "There were both Sioux and Cheyenne warriors in the party that hit the wagon train on the North Platte Road. Plus, it didn't seem to be the usual hit-and-run raid. The Indians had the train under attack for quite a while, or we would never have reached the site in time to engage any warriors."

Ted briefly recounted the events of the short, intense battle and summarized the casualties: thirty members of the wagon train killed or seriously injured, ten braves killed in the surprise attack plus seven killed before the troops arrived, and only one military man wounded.

"We were outnumbered three to one, Abel, but when the Indians saw they were up against the Third, they broke off the battle in a hurry."

The door of the office suddenly burst open, and small feet pounded across the floor. Little William Ted Henderson clambered up in his father's lap and nestled down contentedly. A moment later, Wilma peered into the office.

"Sorry, Ted," she said. "When he found out Daddy was home, he caught me napping and made a beeline for your office."

Abel grinned broadly. "It's all right, Wilma. I don't think a two-year-old—even little Wild Bill here—is going to be much of a threat to military security. Ted, you go on home and get some rest. I'll wrap up here."

Ted nodded as he rose, hoisted the child up on his shoulders, and placed his free hand around his wife's waist.

The trio was halfway home when Ted heard his name called.

"Sorry to bother you, Colonel Henderson," said a slightly built corporal, his uniform still dusty from a long ride. "But I have a problem I need your help on."

"Of course, Bernie. What is it?"

Bernie Christian, who had been among the first of the galvanized Yankees—former Confederate soldiers who volunteered for duty with the Union forces rather than remain prisoners of war—twisted his campaign hat in sweaty fingers. Twice decorated for bravery in action since joining the Third, young Christian had squelched all suspicions about his allegiance and earned the respect of the whole regiment.

"One of the horses, sir. I'm afraid he's got wind-broke during this last patrol. You know how I feel about my horses, Colonel"—Ted had to suppress a smile since the corporal considered every horse in the regiment his—"and I was wondering, do we have to destroy him?"

Ted pondered the question for a moment. It was a painful but pragmatic procedure to destroy horses unfit for duty. Yet there were exceptions to every army rule. "Use your own judgment, Bernie. If the horse has served well, retire him to pasture."

Christian's face lit up with a huge grin, despite eyes bloodshot from exhaustion. "Thank you, Colonel."

The corporal started toward the stables but turned at Ted's call. "Bernie—what horse is it?"

"Old Widowmaker, sir."

"Why didn't you say so in the first place, Corporal?" Ted asked somewhat sharply.

Christian swallowed. "Because, sir, I didn't want any personal feelings to influence your decision."

"Spread the word, Bernie. If any civilian or any military man below the rank of commander in chief—the President himself—touches that horse, he will deal with me personally."

"Yes, sir. I'll watch out for him myself," replied an obviously relieved Christian as he hurried about his business.

The Hendersons walked a few steps in silence. Then Wilma said softly, "Old Widowmaker was Frank Armbrister's favorite mount, wasn't he?"

"Yes, he was."

The colonel and his wife made the rest of the trip home in silence. Both of them were thinking about the former Pony Express comrade of Ted's. Frank Armbrister had risen to the rank of sergeant major before being cut down in a heroic one-man charge in the Canyon de Chelly battle against the Navajo. Though it cost Frank's life, he had broken up a renegade Navajo ambush and saved more than a dozen lives. He had been the first Medal of Honor winner in the ranks of the Third Regiment.

"Ted," Wilma said, swinging open the door to their home, "would it have made a difference if you had known the horse was Old Widowmaker to begin with?"

"Without question. Close friends and good horses are

rare. Frank never lived to see retirement, but his favorite mount certainly will." Ted swung William Ted down from his shoulders to the floor.

Wilma impulsively kissed her husband's cheek.

"What was that all about?" the surprised colonel asked.

"For Old Widowmaker. For Frank's memory. And for being the kind of man you are, Ted Henderson. Loyal to friends and the soldiers under your command. That's why they follow you wherever you lead. You said a moment ago that good horses and close friends are hard to find. I'll expand on that: Good husbands and good commanders are even more rare."

Ted sank heavily into his favorite overstuffed chair, letting the fatigue slip from his shoulders. Little William Ted reached out and touched a finger to one of his father's eyes.

"Is Daddy tired?"

Ted put the youngster on his lap and held him close. "Yes, Wild Bill. Daddy is tired."

"Can't we play?"

"How about tomorrow, son?"

The child nodded solemnly, showing no disappointment.

"You rest, Daddy. We play later." William Ted slid from his father's lap and soon busied himself with some wooden chips in the corner of the room.

Wilma was filled with tenderness and warmth as she surveyed the scene: her husband nodding in his favorite chair as their son built a make-believe fort from the small pieces of kindling in the woodbox. Ted had been away to the south, fighting alongside Kit Carson, when their son had been born. Wilma remembered her agonized concern over how the two would react when Ted once more rode home to the child, who had been almost a year old by then. But her worries were groundless. Now the bond between them seemed closer than most father-son relationships.

In Wilma Henderson's mind, the cloud on this scene of bliss was Ted's growing unrest over the state of affairs on the Plains.

She crossed to his chair and awakened her husband with a gentle kiss on the forehead. "You had better stretch out on the bed, dear," she said with a soft smile. "Even a legend has to rest sometime."

* * *

The return of Kit Carson's patrol, with the woman and child rescued from the Kiowa, caused a brief stir in Fort Sumner, but interest soon faded as Carson turned the massacre survivors over to the wife of the harried Indian agent. The agent's wife shooed away the curious and took the pair beneath her own mothering wings with the promise to care for them until safe escort could be provided for a continuation of their interrupted journey.

Carson had barely settled into his rough headquarters at Fort Sumner when the rugged, muttonchop-whiskered face of General James Carleton appeared in the open doorway. The intense, craggy face bore a rare grin.

"Hello, Kit," Carleton said, stripping a riding glove from an oversized hand. "How is my number one Indian fighter?"

Carson came to his feet, warmly greeting the former commander of the California Column and architect of the Navajo campaign.

"Good to see you again, General," Kit said, "but I'm a little surprised to see you out this way."

The smile faded from the general's face. Kit Carson realized that this was no social visit and that there would be no time spent reminiscing over their experiences against the Apache and Navajo.

James H. Carleton was a working officer, not a political one, and seldom given to small talk. As Kit expected, the general went straight to the heart of the matter.

"Kit, I have a job for you," he said, settling into a rawhide chair near Carson's desk. "It's a difficult assignment—almost an impossible one, in fact. That's why I came in person." General Carleton produced a thick packet from beneath his uniform tunic and tapped the bundle against his palm. "This is the plan for bringing the Plains Indians under control from border to border. I need you, with your experience and understanding of Indians, to play a major role. It's always been my thinking that the best man available should be offered command when the road ahead looks rocky."

Carleton waved a hand as Carson tried to speak. "Let me say now that you may refuse the assignment if you wish. God knows, Kit, you've done enough for your nation already—and no one will think the less of you should you refuse."

The ex-frontiersman nodded. "I appreciate being given the option. Now, what's the job?"

A few minutes later, Kit Carson leaned over a map, allowing himself a mental whistle as he evaluated the proposal.

"In summary," Carleton was saying, "you would be in overall command of the Indian campaign of almost half the southern portion of the Missouri Valley and southern Plains from the Republican River in Kansas all the way to the Mexican border. With Colorado, New Mexico, and Arizona territories thrown in for good measure, in case you get bored."

Carleton jabbed a finger at Fort Laramie. "In the northern area, we have two Indian campaigners who have almost reached your own stature, Kit. The Dakotas and the Nebraska, and Montana territories would be left to the overall command of Colonel Ted Henderson, whom we both know well from the Apache and Navajo campaigns. I understand his second in command, a lieutenant colonel named Abel Hubbard, has earned himself quite a reputation as an Indian fighter. I've never had the pleasure of meeting Hubbard myself, but I've heard nothing but good things of the man."

Carleton placed a weathered hand on the packet he had brought. "It falls somewhat short of ideal from a military standpoint," he said, "because there is so much territory for each commander to cover, few experienced Indian fighters, thin supply lines, and mostly green troops who have yet to see a feather, let alone the man behind the bow.

"Yet," the general continued, "we still have an outside chance to bring peace to the whole of the Missouri Valley and the mountain states—with the right people at the reins. The one thing we don't need right now is some Indian-hater or glory-hunter stirring up the tribes still more. You have the credentials. So do Henderson and Hubbard."

"Have they been informed of the proposal?" Carson asked.

Carleton shook his head. "Not yet. I was hoping you would take it upon yourself to inform them."

Carson scratched an ear as he idly scanned the map. "We'll need centralized bases of operations," he said. "For the southern campaign, Fort Garland in south-central Colorado would seem to me most logical. And Fort Laramie is well located on the major roads to the north."

"Does that mean you will accept the assignment?" Carleton asked.

The former frontiersman sighed. "I had hoped to be able to hang up my pistols and saber soon. But you're right,

General. This country is a powder keg, and we need people who won't light the fuse. Yes, I'll do it—or at least try. I'll begin preparations immediately to move my headquarters to Fort Garland, then call on Henderson and Hubbard to ask their help. Perhaps, if we're lucky, we can head off any major Indian wars and see that the red man gets as good a deal as we can manage."

"Excellent, Kit!" Carleton said with a rare display of emotion. "I was hoping against hope you would take the job."

Kit Carson breathed a heavy sigh. "Plans on paper are one thing, General. Human beings are another, and sometimes neither has a blessed thing to do with each other. But I'll do the best I can."

"That," General Carleton said, "is all that could be asked of any soldier, or any man. Now that this is settled, I can be on my way."

"General, I'd offer you a drink, but I don't use liquor or keep it on the post," Kit said. "If there's anything else I can offer you . . ."

Carleton shook his head. "I've got all I came for, Kit—the man I needed to take over an impossible job and do it."

With Carleton's promise to provide all the support possible still in mind, Kit Carson began the tedious, detailed process of preparing to move a military command from one headquarters to another.

He—and most of the men of the First New Mexico Volunteers who had been stationed at the Bosque Redondo—would not be especially unhappy to ride from this place, Carson thought. Few of the soldiers had remained indifferent as the Navajo and Apache tried to adapt to their new home. But the Navajo in particular suffered. Expert farmers in their own right, the Navajo valiantly struggled to adopt the white man's agricultural methods. Unfortunately, even the weather seemed to conspire against them. Carson knew how a move to an alien land and alien culture could send any human being staggering. It would be the same thing as moving him and the other mountain men lock, stock, and grubsack to some place as hostile as New York or Chicago or Saint Louis and expecting them to survive and prosper.

No, Carson thought, *I don't think many of my boys will mind moving even if it does mean possible fighting ahead.* Leaving the details of mobilizing the troops to junior officers and non-coms, he puttered about his quarters gathering his personal items. They were few. He believed in caring for his own equipment and so was in the process of oiling the stirrup leathers of his saddle when someone knocked at the door.

At Kit's call a massive frame almost blocked out the light in the doorway. It was Lieutenant Kevin O'Reilly. "Come in, Lieutenant," he called.

O'Reilly saluted his commanding officer, then removed his campaign hat as he stepped inside, still limping a bit from the wound he had suffered in the Canyon de Chelly invasion. Kit noticed that O'Reilly was crushing and twisting the hat in his massive hands, a sure sign that something was bothering the lieutenant.

"Something on your mind, Lieutenant O'Reilly?"

"Colonel Carson, sir—I hate to ask, but—"

"Go ahead, son. The only thing a soldier should ever hate to ask is 'where did the bullet come out?'" the colonel said encouragingly.

"Well, sir, you know about Wind Flower and me. . . ."

Carson knew the story well; it had become almost a legend on the frontier: how an Irish soldier had twice saved the life, and finally the honor as well, of the daughter of the late Chief Gallegos, perhaps the bravest warrior among the Navajo; how the Irishman, though himself wounded, had searched for her during the four hundred or so miles of the painful Long Walk from Navajo country to the Bosque Redondo reservation; and finally, how Kevin O'Reilly had slain a renegade Indian about to attack the young woman.

"I am familiar with your predicament, Lieutenant O'Reilly. Do you wish to stay behind, to be near her, instead of moving out with the rest of our unit?"

O'Reilly shook his head. "Not exactly, sir." The young officer took a deep breath and plunged on. "Wind Flower has finally consented to marry me, Colonel. The Navajo have chosen new leaders, and she feels her work here is now done. I—want to resign my commission, marry Wind Flower, and make a life outside the service."

Kit leaned back in his chair, wiping the oil from his fingers with a rag as he let the stirrup of the saddle drop.

"Well, Lieutenant," he said, slowly standing—which put the top of his head somewhere near O'Reilly's shoulder, "I really hate to lose a good officer. But congratulations, and of course your request will be honored." Kit stuck out a hand still a bit slippery with oil and found it almost swallowed in

O'Reilly's massive fist. "I'd like to attend the ceremony if it's performed before we move out."

Relief flooded O'Reilly's face. "Certainly, Colonel. The ceremony will be tomorrow night, and Wind Flower and I would be honored by your presence."

"Kevin, are you fully aware of the problems you and Wind Flower may face?" Carson asked. "In the old days, you know, it wasn't unusual for a man to take an Indian to wife. But times are changing, and feelings are growing stronger on both sides."

O'Reilly nodded emphatically. "Yes, sir. We expect an occasional cactus in the garden. We've spent many hours talking about just such things. We believe we can handle it." The broad Irish face, which still tended to sunburn even after such a long time in the wind and weather, seemed to redden a bit more. "After all, Colonel, we love each other very much. . . ."

Carson waved a hand. "Kevin, don't ever feel embarrassed for saying you're in love. Especially to her—and tell her often. There may be times it's all you will have to see you past the rough spots. You've chosen a strong and beautiful young woman. Take good care of her."

"You can count on that, sir."

"What are your plans, if I may be so nosy as to ask? How will you make your living, if not in the army?" Carson smiled ruefully. "Soldiering really isn't a trade worth much in the outside world."

With the most difficult question now settled, Kevin O'Reilly seemed almost anxious to talk. "I've been in touch with Colonel Henderson, sir. You know, he owns a ranch in Wyoming, but he had to abandon the place when hostilities broke out. And what with his army duties and all, he's never managed to get back to ranching.

"Sir, we Irishmen are said to be stubborn enough to farm anything, and I know enough about horses and cows to make a ranch go. Colonel Henderson has agreed to let Wind Flower and me operate his ranch in return for a small share of the profits—if we make any."

Carson nodded. "I know Ted's place. Knew it even before he found it. It's a prime ranching spot. But there will be problems. While it's a good, well-built, and easily defended house, it *is* isolated. You could have trouble with Indian or white raiders—or even with those who just hate Indians."

"We're aware of the dangers, sir. And I think it's worth the gamble. When Colonel Henderson wants his place back, we should have enough money to buy our own. I've saved some already—where would a soldier on the frontier spend money if he doesn't gamble or drink?"

Carson smiled. "Then it's all set, Kevin. Except for one thing. As of sundown today, you will no longer be in the First New Mexico. From that point on, I would like to be addressed as 'Kit'—not 'sir,' or 'colonel,' just as a friend. Agreed?"

"Yes, sir." O'Reilly grinned broadly and started for the door. "Colonel Carson," he said turning back, "I hope you don't think I dislike the army. It has been my lot for a few years, and not many soldiers have had the honor of serving under commanders such as General Carleton and yourself, sir. I've learned a lot more than just how to fight. . . ." The words trailed off rather helplessly.

Carson slowly raised his right hand in salute. "Thank you, Lieutenant. You're a top-notch soldier. If the ranch doesn't work out, you'll always have a place in any command of mine. Now, begone with you, Irishman. Go tell your pretty bride-to-be that you have my personal blessing for a long and fruitful life together."

Kit grinned at the sudden, happy whoop that came a few seconds after the young officer walked from the office. There were times, he thought, when a man could be excused from being "an officer and a gentleman."

Thinking about the happy couple, he settled back to work on the saddle. For a moment he felt a strong pang of loneliness at the separation from his own dark-haired Josefa. He wondered what she and the kids were doing at the moment—chores, play, or studies? At least, he consoled himself, with the change of command posts, he could spend a few days with his family.

Colonel Kit Carson had attended society weddings in Santa Fe and short ceremonies in lonely frontier outposts, yet he still was impressed with the stark simplicity and reverence of the Navajo wedding that took place the next day. The small, dark, and serenely beautiful Wind Flower stood beside the strapping Irishman amid the uplifting chants of the Navajo women. When the ceremonial blanket was draped across both their shoulders, Kit seemed to feel physically a benevolent presence in the air.

The newlyweds made their way to the temporary lodge that had been set aside for their nuptial night, she with the proud carriage of the daughter of the powerful war chief Gallegos, he attempting to restrain his exuberance at finally capturing the one prize that had eluded him for so long.

"Walk in happiness, my friends," Kit Carson said softly, "and do not hold it against me that I envy you your youth."

The door flap of the wedding lodge closed, and the chants of the Navajo women grew soft and lovely against the night. The ancient wishes and prayers for the new couple gradually faded, and the wedding party quietly dispersed.

Carson remained seated for a few moments, the solemn tenderness of the occasion again having stirred memories of his beloved Josefa. He hoped that the legend that had begun with the romance of the chief's daughter and the Irish lieutenant would continue to grow, a frontier love story played out amid the tragedy and drama of war and personal conflict.

In ex-lieutenant Kevin O'Reilly's final army pay envelope, his colonel had placed a gift of a hundred dollars. Despite the dangers they faced, Kit felt in his heart that the couple would survive and prosper in their new venture.

If I must lose a fine young officer, he thought, *I would much rather lose him to love than to anything else.*

Many farewells were said the next morning, for Carson and the members of the First New Mexico Volunteers had found new friends at the Bosque Redondo—not only among the Navajo, but also among the truculent Apache.

At the head of the assembled column, Kit Carson said his good-byes to Kevin O'Reilly and his new wife. Before signalling his own troops forward, he watched for a moment as the couple rode alone in the direction of Fort Laramie and a new life.

"Watch over them, Ted Henderson," he said to himself. "If, that is, the Indians around Laramie give you time."

He wiped the first few drops of the day's sweat from his neck with a kerchief. Colonel Ted Henderson was apt to be doing some sweating of his own, he thought. For Laramie would be one tough post to handle if a number of the northern Plains tribes took up the war ax.

Then he raised a hand and signaled his own troops forward to an equally new home and an even more uncertain future.

Two

Sergeant Major Albert Jonas glared at the bearded man on the wagon seat and gritted his teeth in a not-too-successful attempt to control his rising fury. The bearded man stared back, an insolent challenge in the smoke-gray eyes.

Behind the wagon four men sat uneasily astride rangy horses, their eyes darting from the two men up front to the circle of blue-clad troopers surrounding the small party. The civilians carefully kept their hands clear of weapons, painfully aware of the muzzles of army carbines slung casually across the pommels of saddles or resting in the crook of elbows.

"For one last time—and I ain't going to ask you again—what are you doin' in Cheyenne country with a wagon?" Albert Jonas's tone of voice left no doubt that he meant business. Still, the bearded man remained defiant.

"Ain't none of the army's concern," the man on the wagon said. "You s'posed to be protectin' white folks, not pointin' guns at 'em. 'Sides, I got a permit to trade with the Injuns." He fumbled in a shirt pocket and produced a ragged piece of paper.

Jonas swung down from the broad back of his big bay, reaching the wagon in two strides. He took the paper, glanced at it, then shook his head.

"I don't know where you got this, Bagley—if that's what your real name is—but you're way out of your trade area. This ain't Kansas." The sergeant handed the sweat-stained paper back to the man on the wagon. "I reckon you won't object if we take a look at these trade goods?"

Bagley's temper flared. "Listen, nigger, you touch one blanket—" He never finished the statement. A ham-sized fist reached up, grabbed Bagley's shirt collar, and yanked him from

29

the wagon. Bagley was a big, solid man, but he was lifted onto his toes by only the left hand of the black man.

"Bagley," Albert Jonas said in a frighteningly soft voice, "I may be a nigger, but I'm damn choosy about who calls me one." He glared into the bearded man's eyes for a moment, then tossed him aside as if he were a rag doll. Bagley tumbled heavily into the dirt.

Jonas flipped the canvas cover from a corner of the wagon bed and rummaged through the contents. He motioned to a nearby cavalryman.

"Smith," Jonas said, "come take a look. Tell us all what we got here."

Smith dismounted, then peered into the wagon. Jonas saw the trooper's unshaven jaw tighten. "Blankets on top," Smith said, "whiskey and guns, powder and ball below." He pulled a rifle from the wagon. "Cap-and-ball Springfield," he said. "Looks like our trader friend here got hold of some army issue rifles."

Jonas snorted in disgust. "Disarm the whole bunch, Smith. Rope 'em together and we'll let Colonel Henderson decide whether to hang 'em or not—"

"Sergeant! Watch out!"

At the cry from the ranks, Albert Jonas spun on a heel, then twisted aside. The knife held in Bagley's big fist nicked Jonas's campaign tunic. Jonas clamped a heavy hand on the teamster's wrist, then slammed a short, choppy right into the side of Bagley's neck. The bearded man grunted as his knees buckled from the impact.

Jonas wrapped his right arm over and then beneath Bagley's knife arm. Grasping his own left wrist with his right hand, he gave a sharp tug.

The trapped elbow snapped loudly, and the civilians all winced. Bagley screamed, then sank to his knees, cradling his broken arm against his body.

Jonas casually turned away. "Wrap 'em up, Smith. Take the ammo and the rifles, then torch the wagon."

He reached down and with one hand hauled the whimpering man to his feet. "And be careful, Bagley, who you call a nigger." He shoved the stumbling man toward the cluster of civilians.

"Any other of you boys get out of line," Jonas said quietly, "you'll be in worst shape than old Bagley here."

Smith had unhitched the team of horses from the wagon and poured one of the kegs of gunpowder into the vehicle. The trooper glanced up at Jonas. "Better get a move on, fellows," he said. "This thing's gonna make a big boom."

From a hundred yards away, Jonas and his patrol, the bound captives in the middle of the group, watched as Smith remounted. He leaned from the saddle for a moment, then spurred his horse hard away from the wagon.

It was a gratifying blast, Jonas thought, watching smoke rise from the rubble, then flatten out on the stiffening breeze. Satisfied the blaze would not spread and trigger a devastating prairie fire, Jonas waved the patrol back toward Laramie.

A short time later, Colonel Ted Henderson stood outside the post hospital, wincing occasionally as an agonized moan drifted through the open windows. Bagley was having a rather bad time of it, Ted thought.

"Think I was maybe too rough on him, Colonel?" Albert Jonas asked.

"I think that under the circumstances your Mr. Bagley came off most fortunately, Sergeant," Ted said. "Your self-control was better than mine would have been."

Jonas shrugged. "When I lie, I want to make it worth my time, so I won't say I didn't want to kill that coyote. But it seems I do get a bit queasy in the belly when I have to blow out somebody's light." He sighed. "If you don't need me for a spell, Colonel, I'd like to check on my men."

Ted clapped the sergeant on a rocklike shoulder. "Sure, Albert. And you did a fine job out there."

"Just another day's work, sir," Jonas said, then turned and walked away.

The post surgeon, Dr. Mason, emerged from the infirmary, wiping his forehead with a cloth. Bagley, his face ashen, followed in the grasp of a guard. The teamster cradled his splinted and bandaged elbow in its sling.

"He's all yours, Colonel, and good riddance," Dr. Mason said.

Ted nodded his thanks to the doctor, then stepped up to Bagley. "Before you head for the stockade, Bagley, there's someone I want you to meet," Ted said. "Follow me, please. And from the expression on your guard's face, I don't think it would be wise to try anything."

Ted knew the guard had lost two good friends to Indians

whose guns had been supplied by traders, and he suspected the guard wanted nothing more than an excuse to plant a slug in Bagley's brain.

The trio made their way to the refugee compound. Ted stopped a dozen strides from where a young girl sat, most of her head swathed in bandages. He pointed toward the girl.

"Her name is Nancy. She is seven years old, Bagley—and blinded for life. Both eyes were shot away, along with the bridge of her nose, by a rifle ball fired by an Indian during an attack on a wagon train. If I could prove that the Indian who fired the shot that disfigured and blinded Nancy had gotten his rifle from you, I would personally execute you right where we stand. This, Bagley, is the harvest innocent people reap from the seeds you sow for profit." Ted turned to the guard. "Take him to the stockade, please." Ted spun on a heel and stalked back to his own quarters.

Wilma was putting away the last of the dinner dishes when her husband entered. She saw the rage simmering in his eyes. She crossed to him, kissing him lightly on the cheek. She had watched his mood darken almost daily in the week since the attack on the wagon train. Yet she had not pushed for a reason. In time, when he was ready, Ted would confide in her, drawing on her strength and advice.

"Where is that horrid man, the one Albert brought in?" she asked.

"Safely locked up," Ted said, placing his hat on a rack of deer antlers near the door. "Unfortunately, there are still scores like Bagley moving among the Indians." He slumped heavily in a chair. "If I didn't know what liquor does to me, I would have one very stiff drink right now."

Wilma felt her heart go out to her husband. He was caught in an almost impossible situation, and she knew even the strongest of men could cope with only so much.

"What will become of this Bagley?"

"He'll stand trial," Ted said, "but not here. Even scum like that deserve a fair hearing, and he certainly wouldn't get one here in Laramie. I'll send him under guard to Fort Leavenworth, along with the statements of Albert Jonas and the other members of the patrol."

Wilma busied herself at the stove, and soon the aroma of steeping tea filled the room. She had discovered that while Ted preferred the flavor of coffee, he enjoyed hot tea, and it seemed to make his nights less disturbed by bad dreams.

"Wilma, I'm confused," Ted said, his voice heavy. "I don't know if I'm on the wrong side, the right side—or even if there *is* a right and wrong in these Indian troubles. Both sides, red and white, have wronged and been wronged. Both have broken promises and committed unspeakable, inhuman outrages against the other. Perhaps," he said, sighing, "I'm unfit for a command such as this."

"Nonsense," Wilma said instantly. "Few men have such a complete understanding of the Indian's thinking and his culture as you do. Few have such a grasp of the forces at work here in the West." She poured tea into fine porcelain cups, handing one to Ted and sitting next to him.

"One thing I know, Ted Henderson—there is no better man to tackle a distasteful and frustrating job. Since I've known you, there has been only one time that you've tried to run from a problem. And I just can't see you doing that again."

A rapid patter of small feet on the walk outside was followed by the slam of the door closing. Little William Ted Henderson burst into the room and started toward his father, almost vaulting into Ted's lap. Ted hugged the child close, ignoring the usual accumulation of dirt picked up by any active boy.

At times, Wilma thought, the youngster seemed to physically resemble his namesake, the late Colonel William "Wild Bill" Robinson. The child bore no blood relation to the former commander of the Third Regiment, but sometimes a certain glint in his eye, a determined set of his jaw when the blocks would not stack right, conjured up a vision of the colonel.

Wild Bill Robinson's death had left a void in all their lives. It had been the colonel who had first treated Wilma as a lady instead of the owner of a Laramie house of ill repute. Both Ted and Abel Hubbard, Robinson's son-in-law, obviously had been influenced by the colonel's approach to soldiering. The two officers led instead of ordered and had little use for military politics, and they each had a deep concern for the welfare of the common soldier. Like Robinson, they were bulldogs on the trail, almost tireless in the saddle, and seldom given to impulsive action where battles were concerned. Perhaps,

Wilma concluded, the colonel could not have left a better legacy.

"Bath time, Bill," she said to the youngster, who made a face in reply.

Ted found himself chuckling at his son despite the problems and uncertainties that whirled in his brain. *Leave it to a child to put things in perspective*, he thought. *If the world were riding on the brink of disaster, the thought of a bath was even worse*. He rumpled his son's hair as he kissed a gritty cheek. Ted wondered what the future held for his son. Being a soldier had its drawbacks, but few civilians knew the simple joys of life better than the military man. A man who knows he might not see the sun set again cherishes the quiet moments with loved ones.

Ted watched contentedly as Wilma poured a pail of hot water into the washtub that served as Bill's bath and tested the temperature with an elbow. She brushed a strand of hair from her forehead, then turned and held out her hands to the child.

Bill, the expression on his face a miniature duplicate of a man bound for the gallows, reluctantly climbed from his father's lap and crossed the room to his mother.

Moments later, the well-soaped youngster was playing with a sponge and giggling. Wilma finished washing Bill and left the child to play his water games. Drying her hands on her apron, she returned to her chair at Ted's side.

"Wilma, I think it might be wise for you and Bill to go back East for a time," he said seriously. "If I can't talk some sense into the skulls of both the red man and the so-called leaders of the United States government, we could be facing an all-out, no-quarter war in the Plains. If the Indians do combine forces, they could be more than my small command can handle. There could even be a danger of direct attacks on Fort Laramie." He paused for a deep breath.

Wilma shook her head emphatically. Her deep violet eyes reflected the determination that had carried her through numerous crises. "Where you are, that's where we will be," she said firmly. "We're a family now, and a family we will remain. We exchanged vows to share the good and the bad, and we will do exactly that, Ted. I'll hear no more talk of separation in this house!"

Ted's answering sigh was one of relief, it seemed to

Wilma. It was as though he had asked the question he feared to ask but had heard the answer he wanted to hear.

He reached over and gently pulled her to him. Their kiss was soft at first, then deepened as Ted felt the warmth of his own desire answered in her lips. Finally, reluctantly, he drew back.

"I love you, Wilma. I hope you don't get tired of my saying it."

Wilma's eyes sparkled. "Never, Ted. Never."

A loud giggle from the washtub interrupted the moment but not the mood. "Our audience seems to have finished his bath," Wilma said. Her voice dropped to a seductive whisper. "It's Wild Bill's bedtime, and I love you very much. Think we should build him a little sister?"

Ted's eyebrows lifted in surprise. "I didn't know you wanted another baby."

Wilma's wink bordered on outright lechery. "I wouldn't mind, of course. And with you, my rugged lover, I would certainly enjoy trying. . . ."

Ted grinned. "Do I still have my choice of any woman in your house?"

She nodded. "Of course. If you see one that suits your fancy."

He placed a playful finger on the end of her nose. "Then I'll take this one," he said, "if the price is right."

"For you, sir, the best of deals. Now if you will excuse me, I will attend to the details of putting my other man comfortably to bed."

Ted watched his wife cross to the bathtub, her mature but firm hips swaying gracefully. *Colonel Henderson,* he told himself silently, *you are one lucky man.*

Later, as Wilma lay relaxed and sated, savoring the cool, gentle breeze drifting through the partially opened bedroom window, she understood fully the reason behind Ted's question about sending them back East.

Ted's nightmares had been returning: the suppressed but unforgettable scene of the carnage in the ranch house, the shock of finding his beautiful blond wife and daughter, Crissie, brutally butchered. Wilma knew that part of Ted's concern for his new family was based on his fear of losing them, too.

As she drifted toward sleep, Wilma vowed to redouble her efforts to keep their son—and herself—from harm's way.

Even a man as strong as Ted Henderson had weaknesses. *And if a man had to have weaknesses,* she thought, *devotion to and love of his family were the most excusable.*

Dawn was still two hours away when Wilma felt Ted slide quietly from the bed. He dressed in the dark, went to the kitchen, and soon the sliver of light from the oil lamp shining beneath the bedroom door was joined by the rich scent of coffee brewing. Wilma stretched languidly—then started at the loud knock on the outside door.

"Colonel Henderson! Come quick, please! The hospital—"

Wilma recognized the voice of the corporal of the guard. She slid from the bed, quickly donned a housecoat, and entered the kitchen as Ted reached for his hat.

"Anything I can do, dear?" she asked.

He shook his head. "I'll be back as soon as possible," he said, giving her a quick kiss before the door closed behind him.

In the post hospital, Dr. Mason was working feverishly over the squirming body of a middle-aged woman. The physician glanced up as Ted entered the room.

"Tomahawk," the doctor said. "Made a terrible mess." He waved a scalpel toward the corner of the building. "Those two brought her in."

Ted turned to the teamsters who sat, faces ashen, on a low bench. "What happened?"

"We come acrost 'em 'bout midnight," one of the men said. "We was travelin' at night cause it's safer and we didn't have no guard. Anyways, we come up on this wrecked wagon. Looked like Injuns hit 'em jist afore sundown. Kilt five, three men, two kids—jist babies—guess they left her for dead, too. We brung her here fast as our mules could travel."

Ted's eyes narrowed. "Any clue as to what tribe?"

"Musta been Sioux," the second man said. "None of the dead ones was cut up, and we heared the Sioux been about where we found 'em."

The colonel nodded his thanks. "If you need fresh animals, you're welcome to replacements from the army herd. Or if you wish, you may stay at Fort Laramie as long as you like."

"Thanks, Colonel," the first teamster said. "I think we'll

jist stick around here a while. Gettin' to be so many Injuns out there I ain't too keen on travelin' without some help."

Ted walked to Dr. Mason's side. He felt his stomach churn at the gory wound on the woman's head. "Can she talk, Doc?"

"Some. Got her full of opium to ease the pain."

"Ma'am? Can you hear me?" Ted asked.

The woman groaned, mumbling something.

"What happened? Was it Indians?" Ted asked anxiously.

"Yes." The woman's voice was so faint he had to lean close.

"Can you tell me anything about them? How they were dressed, were they wearing paint on their faces?"

"One—one blue eyes," the woman muttered. "Never seen—blue-eyed Indian before. No paint. Oh, God—my husband—babies . . ." The woman shuddered, then lay still. The surgeon lowered his ear to her chest, then slowly pulled a blood-spattered sheet over her face.

"Sorry, Ted." Dr. Mason dipped his hands in a nearby pail of water and began scrubbing the blood from his fingers. "Before she went onto the table, she said something about that blue-eyed Indian. Something to the effect that he spoke fluent English, asked for tobacco, and seemed friendly. When he struck the flint onto his pipe, the others hit the wagon."

Ted nodded. He knew most of the prominent chiefs and warriors in the region, but none had blue eyes *and* talked fluent English. Also, the attack had a different flavor from most Sioux raids. *Maybe*, he thought, *we have a new force at work here, perhaps a half-breed renegade or a captive raised as an Indian*. Any warrior of proven status could lead a raiding party, so it would not necessarily have been a chief. He turned to the surgeon.

"You look tired, Doc," Ted said.

Dr. Mason sighed. "Guess I have a reason to be. The whole medical staff is running on coffee and determination, what with all these raids of late. We've lost seventeen patients in the last ten days, and I know of at least forty other people who've been killed by Indians."

Ted put a hand on the surgeon's shoulder. "Go try and get some rest, Doc. I'll see if I can't get some help for you. I'm afraid it will get worse before it gets better."

Outside the hospital, Colonel Henderson drew a deep breath of the cool predawn air, clearing the medicinal smell of the infirmary from his lungs. Of all the jobs in the army, he knew the surgeons had the worst. They lived with the results of war and disease and accident every day, and each death seemed to represent a personal defeat.

He leaned against the corner of a barracks and watched the post come alive to a new day. The eastern sky lightened, and finally the first rays of sun brushed the tops of the high country to the west. Even from such a distance, Ted could make out the snowbanks that defied the hottest of summers in the thin air atop the peaks. The sight triggered a fleeting impulse—to saddle his horse and take to the mountains, where a man had room to think. The army might control his body, and Wilma and the baby had his love, but the mountains still held his spirit.

At the moment he wanted nothing more than an extended hunting trip with the Cheyenne brave known as Yellow Crow. Ted missed the company of his blood brother, the Indian who was also godfather to young William Ted. Sometime soon, Ted promised himself. . . .

Yellow Crow's only visit to the post since their parting at the end of the Navajo campaign had been too brief. Yellow Crow had ridden once more into the mountains and prairies with the declared intention of working toward peace among the varied Indian tribes. While Ted freely admitted his resentment toward the forces of history that were keeping him from riding at the stirrup of his friend and brother, he also admitted that if any one man could convince the Indians that peace was much preferred to war, it would be Yellow Crow.

"Good hunting, brother," Ted said to the distant peaks. "May the spirits smile upon you and your medicine be strong until we meet again."

On the edge of a shallow canyon slicing through a wide plateau between the foothills and the high mountains beyond, Yellow Crow silently nocked an arrow. The stalk had been long, but now the prey was in sight.

The Indian studied the cluster of trees only yards ahead. Keen eyes tracked the almost indistinct ripple of movement among the smaller saplings. Then the underbrush parted. Smooth muscles knotted beneath bronze skin as Yellow Crow drew his bow to its full power, a feat few men could perform. The muted thump of the bowstring sent the arrow on its brief flight. A split second later the Indian grunted in satisfaction as the arrow struck its mark with a *whump*.

The fat mule deer died almost instantly, its heart pierced clean by the driving force of the arrow.

The Cheyenne slung the bow across his shoulders and slid his skinning knife from its sheath. The spirits had guided the arrow well. Bellies would be filled that night.

Yellow Crow raised his eyes to the heavens, intoning the chant that would carry the dead animal's spirit to a land of rich grass and warm suns. Then he expertly field-dressed the prime young buck. Retrieving his palomino gelding from a hundred yards away, the Cheyenne quieted the nervous, snorting animal with a single word. He picked up the two-hundred-pound deer and effortlessly swung it into place behind the saddle.

Unwilling to burden the palomino with a double load, Yellow Crow picked up the reins and led the gelding toward the huddle of tipis in the distance. The Cheyenne's stride was the ground-covering walk of a man as much at home afoot as on horseback. The signs were good that day, he thought. The feel of his medicine was strong. It would be a good day for talk.

Split Hand, chief of the small Northern Cheyenne band, greeted Yellow Crow personally. Though Yellow Crow seldom smoked, he accepted the small sack of tobacco in exchange for the gift of the deer in order not to offend the chief. Split Hand directed the distribution of the meat in the prescribed fashion of a Cheyenne chief. He asked only that a small portion be saved for his own family's use. Then he motioned Yellow Crow inside the tipi.

"What brings my brother to Split Hand's camp?" the chief asked after both men had settled comfortably onto buffalo robes flanking the small fire in the center of the tipi.

"Yellow Crow comes to seek peace between the Cheyenne and the white man."

Split Hand's bushy, graying eyebrows lifted. "The name of Yellow Crow is well know among the many bands of the Cheyenne. Does Yellow Crow come as a Cheyenne or as a messenger of the white man with whom he has ridden?"

"As a Cheyenne," Yellow Crow replied. "The Cheyenne will suffer greatly in a big war with the white man. Split Hand is noted as a famed peace chief. He knows the value of the friendship of the white man and of the danger in having him as an enemy."

Split Hand nodded somberly. "It is true that more can be saved in peace than in war. Yet there are many, more powerful than Split Hand, who pledge to take up the lance. Do we not outnumber the white soldiers? There is talk among the Cheyenne, the Sioux, and the Arapaho, even some of the Ute, that now is the time to strike—to sweep the Plains free of the white disease that spreads across Indian lands. While the white soldiers wear different war shirts and fight a great war among themselves, is it not the time for the Indian to strike?" Split Hand sighed heavily. "These are the arguments for war. Those who would take up the lance say the white man's peace is one that favors only the white man, not the red."

Yellow Crow's face remained impassive. He had heard the same logic in many camps. "There may be a seed of truth in what our people say," Yellow Crow said. "But the whites will not fight each other forever. When their war is ended, they will again join against the Indian. The time to sue for peace is now." Yellow Crow paused for a moment as Split Hand's brow furrowed. Yellow Crow knew Split Hand as a logical man and a proven leader of his people. And though his band might be small, his voice in council was not.

"Is it not better," Yellow Crow asked, "to deal from a position of strength when treating for peace? The whites know of the Cheyenne's bravery as warriors. The Sioux are many, and almost as good as the Cheyenne in battle. Yellow Crow believes they will listen now. But with the change of each season, the chances for a just peace melt as the snows."

The chief picked up a small stick and began tracing random patterns in the ashes at the fringe of the fire.

At length he looked up. "Split Hand finds no flaw in Yellow Crow's thoughts," he said, "for they are those in my own mind. You have spoken with others?"

Yellow Crow nodded. "At this moment Black Kettle and his band are camped in peace along the South Platte, almost within the shadows of the gates of Fort Laramie. They have been well treated. Other bands also have chosen the way of peace. Soon there will be a major council of the Cheyenne. At that council Yellow Crow will plead for peace."

Split Hand's eyes narrowed slightly as he stared for a moment at the warrior. "Does Yellow Crow think the blood brother of a white soldier will be heard at such a council?"

"He will be heard," Yellow Crow said. "The blood brother

Ted Henderson is known as a man of his word. It is Yellow Crow's hope he will be there also. He is a just man. At such a meeting each side shall voice its desires and complaints. Then, perhaps, we will have peace."

Split Hand sighed. "The question will be placed before the band," he said. "If all agree, Split Hand's people will not pick up the war lance. If all agree, he too shall speak for peace at the council."

The chief produced a pipe and offered it to the four winds. "Yellow Crow and Split Hand will smoke," he said, "in the hope that only tobacco will burn on the prairie."

"It is good," Yellow Crow said, accepting the offered pipe. "Blood brother Ted Henderson will be told."

"Yellow Crow rides back to Fort Laramie?"

"Soon. There is much work to be done yet. When the circle is complete and Yellow Crow has spoken with more chiefs of the Northern Cheyenne, he will return to Fort Laramie. It has been too long since seeing the young godson." Yellow Crow smiled through the wisp of smoke from the pipe. "Godson already is two summers old," he said. "It is time for him to learn to ride the pony, Cheyenne-style. At the camp of Black Kettle, Yellow Crow shall trade for a pony worthy of such a fine young warrior."

Wilma Henderson was seated at her dressing table, struggling with an especially rebellious wisp of hair. Finally she regained control of it, then crossed to the closet to lay out her best, and favorite, dress.

It was not often she and Ted could enjoy the luxury of a meal in Vi Robinson's hotel, especially in the company of Abel and Judy Hubbard. Ted and his second in command were seldom on the post at the same time, since one or the other usually was out on patrol.

Wilma slipped into the dress, which was Ted's favorite as well, and allowed herself a touch of vanity. She could still wear the same clothes she owned before the birth of Bill. It had not been easy. She recalled the long walks and extended rides— and the skipped desserts—that had been needed to restore her figure to nearly its original shape. The long rides also had helped keep Ted's prized stallion in shape as well.

She was straightening the fit of the bodice when she

became aware someone was watching her. Ted was leaning against the closed door, an easy smile on his lips, his eyes soft.

"Wilma, I wish I knew how you grow more beautiful every day," he said huskily.

She crossed to him and took her husband in her arms. "Perhaps, sir," she said, "your evaluation is slightly tainted from too many days in the saddle miles from any white women. But I thank you." She kissed him, long and deep, enjoying the man-smell of horse and sweat and gunpowder. Then she playfully pushed him away. "I will thank you, sir, to keep your hands to yourself until after dinner. I have invested too much time sprucing up the product to have it spoiled so casually. Besides, you could do with a shave."

Ted reluctantly agreed. He went to the kitchen to heat water, and Wilma soon came in with his fresh uniform.

"Ted," she said after a short silence, "we're going to have to make it a point to see more of Vi Robinson. I'm afraid we sometimes take her strength for granted when really we ought to be supportive of her."

Ted nodded. "You're right, of course," he said. "She's a remarkable woman and has always been a good friend to us. Not many women could go through what she did and still not be bitter. She provided a valuable service to the Pony Express, running the relay station when her first husband drank himself into a stupor and later, when he was killed by Confederates. Then to be widowed a second time so soon after—"

"Yes. When Colonel Robinson was killed and Judy's mind deserted her as a result, I think we all leaned on Vi for emotional support. I don't know where she finds the strength." Wilma handed her husband a towel, shaving mug, and razor. "Vi seems to have bloomed once more since she was made manager of the Laramie Hotel. I'm glad Mr. Russell built a hotel in Laramie as well as Denver and asked Vi to be in charge."

"William Hepburn Russell never forgets a friend or a promise," Ted said between swipes with the razor. "And it has paid off for him, too. Since Vi took over the hotel, it has become one of the most famous between Saint Louis and Sacramento." He wiped the last of the lather from his chin and slipped into a fresh uniform.

Within moments they were strolling the busy main

thoroughfare, headed for the hotel. The growing tension in the countryside was apparent on the streets of Fort Laramie.

Most of the civilians, Ted noticed, carried weapons of some sort, ranging from ancient muzzle-loaders to shotguns and modern repeating rifles, and most had revolvers thrust into waistbands as well. Here and there an Indian from one of the peaceful bands or allied tribes went about the business of trading. The Indians ignored the not-infrequent, hostile stares of some civilians who could not tell one tribe from another. Ted reminded himself to call on a few of the merchants the next day; he had heard the Indians were being cheated in certain establishments, and he would not tolerate such actions. As post commander he had the power to enforce equal treatment of the red man or ask the proprietor of the offending business to take his wares elsewhere.

Judy and Abel Hubbard already had arrived when the Hendersons reached the Laramie Hotel. Vi Robinson greeted them warmly, a firm handshake for Ted and a brief embrace for Wilma.

"Your table is ready and waiting," she told them. "Ted, you have your choice tonight of pot roast, broiled prairie chicken, or prime elk steak."

Ted sighed contentedly. "Just one more decision to make," he said, smiling at Vi. "And I thought I had left all those problems behind for the day. If the meal is up to your usual standards, Vi, I may wind up having two of each."

Protesting that business was too brisk for her to join them except for coffee and dessert, Vi led the two couples to a table before the big bay window. There they would have an excellent view of the town outside, yet enjoy relative privacy. Vi Robinson, Ted noted, was not a conventionally beautiful woman, but she was very attractive. Her slim but womanly figure, expressive eyes, and quick smile drew admiring glances from the men around the room.

But it was Judy, Vi's stepdaughter, who almost brought conversation to a halt as they made their way across the room. The indigo gown, demure by her former standards, clung to a marvelous figure and perfectly contrasted with her rich blond hair and fair skin. The color of the dress seemed to deepen the natural blue of her eyes. Ted saw that one guest in particular was studying Judy a bit more openly than could be considered polite. Judy's husband noticed, too, and a thinly veiled warning in Abel's glance sent the guest's attention back to the food on his plate.

Ted hoped that one day his friend would learn to cope with the problems that being married to a beauty brought. In the field he was an excellent commander, always planning ahead, and he was a tactical master at Indian fighting. But where Judy was concerned, Abel's temper was short. Ted sometimes wondered if his friend had completely forgiven his wife for her childlike, innocent escapade with Colin Dibley. She had not known that Dibley was a Confederate agent. Thinking Dibley's motives were only chivalrous, she had agreed to accompany him to Sante Fe to surprise Abel, whose Third Cavalry relief column was battling the combined Rebel-Texas forces.

The incident had ended in tragedy when Dibley turned on her, used her, even vilely branded her thigh, and finally set her up as bait in a trap to halt the Third in its tracks and permit a Confederate breakthrough. The trap had left Colonel Wild Bill Robinson dead and sent Judy out of her mind with grief and guilt. Ted Henderson was not one who enjoyed killing, but he found some satisfaction in the fact it had been his shot that felled the treacherous Dibley.

The tragedy had quieted Judy's flirtatious and impulsive manner. Ted knew Abel's love for Judy remained strong but that the seeds of suspicion were hard to kill once planted.

Ted forced his attention back to the handwritten menu as the women made their "oohs" and "aahs" over the fine linen, first-rate silver, and high-quality European glassware on the table. William Hepburn Russell never went second class with his enterprises, and the founder of the short-lived Pony Express had remained in character with the construction of the Laramie Hotel.

However, Russell had done one thing that embarrassed Ted slightly. In his flair for the dramatic—and from a practical standpoint to keep his less glamorous but profitable freight business before the public eye—Russell had decorated the walls of the Laramie Hotel with drawings and paintings of Pony Express riders. Above the massive marble of the main fireplace, the likeness of a slightly younger Ted Henderson astride a rangy horse glared out over the crowd. In their infrequent visits to the dining room, Ted had noticed a number of patrons studying the drawing, then turning and looking at him.

Russell's Pony Express had served several purposes, not the least of which was keeping communication lines open from coast to coast in the days before the current War Between the States broke out. If it had been a "publicity gimmick," as some charged, it had been a valuable one to the country, even though it lost money from the first day. And it had given one grieving Ted Henderson a job that fit his talents and his mood—something to do besides drink after his first wife and child had been murdered.

Ted supposed he owed Russell at least a painting over a fireplace.

"Something from the bar while you wait?" Vi herself had decided to attend her friends. Ted smiled up at her and shook his head.

"Just water will be fine," he said. "I had enough of the other in my younger days."

The women ordered the California white wine, which they pronounced excellent, while Abel absently swirled a single shot of whiskey in his glass. Something was gnawing at his second in command, Ted knew. Neither man was much good at small talk, so they left most of the predinner chatter to the women.

The meal was superb by any standards, and Judy was the first to give up. "I must have eaten more than two field hands," she said, then sighed contentedly.

Vi's offered desserts were waved away as the stuffed party concluded the meal. The hotel proprietress took a chair. "I suppose the place can run itself for a few minutes without me," she said.

After a few brief but sincere compliments had been exchanged, Vi turned to Ted. "From the conversations I've overheard in here," she said, "things must be going badly in the territory. Are we building toward still more Indian troubles?"

Ted sighed. "I wish I knew for sure, Vi. I know we have had more and more raids. It's getting to be a full-time job just to keep the telegraph lines open and the mail running through here." Briefly he told her of the threat that would be posed if the various tribes banded together against the whites.

"But there are so many Indian tribes and factions that it

seems unlikely they would all go on the warpath together," Vi
protested.

"Left to themselves, they probably wouldn't," Abel
agreed. "But we have more evidence all along that some force,
or someone, is working toward such an alliance."

"Confederate influence again?" Vi's question was spoken
softly, and Ted could detect no bitterness, despite the fact that
Confederate agents had left her a widow twice.

Abel nodded solemnly. "It may go beyond even the
Rebels," he said. "We just don't know enough to put the puzzle
together now."

"To be truthful, I can't really blame the Indians, although
I do not condone their barbaric acts," Vi said. "The Oregon
Trail split their hunting grounds, then the telegraph came.
Settlers are moving in from both the east and west as word of
land for the taking spreads. And some of the new arrivals are
desperate, people displaced by the war and hungry for a new
life, or just riffraff seeking gold on Indian lands."

Vi shook her head sadly. "If my culture and the food for
my family were threatened, I suppose I would fight, too."

"There's been wrong on both sides," Wilma added. "There
are a number of tribes and bands who profess peace in the
autumn—before the hunger and cold of winter set in—obtain
rations and supplies, then go back to raiding the next spring.
The Plains Indian has his own sense of law and justice, and a
mark on a piece of paper can be ignored by a red man as easily
as by a white."

Ted helped himself to a cup of tea from the silver pot on
the table. "One thing that has me concerned," he said, "is the
growing anti-Indian sentiment. The peaceful bands who have
never caused anyone pain could be in jeopardy if the dedicated
Indian haters—or someone intensely stupid—should decide
all Indians are alike and attack the peaceful villages."

Vi nodded. "It's true that as the population of the region
grows, people will be moving in who don't know one Indian
from another. Or perhaps someone who has lost a family or
friends to warring tribes might go on a rampage—" A touch on
her shoulder interrupted the sentence. A waiter leaned down
and whispered something that made Vi's eyes brighten.

"Ted," she said, a new lightness in her tone, "it seems you
have a visitor. A big, strapping man and a young Navajo
woman have asked to see you."

Ted's chair almost tipped over as he jumped up. "It's them, Wilma—the O'Reilly couple. I wasn't expecting them for a week yet."

"Wonderful!" Wilma exclaimed. "I've so been looking forward to meeting them! Don't just stand there, Ted—go invite them to join us!"

Kevin O'Reilly looked even bigger in civilian clothes than in uniform, Ted thought.

"Welcome to Laramie, Kevin. You're looking well," Ted said warmly. He turned to the slender woman at O'Reilly's side. "It is a delight to see you again, Wind Flower," he said in his fluent Navajo.

"Is nice to see you too, Colonel," Wind Flower replied in English. "You treat Navajo well during Long Walk. Navajo not forget." She extended a deceptively dainty hand. Ted could feel the strength in the delicate fingers—not, he thought, a physical power so much as an inner force. "Excuse English," Wind Flower continued. "Kevin patient teacher, but is hard language. Many funny words."

Ted smiled at her. "Don't apologize, Wind Flower. You are doing remarkably well. You'll be teaching the language soon, I would wager. Now, please, join us for dinner. I'm afraid we've finished, but we are in no hurry to get home."

Looking embarrassed, Kevin shook his head. "Thanks, Colonel," he said, "but we've already eaten at the post. We—didn't think we should be spending much money on expensive meals just yet."

"Then join us for coffee, at least. There are some people I'd like you to meet."

Ted led the young couple through the crowded dining room. Despite the sea of white faces—some curious, a few hostile—Wind Flower showed no signs of shyness or apprehension, but moved with the grace and self-confidence befitting the daughter of a Navajo warrior chief.

"Kevin O'Reilly, Mrs. O'Reilly, may I present my wife, Wilma."

Wilma greeted the two warmly. "From your letters, Kevin, it seems that I have known you for years, and Ted has talked so much of you both. He told me Wind Flower was beautiful, but I think he's guilty of understatement."

Kevin seemed to quickly overcome his natural shyness, and soon the conversation took a lively turn as the two new arrivals recounted their long journey from the Bosque Redondo. "Once," Kevin said, "we rode through the edge of the southern buffalo herd. It took almost two days—" He stopped speaking as a sharp-faced, swarthy man dressed in the coarsely woven clothing of a teamster approached the table.

Kevin stiffened as the teamster glared at Wind Flower, his face full of hate.

"Something I can do for you, sir?" Vi Robinson asked calmly.

"Yeah. You can get this stinkin' redskin squaw outta here," the teamster said, his voice loud enough to reach the most distant corner of the dining room. "I don't care to catch no lice from eatin' here!"

Kevin started out of his seat, rage flaring in his narrowed eyes. But Wind Flower's hand on one arm and Vi's on the other eased him back into his chair.

"Sir," Vi said, "You are either drunk or stupid, and I will have neither in my hotel. Control yourself or I will have to ask you to leave."

"Not till I said my piece," the teamster growled. "I ain't sharin' no room with no damned Injun! Ain't no white man should, neither." He glared at Kevin. "Squaw man!" The words were clearly a challenge.

Kevin sprang to his feet, fists bunched, his face livid with anger.

Vi calmly stepped between the two men. "Leave this to me, Mr. O'Reilly," she said. "After all, it is my place of business." She stared at the sharp-faced man for an instant. All over the room conversations stopped, and utensils fell quiet as the other customers watched the drama unfold. "Sir, you have overstepped your bounds as a customer and as a man. Now, leave my hotel—and don't ever return!" Vi commanded.

"You tellin' me you'd rather feed some dirty-blanket squaw than a white man?"

Ted quietly slid his chair back and stood. If Vi needed help, it should come from some direction other than the big Irishman. There was no doubt in Ted's mind that Kevin O'Reilly would tear the teamster limb from limb.

"I'm telling you," Vi said, "that I prefer my customers to be civilized. Now, get out!"

Ted took one easy stride forward and placed a hand on the teamster's shoulder at the base of the neck. The man started at the unexpected touch, then gasped in pain as Ted dug his fingers into the nerve complex just above the collarbone. As he tightened his grip still more, the teamster's eyes widened, and color began to drain from his face. "If you do not leave immediately, I will personally place any undamaged parts of you in the post stockade. Do I make myself clear?" Ted asked quietly.

Ted took the strangled grunt as an affirmative answer. Keeping his solid grip on the man's neck and shoulder, he steered the teamster toward the door. "Consider yourself lucky," he said as they picked their way through the silent crowd. "That big Irishman would have broken every bone in your body and picked his teeth with the slivers."

A customer who had been about to depart when the fuss broke out held the door open. Ted led the teamster into the street and several strides from the hotel. Then he released his grip.

The teamster turned, started to swing his fist, and caught a slashing right in the belly. The air left in a rush as the man doubled over. Ted looked at him almost casually, then ripped a wicked left to the temple. The teamster dropped facedown into the dust.

Ted grabbed an arm and yanked the stunned man erect. "Get out of Laramie," he said. "Go back to your Indian-hating friends. If I ever see your face around here again, I'll remove it from your body." He spun the troublemaker about and sent him on his way with a quick boot to the backside.

Rubbing the bruised knuckles on his left hand, Ted went back into the hotel. He approached the table in time to hear Wind Flower say, "We go now, Kevin. I not wish to cause trouble."

Vi Robinson waved the young woman back to her seat. "You will do no such thing, dear. You are a guest in my hotel." Vi raised her voice so that it carried throughout the still quiet dining room. "If any others among you object to this woman's presence, you have my invitation to leave as well!"

For a moment no one stirred. Then, at a small table in a corner, a woman stood and began to applaud.

Within moments all the guests were on their feet, the dining room echoing with their cheers of approval.

Vi's face flushed in sudden embarrassment. She stood silently for a few seconds, overwhelmed at the response, then raised a hand for quiet. "Thank you, my friends. Let's get on with the evening."

She touched Ted's arm. "Thanks, Colonel. That could have gotten a bit sticky without your help. And," she said, grinning with delight, "if I ever need a bouncer and you happen to be out of a job, come calling. Now if you people will excuse me, I had best go run my hotel."

Kevin O'Reilly draped a burly arm over Wind Flower's slim shoulders. "We knew it would happen sooner or later," he said. "I think I might have killed that man."

Wilma smiled at the two newlyweds. "Rest assured, Kevin, that you *will* find the strength to cope with such a situation—and it will happen again." She nodded toward Wind Flower. "Just remember your wife is worth that extra effort." She turned to Ted. "Are you all right, dear?"

"Yes. Just bruised some knuckles a little to prove a point. Abel, remind me to check up on that man. He's the sort we don't need here at the moment."

The incident quickly slipped from the conversation as Judy and Wilma became involved in a spirited discussion with Wind Flower on Navajo customs and recent happenings in Laramie. The men turned to other matters.

"Colonel Carson sends his compliments, sir," Kevin said to Ted. "He has asked me to tell you he plans a visit here soon, to map out an overall plan to bring peace between the red man and the whites."

"How is Kit?" Ted asked eagerly.

"Physically fit and as busy as ever, Colonel. He's had his hands full with the Kiowa, the Kiowa-Apache, and the Comanche. Some of the smaller bands have asked for peace, but the southern Plains are anything but dull at the moment."

Wilma called the dinner to an end. "Kevin, Wind Flower—do you have a place to stay?"

At Kevin's nod Wilma suggested they retire to the Henderson quarters for a late coffee and to discuss the details on the ranch operation.

During the brief walk to the Henderson home, Ted told Kevin that Wilma had been the one to study his proposal to lease the ranch.

"She's the member of this family with a nose for business," Ted added. "Money never has meant much to me, so I seldom had occasion to learn to handle it. I think you'll like Wilma's proposal."

Anna Keller saw the light in the Henderson window and brought young William Ted home. Kevin and Wind Flower took an immediate liking to the youngster, and in a short time he was nestled sleepily in Wind Flower's lap.

"Now, down to business," Wilma said. She produced a few papers on which columns of figures shared space with her elaborate doodlings.

"Ted and I figure you may need a bigger cash flow to make the ranch operate at a profit," Wilma explained, "so we have decided that instead of a sixty-forty split of any net earnings, we would prefer that you retain eighty percent and our share would be twenty."

She waved away Kevin's attempt to protest. "Actually, we should be paying you a salary for living on the place and keeping things in shape. A home can get so rundown when it stays vacant. And it looks like we may be away for quite some time yet, with the Indian troubles and all.

"We propose," she added, "to add three thousand dollars to your savings as our share of the investment in the ranch."

Kevin's jaw dropped. "Three—*thousand*?"

Wilma nodded. "You may well need it, Kevin. It's difficult to turn a profit on a ranch the first couple of years, what with the price of replacement cattle and purchases to make repairs. Besides, we don't need the money right now. We aren't rich, but by frontier standards we're in better shape than most. And I've always believed in putting surplus capital to work."

"Kevin," Ted said, "I would recommend you concentrate on developing the cow-calf end of the operation. Buy a few head of steer—giving beef to a hungry Indian is a much better investment than having your entire herd stolen. Also, I wouldn't stock too many horses. They are too tempting a target to both the Indians and a lot of white men in this area."

Kevin nodded his agreement.

"One more thing," Ted added. "You are fully aware of the dangers involved in ranching in an isolated spot. I can't offer you much in the way of protection because I'm short of men to begin with. You'll be pretty much on your own there. There will be renegade Indians, white outlaws—even people who will try to make life miserable for Wind Flower simply because they don't like the color of her skin. Plus you will have the weather to contend with. In good years the ranch practically runs itself. But I've seen some signs that we may be in for a bad winter.

"Kevin, are you sure—absolutely sure—that you're ready and willing to take the risk?"

"Yes, Colonel. Wind Flower and I have examined everything that could go wrong. We're determined to make a go of it, and this is our best chance," O'Reilly said, putting an arm around his wife.

Ted glanced at Wilma, and they nodded as one.

"Then the terms are satisfactory?"

"More than satisfactory, Colonel. I feel a little bit like a charity case, in fact. Suppose we don't make it?" Kevin asked anxiously.

Ted shrugged. "Then you don't make it. A lot of enterprises fail. But I have an idea you've enough of the stubborn Irish temperament to make this one work."

Kevin grinned and for the first time looked relaxed. "Will you draw up the papers, Mrs. Henderson?"

"Your word is our contract," Wilma said. "Just let us know if you need anything, and at the end of the year tell us whether we made or lost money. You don't seem to be the type to cheat anyone."

Ted leaned back in his chair, fingertips forming a steeple. "Kevin," he said, "it might help head off some potential problems if I, along with a small escort, accompanied you and Wind Flower to the ranch. It would at least put out the word that you have the protection—if we can provide it—of the Third Regiment. Most of the Indian tribes, and a majority of the rustlers as well, have a healthy respect for my men. A small show of support certainly wouldn't hurt."

"Thanks again, Colonel." Kevin rose as Wilma gathered her now-sleeping son from Wind Flower's lap and carted the youngster off to bed.

"Just do me a couple of favors, Kevin."

"Certainly, sir."

"For openers, stop calling me 'sir' and 'colonel.' You're a civilian now. The army named me Colonel Ted Henderson, but my mother named me just plain old Ted. Let's use first names from now on.

"Secondly, you and Wind Flower keep your hair."

"We'll do our best in that respect, Col—Ted."

Wind Flower wrapped her light shawl about her shoulders and placed a delicate hand on Ted's arm.

"You are very kind man," she said. "I proud to call you friend."

Ted patted her hand gently. "And I you, Wind Flower. May the spirits walk beside you and sing of fine harvests." He turned to the big Irishman at his side.

"Kevin, if it's all right with you, we'll start to the ranch tomorrow morning, since it's a long ride and could hold some danger. So, you'll need to buy any supplies you don't have as soon as the merchants open. I have a wagon here that belongs at the ranch. You might as well take it." Ted crossed the room and swung open the door. "Also," he added, "keep your weapons handy."

Kevin grinned. "Ever hear of an ex-army man who didn't keep his horses healthy and his powder dry?"

Wilma came into Ted's arms after the door closed. "They are every bit as nice as you told me they were, darling," she said. "I certainly hope no ill befalls them."

"So do I. In that isolated spot they'll be so vulnerable." He held her close. "It couldn't hurt a bit if you mentioned them in your prayers from time to time. You know the old saying about the ill wind that blows nobody good? I can't say why, exactly, but I have a feeling in my bones that the breeze may be freshening. I just hope it isn't going to develop into a truly ill wind."

Three

"**D**o the leaders of the great Sioux nation tremble as the grass before a mere breeze?"

The warrior known as Long Walker paused, fully aware that his words walked the thin line between challenge and insult—and that this was precisely the wrong group to insult.

His eyes, a startling blue against the deep bronze of his face, swept the half-circle of Sioux chiefs, subchiefs, and war society leaders. Among them were representatives of the Brule, Oglala, Hunkpapa, Teton, and the remnants of the Santee band. It was the largest gathering yet of the leaders of the powerful Indian nation. Long Walker had invested many days and ridden long distances to organize the council, and he was well aware the success of his mission depended on the arguments he set forth here.

"No, the Sioux do not tremble. There are no braver warriors than the Sioux, and Long Walker is honored to have gained a place among the tribe."

Long Walker drew himself to his full six feet in height, his muscles rippling across a heavy chest that bore a still-healing red gash from a recent wound.

"All must band together *now*, brothers. Individual groups can kill only a few white soldiers, a few settlers and miners who have taken Sioux lands as their own. But listen now, and listen well. If all join forces, the power of the nation will be such that warriors can sweep the Sioux lands free of *all* whites. Only then will the red man be able to ride once more where he chooses. Only then will the red man be able to hunt where the buffalo and the deer take him and keep his family fed. The wagons that destroy the lands will disappear, and the forts of the soldiers will lie in ashes."

Long Walker paused, letting his words sink into the minds of those gathered about the council fire.

"The time to strike is *now*," Long Walker said, slashing his hand across his throat. "The time is now because the white soldiers fight each other in a great war beyond the wide river. When that war ends, they will turn on the Sioux. The old ways, the good ways, will be gone forever. This can be stopped if the war pipe is smoked by all before the sun sets on this day."

Long Walker saw with satisfaction that some heads nodded in agreement. Yet others showed no expression.

"How is it that Long Walker knows what is in the mind of the white man?" The speaker was a battle-scarred Teton senior warrior known to Long Walker only by reputation as a fierce fighter.

"Long Walker has lived many years with the white man," the blue-eyed Indian replied. "Long Walker went to the white man's school, studied his ways of war, learned his language, his history. But Long Walker's heart remained red, and everything was done with the plan of returning to his people and bringing strong medicine with the knowledge he had gained."

"Long Walker says he returns to his people," the Teton warrior retorted. "Yet Long Walker is not of the Sioux. His eyes are those of the white man. Why should his promise of strong medicine be trusted?"

A ripple of agreement spread through the gathering. Long Walker raised a hand, waiting until the murmurs subsided.

"The words are true in part," he said. "They are questions Long Walker would ask himself, if he wore your moccasins. By birth he is not a Sioux, but a Seminole. This is strong medicine, for the Seminole never signed a treaty of peace with the white man, and many soldiers were slain by only a handful of Seminole warriors. Some of the tribe remain in the land called Florida, still unconquered. Many have been moved to a reservation. There Long Walker has seen them suffer at the hands of the white man."

Abruptly Long Walker stopped speaking. In deliberate strides he walked around the assembled Indians, then stopped at the place he had begun.

"The circle just walked," he said, "represents the land now called Sioux country. The spot beneath this foot represents the reservation where all Sioux will be sent if the white man is not crushed and driven away. Is there a man here who wishes to live beneath Long Walker's foot? For that is the plan of the Great Father in Washington."

Around the circle, heads shook in astonishment. "The Sioux cannot live in such a small space," a voice from the crowd said.

"Such was the fate of many of the Seminole tribesmen," Long Walker pointed out. "When the Sioux are on this small spot of earth, they will be forced to dig in the dirt like badgers. They will be farmers. They will have no weapons. They will be allowed no horses. They will be promised food, but the promise will be empty. Women and children will die of heat and disease."

Long Walker raised his arms wide, in an embracing motion. "Brothers, hear me! This must not happen!"

This time, the mutters of agreement were louder and more forceful.

"Long Walker's father was a Seminole warrior, of whom songs are still sung in his honor. Long Walker's mother was a white captive. He himself was captured during a battle with soldiers. He had seen but thirteen summers, yet he went with war parties to kill soldiers. One day Seminole medicine was bad. In the battle all were killed except Long Walker. He fought hard, but when the whites saw that his eyes were blue, they did not kill him. He was taken far from his homeland. For years his heart cried beneath the white man's foot. Now he has found a new homeland, new brothers. He will not see it taken away. Long Walker will fight and die for it."

At one side of the crowd, a young Santee brave, Quick Arrow, stood. "What Long Walker says is true," he said. "In the moons Long Walker has lived with the red man, Quick Arrow has ridden with Long Walker on many raids. He has counted many coups, taken many scalps and guns. He has told me the story of his escape from the whites, and his words ring true. He was given his name after he came to the Sioux on foot, walking all the way from a distant place named Virginia far beyond the big river. None who know Long Walker question his courage in battle. His medicine is indeed strong."

Long Walker strode to the large tipi—the temporary lodge—where he had waited for the Indian leaders to assemble. He plucked a lance from alongside the tipi, then turned to the group, the lance held high overhead.

"Brothers, the day of the lance in war is near an end. The Sioux must have guns. Long Walker can get them. Among the whites are a few who secretly support the Indian cause. From them Long Walker will receive many guns and bullets—not old muzzle-loaders, but fine new rifles and pistols. At this moment, the first of these guns are on their way to Sioux country. By the time the cottonwoods turn color, more guns will have arrived. This is the promise and the medicine Long Walker brings before this council."

Then Long Walker suddenly lowered the lance and, with a surprising power, drove it into the earth. The blade of the lance was all but buried in the dirt, the single eagle feather on the end of the shaft fluttering with the vibrations.

Long Walker folded his arms across his broad chest. "Will the Sioux join as a single band and drive the whites from the Indians' homeland? Or do the Sioux choose to wait until they are driven like cattle at the point of soldiers' rifles to a place where freedom will be but a memory in the minds of our elders?"

The questions triggered a spirited discussion among warriors and chiefs.

"One moment!"

The cry from the ranks brought an abrupt silence. Long Walker turned to the speaker, and his heart skipped a beat. He looked into the square, wide-nosed face of Sitting Bull, who, though barely thirty years old, had risen to chief of the Hunkpapa Sioux. Among the Sioux, Sitting Bull was known to have almost supernatural powers. It was said he spoke with the gods, and his visions were legend in both content and accuracy. Long Walker had counted heavily upon gaining the support of Sitting Bull. His reputation as a great warrior and leader already had established him as a powerful force among the Plains Indians of all tribes.

"Sitting Bull does not question Long Walker's words or his medicine," the chief said. "He will stand in no man's way if he chooses the war pipe. But Sitting Bull will not smoke for the Hunkpapa on this day. He will carry the message to his people and await a medicine sign. Perhaps there is yet a chance to live in peace with the white man. This he does not know."

Sitting Bull quickly gathered the few personal items he had brought to the council and strode toward his horse tethered nearby.

One by one, other chiefs of the major bands followed Sitting Bull from the council. Yet some remained. *Enough,* Long Walker thought, *for a beginning.* With those who stayed he was sure he could field a force of several hundred warriors. And as stories of their plunder spread, more would come. Eventually even Sitting Bull must pick up the war pipe.

Long Walker dismissed the Hunkpapa chief's decision from his mind. He was satisfied. His contacts among the Confederacy would be pleased at his progress in such a short time and would continue to supply arms and ammunition.

Long Walker entered his tipi, emerging a moment later with the carefully wrapped ceremonial pipe. He held the pipe to the four winds as the remaining war chiefs and senior warriors gathered into the traditional circle.

With the gods appeased, the pipe passed from hand to hand. Long Walker understood now why the spirits had stayed the hand of the white soldier about to kill him so many years ago. The spirits had led him into the white man's camp, giving him the strength and the wisdom to use the knowledge the white man had to offer.

Long Walker remembered the bitter years when he had endured the teaching of the white man's ways and outwardly became a "tame" Indian, in order to gain knowledge of his enemy. But within his massive chest beat the heart of a free Indian.

When the agents of the Confederacy had approached him in his third year of study at the Virginia Military Academy, it was as though the gods were playing a joke on the whites. In exchange for Long Walker's service in agitating the Plains Indians, the Confederates had promised the return of the surviving Seminole to their homeland. There would be guns, ammunition, and protection for the tribe from both white man and red. The old ways would return to the Seminole.

The Seminole were no longer truly a people, Long Walker reflected bitterly. But in the offer of the Confederates was born a new vision—a vast Indian nation in the wide center of the country, presided over by a wealthy and powerful chief.

That chief's name would be Long Walker.

All he had to do was create an Indian war, disrupt communications across the Plains, harass the soldiers and settlers, and divert supplies and men from the fighting in the

East. That the Confederacy might lose the war did not matter to Long Walker. By then, the Plains would be his.

The pipe traveled the circle and once more was in Long Walker's hands. He lifted the sacred instrument above his head.

"Death to the white man!" he cried.

A resounding chorus of war whoops echoing across the encampment seemed to swell and grow, until Long Walker believed it must be heard across the entire Plains.

Long Walker waited patiently until the war cries began to fade, then raised a hand for silence. "Brothers," he said, "within an hour's ride of this spot is a cache of fine new weapons. There are several new rifles of a golden color metal above the trigger that shoot many times before they must be reloaded. There is much ammunition for these rifles, and pistols as well."

He paused until the excited ripple of voices had stilled. Long Walker, an expert shot with the new Henry .44 repeater, knew some time must pass before other Indians became marksmen. But the many-shot rifles would bring fear to the hearts of the whites and reinforce his own position of strength within the newly formed alliance.

"Long Walker will now demonstrate such a weapon," he said, reaching into his tipi. Sun glinted from the brass receiver of the rimfire repeater. Long Walker stooped and plucked a large piece of wood from the pile beside the fire. He stepped off fifty paces and placed the wood upon the ground.

Slowly he made his way back to the curious warriors clustered about the dying council fire. Suddenly he spun, raised the rifle to his shoulder, and squeezed the trigger in one smooth motion. The piece of wood toppled. Rapidly Long Walker worked the lever action, feeding cartridges into the chamber of the Henry and firing. Each shot found its mark.

As he lowered the rifle, he listened to the murmurs of wonderment among the warriors.

"Long Walker has as many of these as all his toes and fingers," he said, "and more are on the way. The rifles already here Long Walker gives as gifts to his fellow warriors who have killed the most white men. As the rifles arrive, others will be given to those who have counted the most coups."

Long Walker's distribution method was carefully chosen. Among the Sioux, and most other Plains tribes, "counting coups"—the touching of a living or dead enemy before other members of the raiding party—with a stick, lance, or hand was the sign of ultimate bravery. However, many Indians placed so much value on counting coups they forgot to kill the enemy. Placing the new rifles in the hands of those who had killed the most enemies would elevate them above those who had only counted coups. The importance of counting coups would begin to diminish, the first step in breaking long-standing codes of warfare and bringing the Indian a bit closer to fighting like the white man. From there, he would take one step at a time until the Indians understood siege tactics, learned how to capture the soldier's cannon and how to use them, and the basics of both cavalry and fortification defense and maneuvers.

"It is but a small beginning," Long Walker said, lifting the Henry rifle high. "But one day all Indians will have such weapons. In the meantime, the Sioux will carry death to the white man with lance, bow and arrow, and tomahawk." He lowered the rifle slowly until it was cradled in his arms, the barrel still warm from the rapid-fire shooting display.

"Now it is time to select a leader," Long Walker said solemnly. "His first official duty will be distribution of the new weapons."

The awed Indians, led by Quick Arrow, who had risen in Long Walker's support earlier, chose the blue-eyed Seminole as their leader in Sioux fashion—not by vote, but by repeated oratory, praising his prowess as a warrior and his medicine. Not a dissenting voice was raised.

"Long Walker is honored, brothers," he said as the last of the orations reached its end. "Now, it is time to prepare to ride the path of war against the whites." He raised his eyes to the sky. "Wakan-Tanka," he cried, addressing the supreme being of the Sioux, "it is Long Walker's vow that the lands now known to the whites as the Dakota, Montana, and Kansas territories shall be swept clean of the pale faces. Once again your eagles may soar far across the heavens and find no man save the Indian."

Colonel Ted Henderson landed with an unofficerlike *thump* in the dirt of the Fort Laramie parade ground. He rolled onto his side, propped his head on an elbow, and watched the pitching stallion head back toward the stable.

Grinning and unhurt, Ted got to his feet and watched as

little Bernie Christian expertly wheeled his own mount, rode alongside the stallion, and gathered up the trailing reins. The corporal was trying hard not to smile as he led the snorting stallion back to Ted.

"Little too much horse for you, Colonel?" Corporal Christian asked, eyes sparkling. "I can always get Miss Wilma to top him out for you."

Ted shook his head, still smiling, and not the least embarrassed at being bucked off his prized mount.

"Just a little game we play, Bernie," he said, replacing the reins and measuring them carefully as Christian held the stallion snug alongside his own bay. "He gets to feeling a little too spunky sometimes. Too much feed and fun with the mares, I guess."

Ted slipped a boot into the stirrup of the wide-horned, Spanish-made saddle. The stallion's nostrils flared. "I'm ahead of him four-to-two over the years. Let's go for five." He swung into the saddle, picked up the other stirrup with a toe, and settled his foot firmly.

"Let him go, Bernie."

The black stallion bogged his head and bucked again, but this time Ted had the rhythm of the horse's pitching. The black tried one last twisting, high-kicking jump, then abruptly settled down. The small, foxy ears came up from the thick-muscled neck and pointed straight ahead. Ted relaxed in the saddle, knowing the horse would not try to pitch again. He kneed the mount toward the boardwalk, where Wilma and William Ted had been watching.

"Are you all right, darling?" Wilma asked anxiously.

"Sure. It isn't the first time this saddle leaked and probably won't be the last," he said, winking.

"Daddy got dirty," Bill said, laughing.

"True enough, son. Now you mind your mother while Daddy's gone to help Kevin and Wind Flower settle in at the ranch."

Wilma's eyes looked a bit misty. "I wish we could go along. It's been such a long time since I've seen the place."

Ted shook his head. "It's better that you and Wild Bill stay here," he insisted gently. "There may be trouble ahead. And if the place is too run-down, I know how much it would hurt you to see it. You two will be safe here, and I'll be back soon." He leaned down and kissed the top of her head. "If you need anything, Abel will see to it."

Ted reined his stallion toward the Fort Laramie gates. In the distance he heard the lowing of cows in O'Reilly's new herd. Corporal Christian rode up beside Ted as they passed through the gates. The black stallion backed his ears at Christian's gelding but made no move to bite; he knew full well the man on his back was now in control.

"Sir," Christian said, "that's an awful valuable animal you're riding. Are you sure it's a good idea to take the foundation stud from your herd out on escort duty in possibly hostile territory?"

Ted brushed a bit of dust from his shoulder. "He needs it, Bernie. It's between breeding seasons, and I don't want him to forget everything he knows. Besides, I like the feel of him under me."

"Mighty fine piece of horseflesh," the corporal said admiringly. "He sure can pitch some. Don't know how you rode him."

"He's given me some practice," Ted said, leaning forward slightly to pat the heavy muscles in the horse's neck. "It's out of his system now. He'll be fine."

Ted and Christian neared the small herd of stocker cattle. Kevin had chosen well, Ted thought as he studied the herd. The animals, mostly mother cows, were solid, heavy-boned stock, capable of surviving the bitter Wyoming winters with a minimum of human help. Some had calves at their sides, and all had been bred again, so Kevin had acquired at least a few two-for-one packages. The two herd bulls were the short-tempered type with upward-curving horns. Ted knew they would be more than adequate protection from predators during calving time, when both mother and calf were most susceptible to attack. If all went well, the ranch might even turn a profit the first year, he decided.

Kevin O'Reilly, scouts Carl Keller and Pappy Lehman, along with three experienced drovers wearing the uniform of the Third Cavalry, kept the stock under loose but firm control. Wind Flower sat on the wagon seat, the reins of the four-horse hitch held in her small but steady hands.

Following his long-standing custom, Ted took the point as the herd moved out. As the sight of the fort faded in the distance, Carl Keller moved to the front of the herd, leaving

Ted free to range far afield on scout, checking for potential trouble along the rough but passable road leading to the ranch.

The short trip was without incident until they were a few miles from the ranch. Ted was ranging a half-mile ahead of the slow-moving herd and wagon when he suddenly stiffened in the saddle. In the dew on the ground before him were hoofprints—unshod ponies. A few seconds later the *chiiing* call of the blue quail cut the still morning air. Ted's hand drifted to his carbine in its saddle scabbard. He knew there were no blue quail in this particular area where the trail narrowed into a steep pass.

Giving no sign of outward suspicion, Ted kneed his black stallion in a slow half-circle, mentally marking the location of the call of each "quail." As soon as he was out of sight of the pass, he eased the stallion into a fast trot. He waved to Carl Keller as he approached the herd.

"Trouble ahead, Carl," Ted called as he drew near.

"Injuns?"

"Probably. Most likely Arapaho, could be Ute. They're strung out along the sides of the pass." Quickly he briefed the veteran scout on the probable position of the Indians.

"Think you and Pappy can take care of them once I draw them out into the open?" Ted asked.

Studying the terrain ahead, Keller nodded. "Two high knolls up ahead, one each side of the road. Reckon me an' Pappy could heat things up a tad with one of us on each hill." The scout's brow furrowed as he eyed Ted. "Don't you take no chances, Ted Henderson. Anything happen to you and that there stud hoss, Wilma'd have my hide."

"I'll take it safe," Ted said. "This stallion and I know every inch of that pass." He checked the loads in his carbine and pistol. "I'll tell the other riders to take it slow with the herd and give you and Pappy about a half hour to ease onto those peaks."

"Good enough," Keller said. He waved the other scout alongside, and after a brief conference, the two buckskin-clad riders disappeared into the tangle of rocks flanking the winding road.

Ted wiped nervous sweat from his palms a few minutes later as he checked his pocket watch for the final time. Then he firmly kneed the big black toward the pass. A scant twenty yards ahead, the stallion's soft snuffle and a flicker of movement alongside the road sent Ted into motion. He kicked the horse into a dead run as he palmed his revolver and thumbed the weapon to full cock.

A rifle ball cracked near his head. Abruptly he wheeled his horse from the trail proper and sent the animal plunging through the brush and boulders, trusting the stallion's natural sense of balance and footing to keep them from grief.

The tactic caught the first Indian by surprise. The brave was crouched low behind a rock, fumbling with the powder flask of an old muzzle-loader. The Ute glanced up, eyes wide, at the approaching thunder of hooves. Ted's pistol shot took the Indian full in the chest, tumbling him into the dust.

Another Indian sprang from behind a nearby rock, drawing his bow. Ted rammed a knee into the stallion's side. The horse instantly changed course and was upon the brave in two strides. The stallion's massive chest rammed into the Indian, spilling him beneath churning hooves.

Ted reined the black to a sliding halt in the safety of a clump of boulders. Across the road another brave stood, attempting to aim a rifle, then tumbled backward. A split second later came the heavy roar of Pappy's big rifle. Ted turned quickly as the solid *thump* of a slug against flesh sounded behind him. An Indian staggered and fell as the sharp report of Carl Keller's Spencer repeater bounced from the canyon walls.

Stones rattled from above and beyond Ted's right shoulder. He twisted in the saddle and pulled the trigger, knowing as he did so he had rushed the shot. A Ute, diving from the top of a boulder, struck him in the chest. Instinctively Ted kicked free of the saddle, rolling with the blow. He landed heavily on his back, knocking the air from his lungs. But the Ute had been unable to hold on to Ted, and the Indian's charge carried him a dozen feet away. The Indian rolled to his feet, knife in hand, and rushed the momentarily stunned Ted. Ted realized he would never be able to cock and fire the single-action Colt in time.

Sensing a quick victory, the Ute raised his knife for a downward slash. Ted twisted aside, sweeping the back of his cavalry boot against the Indian's nearest ankle. The Ute stumbled and went down near the nervous, stomping hooves of Ted's stallion. Ted cursed. He could not fire without endangering his horse.

He tossed his useless pistol aside and swept the razor-edged skinning knife from its scabbard at his belt. Scrambling to his feet, Ted stared into the black eyes of the Indian and waited, his knees flexed for action.

The Ute's attack came with a swiftness that almost caught Ted by surprise. Ted pivoted on his left foot, letting the point of the Indian's knife slide past. Then he ripped upward with his own blade. Ted felt the jar in his arm as the knife penetrated the Indian's body to the bone. The Ute sagged as Ted yanked his knife free and stepped back, poised for another attack.

There was none. The brief encounter ended with a soft gurgle and a spreading stain on the Indian's chest.

Ted heard hoofbeats fading in the distance as the surviving Indians swiftly retreated. The blast of Pappy's rifle hurried them on their way.

Ted quieted his snorting, wide-eyed stallion. He retrieved his revolver, brushing away the dust and grit from the weapon. Satisfied it was undamaged, he cocked the handgun—just in case.

"Ease off on the trigger!" Kevin O'Reilly called from close by. Ted lowered the hammer and holstered the gun.

O'Reilly walked to the Indian, flipped the heavy body over as casually as a man turning a blanket, and whistled.

"Opened him up like a hog for smoking," the Irishman said. "You handle a knife well for a white man, Ted Henderson."

"I must admit it isn't my favorite weapon," Ted replied, wiping the blade clean on a clump of grass and returning the weapon to its sheath. "But it beats the devil out of nothing. Is anyone hurt?"

"Just a few Indians," O'Reilly said casually. "You, Carl, and Pappy kind of left the rest of us with nobody to fight—although I'm in no rush, I must say. I'm sure my time will come soon enough." He peered closely at the dead Indian. "Ute, isn't he?"

Ted nodded while checking his stallion for any wounds. The horse was uninjured.

"No war paint," Ted said, "so it appears to have been a hunting party. We just happened to come along at the right time, and it's difficult for a Ute to resist a chance to lift a few white scalps—and to get some horses and a woman in the bargain." He frowned at Kevin. "How is Wind Flower taking this?"

O'Reilly smiled. "She's a veteran. Calm as a beaver pond on a still day and working on an injured Indian who looks like he got hit by a wagon team."

"In a manner of speaking, he did," Ted said. "My horse ran over him. I didn't get a good look at the Indian, but there was something familiar about him. Let's go take a look."

Wind Flower was ministering to the unconscious Ute when Ted and Kevin reached the scene. A small cut alongside the injured man's head still seeped blood, apparently the result of a glancing blow from the stallion's hoof. Ted stooped and peered into the Indian's face for a brief moment.

"I thought so," he said. "This is Strong Bow, a senior warrior among his tribe." He glanced at Wind Flower. "How badly hurt is he?"

"Not badly, but he will feel much pain for some time," Wind Flower replied in her own tongue. "Wind Flower thinks he has some broken ribs and his head will ache when he awakens."

"So what do we do with him, Ted?" Kevin asked in English.

"I suppose we'll take him back to the fort as a captive. There's little else we can do," Ted replied.

"Wind Flower has an idea," the young Navajo woman said.

Ted raised an eyebrow.

"Are the Ute not a superstitious people? With a great fear of evil spirits?"

Intrigued, Ted nodded.

"Then, let us give him a spirit to remember." Wind Flower outlined her plan, which they hurried to put into operation before Strong Bow regained consciousness.

They had scarcely finished when the Ute moaned and stirred, fighting his way back to consciousness. The hastily erected tent in which he lay was almost pitch-black, with only a single small candle sending shadows dancing along the wall. Ted, whose command of the Ute language was fluent, knelt near Strong Bow's head just outside the tent.

Strong Bow awoke with a fire in his chest, and for a moment his eyes would not focus. Then the apparition before him snapped together. Half a face streaked with white paint stood in stark relief against the frightening gloom. Atop the half-face, a pair of buffalo horns curved, one up, one down. Strong Bow cringed against the blanket on which he lay. He must be in the Spirit World, he thought, still groggy. A strange smell and swirling smoke eddied about.

Strong Bow tried to extend a hand to ward off the apparition, but fright paralyzed his muscles. The apparition spoke in a strange tongue, and Strong Bow recognized only his own name. Then the words, in his own language, seemed to form from nothingness in the swirl of smoke about his head.

"Strong Bow has violated the sacred ground of the Black Spirit," the voice said, although the apparition's lips did not move. "The Black Spirit is unhappy with Strong Bow and his tribe."

Ted, kneeling outside the tent, awaited Wind Flower's next comment in Navajo, which he then would translate into Ute, his voice at a low and ominous pitch.

"The Black Spirit has sent his Medicine Woman to the sacred ground, and Strong Bow greets her with guns. For this the Black Spirit, taking the form of a great horse, has driven Strong Bow to the ground. The Black Spirit's first desire was to kill Strong Bow and condemn his soul to the World Between Lives forever."

The wide-eyed Ute watched as a seemingly disembodied hand floated above the candle. He gasped in fear, then clutched his chest in pain.

"But the Black Spirit has decided instead that Strong Bow shall live," the voice continued, "but he shall not go unpunished. For the next moon, each time Strong Bow draws a breath, he will remember the words of the Black Spirit from the fire in his chest.

"He will go to his people and say, 'The Black Spirit rides the valley where the white man and the Indian woman live. The lodge of the Medicine Woman and the white man is sacred ground of the Black Spirit. Any Ute who ventures near shall be stricken blind and cast into the World Between, his spirit to wander there in darkness forever.' This you will tell your people, for you have seen the Black Spirit in two forms this day."

Ted had to choke back a laugh as he translated Wind Flower's words. *She may be more of a medicine woman than she realizes,* he thought.

"Should Strong Bow fail in this mission, the Black Spirit shall appear once more," the apparition continued. "Upon that day, Strong Bow shall be condemned.

"No man has seen the Black Spirit and lived. Strong Bow must drink of the spirit waters." The hand that seemed to have no arm reappeared, a large gourd held toward the horrified Ute. "Taste of the bitter waters. Sleep. When you awaken, the sky will once more be blue, the water again will run. And Strong Bow will remember in detail this visit with the Black Spirit."

Strong Bow took the gourd with trembling fingers. The black liquid inside sloshed over one side of the container as he raised it to his lips.

"Drink," the spirit-vision commanded. "And come no more to the sacred valley below this pass."

Strong Bow sipped at the bitter, fiery liquid.

"Drink!"

He downed the contents in large, rapid swallows. Within moments, the spirit-vision began to waver like the water-that-wasn't-water on the deserts on a summer day. Then Strong Bow found himself sliding back into the terrible blackness.

Wind Flower waited until she was sure the young warrior slept soundly, then she tossed back the flap of the tent and breathed deeply.

Grinning broadly, Ted helped Kevin carry the sleeping brave from the tent and place him beneath a stunted pine tree. Quickly they struck the tent, returned it to the wagon, and set out for the ranch.

"I think the black paint takes many sunsets to remove from face and arms," Wind Flower said in English with some dismay.

Ted, riding alongside the wagon, smiled at her. "That was an inspired performance," he said. "Strong Bow will be one frightened brave for many moons to come."

Wind Flower shrugged. "The granddaughter of a Navajo medicine man learns of creating illusions and of herbs and plants that cause one to sleep, to awake, to see visions, and to lessen pain."

"Still, I am impressed. I must admit I have never heard of the Black Spirit," Ted said thoughtfully.

"Nor had I," Wind Flower replied with a smile. "But Strong Bow now has seen the Black Spirit. And he will remember it until the day he dies." Without much success, she continued scrubbing at the paint covering half her face.

"It isn't much farther to the ranch," Ted said. "Perhaps you'll have more success cleaning up there." He leaned over, patted Wind Flower's arm, then laughed. "You do look a bit spooky, at that."

He kneed his horse alongside Kevin's. "Well, my big Irish friend, it looks as though your Medicine Woman has given you a big boost toward survival. If I know the Ute, you will have no trouble with them while the Black Spirit walks the valley."

Kevin cast an admiring glance over his shoulder toward the wagon and Wind Flower. "She is something, isn't she? Now if we could just figure some way to put the fear into the Cheyenne, Sioux, Arapaho, and a few other assorted tribes, we'd be in good shape."

As they topped the ridge overlooking the ranch, Ted felt a tingle of anticipation at the familiar sight and had to check his first urge to send the stallion galloping over the grasslands they had ridden together so many times in the past.

From the ridge he could see Bernie Christian, who had gone ahead with the others while Wind Flower worked her magic. He was struggling to place a fallen timber back into the rail corral. The others had turned the cows onto the lush pastures.

Hoofbeats announced the return of Pappy Lehman and Carl Keller. The two scouts had followed the fleeing Indians to make sure they did not return.

"Them Utes just kept on hightailin' it," Pappy said. "Reckon they had enough of fightin'. Be a long time before any self-respectin' brave will follow any of them warriors on the trail. They lost much medicine there in the pass."

Everyone turned to putting the ranch in the beginnings of working order, and by sunset all was in reasonably good shape.

Ted declined Wind Flower's offer to spend the night in the spare room. To do so without Wilma would somehow seem sacrilegious. Instead, he settled into his bedroll beneath the broad expanse of stars. Above him, the Milky Way, known to the Cheyenne as the Hanging Road, a pathway from Earth to Heaven, whitewashed a major section of the clear Wyoming sky.

* * *

"Does the Cheyenne known as Yellow Crow pretend to know the wishes of Wise One Above? Or is he but too long in the lodge of the white man?"

Yellow Crow slowly turned to face the challenger. He kept his own expression impassive despite his instinctive dislike for the Arapaho warrior, Howling Wolf.

Yellow Crow had expected arguments from the Arapaho invited to the council. He himself had ridden against those very braves to whom he now appealed for peace. However, he had not expected the challenge to be delivered in so sarcastic a tone.

"Yellow Crow does not speak for the highest god of the Cheyenne," he said to the heavily muscled Arapaho. "Yellow Crow makes no claim to having seen a vision by Wise One Above. Yet visions are not needed to see the value of peace and the hardships of war."

Howling Wolf merely snorted and returned to his seat. Yellow Crow was sure he would hear more from the ill-tempered Arapaho before the council had ended.

"It is said among some tribes that the whites can be driven for all times from the Plains," Yellow Crow continued. "Those who call for war would have all believe the white soldier is weak in numbers and spirit. This is not so. He is a fierce and determined warrior. Though his numbers now are small, it will not always be so. In war, many Cheyenne would walk the Hanging Road to the world above. Death holds no fear for the warriors of either tribe here. But what of your women, who will be left behind to gash their flesh and cry over their dead? Who will hunt for meat for the bellies of the young ones?"

"Yellow Crow speaks the truth," a voice from nearby said. Split Hand, with whom Yellow Crow had shared the success of his recent hunt, rose to address the group.

"When the white man's war ends, more bluecoats will come to the country of the Cheyenne—and the Arapaho," Split Hand said pointedly. "The red man has many brave warriors. So does the white man. The red man has fine ponies, bows and arrows that fly true, sharp lances, and good medicine. But the white man does not seek the glory of the coup. He seeks the death of his enemy and will be satisfied with no less. His big guns on wheels are bad medicine for the Indian." The chief looked intently at the Cheyenne and Arapaho braves gathered around the council fire.

"Split Hand agrees with Yellow Crow. Now is the time to treat for peace with the white man. At the moment our numbers are greater. The chances for a just peace will never be better. Split Hand will cast aside the war paint." The chief of the small Northern Cheyenne band sat down, his decision made.

While Yellow Crow was grateful for Split Hand's support, as well as that of other braves whose voices had been raised for peace, but he sensed in the undercurrent of conversations that few had listened well. Perhaps pride simply would not permit them to admit the truth.

All the old arguments had been brought out once more: treaties and promises made and broken, the invasion of Indian lands by the hated seekers of metals from the earth, and the roads that frightened the buffalo. Yellow Crow had pointed out the fate of the Apache and the Navajo, emphasizing that had those two tribes treated for peace, instead of raiding and plundering, they might have a place in their ancestral homelands instead of being placed on the despised reservation.

"Why should any listen to this white man's tame Indian?" Howling Wolf was on his feet again, pointing an accusing finger at Yellow Crow. "Has not this Cheyenne, who would have us believe he is a great warrior, ridden at the side of the long knives against our own people? Howling Wolf spits on Yellow Crow's words."

Yellow Crow fought back a flash of anger. "It is true Yellow Crow has ridden with the white soldiers. It is true Yellow Crow has killed Arapaho warriors—but only those who did not keep their word to the white man, who raided and killed women and children. This does not change the color of Yellow Crow's skin nor his heart. He is Cheyenne. He will always be Cheyenne. And Yellow Crow is no man's 'tame Indian.'"

Howling Wolf snorted. "Is Yellow Crow not the blood brother to the chief of the long knives at Fort Laramie?"

"This, too, is true," Yellow Crow said, as much to the other members of the council as to Howling Wolf. "He is blood brother to Ted Henderson. Henderson would be a friend to the Indian. His heart is heavy when he takes the field against the red man. The colonel of cavalry will do what he can to see that the Cheyenne and Arapaho are treated fairly in time of peace."

Yellow Crow paused, looking over the sea of faces. "But if the Indian chooses the path of war, the blood brother of Yellow Crow will find and punish the warriors who wear paint. He may be a white man but make no mistake—he is a warrior. The red man would do well to turn to Ted Henderson in friendship, for he is not a man to have as an enemy."

Big Nose, whose powerful band of Northern Cheyenne could swing the day toward either peace or war, sat impassively. He had neither spoken nor changed expression since the talks began, and Yellow Crow had no way of knowing what was in his heart.

"Once more, I spit upon the words of Yellow Crow," Howling Wolf cried in a loud voice. The Arapaho turned toward the gathering, waving a muscular arm in Yellow Crow's direction. "Is this Cheyenne not like the fruit from the trees in the time before the leaves fall—red on the outside and white beneath the skin?"

Howling Wolf slowly turned to face Yellow Crow. "Yellow Crow is a squaw," he said. "He flees in the face of the enemy. Yellow Crow claims his medicine is strong for having lived among the long knives. Howling Wolf says his medicine is stronger."

Yellow Crow controlled his anger with effort. He sensed a confrontation coming that would be more than words. Already he had endured many insults at the hands of this Arapaho. He had no intentions of hearing more.

"Howling Wolf challenges the Cheyenne to prove his medicine," The Arapaho said loudly. "A test of strength. Howling Wolf's medicine is stronger!"

Yellow Crow saw the scheming glint in the Arapaho's eyes and knew the proposed test of strength was, in Howling Wolf's mind, a challenge to the death. It was a time to be wary, for Howling Wolf's reputation as a man of strength and a fine fighter was surpassed only by his reputation for treachery in combat.

"And if Yellow Crow accepts the challenge? For what prize will this game of strength be played?" The Cheyenne kept his voice as even and unconcerned as possible.

"Should the Cheyenne win," Howling Wolf said, "Howling Wolf's band will join those who ask for peace. Should Howling Wolf win, he will lead his people in war against the whites."

Yellow Crow glanced in the direction of Big Nose. The chief's face remained impassive, but Yellow Crow caught the glint of interest in Big Nose's eyes. Yellow Crow knew the chief was a man of action more than words. He also held no particular love for the Arapaho, even though he had agreed to an alliance with the neighboring tribe. Perhaps, Yellow Crow thought, the chief could be swayed. . . .

"Then Howling Wolf's challenge is accepted," Yellow Crow announced.

An excited murmur rippled through the crowd round the council fire.

"If Howling Wolf does not care for the fate of his people," Yellow Crow said, "the Cheyenne do."

Preparations for the contest took very little time. As Howling Wolf pulled his buckskin shirt over his head, Yellow Crow removed his knife from its sheath and placed it beside the council fire. A small clearing was prepared a few feet from the blaze. Howling Wolf made a great show of placing his own knife alongside Yellow Crow's. The Cheyenne had no doubt that the display was for his benefit. And he did not for a moment doubt that Howling Wolf had another knife concealed somewhere on his body.

Only a few minutes had passed, but already the wagering was intense. An Indian could scarcely control the impulse to gamble on anything, and a test of strength held the greatest appeal of all.

Howling Wolf stepped to the edge of the clearing, a grim smile twisting his oval face. "Many Cheyenne ponies will change ownership in this contest, Yellow Crow," the Arapaho sneered.

"Perhaps," Yellow Crow said simply. He studied the man across from him carefully. Howling Wolf's powerful muscles rippled on his scarred torso and formed ridges across his flat stomach. His arms were even larger by proportion, and his thighs heavy. The Arapaho would outweigh Yellow Crow by a good forty pounds. But the development of his body would limit the speed of the Arapaho, and the taller Yellow Crow held an advantage in reach. Despite the power and endurance in his own smoothly muscled body, Yellow Crow realized he must stay away from those powerful arms if he was to win the contest.

The two combatants closed to within six feet and began to

circle each other cautiously, each waiting for an opening. The cries of the bettors created a growing din.

Suddenly Howling Wolf charged. As Yellow Crow suspected, the heavily muscled brave was somewhat slow. Yellow Crow waited until the last moment, then sidestepped the charge and delivered the greatest insult of all—a moccasin kick to the rump—as Howling Wolf's rush carried him past.

The kick was part of Yellow Crow's plan of attack; a furious man makes mistakes. He cleared his own mind of all thoughts, trusting his instincts and years of training.

The Arapaho's eyes blazed in fury at the insulting kick. He circled warily, aware now of the speed of the Cheyenne. Howling Wolf feinted a charge to the right, then reached out with his left hand to grab Yellow Crow's wrist. Instead, the Cheyenne seized the advantage by stepping forward and driving a fist to the bridge of his opponent's nose, followed by a hard right to the midsection.

Howling Wolf stumbled back, stunned, and Yellow Crow realized his opponent was unfamiliar with the fistfighting the white man called boxing. Yellow Crow lifted his weight over the balls of his feet, prepared for the next charge. But when it came, his left foot slipped in the loose sand, and a massive jolt from Howling Wolf's outstretched arm sent the Cheyenne tumbling.

Before he could recover, Howling Wolf was on him, reaching for his throat. Yellow Crow placed a foot against his opponent's hip and heaved. The Arapaho twisted, let the foot slide harmlessly off, and closed both hands around Yellow Crow's neck.

The Cheyenne felt the power in his opponent's hands even as he tensed the muscles of his neck to minimize the danger of the grip. Sensing an opening, Yellow Crow rammed a knee upward and heard a muffled grunt of pain as his knee grazed Howling Wolf's upper thigh and thumped into his groin. The Arapaho's grip on Yellow Crow's neck loosened for an instant, which was all the time Yellow Crow needed. The Cheyenne swept Howling Wolf's hands aside and spun away, coming to his feet.

The exertion and the blow to the groin had left Howling Wolf gasping for air. A small stream of blood trickled from one nostril. Suddenly Yellow Crow struck out with a left, his fist striking Howling Wolf in the eye. The Arapaho's head snapped

back, and Yellow Crow immediately hammered a heavy fist
into the exposed front of Howling Wolf's neck. With a
strangled cry, the Arapaho fell forward. Yellow Crow started to
step back and let the man hit the ground when he realized his
mistake—the Arapaho was not as badly hurt as the Cheyenne
had thought.

Howling Wolf's heavy arms clamped around Yellow Crow's
chest, pulling his body into the Arapaho's wide torso. The
pressure built until Yellow Crow could not breathe. He knew
he must act quickly, or his backbone would snap. Cupping
both hands, Yellow Crow suddenly clapped them against
Howling Wolf's ears. The Arapaho screamed as his eardrums
ruptured. He released Yellow Crow and staggered back, dazed
and in pain.

Howling Wolf's hand slid into an opening in his leggings.
Then the firelight glinted on a slender skinning knife. The tip
of the blade flicked forward, and Yellow Crow skipped
backward, but not soon enough. The knifepoint slashed a
crimson trail across his chest.

An unearthly quiet fell over the assembled crowd at the
sudden appearance of the concealed knife. Only the heavy
breathing of the combatants, warily circling each other at the
edge of the clearing, broke the silence.

Howling Wolf charged, swinging the knife at Yellow
Crow's rib cage. Instead of retreating, the Cheyenne stepped
forward, striking downward with the edge of his left hand. He
felt the solid blow as his hand struck the wrist holding the
knife. Out of the corner of his eye, he saw the weapon slip
from numbed fingers onto the ground.

Yellow Crow wrapped his right arm around the back of the
Arapaho's neck, dropped to one knee, and threw Howling Wolf
heavily to the ground.

Under the ordinary rules of tests, the match would have
been over. But the sneak knife had broken the rules. The
entire encampment knew this had now become a battle to the
death.

Yellow Crow's fingers touched the haft of the knife.
Scooping it up, he held the point under Howling Wolf's chin.
The glazed eyes of the Arapaho gradually focused, and
although Howling Wolf knew death was near, there was no
fright in his eyes. Yellow Crow grabbed the Arapaho's right
wrist, pinning it to the ground. A quick swipe of the knife

opened a small cut in the fleshy part of the hand below Howling Wolf's thumb. Yellow Crow drew his own hand across the cut on his chest, then clamped the hand over the cut on Howling Wolf's thumb. Then he tossed the knife aside.

His chest heaving from exertion and his ribs aching from the crushing bear hug, Yellow Crow stood on unsteady legs, facing the council delegates.

"Hear me, oh, brothers!" Yellow Crow's voice rang over the quiet camp. "It was Yellow Crow's right to take the life of the Arapaho Howling Wolf! Instead, Yellow Crow chose to mingle their blood. Despite his treachery in a contest of strength, Yellow Crow would have Howling Wolf as a blood brother, rather than send him to his death!"

The Cheyenne paused, still gasping air. "This does not prove Yellow Crow's personal medicine! It proves the more powerful medicine of peace. Is it not better to befriend an enemy when more is to be gained by friendship than from war and death?"

Yellow Crow ignored the sharp sting of the shallow knife cut across his chest. "Now, Howling Wolf's people must ride the trail of peace as he promised! Is this not a sign? Do Yellow Crow's words still fall on deaf ears?"

He glanced over his shoulder at Howling Wolf, who had struggled to his feet and stood glowering at the Cheyenne. Yellow Crow knew the treacherous Arapaho would ignore the blood bond, but the outcome of the fight had greatly lessened his power among his people. They would sue for peace as promised, with or without Howling Wolf. And undoubtedly other leaders had been influenced by the outcome as well.

"Yellow Crow has made his call to the Northern Cheyenne and the Arapaho to ride not the war trail," Yellow Crow said. "He now leaves the final decision to the council."

The arguments and discussions lasted until dawn. Finally Big Nose turned to Yellow Crow. "Big Nose will not ask for peace, despite the medicine shown in Yellow Crow's fight with the Arapaho. But he will not lead his people into war." The powerful chief rose. "Big Nose shall remain neutral, choosing neither peace nor war, until the snows yet to come have melted in the sun of the time when new grass rises. Big Nose shall not attack the white man unless he first attacks. Nor will Big Nose join the peace talks until the new grass, or until he has seen a vision pointing out the proper road for his people to follow." Abruptly the chief walked from the council lodge.

Yellow Crow felt neither satisfaction nor disappointment at Big Nose's declaration. What would be would be. At least he had bought some time. Big Nose was a logical man, and eventually he might come to see that the path to peace was the smoother. And in the meantime, Big Nose would not be tempted to join the movement toward war.

The leader of a smaller band of Northern Cheyenne, Sees-Visions, rose. "Sees-Visions will follow Yellow Crow to the peace talks," he said. "Our people are few and have little to lose."

One by one, other warriors or chiefs stood and declared their intentions. A few would seek peace. Many would simply wait and see. Most disturbing to Yellow Crow, however, was the increasingly militant attitude of the Cheyenne Dog Soldiers. The members of the elite society were among the finest warriors of the Plains. To a man, they vowed to choose the war ax and to smoke with the Sioux led by the blue-eyed Indian.

After the last of the delegates to Big Nose's council left the lodge, Yellow Crow sat for a long time, staring into the dying embers of the fire. He knew his attempt had been neither a complete success nor a failure. His words and actions would hold some of the undecided bands in check, at least for a time.

His work at the council done, Yellow Crow should have felt some sense of satisfaction. Yet the disturbing memory of his dream returned.

In Yellow Crow's dream, a big black crow had alighted between two rows of corn—one row red, one white. The bird had studied the kernels, and it seemed confused. It turned first to one row, then to the other, but for several minutes made no move toward either red or white grains.

Then the crow seemed to realize what had disturbed the order of things. In the row of red corn were two kernels that did not seem to belong. One was white. The other was half-red, half-white. The bird picked the white kernel up in its beak and placed it back with its white brothers. Then it plucked the curious red and white kernel from the ground and started toward the row of white corn.

The bird, still holding the corn, stood above the white row for a moment. Then it returned to the red row, where again it stood, cocking its head as if undecided. Finally, the crow dropped its head and placed the two-colored corn halfway between the red and white rows.

Still the bird was not satisfied. A long moment passed. Then the crow once more picked up the red-and-white corn and, walking slowly, carried the bit of grain back to the red line and placed it in its former position.

With a hoarse cry, the crow then looked at an Indian standing nearby. Yellow Crow was sure he had seen a tear in the bird's eye before the creature flew away.

Yellow Crow rose from beside the dying council fire and brushed the sand from his backside. It was time for a visit to Fort Laramie. Since the dream, the urge to see his blood brother, Ted Henderson, and his young godson beat strong in Yellow Crow's breast.

And in the camp of Black Kettle along the South Platte not far from Laramie lived an ancient grandmother whose knowledge of dream magic was legend. Yellow Crow would go to her with his dream, but he would do so with reluctance.

Yellow Crow was sure the bird dream had revealed his own future. Torn between two cultures, he must eventually return to the camp of the red man. Yet the presence of the white corn in the red row was not so clear. Could it be that the white corn was Ted Henderson, and that his spirit had been turned against the Cheyenne by some powerful force? Perhaps Dream Woman knew the answer.

Before the new sun was a handspan from the eastern horizon, the lean Cheyenne warrior was astride his powerful palomino gelding, headed southeast toward Laramie.

Four

"**S**ergeant Major Albert Jonas, I do declare, you tear up more good shirts than any two men I ever seen." Sally Coker's face, the color of creamed coffee, crinkled into a slight frown as she looked up from the pile of fabric on the table before her. "What is it this time, Sergeant? Bust the back outta another one?"

Albert Jonas shuffled his feet like a schoolboy who had just been scolded by the teacher and wondered why he felt a tickle of nervousness behind his belt buckle every time he was in Sally's presence. The same sergeant major who could bark out orders that could be heard across most of Laramie was almost tongue-tied when facing the young seamstress. Sally Coker had arrived in Laramie shortly before Jonas had returned from the Navajo campaign. Her talent with a needle and thread had quickly established her as a successful seamstress in the growing town. Jonas had heard she was an escaped slave from a Southern plantation, but another story indicated she had been granted her freedom voluntarily. The big man had long since decided it did not matter. She was in Laramie, and she was the most beautiful thing he had ever seen.

"Now, Miss Sally, you know I can't help it if the army doesn't see fit to make shirts big enough for me." Jonas looked over the pile of clothing on the table. "Looks like you've been mighty busy, Miss Sally. You want me to come back later, I will."

Sally did little to settle Jonas's uneasiness when she shook out the garment she had been working on and held it up to the light, checking her handicraft. It was a camisole, and it looked about her size. Jonas quickly put aside the vision that started

79

to form in his mind. His ebony skin covered his sudden flush of embarrassment.

"No, Sergeant," Sally said. "Might as well leave it here. I'll fix the rip soon's I can." Sally put down her needle and stood. She was a tall woman, nearly five-ten, with brown eyes flecked with gold. The loose-fitting work dress she wore did little to hide her lush body.

"It's not exactly a rip this time, Miss Sally," Jonas said, handing her his campaign tunic. Sally shook his head, making clucking sounds with her tongue as she poked a finger through a half-inch hole in the side of the tunic.

"You been out chasin' Indians again?" she asked.

"It's what they pay me for, Miss Sally."

"And you near enough got yourself killed this time, Albert Jonas. This here's a bullet hole, ain't it?"

Jonas nodded. "Might have some powder burns around it, too. Was awful close."

Sally snorted. "Close, I reckon. Another four inches and you'd be dead now, Sergeant. I'll patch it up. Cost you a dime."

Albert Jonas steeled himself for the plunge, thinking it was easier to face a dozen mad Cheyenne than this woman; at least with the Indians you usually knew what to expect.

"Miss Sally," Jonas said, almost physically forcing the words, "I've been watchin' you ever since I got back from New Mexico. You're an easy woman to admire, Sally Coker, and I'd be honored if you'd let me come callin'."

The young woman's eyebrows arched in surprise. "You mean come a-courtin', Albert?"

"Yes.. I reckon that's what I really mean."

Sally shook her head emphatically. "No. Now, I'll admit you're a fine-lookin' man, Albert Jonas, and you'd make some lucky woman a fine husband. But I got no room in my future for soldiers. When the time comes, I'm gonna raise me some kids, educate 'em proper. I ain't gonna be wearin' no widow's weeds a week after a weddin'. Woman would be a durn fool, pure and simple, to marry a soldier."

Jonas raised a hand in supplication. "Now, Miss Sally—"

"Don't you 'Miss Sally' me, Sergeant." She tossed the bullet-pierced tunic atop the waiting pile of mending. "Now, if you was a blacksmith or a wheelwright or even a farmer—some trade with a future where you could keep your hair on—I just might say come a-callin', Albert. But I ain't marryin', nor even courtin', no soldier."

"Miss Sally, be reasonable," Jonas said, his heart sinking. "I can't give up the army. It's the only life I know. I'm no farmer, never could be. And a sergeant major makes as good a livin' as a blacksmith or a wheelwright."

Sally's rejection was gentle but final. "I want to be a young mother, Albert—not a young widow. I ain't havin' no truck with soldiers. I've had enough grief in my life already." She sat down and picked up a needle. "Now I don't want to hurt your feelin's, Albert. You may be big as a house, but you'd make a gentle husband and a good daddy, I think. Was your situation different, I'd say come a-callin' tonight. But it ain't." She expertly threaded the needle, plucked a garment from the pile, and started to work.

Jonas stood for an awkward moment. "Miss Sally," he said finally, "there's one thing you don't know about me. I'm sort of like a coon on a log in the middle of a creek. No matter how many dogs you send after him, that old coon wins nine times outta ten. I'm just as stubborn as that coon, Sally Coker, and I won't quit pesterin' you till you say come ahead." He turned toward the door, then stopped. "I'll be back, Miss Sally. And not to just pick up my shirt, neither. I think you're worth crawlin' out on that log in the creek for, and let the dogs come on!"

Jonas stepped into the dusty Laramie street. He did not see Sally's smile or hear her quietly humming. "If you wasn't a soldier, Albert Jonas," she whispered, "I'd be on you like a chicken on a grasshopper."

A commotion in the street ahead took Jonas's mind from Sally Coker's rejection. A small figure in buckskin astride a big sorrel horse led a procession of noisy children down the street; the man ignored the openmouthed stares of gawkers along the sidewalks. Jonas grinned widely.

"Kit!" he called, stepping into the middle of the street. "Kit Carson!" Then, suddenly remembering military decorum, Jonas saluted smartly. "Colonel Carson, I mean, sir—"

The weathered face of the ex-frontiersman grinned down at Jonas. Kit Carson snapped a salute, then extended a hand. "Good to see you again, Sergeant Jonas," he said. "Glad to see you've still got that curly hair on your head."

"It'll take a heap a' Indians to lift this scalp, Colonel. You'll be wantin' to speak with Colonel Henderson, I suppose."

Carson nodded, then glanced at the children standing in awe a few feet away. "What's all the commotion about, Sergeant?"

Jonas puzzled over the question for a brief moment, then finally understood and grinned. "The commotion's over you, sir. Not many people around Laramie expected to see a real, live legend. I reckon you're goin' to have trouble riding anywhere without drawin' a crowd. Now, if you'll follow me, Colonel, we'll take your horse to the stables and see if we can stir up Colonel Henderson."

Carson and Henderson, close friends and campaigners whose respect for each other had grown daily during the Glorieta Pass battle and later in the Indian campaigns to the south, greeted each other with a warm embrace that would have been considered unmilitary by those not acquainted with the two men.

Inside Ted's office Kit sank wearily into a chair. Ted, knowing Carson's favorite drink, produced a dipper of cool mountain stream water. His guest sipped it, savoring each swallow, then tipped the gourd dipper up, draining the contents. "No better water in the world than that which flows in the high country," Carson said.

Albert Jonas cleared his throat. "If you'll excuse me, I'll get on about my duties."

Carson interrupted with a brusque wave of a hand. "Please sit down, Jonas. Ted and I both know who really runs the army—the sergeant majors. I would be pleased to have you sit in."

Jonas placed his hat on a nearby rack and took a seat at Carson's right hand.

"Is Abel Hubbard available?" the ex-frontiersman asked Ted.

Ted shook his head. "He's out on patrol again. That young man seems to live in the saddle these days."

"I know the feeling all too well," Carson said, sighing wearily. "And saddles get harder as the years go by.

"Well, you know full well neither of us can indulge in the luxury of social visits, so we might as well get down to loading the powder wagon." Carson tugged at a corner of his mustache. "What's your situation here, Ted?"

The Fort Laramie commander briefed Carson as succinctly as possible, touching on a few of the major hit-and-run raids, the long pursuits with only small successes. "What has me concerned, Kit, is that things seem to be much worse to the east," he added. "When we've been able to keep the telegraph lines open, I've received numerous reports of devastation and havoc in Kansas and northern Nebraska. And I've had one startling dispatch from Fort Scott, which actually came under attack by raiders led by the Sioux. The commander there said the Indians, or quite a few of them, at least, were armed with the new Henry repeating rifles."

Carson raised an eyebrow. "Where do you suppose they're getting such weapons?"

"That's one of the things I've been trying to find out, Kit. I've tried to get some Henrys for my own troops, and the army keeps insisting none are available! The Indians have found a way to get them, obviously, in addition to some older rifles. At the moment the percentage of armed Indians among the Plains tribes is small, thank heaven. If all the braves were armed . . ." He let the statement trail away.

Carson began pacing the floor as he told Ted of his own patrols in the southern Plains. "Many of the Indians were as well—or better—equipped than my own men," he said.

After a detailed discussion, the two commanders reached a decision: The Plains, from border to border, were a potential prairie fire, awaiting only the touch of a match to explode.

The shadows outside were lengthening when Kit produced a thick packet from a tunic pocket. "General Carleton has proposed a plan that he hopes will bring peace to the Plains," he said, tossing the packet to Ted. "We will go over the plan in detail tomorrow, but briefly the overall approach is this: My forces in the south and yours in the north are to apply as much pressure as possible to the warring bands and in the meantime parley with those who have not taken to war paint."

Carson helped himself to another dipper of water. "In exchange for a peaceful settlement, the tribes will be guaranteed ownership of most of their current homelands, hunting rights over a wide area, and food and supplies from the government during bad winters or poor hunting seasons." The wiry ex-scout shook his head. "Proposals on paper are one thing," he said, "and plans in the field are another. But no plan is perfect when it is opposed by an angry warrior." Carson turned to Jonas. "What do you think, Sergeant?"

Albert Jonas tugged at an earlobe thoughtfully. "Colonel Carson, I'm thinking we're goin' to need some help," he replied.

"But there are no regular army troops available for duty in the West, and as a rule the volunteers cause more trouble than they're worth," Carson reminded him.

"I mean help from another place," Jonas said. "The Shoshone have no use for the Sioux or the Cheyenne. They've been enemies of those two tribes since the first sun come up, I reckon." Jonas hesitated, wondering if he was overstepping his bounds as a mere non-com in the presence of two field-rank officers.

The two colonels exchanged glances. "Please continue, Sergeant," Ted said.

"Well, sir, I've been patrolling in Shoshone territory pretty regular, and I've made a friend or two here and there. Say what you want about the Shoshone, but nobody can claim they can't track or fight. Sure would be nice to have them on our side, Colonel Henderson. Say the word and I'll see if I can't talk some of them into lending a hand."

Ted turned to the map behind his desk, on which he had penciled the names and primary ranges of the principal Indian tribes of the region. He studied the map for a moment, then turned back to Jonas.

"The Shoshone would be valuable as allies, Sergeant. They may be a small tribe, but they're fine warriors, and they hold some crucial ground. They could give us a slight edge by keeping the Arapaho from ranging north and the Sioux and Cheyenne from pushing farther west. By all means, see what you can do."

Jonas stood, plucked his campaign hat from the rack, and with a salute said, "Yes, sir. I'll get right on it."

Ted glanced out the window. "It's getting on toward dinner time, Kit, and I expect your ribs are showing after a long ride. Vi Robinson sets a fine table at the Laramie Hotel. Albert, will you join us for dinner?"

The sergeant major declined with the faintest of grins. "Meaning no disrespect, sir, and thank you for the invitation, but a sergeant's place is with his men." He saluted again and softly closed the door behind him.

"Good man," Kit Carson said, gathering up his own hat. "Wish we had more like him. Ted, I need to get some things from my saddlebags at the stable before dinner."

The streets of Laramie seemed more subdued than usual, and the two men had almost reached the stable area when they were suddenly accosted.

"Carson!"

The tone of the call brought Ted and Kit to an abrupt stop. Ted felt a tingle along his forearms, his own warning signal of danger. Together, the two officers turned toward the sound.

Two men stood in the street, an obvious challenge in their stance. The younger man, scarcely more than a boy, held a rifle pointed in their direction. The other man was the sharp-faced, swarthy teamster whom Ted had forcibly ejected from the hotel after the scene involving Wind Flower. His hand held the butt of a pistol in his waistband.

"Something I can do for you gentlemen?" Kit Carson's tone was conversational, but Ted caught the undercurrent of tension in the ex-frontiersman's voice. Instinctively Ted stepped a pace away from Carson. If trouble was on their minds, at least the men in the street would have to choose between them.

"Yeah, Carson!" The younger man's voice was high-pitched with hate and bordered on the irrational. "You damn Injun lover, you can die!" The rifle barrel started to swing in Carson's direction. Ted cursed silently as he realized his own Colt Dragoon was snugly strapped into its holster by the thong around the hammer. Both the men in the street would be able to fire before he could even draw his own weapon.

The teamster's pistol was halfway out of his belt when the unexpected blast of a big-bore rifle shattered the evening. The youth carrying the long gun staggered back under the impact of a heavy slug. Ted sensed rather than saw a metallic object suddenly appear in Carson's hand. He heard the flat *crack* of a small-bore pistol, and the teamster shuddered. Then Ted's own heavy pistol was free of the holster. He shot, and the teamster flopped backward as though hit by a broadax.

Carson's handgun barked again, a split second before the big rifle somewhere behind them sounded again. The youth's rifle flew from his hands, and he tumbled into the dust.

The incident had taken only seconds, but Ted felt he had been standing in the street for hours. Both men lay dead; the teamster with two bullet holes and the youth with three.

Ted glanced at Carson, and both men turned to see Corporal Bernie Christian emerge from the stable entrance, smoke still curling from the muzzle of his Spencer .56.

"Evening, Colonel Carson," Christian said as he drew even with the officers. "You'll excuse me if I don't salute for a few minutes?"

"Son, you've already saluted with that Spencer—and thanks," Carson said. Ted could hear doors opening and the excited babble of voices from neighboring buildings.

Carson casually broke the action of his small handgun, removed the spent shells, and dropped two more cartridges into place. He slid the weapon back into its low-cut holster. "Smith and Wesson thirty-two rimfire," he said in answer to Ted's unasked question. "Faster than that cannon you carry, but nowhere near as much a man stopper."

He turned to Christian, who was examining the bodies. "What was that all about, Corporal?"

"No idea, sir," Christian answered. "I was checking the horses and just happened to be on my way out when those two stepped into the street. Had my rifle with me and a clear field of fire."

"And lucky for us it was, son," Carson said. "They would have gotten one of us for sure if you hadn't stopped the rifleman."

Christian stood, holding a handful of gold coins toward Ted and Kit. "Don't know these two," he said, "but they were packing a bunch of money. Looks like new gold to me."

The corporal of the guard arrived at the scene on a dead run, and within moments Ted was reliving the battle for the benefit of the guard and the soldiers who had gathered around. In the excitement no one noticed the well-dressed civilian emerge from a nearby alley and slowly walk away.

"I knew the older one, sort of," Ted said, recounting the incident in the hotel to Kit. "He didn't seem to be the type who would set up a gunfight just to settle a score."

Carson shook his head. "It's just a wild idea, Ted, but can you think of a quicker way to get rid of two fairly well-known field commanders than to gun them down—or have it done for money?"

Ted had to agree it was possible, and the idea gained some weight when the corporal of the guard reported two saddled horses and a loaded pack mule had been found just outside the stockade walls. A couple of the older posts in the wall had been broken, providing a means of quick escape without having to pass through the guarded gates.

"I don't want to spoil your delayed supper, Kit," Ted said, taking the dead rifleman's weapon from a trooper who had picked it up, "but take a look at this."

Carson hefted the weapon. "Henry forty-four, rimfire repeater. Do you suppose—?"

"Anything is possible. These Henrys are all numbered. And if we had one of the weapons the Indians seem to be breeding somewhere, a comparison of the numbers might be interesting." Ted felt a gentle tug at his sleeve.

"Colonel Henderson," Bernie Christian said, "if I might have a private word with you and Colonel Carson?"

The three men moved apart from the throng.

"I know for a fact that it isn't unusual for the Confederate Army—or even civilians or groups in the South—to offer a price for a Union officer's head," Christian said. "It could be there's a bounty out on one or both of you." Christian scuffed the toe of his boot in the sand of the compound. "Going rate last I heard was two hundred for a general—paid in advance. And those two were packing over five hundred dollars *each*."

The frown lines deepened along Ted's forehead. "It isn't beyond reason. Kit and I both have enemies on both sides of the fence. Thanks for the warning, Bernie."

The corporal, a touch of embarrassment in his voice, said, "I'd just hate to lose either of the two best officers I've ever served with. Y'all best keep a watch on your back trail."

Ted and Kit stood for a moment in silence, watching Bernie make his way back to the crowd in the street.

Carson finally spoke. "Given the circumstances here today, Christian may be right. Unless that kid with the Henry was looking to build a reputation by killing me in a shootout, I think they went about this thing all wrong. If you wanted us killed, how would you go about hiring it done?"

"A lot cheaper," Ted said without hesitation. "I'd hire a couple of drifters or a pair of Indians for fifty dollars each, hand them a shotgun, and let them cut loose from an alley somewhere."

"Exactly," Carson said emphatically. "You and I think like Westerners—frontier types. This setup was just complicated enough to leave me thinking it might be an outside plan, somebody from back East or down South." A slight grin lifted the corners of the ex-scout's mouth. "Besides, I think we were a little overpriced. Oh, well. You still hungry?"

Ted was mildly surprised to discover that despite the coppery taste bloodshed left in his mouth, his belly still felt as empty as ever. While Carson finished his errand at the stables,

Ted gave instructions for the disposal of the two dead gunmen. Neither of them had carried any kind of papers or identification. With the Henry rifle safely locked in the gun rack in his office, the Fort Laramie commander and the ex-frontiersman made their way to the Laramie Hotel.

The story of the gunfight had preceded them, and they were greeted by a shaken Wilma Henderson and an ashen-faced Vi Robinson. Little William Ted was there, too, busily gnawing on a chicken leg.

After assuring the women all was fine, Ted introduced Kit Carson. William Ted offered the scout a manly, if greasy-fingered, hand.

Vi had prepared a table in a private dining room so that the two officers would not be disturbed by well-wishers or the inevitable curiosity seekers wanting to catch a glimpse of the legendary Kit Carson.

After dinner Ted and Kit turned once more to business and, to the surprise of neither, discovered they were in complete agreement that the key to a peaceful settlement with the Indians rested with the selection of proper reservations. The Indians must be assured that their sacred grounds and hunting rights would not be disturbed and that any lands ceded by the tribes would be purchased at a fair price.

Ted was distressed to learn that the Navajo were faring poorly on the Bosque Redondo. Expert farmers in their way, the Navajo were having much difficulty adapting to the white man's agricultural methods. Complicating the problem was the arid and generally infertile soil of the reservation. Living conditions, Kit added, were no better. The fort itself had been constructed, but no provision had been made for housing the Indians. The residents of the reservation faced a miserable winter, huddled in scooped-out holes in the earth and covered with whatever material could be scrounged for roofing. The people were hungry, since promised supplies either had not arrived or had been inadequate, and the new hunting grounds were not as plentiful as their old ones had been.

"There is a message to be learned from the Bosque Redondo," Kit concluded. "I hesitate to criticize a fellow officer, and particularly James Carleton. But the reservation was chosen without the needs of the Indian in mind. The consequences could be disastrous. The Apache in particular are unruly and resentful. I'm afraid they may bolt the reservation and return to their homeland. I pity the troops who have to try to dig the Apache out of those canyons and deserts again."

Wilma reluctantly excused herself to put the dozing Bill to bed. Vi had been called elsewhere to attend to some crisis, but she had insisted Kit take a room in the hotel instead of staying in the barracks. He at first resisted but finally gave in, thankful for a real bed rather than a bunk.

"Will we have the backing of Washington in treating with the Indians, Kit? Or will they ignore any peace treaties we might negotiate on the Plains?" Ted asked.

Carson shook his head sadly. "I just don't know. I'll be doing my best, as I know you will, to see that the government comes through on its promises. Given our past national history in dealing with Indians, though, I wouldn't bet on it. And it will be our personal reputations with the Indians on the line. If Washington makes a mess of things, the red man will think it's our doing, that our word is no longer good."

Carson pushed back his chair, yawned, and stretched. "It's been a long, busy day, Ted. I think we'd best get some rest while we can. There may not be too many opportunities in the near future."

When Ted came home, Wilma already had settled into bed. Ted checked on his son and placed a gentle kiss on his pink cheek. Sleep had, for the moment at least, escaped Wilma.

"Darling, I'm frightened," she said as Ted slipped into bed. "There's more to this business today than you've told me, isn't there?"

Though he did not want to worry Wilma, Ted had always been honest with her, so he filled in the details, complete with suspicions and speculation.

"I must admit I'm a bit edgy myself," he concluded. "Not for my own safety, but for yours and Wild Bill's. I can cope with bullets and arrows and take my chances, but I'm not sure I could handle it if anything happened to you two."

She snuggled close to his side. "Try not to worry about us, honey. Just promise you'll take care of yourself. So you can come back home to us." She stretched her body full against his. Their gentle kisses began to grow more urgent. Ted finally moved his lips to her ear as his hand stroked the curve of her hip and thigh.

"It must be difficult for you, sweetheart," he whispered.

"Being the wife of a warrior has to be much more painful than being the warrior."

She clasped him tighter. "You are worth the worry and the bother, sir. And every night you're home is a honeymoon for me. Now, shut up and do your duty, Colonel."

The blue-eyed Indian known as Long Walker carefully parted the tall grass with the barrel of his rifle and grunted in satisfaction. The pack train of some thirty animals, all heavily laden, had fully emerged from the brush and stunted trees on the remote tributary of the upper Missouri River. A dozen men rode alongside the pack animals, and in front of the column was a familiar figure on a big gray horse.

Long Walker retrieved his own mount and galloped to meet the pack train. He pulled his horse to a sliding stop before the man on the gray, and for a long moment the two men stared at each other silently. Despite the warmth of the afternoon sun, the man on the gray wore the jacket of his expensive vested suit buttoned below a blue cravat.

"You are late," Long Walker said, disdaining any other greeting. "My warriors have been kept waiting for two days. They are getting restless."

The man on the gray shrugged. "It couldn't be helped. The commander of volunteers at Fort Sully decided to raise his price for letting us pass safely."

Long Walker snorted. "Bribery is your problem, not mine. Did you bring all the rifles?"

"Only sixty of the new Henrys were available, with two hundred rounds of ammunition for each. The rest of the rifles are cap and ball."

The Indian's blue eyes snapped angrily. "Our deal was for one hundred repeaters and five hundred rounds of ammunition each. Why aren't they all here?"

The man on the gray tensed at the challenge. "In case you haven't heard, Long Walker, there is a war going on. Modern weapons are hard to locate and expensive to buy." A well-manicured hand dropped toward his hip.

"Touch that weapon and I will kill you on the spot," Long Walker said quietly.

The white man's youthful-looking face twisted in a sneer, distorting his otherwise handsome features. "And then who would be your contact for supplies and arms?" he asked pointedly. Even as he asked the question, however, his hand reappeared on the silver horn of his expensive saddle.

"It would not be hard to find another contact," Long Walker said, staring into the green eyes of the pack train leader. "Have you made arrangements for the next shipment?"

The man on the gray relaxed. "Yes. Two hundred Henry rifles, some of the new Winchester repeaters, and a great deal of ammunition will be on its way from Mobile within a month. Such a volume of goods would be impossible to pack in by mule, so the shipment will be moving by wagon train from the railhead at Atchison along the Overland Stage Route. You'll be advised in our usual manner when the wagons are clear of Atchison."

The horseman plucked a cigar from his breast pocket, touched a match to the thin-rolled tobacco, and breathed a cloud of smoke. "The wagon master was something of a problem, Long Walker. I think a raid, with no survivors, would solve some problems for both of us," he suggested casually.

"Agreed."

"How goes the hunting?" the white man asked.

"It goes well," Long Walker replied. "My men have taken a number of scalps, and our raid on Fort Scott was successful even though the soldiers think they fought us off. We now have a fair-sized herd of shod army horses, courtesy of the Union. Enough to convince Big Nose of the Cheyenne and Sitting Bull of the Sioux to join with us."

The green-eyed man nodded. "Good. How soon do you plan to open your major campaigns?"

Long Walker waved toward the pack mules. "A couple of days after the guns are distributed. There will be few sunrises without new graves on the Plains. Have your men unload the mules here. My warriors are but ten minutes' ride away. In fact, you just rode through most of the band."

The white man's green eyes widened in astonishment. "We saw no sign of Indians!"

"Should I have suspected any kind of treachery, you would have seen more Indians than you ever thought possible, my Rebel friend." Long Walker's voice was clearly mocking, but the horseman let the remark slide. He called to one of his riders to begin unloading, then swung down from his gray.

"Do you want to check the merchandise?" he asked.

"I don't think it necessary," Long Walker replied, slipping

from his horse. "I think you realize what would happen if it is not all here."

"Long Walker, I would value your suggestion on a problem we have," the Southerner said. "The commander at Fort Laramie—"

"Colonel Ted Henderson," Long Walker interrupted. "He is apt to become a thorn in your side."

"Yes. And for that reason we want him removed. Along with his second in command, Abel Hubbard, if possible. But Henderson is our prime target."

"Why not just have him killed?" the Indian asked.

The man in the suit squinted through the cigar smoke. "It's a bit more complicated than that. Besides, it has already been tried unsuccessfully. Now he will be on his guard. His death from an ambush would serve us no purpose, either, because the men of his command are devoted to him and would fight even harder to avenge the loss of their commanding officer. We would be much better off if he could simply be neutralized."

The two men squatted on the ground and talked until the unloading of the pack train was finally completed.

"I will give the matter some attention," Long Walker said. "There is always a way. Each man has a weakness. I will find it and be in touch with you." Long Walker's smile was more a sneer. "In the meantime, I have a few whites to kill. This new commander at Fort Sully—the greedy one—would you like to have him punished?"

"Enough to offer you a personal bonus," the visitor said. "It would be an effective warning to others on our payroll not to get too greedy."

The Indian stood. "Consider it done. It will be a good place to start; my braves can become accustomed to the new rifles. Then we will be ready for bigger game. I think it best that you leave now. We have much to do, and the sooner you have left this area the safer it will be for both of us. We shall meet again in, say, three weeks? At the usual place?"

"I will be there." The man pulled down his hat and mounted his gray. "In the meantime, good hunting, Long Walker."

The blue-eyed Indian waited until the riders from the pack train had moved well away from the scene, then waved his hand twice above his head.

Within moments, scores of braves appeared on the scene.

Long Walker took charge of distributing the weapons, and as promised, the warriors who had killed the most whites received the fine new repeating rifles. By nightfall the newly armed band was on its way to Fort Sully.

At dawn the Indians were hidden within sight of their target. Long Walker waited patiently until the men on the fort's wood detail had drawn near enough that he could hear their mutterings and grumblings. Long Walker recognized them as soldiers of the Sixth Iowa Volunteers. They were new to the area and inexperienced as Indian fighters. It was a good sign.

He raised a hand, cautioning his eager braves to be patient for a few moments more. He lined the sights of his rifle on the soldier trailing behind the second wagon. Long Walker waited until the infantryman had passed by, the X where his suspenders crossed his back providing a natural target. Slowly the Indian squeezed the trigger.

The Henry bucked against Long Walker's shoulder, and the soldier pitched forward. The shot triggered a volley from the concealed braves along either side of the trail. Within seconds the wood detail was wiped out. Yelling and whooping braves dashed from one body to another, lifting scalps, stripping clothing, ammunition pouches, weapons, and finally hacking away at the mutilated remains of the ill-fated detail.

Long Walker waited until the initial burst of enthusiasm over the victory had passed, then summoned to his side a half-dozen braves chosen for their horsemanship and bravery.

A quarter mile to the north and almost a mile from the fort, a force of five hundred of Long Walker's warriors lined the sides of a shallow valley. It was to that spot Long Walker and his six men would lead their pursuers from the fort—right into the carefully planned ambush.

With Long Walker in the lead, the half-dozen Indians charged the entrance to the fort. They had almost reached the gates when it appeared to the wildly firing volunteers inside the fort that the Indians suddenly panicked. Long Walker wheeled his pony and set the pace as the small war party fled the scene. Few of the rifle balls fired from the fort even came close to hitting their marks.

Just out of range of the soldiers' rifles, Long Walker waved his party to a stop and set them to milling about as though confused. His patience with the indecision of the soldiers was beginning to wear thin when the fort gates suddenly swung open. Out thundered a group of mounted men. Long Walker smiled; the soldiers had taken the bait. He delayed long enough to estimate the force at two companies, then wheeled his horse, and quirted the animal toward the shallow valley.

The six Indians bent low over the backs of their mounts, appearing to flee for their lives. Yet each of the Sioux held his animal carefully in check. As they entered the valley, Long Walker and the others slowed their mounts even more, letting the soldiers believe they were gaining ground.

The first of the cavalry volunteers swept into the valley, followed by the disorganized remainder of the two companies. Long Walker glanced back and saw with satisfaction that a group of four men had fallen behind the rest of the soldiers. Reaching the far end of the shallow valley, Long Walker suddenly stopped his horse, slid from the saddle, and shouldered his rifle. The first slug from his Henry toppled the lead rider from his mount.

Instantly the trap slammed shut.

Fifty braves raced into position behind the soldiers, cutting off any retreat. A blistering volley of rifle fire boomed from the crest of both sides of the valley.

Horses screamed and fell to the ground. The pursuit column, realizing they had blindly ridden into an ambush, dismounted and began a valiant but futile defense. Indian sharpshooters picked off the surviving troopers one by one. Scattered and unable to set up a perimeter of defense, the soldiers were left to make such stands as they could in small groups of five or fewer.

The Sioux, using each low bush or grass clump for cover, closed to within a few yards of the defenders. In one whooping rush, the wave of Indians swept over the remaining pockets of soldiers. It was nearly over.

Long Walker reached the isolated soldiers at the rear of the column just as a brave raised a pistol to finish off the last trooper, who stood clicking his empty revolver at the Indian in panic.

A cry from Long Walker stayed the brave's hand. "Do not kill this one! He is of more use as a captive. Bind his wrists and mount him on an army horse."

Reluctantly the brave did as he was told. With the stunned soldier firmly strapped to a horse, Long Walker squatted in the grass and listened to the victorious war whoops ring across the valley. He was pleased. His plan was working perfectly. Now he had the final items he needed to draw Sitting Bull and Big Nose into the war against the whites.

He had a captive soldier and many army rifles.

Leaving the main body of Indians under the command of one of his top warriors, Long Walker led the white captive and a heavily laden packhorse northward along the Missouri River.

At noon the next day, Long Walker touched flint to steel and ignited the small signal fire atop a low, rocky mesa. He settled back to await the arrival of the half-dozen outcasts—three Pawnee, a Ute, and two Crow braves who had all been banned from their own tribes for crimes against their fellow tribesmen. Long Walker did not relish working with the outlaws. He knew that, to a man, they were insane in one way or another. But men with no conscience fit his needs, and if the plan should go awry, they were easily expendable. Besides, they could be expected to relish performing atrocities no self-respecting Sioux or Cheyenne would even consider. The fact that they would be well paid for their services should only inflame them.

Tired of the captive soldier's constant whining and begging, Long Walker fought an urge to slit the man's throat. Instead, he roughly gagged the man with a strip of cloth and deprived him of any food or water.

By nightfall the six outlaws had arrived. Extensively trained in languages of the Plains Indians by the Confederates, Long Walker greeted each man in his own tongue.

Early the next afternoon, Long Walker had located what he needed, a small family group, only four tipis, of Hunkpapa Sioux camped near a thicket of ripening berries. The laughter of the women as they gathered berries to be dried for winter use drifted toward him on the growing breeze.

Long Walker tied the captive soldier securely to a small, well-concealed tree. Then, carrying an army issue cap-and-ball Springfield and with an aging .36 navy revolver bearing a USA stamp tucked into his breechcloth, he strolled casually into the small camp. As he had suspected, only two men were guarding the berry-gathering party.

Long Walker raised a hand in salute as one of the braves stepped from a tipi, bow in hand.

"Greetings, brother," Long Walker called in Sioux. "The spirits have smiled this day in letting Long Walker find your camp. Long Walker's horse is dead for two days, and he has many miles to travel."

The Sioux warrior lowered the bow. "Long Walker is welcome in our camp, brother. He may have one of our horses to continue his journey." The brave turned and started to walk past the tipis to the small pony herd beyond. Long Walker casually raised the army rifle and shot the warrior in the back of the head. He tossed the single-shot weapon aside and drew the navy revolver.

Drawn by the sound of the rifle shot, the second brave came into the camp area on the run. Long Walker shot him four times in the chest. The man tumbled into the dust, shuddered once, and lay still.

Long Walker paused for a moment to listen as the six outlaw Indians pounced on the berry-gathering party. From the sounds in the thicket, he could reconstruct the scene as the attackers overpowered the unarmed women. The old and the ugly were shot on the spot, the younger and prettier ones violated, then slain.

As the sounds of the murderous orgy continued, Long Walker retrieved the captive soldier and led him to the center of the camp. Still bound and gagged, the wide-eyed soldier could only make terrified gurgling noises as Long Walker picked up the dead Sioux brave's bow and nocked an arrow. He smiled evilly at the soldier, then sent the arrowhead deep into the doomed man's heart.

Long Walker dropped the bow by the dead Indian, then slashed the soldier's bonds and gag, storing them carefully in a pouch slung over his shoulder. With great satisfaction he stepped back to study the scene.

It appeared that the camp had been attacked by soldiers and that one was killed; the dead women in the berry thicket, along with the bodies of their babies, would complete the deception he was building. Not even Sitting Bull would fail to be enraged at the devastation. Retaliation against the soldiers would be the only answer to such carnage.

Long Walker mounted the dead soldier's horse and rode at a gallop several times across the campground and toward the thicket, obliterating signs of his own passage and completing the illusion of a mounted attack by soldiers.

Then he rejoined the sated, blood-smeared outlaw braves. "There are none left alive?" he asked the scarred Pawnee, who had been cast from his tribe for rape and murder.

"None."

"It is good. Now let us regroup and make for the country

of the Cheyenne. There we shall find another small band with many women for your entertainment. Then you will have your reward, a fine new repeating rifle, ammunition, and three good war ponies each."

The scarred Pawnee eyed Long Walker. "And what reward will you receive?"

"It is a long story," Long Walker replied, his blue eyes angry. "And one that does not concern you." The barely veiled threat silenced the Pawnee.

His reward, Long Walker told himself, would be far greater than any of these half-wit outlaws suspected. His reward would be power—and control of the rich Plains. A kingdom such as those he had read of in the white man's books would be his—a land rich in gold and silver, teeming with wild game. Tributes of money and horses from certain white men also would be his in exchange for passage to the ore fields or to move freight across his kingdom.

When Sitting Bull learned of the atrocity comitted by the "white soldiers" and a similar fate befell one of Big Nose's small bands, the grand scheme would be in motion at last.

Long Walker swung onto his horse and reined the animal toward Cheyenne country. By now the warriors he had left behind after the Fort Sully attack would be well on their way toward the Overland Trail. In their wake, the communication lines of the white man would lie in ruins, ranches and farms sacked and burned.

Still, Long Walker resolved he would not count his winnings until the game had ended. He knew the Confederacy would likely fall before the superior manpower and production facilities of the Union. Until then, he would use the Confederacy even as they thought they were using him. But he knew instinctively he must move with speed, driving out the whites and establishing his kingdom before the war between the North and South came to an end.

He glanced in the direction of Fort Laramie and frowned. There still remained the problem of Ted Henderson. But the glimmerings of an idea already were taking shape in the blue-eyed Indian's mind.

Wilma Henderson's breath caught in her throat as Yellow Crow's bronze arm boosted little William Ted onto the back of the sorrel and white paint pony. Instinctively she started toward her son, but her husband grasped her arm firmly.

"Leave them be, Wilma," Ted said. "The pony is Yellow Crow's gift to his godson, and Little Bill couldn't be in better hands."

"But, Ted! He's—so young."

"He's going on three, dear," Ted said. "That's about the time the Cheyenne begin training their boys in horsemanship. Yellow Crow isn't going to let anything happen to our son."

The child's exuberance at the arrival of Yellow Crow and the gift of the paint pony subsided a bit when he actually found himself on the back of the animal. Little Bill's face took on a manly expression as he exchanged short sentences with his Cheyenne godfather. They spoke alternately in English, Cheyenne, and a bit of Arapaho when the boy could not find the proper word. Wilma realized with a start their son was rapidly becoming multilingual.

Yellow Crow, his instructions to the boy concluded, mounted his own palomino gelding. They rode side by side along the parade ground, the tall Cheyenne occasionally leaning down for an earnest word with the small boy. Before they had completed the first circuit of the parade ground, Wilma could see her son's confidence growing almost by the stride as he learned first one and then another technique for keeping his pony under control.

At the end of Bill's first ride, Yellow Crow stopped his palomino in front of the Hendersons' quarters, dismounted, and left the youngster to ride alone.

"Young godson learn quick," Yellow Crow said with a rare grin of delight. "Handle horse like born to ride. Maybe in blood. Maybe in wisdom of godfather." The Cheyenne closed one eye in a slow wink at Ted, unnoticed by Wilma, who was intently following the progress of her son and his paint. "Spotted horse gentle," he told Ted. "Teach young warrior much. Not pitch."

Ted clapped the back of his blood brother. "Yellow Crow has brought many welcome gifts on his return," he said in Cheyenne. "Perhaps this time he will stay for a few moons; it is long since we have hunted together." Ted looked at the small figure on horseback. The boy already had picked up the rhythm of the horse's movements and was putting the animal through a slow figure-eight pattern at the far end of the compound. "This time, Yellow Crow's godson will accompany us," Ted added. "It is time he tasted the high country air, the thrill of the hunt, and the beauty of our mountains."

Ted felt the solid muscles beneath his hand tense. "It is not the will of the spirits that we ride together on the hunt this time," Yellow Crow said regretfully. "Soon more Cheyenne and Arapaho arrive to join the peaceful Indians in Black Kettle's camp. Much remains to be done. Perhaps other bands may yet be persuaded not to raise the war ax."

Abruptly Yellow Crow stepped from the boardwalk and waved to the boy on horseback. William Ted turned the pony, and the two new friends made their way back to the group. Wilma reached up to help her son down but stopped at a word from Yellow Crow.

"Let godson do dismount himself," the Cheyenne said.

The boy sat astride the pony for a moment, measuring the distance to the ground, his young face furrowed in thought. Then he leaned forward, grasped a handful of the pony's mane, and, using the long horsehair as a handhold, slid to the ground.

Yellow Crow grunted in satisfaction. "William Ted do well," he said to the boy. "Now he must learn to care for pony. Not just ride and turn loose. Take pony to stable. Yellow Crow be along quick to tell more."

Wilma stepped to Yellow Crow and kissed the Cheyenne on the cheek. "Thank you for the gift of the pony," she said. "Your godson appears to have the makings of a fine horseman—thanks to instructions from you. Now if you will excuse me, gentlemen, I will go and prepare dinner for my three men." Wilma scurried back inside to her stove, obviously relieved that the initial horseback ride had gone so well.

Ted fell into step beside Yellow Crow as the pair made their way toward the stable. "Something is troubling my brother," Ted said in Cheyenne. It was a statement, not a question.

"This is true," Yellow Crow replied. "It is a confusion of the spirit." Briefly he recounted his dream. "Yellow Crow will ask Dream Woman to interpret the details," he concluded, "but he thinks it was a bad dream for Yellow Crow and his blood brother."

Ted knew how much visions meant in the Cheyenne culture, and he had no intention of treating lightly the dream Yellow Crow told him. In fact, the story had shaken Ted more than he wanted to admit since it reflected his own fears. The blood brothers were caught in a crossfire of history, neither completely red nor white in temperament or in heart.

"We don't yet know what forces are really at work on the Plains," Ted said, "and I do not have the gift of seeing into the future. But if your dream is truly as you believe, one thing will remain. Even if one day our horses must take different trails, our spirits shall ride as one forever."

During dinner Ted sensed an uneasiness in Yellow Crow, despite Little Bill's excited babblings over the pony and Wilma's lighthearted manner.

"I'm sorry you missed seeing Kit Carson," Wilma told Yellow Crow over coffee. "He only stayed two days and just rode out yesterday morning. He inquired of you several times."

"Perhaps we will meet again," Yellow Crow said, waving a hand toward the window. "It seems big country. Not so big when two warriors ride trail."

The meal concluded, Ted and the Cheyenne stepped into the growing dusk for a breath of fresh air. Their short stroll was interrupted by the corporal of the guard.

"Sorry to disturb you, sir," the corporal said, "but the telegraph lines to the east have gone dead again. The last message that came through was broken off suddenly, but it indicated a great deal of trouble along the Platte." The corporal handed Ted the incomplete message. Ted glanced at the paper. "Has Colonel Hubbard been informed?"

The corporal nodded. "Yes, sir. He asked me to advise you he will be forming a detail to move out at first light."

"Thank you, Corporal. Tell Colonel Hubbard I will call him before long to discuss the situation."

Ted waited until the non-com was out of earshot, then turned to Yellow Crow. He read from the piece of paper:

"Forts Sully and Riley attacked by Indians last few days. Wagons, farms raided, many civilian casualties. Appear Indians headed your direction. Estimate raiding band numbers in hundreds. Volunteer units forming and ex—"

Ted folded the paper and tucked it into his shirt pocket. "What do you think, Yellow Crow?"

The Cheyenne's face grew even more grim. "Not good. Hard to talk peace when men shoot at each other. Indians raid, white man raids back. Maybe get wrong Indian."

"That," Ted said, "is one of my biggest worries, now that

more and more peaceful Indians are coming to Laramie, thanks in great part to your work. But why the sudden attacks by a large Indian force? Most of the raids up to now have been by small bands, not by forces 'in the hundreds' as the telegram said."

Yellow Crow pivoted on a heel and stared toward the northeast. "Blue-eyed Indian," he said after a brief pause.

Ted started. "There was a word of a blue-eyed Indian in a band that attacked a family not far from here," he said quietly.

"This one bad Indian," Yellow Crow said. "Promise braves new guns, many scalps. At council fires Yellow Crow hear much talk of this blue-eyed one called Long Walker. He has strong words. Many young warriors listen. Maybe enough braves leave own bands and join Long Walker to put small red army in field."

Ted's mind leaped back to his earlier conversation with Kit Carson and the fact that Sioux raiders armed with Henry repeating rifles had attacked Fort Scott. Could the blue-eyed Indian have been among those attackers? If so, it would appear this Long Walker was able to procure new weapons. Those guns had to come from someplace, and Ted knew of no traders in the area who could afford the heavy cash outlay necessary to stock the repeaters. Besides, few Indians could afford to buy them. Evidently Long Walker had strong ties to some large, well-funded organization.

Ted could not shake the sudden feeling that Yellow Crow had just pointed him toward a Confederate agent. A blue-eyed Indian.

"Yellow Crow, I must go now and talk this over with Abel. Lord knows he can handle himself in any scrap, but if Long Walker has put several hundred well-armed warriors in the field, Abel could be riding into a hornets' nest." Ted started to turn away, then stopped. In his concern over the new developments, he had almost forgotten his manners. "You will be our guest here for as long as you can stay, Yellow Crow. My lodge is yours."

The Cheyenne shook his head. "Yellow Crow must go to the camp of Black Kettle." He waved a hand to cut off Ted's protest. "He must make ready for the arrival of more peaceful tribes at Black Kettle's camp," Yellow Crow said. "Also, he goes to trade."

Respecting his friend's wishes, Ted merely nodded and strode toward the commanding officer's quarters, where Abel

Hubbard would be making plans to move against the marauding Indians.

The slightest hint of a smile on his lips, Yellow Crow watched Ted go. Then the Cheyenne retrieved his palomino, and once outside the fort gates, he reined the animal in the direction of Black Kettle's camp along the South Platte River.

When Yellow Crow entered the camp, fires still burned before the lodges. He paused long enough at Black Kettle's tipi to pay his respects, then made his way toward the special lodge.

He felt a sense of relief when he saw a young, slender figure, a water container in her hand, emerge from the lodge. At least she was still there; Crooked Stick had not yet sold or traded the Blackfoot woman.

But Crooked Stick also drove a hard bargain, and the negotiations continued until the night was half gone. In the end, Yellow Crow was pleased. The agreed upon price did not include Yellow Crow's palomino gelding that Crooked Stick had coveted.

The next morning dawned crisp and cool, a solid touch of autumn in the air. At the agreed-upon time, the captive Blackfoot maiden was summoned to the lodge. At Yellow Crow's request, Crooked Stick and his entourage of wives found business outside the large tipi, leaving Yellow Crow alone with the Blackfoot woman. Looking across the remains of the morning fire, Yellow Crow studied the woman and wondered if his gamble would be rewarded.

"Talking Bird, how long have you been a captive of the Cheyenne?" he asked gently.

If she was startled that he spoke in her native Blackfoot tongue, Talking Bird did not show it. "For three summers." Her wide-set black eyes showed no emotion, but Talking Bird felt her heart skip a beat as she glanced at the tall, lean warrior. He was a handsome man in his way, she thought, and his eyes seemed kind.

"Last night," the Cheyenne said, "Yellow Crow arranged your purchase from Crooked Stick."

Talking Bird felt neither surprise nor degradation at the fact she had just been bought like a horse at auction, for it was a way of life among most Plains tribes to buy, sell, and trade captive women. They were, after all, the property of the victor. There was no shame involved.

"Talking Bird will gather her few belongings," she said.

Yellow Crow waved a hand. "Please. Sit down. There is much to discuss."

Talking Bird was momentarily confused. No one said "please" to a slave. Then she sat and waited.

"It is not Yellow Crow's wish to possess slaves or captives," he said. "Yet the winters grow longer. Yellow Crow has no sons, no woman to share his thoughts. There is no time for courtship, and Yellow Crow will be away from the camp of Black Kettle much during the weeks to come. He has watched you for months, Talking Bird. You are young and pretty. There are others perhaps braver, more wealthy, more physically attractive than Yellow Crow."

Talking Bird was momentarily astounded. She had never heard a Cheyenne brave admit that he might be less than perfect. All the braves she had known, even the braves among her own tribe, were vain and boasted until one's stomach turned.

"Among your own people you may have found a man for yourself. Yellow Crow would not interfere with any living creature's freedom. He cannot tie horses and gifts before your lodge, for our people have always been enemies and even today remain so.

"Therefore, Yellow Crow offers you your freedom," he continued. "If you choose to return to your people, he will escort you there in safety. If you choose to stay, he would have you as his wife. The decision is yours and yours alone. Let no one influence you."

Talking Bird opened her mouth to speak, but the Cheyenne raised a hand.

"Do not decide now," he said. "Yellow Crow has arranged that you live here, with Crooked Stick's family, until you have had time to give the matter some thought. Your duties will not change except that you need share no man's blanket. When Yellow Crow next returns, you may inform him of your answer."

The Cheyenne walked to the astounded young woman and looked down at her for a moment. "It is his hope that you will choose to be Yellow Crow's wife," he said, touching her softly on the shoulder. Then he was gone, leaving her alone with her swirling thoughts.

Five

The arrival and departure of patrols from Fort Laramie was an almost constant stream, ebbing and flowing with the tides of violence by marauding Indians and white outlaws, routine escort details, and supply missions. But when Abel Hubbard led his three-hundred-man column toward the gates, practically the entire community gathered to watch. Seldom was such a large force sent afield at one time.

Judy Hubbard forced a bright, encouraging smile onto her face despite the leaden weight in her stomach. As her husband approached, lean and confident in the saddle, she blew a silent kiss in his direction. He touched his hat brim in salute to his wife. As he rode past her, the expression in his eyes seemed to say, "Don't worry, dear. I'll be home safely."

But Judy was not reassured. She knew her husband was an expert soldier, sure of his own abilities, yet cautious in the field. She also knew that anything was possible: a stray bullet, a tomahawk at short range, even a badger hole waiting unseen to trap and bring down a running horse.

Each time Abel rode away it seemed to Judy that a part of her died, only to be resurrected on his safe return. They both had worked so hard to rebuild their marriage, which had been badly shaken in its early months. The thought of losing Abel cut through Judy's heart like a knife. She knew he had forgiven her for her early mistake, but she was not as sure he had forgotten. Silently she renewed her vow never again to give Abel cause for suspicion.

Judy watched her husband as long as she could see him, then turned to look into the faces of the passing troops. She wondered how many of those faces she was seeing for the last time.

"Morning, ladies," Sergeant Major Albert Jonas said as he rode past, doffing his hat and bowing in the saddle as though he were gallantly asking for the next dance instead of possibly riding to his death.

Judy realized the gesture was not meant only for her. She glanced at the woman at her side. Sally Coker, the seamstress whose genuine warmth and gentleness had won the respect of practically everyone in Laramie, had put aside her needle to watch the soldiers depart.

"Sergeant Jonas cuts an imposing figure on horseback, doesn't he?" Judy said.

"Yes'm," Sally replied, "I reckon he does, for a soldier."

"Is he still, as you say, 'pestering' you to come calling, Sally?"

"Yes'm, that he is," the seamstress replied, then sighed. "Lawd, that man is as stubborn as me. I keep tellin' him I ain't gettin' involved with no soldier, and he keeps tellin' me right back I will, sooner or later. I swear, Miss Judy, I don't know which one of us'll quit first."

Judy thought she caught just the hint of wistfulness in Sally's final statement. "You could do worse, Sally," she said. "Albert Jonas is a fine and gentle man. There aren't many of those about, in uniform or out. Colonel Henderson and Abel have told me of some of Sergeant Jonas's exploits, and they have been remarkable."

"Miss Judy, I heard most of them stories myself. He's a good man sure 'nough, and he knows all he's got to do is take off that uniform for good, and I'll open my door to the big ox." Sally turned away. "The Lawd ride with you, Albert Jonas," she prayed.

Despite the heaviness in her own heart, Judy smiled, remembering what Wilma Henderson had once said: "There is no homecoming like that when a soldier comes back from the field." Words Judy now knew to be true.

The dust of the passing column, a hundred fifty mounted men and as many on foot, began to drift over the sidewalk. Judy felt a sneeze coming on and ducked inside a nearby store to escape the dust.

Finally the last supply wagon had passed by as the unit from the Third Cavalry cleared Fort Laramie's protective walls. The heaviness seemed to grow in Judy's heart, and she knew she had to follow Wilma's advice—stay busy when your man is away or go crazy with worry. Judy sighed. At least in

Fort Laramie there was more than enough to do. If Wilma had things under control at the refugee center, there was always the hotel, where Vi welcomed her assistance. It was hard and demanding work, but it kept her hands busy.

Judy cast one last, longing look in the direction her husband had gone, then went in search of Wilma.

Less than a mile beyond the gates of the fort, Abel Hubbard already had deployed his column of troops. He was highly pleased with Albert Jonas's efforts among the Shoshone. Fifty mounted warriors would be ranging far afield in advance of the column, negating chances of a surprise attack. Ted Henderson's crack R Company, led by Sergeant Jonas, preceded the main body of troops. Cavalrymen riding flank protected the infantry and supply wagons.

Abel had a healthy respect for the infantry companies. While the mounted cavalry units seemed to get all the glory, the leg-weary foot soldier was the man who actually won the wars. He marveled at the infantryman's stamina. Many times he had seen an infantry company cover forty miles on forced march and still seem fresh in an engagement with an enemy. Personally, Abel was much happier with a horse between his knees. He settled back in the saddle, steeled for a long ride, and instinctively touched the stock of the Spencer repeater in its scabbard. No field commander in his right mind wanted to meet a force of a thousand Indians head-on, but Abel Hubbard fervently hoped he could get at least one shot at the Indian Ted Henderson described, the one with the blue eyes.

Hubbard's column had been on the move for three days when the Shoshone chief of scouts galloped up, yanking his lathered pony to a stop beside Abel and Albert Jonas.

"Much Indians ahead," the scout said. "Sioux, some Cheyenne. Many new scalps on lances. Smoke we see this morning from freight wagons. No one alive there now. Whiskey smell strong, maybe much drunk Indian up ahead."

"Do you think they've spotted us yet?" Abel asked.

The scout shook his head. "No see yet. They move slow, no hurry. Leave road, go toward place white man call Republican River."

"How many?"

The Shoshone held up two fingers and pointed toward the column of soldiers. "Twice times us," he said.

Abel uncapped his canteen and handed it to the Shoshone. The scout took two long swallows, then returned the container.

Hubbard turned to Albert Jonas. "What do you think, Sergeant?"

"Must be Long Walker and his bunch of devils," Jonas said, his dust-streaked black brows knit in thought. "Can't say as I like the odds, Colonel Hubbard, even though we've faced worse many times. But if these braves have many repeater rifles, they could be a tough nut for us squirrels to bite."

Abel glanced at the sun. "Call a halt and rest the men and horses until nightfall, Sergeant. I have an idea. Keep the scouts out; we don't want to lose contact with the Indians. Pass the word we'll be facing a tough night march. If that is Long Walker's bunch, and if we get lucky and smart, we might just have a little surprise in store come dawn."

Abel Hubbard's luck almost held—but not quite.

The Cheyenne brave called Goat's Neck, awakened in the predawn hours by an overwhelming urge to urinate, crawled from the spot where he had fallen in a drunken stupor from his pony the previous afternoon.

The young warrior emptied his bladder and listened to the pounding of blood inside his aching head. He glanced at the stars and the weak quarter moon to get his bearings and decided he was about a mile north of the planned campsite on the river. Then came another sound—a clink of metal on rock. The noise cut through the Cheyenne's whiskey-induced misery and snapped him alert. He crept to the edge of the shallow depression in which he had fallen.

The sight that awaited him in the faint light jarred Goat's Neck. Only a few hundred yards away, he could make out the distinct forms of horsemen surrounding others traveling on foot. Soldiers! And they were headed toward the Indian camp!

Fortunately for Goat's Neck, he had fallen on the hackamore rein of his pony, preventing the horse from straying. The animal's nostrils flared as it smelled the scent of other horses. Goat's Neck clamped a hand over the horse's muzzle to prevent its nickering and giving away his position. As quickly and quietly as he could, he led the horse away from the slowly approaching line of soldiers until it was safe to mount. Quickly Goat's Neck vaulted aboard his pony and urged the animal toward the encampment on the river.

Goat's Neck's warning quickly brought the rest of the camp awake, and within moments the Indians had organized a rear guard. In Long Walker's absence, his second in command elected flight rather than to face the approaching soldiers head-on. The terrain was not of his choosing, and his warriors still suffered from the effects of alcohol they had plundered from the teamsters' heavily laden wagons. The call went out for a stealthy retreat. Only two dozen Sioux remained behind, rifle muzzles poked over a hastily erected breastwork of sand from the riverbed.

By the time dawn speckled the eastern horizon, Abel Hubbard's scouts were on their way back to the main body of troops with the report that most of the Indians had escaped the carefully planned trap.

Abel's sharp curse cut through the imposed silence of the night march. With just a few more hours, he could have dealt a heavy blow to Long Walker's growing army.

After a short conference with his scouts and non-coms, Abel decided against pursuit. The fleet Indian ponies could easily outrun the slower and heavier cavalry mounts, and the braves could possibly turn on the soldiers from ambush. Besides, if Abel knew Indians, the group would soon begin to divide until only single trails remained. Still, something might be gained from the botched ambush. Ted Henderson wanted Henry rifles from Long Walker's band, and it was logical that the rear guard would be equipped with the repeaters. Perhaps a few captives should be taken.

After persuasive arguments from the Shoshone, Abel gave his Indian allies permission to try and overrun the rear guard. If they met unexpectedly heavy resistance, the soldiers would be thrown into the action. With great reluctance, the Shoshone finally agreed to spare as many Indians as possible for captives. Then they melted away into the surrounding hillside.

The attack by arrows and lances from nearby surprised the Sioux defenders, who had been concentrating on the soldiers just out of rifle range on the ridge above the river. As Abel watched the attack unfold, he marveled at the efficiency of the Shoshone stalk. The Sioux were able to get off only a couple dozen wild shots before the Shoshone completely overran the outpost.

Twenty Sioux were killed and quickly scalped. Four others were bound as captives, and a half-dozen Henry rifles were delivered to the lieutenant colonel.

Weary and disgusted, Abel Hubbard gave his troops a few hours' rest. Then would come the march back to the Overland

Route and the tedious but necessary repair of the downed telegraph lines. Units from other forts and outposts would be working to restore communications as well, but his group faced the longest reconstruction task.

Thanks to adroit tracking by the Shoshone chief of scouts, Abel found out the cause of the plan's failure. He was furious.

"Dammit to hell!" Abel picked up a handful of earth and slammed it into a nearby brush clump. "How am I going to tell Ted Henderson that some drunken Indian's urge to pee blew our one chance to break Long Walker's medicine forever? How many lives will that one Indian taking a leak cost before it's over?"

The lieutenant colonel stalked angrily away. One of the Shoshone started to follow, but a big black hand clamped on his arm.

"Leave him alone, brother," Sergeant Major Albert Jonas said. "He's not angry with you, me, or the world. He's angry with himself 'cause he thinks he's failed. Leave him be. It's not a feeling he has too often."

Colonel Ted Henderson banged a fist down hard on a stack of reports. "Corporal of the guard!" he bellowed.

The startled face of the non-com on duty appeared at Ted's doorway. "Yes, sir?"

"Get Lieutenant Wills over here at once! On the double and in his drawers if you have to!"

The corporal took one look at Ted's face and fled. Within moments, the pink-faced young lieutenant stood before his enraged commander.

"Wills, how do you explain this?" Ted demanded in a voice tight with fury. He jabbed a finger at the report lying on a corner of his desk. "Why did you put Private Edwards on report?"

Flustered and confused, Lieutenant Wills could only stammer. "But, sir—it's all there—improper salute, top button unfastened on tunic—"

Ted had to force himself not to hit the man in front of him. Striking a junior officer was not a minor offense in the U.S. Army. "Wills, I am going to tell you this just once! I expect you to listen. Private Edwards's tunic was unbuttoned because the man was in pain. His salute was improper because, Wills, Private Edwards cannot yet raise his right arm above shoulder height. It was not long ago that a surgeon dug a rifle ball from

Private Edwards's shoulder. It was put there by an Indian."
Ted glowered darkly at the lieutenant. "Private Edwards
should still be in his cot. But the man volunteered to stand
commissary guard watch because that would free a healthy
soldier for duty elsewhere!"

A flush further reddened the cheeks of the young
lieutenant. "I—I didn't know, sir—"

"As an officer in my command, Wills, it is your duty to
know! Before you are ready to lead any troops into the field,
you *will* know each man assigned to you, plus every trooper in
R Company. You will know his personality, likes and dislikes,
family or money troubles. You will know, Lieutenant Wills,
because your very life might well be in the hands of that
trooper you just put on report! I don't think you would like that
situation, would you?"

Sweat broke out on Wills's forehead despite the coolness
inside Ted's office. "Yes, sir. I—I think I owe Private Edwards a
personal apology."

Ted felt the blood pounding in his temples and knew he
would have another headache if he did not calm down. "I think
that would be an excellent idea, Lieutenant Wills. And I think
you should make that apology a sincere one. In the future,
Wills, keep in mind this is the Wyoming Country, not
Washington. Your rank at West Point does not mean one bean
out here until you learn to lead men. Do I make myself clear?"

"Yes, sir! I'm sorry, Colonel—"

"I don't want your apologies, man. I want performance! If
I do not get that performance, you will rue the day the War
Department sent you and your volunteer company to Fort
Laramie! Now, get out of here. Go find Edwards and make
your apology."

Ted watched the door rapidly close behind the lieutenant.
He wondered for a moment if he had been too harsh with the
young officer. No—it was a lesson the youngster would
remember for the rest of his life, a lesson that just might save a
command from being wiped out one day.

He turned to the remainder of the reports. They did little
to improve his dark mood. Ammunition for the Spencers was
running low, two companies of new recruits, which had only
recently arrived in Fort Laramie, were yet to be field
equipped, and that would strain the stockpile of clothing and
blankets. Food supplies were adequate, but barely, for another
four weeks. The new recruits were all volunteers except for

the officers, and to a man they knew nothing about fighting Indians. Communications had not been restored along the Overland Route, and Abel had not yet returned.

But what concerned Ted most of all was the latest report from Yellow Crow. Sitting Bull of the Sioux and Big Nose of the Cheyenne were about to pick up the war pipe because of some stupid atrocity committed by some white men.

He initialed the last document and flung the pen down in disgust. There was only one chance now to avoid an all-out war on the Plains. He himself must take to the saddle and try to restore reason among the more powerful chiefs, who might at this moment be honing a scalping knife.

Ted stalked from the office toward home. Even the warm greeting from Wilma and the dirt-smudged hug from Little Bill did not chase the clouds from his mind. He sank wearily into an overstuffed chair, his son perched on his lap.

"Bad day, dear?" Wilma asked.

"One of the worst yet, darling. Sometimes I wonder why I ever gave up ranching."

A low growl from the mongrel dog named Toby at her feet brought Wind Flower erect, the harness she had been mending quickly forgotten. She listened for a moment, trying to pick up the sound that had gotten the solidly built dog's attention. She knew the animal was not one to sound false warnings. She walked to the front door and glanced about. Approaching across the south meadow were four horsemen. Even at that distance Wind Flower could tell they were white men by the way they rode. The Navajo woman felt no fear. An occasional horseman had visited the isolated ranch house, and Kevin was nearby.

She went to the back window and called softly. At the nearby well Kevin O'Reilly placed a newly drawn bucket of water on the ground. It was not the first time his irrigation of the small garden plot, now brimming with fall vegetables, had been interrupted.

"How many?" Kevin's voice was soft, but the words carried.

"Four. All white men, I think."

Kevin retrieved his new Root Model revolving rifle from where it leaned against the well and made his way into the thick-walled ranch house. At a word from Wind Flower, Toby ceased his growl and crouched as though waiting for the word that would send him on the attack. Wind Flower picked a .36 navy pistol from a shelf and draped a tattered dish towel over the weapon and her right hand.

When the approaching riders had almost reached the house, Kevin stepped onto the front porch, his rifle resting in the crook of an elbow. Wind Flower remained inside with the dog. The apparent leader of the four was a short, wide-shouldered man with a heavy beard.

"Howdy, neighbor," the bearded one said. "Got any coffee to spare?"

Kevin felt his nerves tighten. Something about this bunch spelled trouble. He slipped a thumb over the hammer of the revolving rifle, ready to bring the weapon to full cock if need be. Kevin shook his head and forced an apologetic grin.

"Sorry," he said, "but we ran out a few days ago and haven't had a chance to buy more."

As he spoke, Kevin became aware that one of the horsemen had drifted off to one side. The man carried a shotgun, and it was pointed in Kevin's general direction. The Irishman took a calculated step forward, placing a heavy porch timber between himself and the man with the gun. "We have plenty of fresh water in the creek over there. You're welcome to that," he added.

The bearded man's eyes glinted beneath the wide brim of a battered hat.

"Wasn't really what we come after, anyway," he said. "Me and the boys heard there was Injuns about." He glanced toward the house.

"Haven't seen anyone around here except myself and my wife," Kevin said.

"Funny," one of the other riders, a thin, slouched man, said. "I coulda swore I smelt Injuns. Heered there was a squaw man in this valley. Word is he's a big Irish type. Kinda like you are."

Kevin's concern kept his Irish temper in check. "And what would you be wanting with this man?"

The thin one grinned, exposing ragged and stained teeth. "Nothin' much," he said. "We jist thought this Irishman might share his Injun squaw with some fellow white men."

Kevin suddenly realized the fix he was in. The men obviously had worked together before. They had moved apart gradually until the shotgun covered his left and the fourth rider his right. For a split second Kevin cursed his own stupidity at allowing himself to be flanked. The man at his right probably had his gun drawn by now and was holding it out of sight on the far side of his horse. Kevin realized he could not take on all four riders. He only hoped the lead they could get into him did not hit anything important.

"The Irishman might not be so generous," he said, hoping to keep them occupied until Wind Flower could realize the situation and flee to the barn and her swift bay mare to escape.

He almost turned in surprise and fear when the front door swung open and Wind Flower stepped onto the porch beside him. The woman's appearance drew outright leers from the four riders. "Now that is one fine-lookin' squaw," one of them said.

"Go back in the house, woman," Kevin said. Wind Flower merely looked from one man to another, as though confused at the English words.

"Wind Flower saw you were in difficulty," she said in Navajo. "Perhaps you could use some help. The one on your right has a pistol drawn." At the corner of his vision, Kevin saw the dish towel still draped over Wind Flower's right hand. Her left rested easily atop the cloth. Kevin silently prayed the men did not understand Navajo. "Wind Flower will take the one with the shotgun," his wife continued. "The signal will be when the dog is called."

For a few seconds no one moved. Then Kevin saw the shoulder of the gunman at his right jerk. At that instant Wind Flower yelled a single word, then whipped the dish towel from her hand and flung it beneath the shotgun-bearer's horse. The animal snorted and jumped, the shotgun discharging harmlessly into the dirt. The navy pistol in Wind Flower's hand fired. The rider dropped the shotgun with a howl and tumbled from the bucking horse. Kevin shot at almost the same time. The rider to his right was slammed from his horse by the slug.

The bearded one and the skinny man, fighting to regain control of the horses spooked by the sudden gunfire, reached for their belts.

"Touch it and you're dead!" Wind Flower yelled in English, her navy pistol pointed at the thin one. Kevin had the bearded one in his sights. Both men froze, then slowly raised their hands.

"Gather your dead and wounded," Kevin ordered, "and ride out of here. Now!"

The bearded man's eyes narrowed until they were barely

points of light beneath the hat brim. "You ain't heard the last of this, squaw man!"

At Wind Flower's side the muscular mongrel growled ominously. Kevin could hardly control the impulse to kill both men on the spot, but he knew Wind Flower's horror of unnecessary violence.

"You had best get out before I blow a hole in you the size of your fist!" Kevin said, his voice shaking with anger. "And if you ever come back here, I will personally skin you alive one strip at a time!"

"Better do as the man says, boss," the thin rider said. "I didn't come out here to get a hunk of lead in my belly."

Within moments three riders, one slumped in the saddle, led a fourth horse carrying a dead body back toward the south. Kevin watched until they were far in the distance, then turned to Wind Flower. He gently lifted the revolver from her fingers and lowered the hammer of his own rifle. Pride and love swelled his chest.

"That was a brave thing you did, Wind Flower. You scared me to death, though. You could have been killed!"

She nestled in his arms, and Kevin felt a slight shudder go through her body. When she looked up, there were tears in her eyes.

"My fear of death is of nothing against the fear at the loss of my husband," she said. "I am not brave, Kevin. I am weak of spirit, for to find a man I love and a new life only to lose it would be more than I could bear. They would have to bury me beside you."

Kevin put his arm about her shoulders and led her inside, the mongrel trailing dutifully behind.

Abel Hubbard's safe return to Fort Laramie brought a collective sigh of relief from the community. While his force had not engaged the warring Indians, it had succeeded in dispersing them for the moment. With repair of the telegraph cables, communication lines had been reestablished, and the Overland Route was open for travel.

Veteran observers were aware the situation would worsen, but in the meantime merchants took advantage of the opportunity to replenish their stores, and refugees from farms and ranches along the trail grabbed a chance to flee to the safety of the fort while they still could. Many newcomers in the growing population were destitute, having lost everything to the roving Indian bands. This placed a heavy drain on army stores. Soon harried surgeons reported the first cases of malnutrition among children in the swollen refugee camp.

Of all his concerns, it was this report that distressed Ted Henderson the most. While he was no stranger to privation and hunger himself, the thought of a single child falling ill because of bare larders was intolerable to him.

Abel, having linked up with patrols from Forts Sedgwick and Kearny during his drive against the Indians, reported that few supplies were to be had to the east all the way to Kansas City. The once plentiful hunting grounds now yielded very little game.

Ted and Abel agreed that the only solution was to dispatch a heavily armed wagon train west to Salt Lake City. There, Mormon traders would have ample supplies of goods and ammunition, which could be bought and would reach Laramie before the first blast of the approaching winter struck. In the meantime, Wilma's volunteer group would twist a few arms among local merchants to get food for the refugee children until the supply train returned. The two officers agreed that dispatching two infantry companies for escort would seriously weaken the already shorthanded military post—but that could not be helped.

"One thing we don't have a shortage of," Ted concluded, "is Indians." He rose from behind his desk and walked to the window with its view of the distant mountains. The snowcaps already had begun to creep down the sides of the Rockies. "Long Walker's bunch probably will make a couple more massive sweeps before winter sets in," he said thoughtfully.

Ted returned to his desk and thumped a palm down on a sheaf of papers. "The War Department has, in its questionable wisdom, ordered punitive expeditions against the raiding Indians. That will be your department, Abel. My own efforts will be directed toward talking peace with the major uncommitted bands."

"Still no hope of reinforcements?" Abel asked.

"None," Ted said. "In fact, the War Department as much as told me to shut up, or they will yank the Third from Wyoming and send us all to the eastern front."

Abel snorted in disgust. "It's bad enough to fight Indians without having to fight the government, too. It looks like no one in Washington knows how critical the situation is out here."

Ted nodded sadly. He strode to the gun rack in the corner of the office, plucked one of the captured Henry repeaters from its resting place, and turned the rifle casually in his hands, testing its balance. "This could be one of the biggest threats we've yet faced," he said.

Abel did not reply. There was no need. The numbers stamped into the metal of the rifles captured by Abel were so nearly alike as to be almost sequential, and they were very near the number on the weapon taken from the body of the young gunman after the attack on Ted and Kit Carson. So near, in fact, that they could almost have come from the same box.

At first, the Sioux captured by Abel's Shoshone scouts had stoically refused to speak. But their tongues loosened rapidly when Ted threatened to turn them over to the Shoshone. The captives confirmed that the guns had been distributed by Long Walker. Further, many more guns were on the way, Long Walker had boasted. The Sioux knew no details of when the weapons were to arrive, nor the means of transportation, or the distribution point. Convinced they were telling the truth, Ted reluctantly dropped the line of questioning.

He decided the captured Henry rifles would be handed out to select soldiers, along with ammunition taken from the Sioux rear guard. One of the repeaters went to the Shoshone chief of scouts. Ted kept one for his own use after testing the weapon and finding it more than adequate in firepower, if somewhat lacking in range. Abel declined the offer of a Henry, choosing to stick with the more familiar Spencer.

Ted replaced the rifle in the rack. "Abel, you will be wanting to spend as much time with Judy as possible in the next few days, I expect. We'll both be back in the field soon. Go on home now. I'll finish up the reports and make the duty roster for tomorrow."

Ted held the door open for his second in command, then stepped onto the busy street for a quick look about. A steady stream of pedestrians, wagons, and horsemen plied the major thoroughfares into Fort Laramie, and Ted knew many more were entering the growing town outside the walls.

At least, he thought, Vi's hotel business should be booming.

Vi Robinson watched with growing interest as the new guest signed his name to the register in clear, flowing script. He was medium height, with alert kind hazel eyes bracketed by crow's-foot wrinkles that deepened as he smiled. He was well dressed but not flashy, with broad shoulders and an almost square face framed in gray-streaked brown hair. He was, she decided, probably in his early forties, and quite handsome.

She turned the register. "Welcome to Laramie, Mr. Elkins," she said.

His quick smile revealed a row of even, white teeth. "Please," he said, "if it is not too presumptuous of me, call me Taylor. I've always preferred my first name to be used, especially by such a lovely lady."

Vi felt her cheeks flush at the comment and instinctively knew it was not simple flattery but a sincere compliment.

"Thank you, Mr.—Taylor," she said. "I'm afraid we have only two rooms left. One of them will be rather noisy with the windows open. It's on the corner of the second floor. The other is on the first floor in the back, by the alley and garbage cans. I'm sorry."

"The second-floor room will be most satisfactory," Taylor Elkins said. He took the key with a surprisingly delicate and uncalloused hand. "You must be Vi Robinson," he said.

Vi's eyebrows arched in surprise. "How did you know that, Taylor?"

His laugh was soft. "I'm a newspaper reporter, Mrs. Robinson. It is my business to learn as much as I can about a new assignment beforehand."

"What newspaper are you with?"

"*The Boston Herald*," Elkins replied. "My editors have not been satisfied with the reporting of events on the frontier and have sent me to file stories with some basis in fact. Primarily, I've been sent to cover the Indian troubles. As you may know, my paper is one of the leading voices favoring fair treatment of the Indians. I understand that Colonel Henderson, the commander here, shares that objective."

Vi nodded vigorously. "I'm sure you will find Ted Henderson most cooperative in working with you, Taylor. If you can manage to catch him. He's in the field so much these days. Now, I'll send someone for your luggage."

Elkins held up a palm. "That won't be necessary, Mrs. Robinson. I travel quite lightly, just one suitcase and a few notebooks. I can handle my own." He reached down and plucked a single suitcase from the floor.

"Up the stairs and down the hall to your left," Vi said. "We have a dining room, open most of the day, and a bar if you're thirsty."

"Thank you, Mrs. Robinson. I seldom drink, but if you have the opportunity some time, I would be honored to share a bottle of wine or a dinner with you."

The color returned to Vi's cheeks. "Why, thank you, Taylor. I might just take you up on that invitation."

The reporter touched the brim of his derby hat. "Where might I find the telegraph office?"

"Down the street on the left. If the military office is not in use, Colonel Henderson might permit you to file from his command post."

She watched the Boston newsman make his way up the stairs, marveling at her own response to him. Twice widowed, Vi Robinson had promised herself she would not become involved again. The heartbreak would be too much to bear a third time, and her love for the memory of the late Colonel Wild Bill Robinson still remained strong in her heart.

Yet there was something about this man, a confidence in himself tempered by respect for other people, the gentleness in his hazel eyes and the way his whole face seemed to brighten when he smiled. . . .

"You're acting like a schoolgirl!" she told herself, turning her attention to the front desk. But Taylor Elkins's face kept intruding on her work. The invitation to dinner was more than tempting, she admitted. It had been a long time since she had dined with a single gentleman. There had been offers, but until then, none had appealed to her.

Taylor Elkins turned the key in the door, stepped into the room, and was pleased with what he saw. Windows opened off both sides of the corner, overlooking the street and a wide swath of the community and fort below. It was a perfect observation post.

He placed the suitcase on the small but sturdy bed and laid out his clothing. From the bottom of the case, he took a canvas-wrapped bundle. He spread the covering carefully, then plucked a double-edged, thin-bladed stiletto from its sheath. He tested an edge with his thumb. Satisfied with the touch, he slid the knife into the inside top of his sturdy calfskin boots. The weapon clicked into position as the thin steel spring of the sheath took its grip on his boot.

Next, he picked up a squat, ugly handgun. The specially

made, five-shot revolver with its four-inch barrel nestled perfectly in his hand. The weapon infringed on a dozen or more existing or pending patents, but Elkins had had no trouble finding an expert gunsmith to build the revolver to his specifications. He smiled at the thought he probably was the only man west of the Mississippi who owned a center-fire pistol and reloading tools to fit. He broke the action. The .41-caliber cases seemed out of place in so compact a handgun, but the brute power of the soft-point lead slugs made up for any lack of aesthetics.

Finally, Elkins shrugged out of his jacket and slipped a harness-type arrangement of straps around his chest and shoulder. Into a small holster he dropped a two-shot derringer, then snuggled the small but deadly, short-range pistol comfortably under his left armpit. He returned the loaded larger handgun to the suitcase, unwilling to carry the strange weapon until absolutely necessary. It was the sort of handgun that would be noticed on the frontier, and attention was the last thing Elkins needed at the moment.

He placed a thumbnail at the corner of the suitcase and pressed. The wall gave way, revealing an envelope thick with papers. Although he had practically memorized the contents, Taylor Elkins once more thumbed through the documents. Only one name—Bernie Christian—showed much promise, but judging from the man's record in the Union army, Elkins was sure he would have to look elsewhere for his prey.

Replacing the documents, he walked to the window and stood looking down at the teeming streets of Laramie. Somewhere down there, or at least someplace nearby, was the missing link, he thought. The man, or woman, whom he now stalked. At the moment all he knew of that person was that he was elusive and good at his job. Perhaps, Elkins admitted, as good as he was himself.

He turned from the window, plucked another packet from the suitcase, and casually dropped it into his coat pocket. He grinned as he recalled the displeasure on the face of the owner of *The Boston Herald* as the gentleman signed the letter identifying Taylor Elkins as a reporter for that staid journal. But the owner had owed President Lincoln a favor.

Elkins wondered how displeased the owner of the *Herald* was now, for the spy had soon proved he was a highly competent journalist. He took considerable pride in the fact that his stories were almost never edited and that his pen name above a story was a guarantee of accuracy in reporting. Besides, he enjoyed writing.

He picked up the tools of his secondary trade, a small notebook and a pair of pencils, and went into the streets of Laramie in search of his first story.

He had strolled less than a block before he realized the fort and its people were a literal gold mine of journalistic material.

That part of the job, he thought, would be easy.

Vi Robinson stood at the bay window at one side of the Laramie Hotel and watched the newsman make his way down the street, his derby tipped at a jaunty angle. She blushed as she made her decision. Taylor Elkins was going to have to make good on that promise of dinner, just as soon as business slowed a bit or Judy was free to take over for a couple of hours. After all, she concluded, there certainly was no long-term commitment involved in a simple dinner.

"Woman," Albert Jonas said emphatically, "this time you're gonna listen to me! I swear, you're the most stubborn thing I ever saw, even if you is the prettiest! Now put that blasted needle down an' open your ears. I didn't come here to talk to the top of your head."

With a resigned sigh, Sally Coker set aside the gold-colored gown. She had been expecting Jonas to come calling again. Indian troubles or no, the people of Laramie held a big dance and celebration every harvest moon, and the dance was that night.

"Ain't you ever gonna give up, Sergeant?"

"No. And this time I'm not gonna let you off on account of your tongue, either." Albert wiped his sweaty palms on the legs of his dress trousers, then squared his massive shoulders. "I'm through arguin' with you, Sally. You're goin' to that dance with me tonight if I have to throw you over my shoulder and drag you there kickin' and screamin'."

Sally snorted. "Just what makes you think I'll go with you this time, Sergeant? Do I gotta hit you between the eyes with a board to get your attention?"

"You're goin', woman, because it's time we did some serious talkin'. I'm gonna make you a deal. My enlistment's up next spring"—he raised a hand to shut off Sally's comment—"and I'm makin' no promises neither way right now. What we're gonna do is this, Sally Coker. You're goin' to that dance with me, and in two days me and the colonel are goin' out on patrol. We'll be gone a spell.

"While we're away, you and me both are gonna do some heavy thinkin'. Maybe I'd give up the army for you, maybe not. Maybe you'd marry a soldier, maybe not. But this thing's been draggin' on long enough, and I'm runnin' clean outta patience."

Albert Jonas studied the gold-flecked brown eyes before him and could read nothing there. He did not know what he would do if she turned him down this time; he had not even given that possibility much thought. So he simply stood, stared, and waited.

Finally Sally shrugged. "All right, Albert. I'll go if it'll get you outta my hair for a while. Be at my house come sundown." Abruptly she picked up the golden gown again and resumed sewing.

Albert breathed a huge sigh of relief. "I'll be there, Sally. And—thanks."

She glanced up and scowled. "Don't you thank me yet, Albert. And don't make nothin' out of this it ain't intended to be. You know what I think about soldiers."

"Things change, Sally," the huge man said softly. "And so do people. We'll see." He turned and walked back into the street, his steps suddenly light.

After glancing at the mantel clock nearby, Sally applied her needle to the new gown with a vengeance. She did not have much time left—and it was her own gown. She had not realized until the day before, that she had nothing to wear to the dance. A smile lifted the corners of her full lips. "Albert Jonas," she muttered to herself, "I was beginnin' to think you wasn't comin' by, and this here cloth don't come cheap."

The celebration that evening was in full swing when they arrived, Jonas cutting a striking figure in his full-dress uniform. But most of the eyes in the nearly full barracks turned to the vision on his muscular arm. Sally Coker had chosen well. The new gold gown was a perfect complement to her complexion, and the cut of the dress although demure, clung to the full woman's body beneath. The couple immediately swept onto the dance floor as the regimental band did its best with a waltz.

Wilma Henderson was standing at her husband's side near the table that, in better times, would be groaning with treats but now held only a punch bowl and a few baked goods. She slipped her arm inside Ted's and nodded toward the swirling couple on the dance floor.

"It appears that your sergeant major is one proud man tonight," she said.

"And well he should be," Ted replied. "He has in his arms the most beautiful woman in Laramie—" Wilma's fingers clamped on his forearm in a pinch that brought an involuntary "ouch" from the teasing Ted. "Except, of course, for Wilma Henderson," he added quickly.

The tune resembling a waltz ended, and Albert Jonas bowed gallantly to the woman in gold as the crowd applauded the efforts, if not the musical expertise, of the musicians.

"Didn't know they let niggers into places like this." Ted and Wilma both tensed at the nearby remark.

Ted eased Wilma's hand from his arm and took two quick strides to the speaker, a new arrival in town, who smelled as if he had been sampling the cheapest whiskey in Laramie. Ted looked down at the speaker, an unshaven, coarse-looking man in the rough clothing of a farmer. "Sir," Ted said, his voice barely under control, "if you will take one more careful look, I don't believe you will see any black folks here. Am I correct?"

The man opened his mouth to protest, but something in the eyes of the officer standing before him stayed his tongue. The farmer swallowed. "Yes, sir," he mumbled. "I reckon you're right after all."

"Good. Now the next time I look around, I don't expect to see you here. Drinking is forbidden on post grounds. The side door is right over there," he concluded, pointing.

The door swung shut behind the farmer, and Ted returned to Wilma's side. She hoped the incident would not spoil the evening for him, as there were too few chances to relax these days. Steering him onto the dance floor, she snuggled close and felt the tension gradually leave him as the music swirled around them.

Over his shoulder she saw Judy and Abel Hubbard embrace briefly as the tune ended, then return to their seats against the wall. Judy's golden hair tumbled over the deep blue gown she wore on special occasions. She had hardly settled into her seat when Vi Robinson, accompanied by the new arrival, Taylor Elkins, joined the Hubbards. Vi, Judy thought, had not looked so vibrant and alive in months. And, Judy reflected, it had not taken much persuasion to convince Vi the employees could run the hotel for one night out of the year.

Judy freely admitted she liked Taylor Elkins; there was something about the man that seemed to inspire warmth and confidence. Even Ted and Abel, both suspicious of news reporters, had warmed to Elkins quickly. She hoped something would grow between Vi and the handsome Boston journalist.

Judy greeted Vi affectionately. Then, feeling someone before her, Judy turned from Vi. She looked up into the face of one of the most handsome men she had ever seen, a face that seemed somehow vaguely familiar in its perfectly formed features. The man was dressed in an expensive three-piece suit, a blue cravat contrasting with the green of the eyes.

"Mrs. Hubbard?" The voice was melodic, with just the faintest trace of a Southern drawl.

"Yes?"

"If I might be so bold and if your husband does not object, I would be honored to introduce myself and request the pleasure of the next dance. My name is Calvin Winston, lately of Carolina and en route to California, weather and Indians permitting."

Judy nodded a greeting. "I'm pleased to meet you, Mr. Winston, and flattered at your request. But I only dance with my husband."

"Then he is a most fortunate man," Winston responded. He extended a hand to Abel. "It is a pleasure to meet you, Colonel Hubbard. I have heard a great deal about your success against the Indians here in the Laramie area."

Abel shook hands with a reluctance that Judy did not understand, and quickly released his grip. Perhaps, she thought, Abel was just tired. Surely she had given him no reason to be feeling insecure or jealous with her handling of Winston's request to dance.

"Colonel Hubbard," Winston said, "I hate to bring up business at such a gala occasion, but I would appreciate your advice. Is it safe to travel toward the west?"

Abel shook his head. "I don't advise it, sir, unless you have a sizable armed escort. In addition to the Indians, we unfortunately have a number of robbers and highwaymen about. I can only suggest, of course, but I strongly advise you to stay in Laramie until a suitable escort is headed in your direction."

"Thank you, Colonel. I appreciate your observations and will act accordingly. Perhaps by the time my business here is complete, it will be possible to continue my journey." Winston excused himself with a bow to the two women and moved away.

Abel turned to his wife. "Have you seen him before?"

"No, honey, I haven't."

"He rode into Laramie this afternoon," Vi Robinson volunteered. "He took the last room at the hotel. You should see his horse, a most impressive animal, a big gray."

"Did he say what his business was?" Elkins asked.

Vi thought for a moment. "Yes. He said he was an ore assayer, and he paid two weeks in advance. Said he would be gone for a couple of days at a time and wanted to be sure he would have a room on his return."

The conversation turned to other topics, but Taylor Elkins did not join in unless asked a specific question. Even whirling Vi around the dance floor, Elkins's mind was on the green-eyed man. A lone horseman did not venture far from Fort Laramie in these times. The two ore assayers Elkins had met since being in town had both declared they were not leaving the safety of the fort until this latest rash of Indian troubles was over. Where would he be going for "a couple of days at a time," as Vi had said? Surely not out to buy ore in the mountains. Elkins made a mental note to keep an eye on this young Calvin Winston. There was something about the man's manner that just did not seem to fit, that was too studied, but Elkins could not put his finger on what it was.

With the shortage of women at Fort Laramie, Vi, Wilma, and the glamorous Sally Coker were soon breathless and beginning to feel footsore, dancing with officers and enlisted men alike. Few of the civilians at the dance asked the military wives to dance, an omission that was not lost on Ted Henderson. It was a sad reminder of the unseen but very real barrier between two worlds.

True to her comment to Calvin Winston, however, Judy danced only with her husband. As the evening wore on, she found herself becoming perturbed that she could not keep Calvin Winston from her thoughts. If only she could remember why the man's face seemed so familiar, she thought, perhaps the preoccupation would vanish. Despite the man's obvious physical attractiveness, there was something repulsive about him.

Ted called the party to a halt at midnight, reminding the troopers in attendance to check the duty roster before retiring.

Those selected for patrol duty were to be ready for Boots and Saddles shortly after dawn.

While wives unable to get baby-sitters for the evening bundled up sleepy youngsters, Sergeant Major Albert Jonas escorted Sally Coker home at a brisk walk. Outside her door he paused, unsure of what to do next, and Sally had to bite her cheek to keep from giggling.

She let him squirm on the horns of the dilemma for a few moments, then stood on tiptoe and kissed him lightly on the lips. Pulling back before the surprised sergeant major could take her in his arms, she waved a finger under his nose.

"Now, Albert Jonas, don't you get to thinkin' that proves nothin', either. And you do some studyin' on what you gonna do in the future whilst I do the same. We got us a deal, remember?" She ducked inside and leaned against the closed door, trembling with the flood of emotions triggered by the brief kiss.

Jonas stood for a long moment, fighting the urge to bang on the door and sweep Sally into a tight embrace. Then he turned and slowly made his way back to his own quarters. A small ache along his jawline puzzled him until he realized he had been grinning like a school kid and had not even known it.

Bernie Christian, who had been standing night watch in the commander's office, intercepted Ted and Wilma as the couple approached their quarters.

"Sorry to disturb you, Colonel," Christian said, "but the telegraph operators have been busy since the lines were opened again. I brought along some dispatches you might be interested in." He held out a sheaf of papers. Wilma took them, since Ted's hands were full with their sleeping son.

"Thanks, Bernie," Ted said as he nudged the door open with a toe and allowed Wilma to enter. "Care for a cup of stale coffee?"

Christian smiled. "Thanks for the offer, sir, but I'd best get back on duty. There's plenty of stale coffee at the office."

Ted surrendered the boy to his wife's care, then scanned the papers Christian had brought. He was leaning back in his chair at the table, deep in thought, when Wilma returned from putting Bill down for the night. She studied his intense expression for a few seconds.

"Trouble, dear?"

"By the wagonload," Ted replied. "A large body of Indians

has been sighted east of Fort Randall, headed south. No women and children in the band. I would lay odds that's Long Walker's bunch, regrouped, and looking for mischief. The Indians seem restless everywhere, according to these reports. Council fires are burning brighter in Ute, Arapaho, Sioux, and Cheyenne country."

Ted rose from his chair and took Wilma in his arms. "It looks like there may not be many soldiers in Fort Laramie for a while, Wilma. I'm taking Albert Jonas with me, to try to talk things back into line before every Indian over the age of ten slaps on war paint."

Wilma was suddenly alarmed as her husband's words struck home. "You're going in alone, Ted? Just the two of you? That's—too dangerous—"

"We'll be safer than we would with an escort," Ted said, hoping his words sounded more confident than he felt. "Besides, I don't have the men to spare, and a show of force would only agitate the Indians further. In the meantime, I have to send Abel back into the field to put some pressure on the warriors who won't listen to reason. That could have a sobering influence on the bands that are still undecided about peace or war."

He kissed her lightly on the neck. "There is some good news, though. Fort Bridger scouts report our supply train is nearing the outpost, headed for home. If they can make it through South Pass, we should have beans, bacon, and bullets for a while."

He released Wilma and strode to a window. Although the night shrouded the distant mountains, Ted knew the snows would be near timberline now.

"We're trying to buy some time, darling," he said, staring at the blackness outside. "If we can keep a measure of peace in force until winter sets in, a lot of lives will be spared on both sides."

Wilma, no stranger to the ways of the Plains Indian, knew the tribes retreated to winter camps to wait out the snows. Only the Crow nation sent out war parties in winter, and so far they had kept their distance from the white man. She breathed a silent prayer for an early winter. The lingering sensation of his lips against her neck only served to heighten her dread of what promised to be a long separation and lonely nights of worry.

"Ted, there's something else, isn't there?" she asked.

He turned from the window, and she could see the concern in his eyes. "Yes, there is," he said sadly. "A number of those messages were intended for Fort Garland. Kit Carson may be in deep trouble, and there's nothing I can do to help. Kit has been ordered to attack and destroy a combined force of Kiowa and Comanche. Kit has about seven hundred men, mostly infantry. The Indian force is estimated at three thousand warriors."

Wilma gasped in shock. "I know Colonel Carson has been called a miracle maker, but against those odds. . . ."

Ted gently embraced her again. "I know, Wilma. It's going to be the fight of his life. And if he fails, we've lost more than a good friend. Unless Kit wins, our own future is in danger. If the Indians overwhelm him, the way will be clear for them to sweep north toward us."

A chill autumn wind whipped the short grass of the Texas Panhandle, stripping the remaining leaves from the cottonwoods along the Canadian River breaks and sweeping across the ridge where two men huddled in conversation. Colonel Kit Carson ignored the bite of the breeze as his chief scout completed his report. As Kit had suspected, previous reports of the size of the Indian force closing in had been somewhat inflated, but he was still not in the least reassured.

"Mix of Kioway and Comanch," the wily scout concluded. "Didn't get close enough to tell who's in charge, but your old friend Lone Tree's amongst 'em."

Carson nodded absently, his mind already at work on tactics. Caught in the open, he knew, his small force would be quickly overwhelmed by the Indians. Seven hundred men were no match for some two thousand braves, all well armed and mounted. Carson's own men were seasoned veterans, but he had only two companies of cavalry. Still, with the howitzers, he held one strong card. There was a chance to do some damage before they were overrun.

"How much time do we have, Sam?" he asked.

The scout shrugged. "Three days, maybe. The Injuns hauled up about a day's ride off to make medicine. Probably take 'em a couple of days to get the spirits all stirred up and happy whilst they figger what to do with all our scalps."

Carson made up his mind. A short way downriver were the remains of a long-abandoned trading post. But the crumbling structures offered some protection from the elements and Indian bullets while providing a clear field of fire for both riflemen and cannon crews. Win, lose, or draw, he decided, Adobe Walls, as the post was called, was the only logical spot to make a stand.

Within minutes the column of volunteers was en route toward the crumbling structure just off the banks of the winding Canadian River.

His men slept little for the next two days, and Carson slept even less. Outside the adobe walls of the trading post, earthen breastworks were thrown up. Rifle companies were assigned to certain areas of defense, with the two cavalry patrols in reserve and keeping an avenue of retreat open to the rear. The howitzer crews already had cannon muzzles lined on the only direction from which the attack could come.

Carson did not have to tell his men the seriousness of their situation. They were all veterans. The preparations complete, the soldiers could only catch what little rest was possible and endure the growing tension of impending combat.

They did not have long to wait.

"Here they come!"

The cry from the front ranks sent soldiers scurrying into position. Where only moments before the morning sun had bathed the sides of empty hills, a cloud of dust rose behind the pounding hooves of the massed Comanche war ponies. As the first of the Indians reached the bottom of the hill, the gunnery officer dropped his saber point. The roar of the cannon momentarily covered the war cries of the charging Indians.

The initial shell burst landed squarely amid the front wave of onrushing warriors, sending Comanche ponies squealing to the ground. A blast from a second howitzer ripped a hole in the Indian lines. The gun crews settled into the practiced efficiency of their deadly trade, sending shot after shot into the Indian ranks.

Kit Carson and his riflemen watched as the Comanche charge faltered. But the Indians did not retreat. Instead, holes punched in the line were quickly filled by whooping Kiowa braves. Despite the intense pounding of the howitzer crews, the first swarm of warriors broke through the pall of smoke and dust and the tangle of dead and wounded horses.

Carson's carefully deployed veteran troops selected targets, and as the Indians came within rifle range, a single shot sounded. A painted warrior tumbled over the rump of his pony. The shot touched off a ragged volley from the sharp-shooters in Carson's front lines. Braves in the vanguard of the first wave paid a heavy price for their courage.

Carson lined the sights of his own carbine on a charging warrior, instinctively allowed for lead, angle, and wind drift, and squeezed the trigger. The rifle bucked against his shoulder, and the Indian slid from the back of his pony.

The wildly firing Indians, many armed with rifles and others with handguns, had almost reached the front line of soldiers before the steady hammer of lead balls broke their initial charge. The Indians wheeled their mounts to flee, leaving the battlefield littered with the bodies of horses and men. Carson felt a rifle ball whip past his head. He heard the sickening slap of lead against flesh at his right, followed by a sharp curse from the scout who had taken the hit.

Kit leaped to his feet. Ignoring the bullets kicking sand at his boots, he sprinted the few yards and knelt at the scout's side. The ball had struck Sam in the arm, shattering an elbow. The scout kept up a steady stream of curses as Carson wrapped his kerchief around the wounded man's upper arm and pulled it tight.

"You red bastards," Sam muttered. "I still got one good arm and two six-shooters left, if you wanta come after 'em."

The colonel handed his canteen to the scout, then glanced toward the hills. Already a second wave of Indians had formed and was pounding toward the Adobe Walls entrenchments.

"Looks like they heard you, Sam," he said.

Again the Indians ran the gauntlet of cannon fire, once more racing toward the waiting troops. Caught up in the heat and swirl of battle, Kit Carson could only hope the cavalry troops to the rear were keeping a retreat route open. His small force was in serious trouble.

The second Indian assault wave reached the outer defensive line as the constant crackle of gunfire continued from both sides. Carson saw one soldier drop his empty carbine, pull his pistol, and down two Indians at point-blank range before a lance ended his gallant stand.

As quickly as it had formed, the Indian assault broke. Only an occasional rifle barked as the Kiowa and Comanche fled. The veterans were conserving ammunition, making sure of their targets. At Carson's side the wounded scout snorted.

"They had us in the bog clear to the saddle blanket. Don't

know why they turned and run, but I'm sure glad they did," Sam declared.

Kit pulled his field glass from its case at his belt and trained the instrument on the hillside. "I don't think they went very far, Sam," he said. "Better make sure both pistols are loaded. Looks to me like they're going to try again." Kit slid the field glass back into its case. He had spotted something on the far hill, an Indian mounted on a distinctly marked pony. "Loan me your long gun, Sam? My carbine's a bit short on range, and if I'm going to lose my hair, I intend to settle a score in the process."

"Sure thing, sir. She's primed, loaded, and ready. Throws dead on at a hundred-fifty paces with a six o'clock hold. Got old Lone Tree spotted, have you?"

Carson nodded, hefting the scout's rifle. It felt true to the touch. "Maybe I'll get a crack at him," he said. "I've got to go check on the rest of the troops. Will you make it all right here?"

The scout nodded. "I'll be all right. You go nail yourself an Injun."

After a quick check of the lines, Carson was relieved they had suffered so few casualties, though his losses saddened him.

He picked his way to a spot on the left side of the second defensive embankment and had barely settled in when the Indians launched the third charge. The pounding from the cannon was as intense and even more accurate than before, yet still the Indians broke through the fusillade. Through the dust and smoke, Kit Carson spotted his target. He lined the sights of the borrowed rifle, waited until he was sure of the range, then squeezed the trigger.

The long gun slammed heavily against his shoulder, bellowing smoke. When the scene cleared, the pony with distinctive markings was racing away riderless.

Carson was caught immediately in the noisy, choking melee of close-range combat as a half-dozen Kiowa braves broke through the lines and charged his exposed left flank. Kit hefted his field pistol, a powerful Colt Dragoon that he preferred in prairie fights over the smaller .32 rimfires. His first shot knocked a Kiowa from his horse.

Another Indian charged, and Kit lunged to the side, barely escaping a slug from the warrior's pistol. Kit twisted and brought his pistol into line as the Kiowa turned his pony. Kit stared into the eyes of the man on horseback and pulled the trigger. His heart plummeted as the hammer fell with a dull *click* on a faulty cap. The Indian triumphantly pointed a large-caliber handgun directly between Kit's eyes.

Suddenly the brave straightened, shuddered, then toppled from his pony. A few yards away the wounded scout, Sam, pumped another shot into the Indian's body. He waved his revolver toward his colonel, then turned to fire at another target.

Once more the Indian forces broke under the onslaught of deadly accurate fire from the men in blue. The battered attackers spun their ponies about and raced for the safety of the hills. When they were out of range, Kit stood and surveyed the scene. Scores of war-painted red bodies littered the open field before the Adobe Walls barricades. Wounded ponies threshed about, screaming in agony.

Despite his revulsion at the sight of the carnage, Kit Carson felt a grudging admiration for the Kiowa and Comanche warriors. Expert horsemen, the Comanche in particular disdained personal safety to swoop in toward wounded comrades and swing fellow warriors onto the backs of their horses. When the dust and smoke had drifted from the scene, only the dead and severely wounded warriors remained on the battleground.

Kit made his way to the wounded scout. "That's one I owe you, Sam. That Kiowa had me lined up dead center before you dropped him."

The scout shrugged, then winced at a sudden stab of pain. "Ain't keepin' score, sir," he said. "Would you do me a favor, though? Kinda hard to reload with one hand, and I used up both pistols. Just in case they come back again."

Kit was placing the final cap on Sam's pistols when a young artilleryman, faced smudged with gunpowder residue, appeared at his side.

"Sorry to report, Colonel, that we're completely out of howitzer ammunition. We still have our sidearms, sir, and a bit of fight left. If you wish, we'll join the troops in the front lines."

Carson nodded his thanks. "Your people never wasted a single shell, son. Get the cannon ready to move out, then pick a spot to fight from."

Kit glanced at the midday sun. At least his troops had held their own up to now, and casualties had been remarkably light—a combination of experience, good soldiering, and no small amount of luck, he thought.

One by one the company commanders reported in. Kit had known the situation was grave, but he did not realize how serious until the last non-com echoed the comments of others: "We'll be out of rifle ammunition by sundown, Colonel."

Carson summoned his unit leaders for a brief conference. "We may be in for another attack before nightfall," he said in conclusion. "Hold your fire until the last possible moment. If we're going to leave Adobe Walls, we must make every shot count."

The final assault came at midafternoon, and it seemed to Kit that some of the confidence had faded from the Indians bearing down on the entrenched soldiers. His impression proved correct when the line of whooping warriors, almost upon the defenders, shattered before the roar of carbines and rifles. A second wave of braves momentarily checked their horses, providing stationary targets for the marksmen in the ruins. The hesitation turned into a rout as rifle bullets quickly thinned the warriors' ranks.

An eerie quiet, punctuated only by the groans of the wounded, settled over the Adobe Walls fortification as the Indians broke off the attack. Kit Carson breathed a silent prayer of relief. The Indians had been badly mauled, and if he knew the Kiowa and Comanche, no more attacks would come before dawn. The warriors would spend the fading hours of the day licking their wounds and arguing about whose fault it was that so many Indians had died against so few soldiers.

The cavalry units had been successful in keeping the route to the rear open. Now Carson had a glimmer of hope his command might be saved—even though he had only five rounds for his carbine and ten shots left for his revolver.

At nightfall he sent out the prearranged signal to prepare for a withdrawal. "It's the oldest trick in the book," he said to Sam. "But it just might work."

"Way I see it, sir, we got nothin' to lose. They come back again, they got us." Sam's brows bunched in thought for a moment. "I can't be sure, but I think I spotted a couple of Sioux in that second charge."

Carson stared at the scout. "I was thinking the same thing earlier, but I decided it was just my eyes playing tricks on me. What the deuce would Sioux be doing this far south?"

"Danged if I know," Sam replied, shaking his shaggy head, "but I ain't sure I like the smell of it."

The army's dead were buried in unmarked graves and all

traces of the burial sites obliterated to prevent mutilation of the bodies by the infuriated Indians.

When full darkness settled on the Canadian River, the first campfires were lit, and one by one the soldiers slipped away into the night. The stealthy retreat to the cavalry companies and to safety was orderly. Colonel Kit Carson was the last to leave. Despite the light casualties in the face of overwhelming odds, only eleven soldiers killed and just over seventy wounded, the frontiersman-turned-officer was sad. For the first time in his career, Kit Carson felt he had been whipped on the battlefield. Organizing a retreat after an Indian battle was a new experience for him. And one he did not like.

When dawn broke the next morning, Carson's weary force was several miles from Adobe Walls. The old ruse—leave campfires burning to deceive the enemy and escape under cover of darkness—had worked. Finally sure they had left the Indians far behind, the colonel called a short rest halt.

A long, grueling march still lay before them. Their route went through hostile, barren country, swept by the brisk wind of a new norther driving in from the Plains. Even a small band of warriors would be able to pin down his troops and take a heavy toll. Everyone's aching bones seemed to magnify the distance to Fort Garland and safety.

Kit himself did not rest during the brief stop, but moved among the soldiers, checking on the wounded and offering words of encouragement and praise where warranted. The cavalrymen who had surrendered their mounts to injured foot soldiers were suffering greatly, nursing blisters on their feet unaccustomed to long marches.

At least their luck held. A dispatch rider had gotten through to Fort Garland, and Carson's weary troops rode the last few miles in wagons brought by an escort detail. Only when the column had reached Fort Garland did the colonel discover just how narrow their escape had been. The six hundred or so soldiers who were still able to fight had less than ten pounds of rifle powder among them.

Kit sank exhausted into the chair behind his small desk and summoned his second in command. The major who ran Fort Garland in Carson's absence was jolted by his colonel's appearance. Carson's eyes were sunken from lack of sleep, his cheeks gaunt and unshaven. The smell of black powder residue hung heavy in the tiny office.

"Kit, you'd better get some sleep, and quick. You're out on your feet," the major said.

"There's one thing I want you to do first," Carson said, his voice reflecting his black mood. "I want you to prepare a letter for me. I failed on this assignment. I got my troops into a box, and they were battered. I intend to resign my command."

Shocked speechless, the stunned major stared at his commanding officer. Finally he found his voice.

"Colonel Carson, I have never disobeyed a direct order. Until now. I will not prepare that letter! Not one officer or enlisted man in this post would stand for that. Now, Colonel, you are going to take an order from a junior officer. Get some rest, man!" With that, the major stalked away.

Carson watched him go for a moment. Then he slowly turned to the cot in the corner of his office. He would catch a short nap, visit the men, then deal with his resignation. By the time his head touched the cot, Colonel Kit Carson was fast asleep.

A few hours later, slightly refreshed by the nap and a quick shave, Kit sat down by a cot in the post hospital.

"Hello, Sam," he said. "How're you feeling?"

The scout, his left arm strapped to his chest, fixed a bloodshot and glaring eye on his visitor.

"Colonel Carson, I'm gonna unload your musket, and if you don't like it, you can just go chew on a ramrod." The scout was about to explode with anger, and Kit was taken aback at the obvious hostility.

"I've rode many a mile with you, Kit Carson," Sam said. "And I never figgered you for a quitter. What's this bunch of buffalo droppin's I hear about you wantin' to resign?"

"It's true, Sam. I'm tired of getting men killed."

"Bull!" Sam worried off a small chew from the twist of tobacco he had pulled from a shirt pocket. "You listen to me. Ain't a man here don't feel the same way I do 'bout this. You got us out of a jam at Adobe Walls, and we kicked the redskinned hell out of a buncha Injuns in the process. You hadn't been in charge, we'd of lost seven hundred good soldiers out there."

Kit opened his mouth to speak, but the old scout glared him into silence. "The doc tells me I'm gonna lose this arm. I'll miss it, but I ain't gonna quit livin' and fightin' because of it! And you ain't gonna quit because you got your feelin's hurt when a little bunch of soldiers couldn't mop up on the biggest mess of Injuns ever put together in this country."

The scout's eyes narrowed still more. "Colonel, you owe me one. Said so yourself after I shot that Injun off your tail. Now we're gonna get even. You pay off by stayin' on the job, damn you!"

Carson tried to be angry with Sam, but he could not pull it off.

"Sam's right, Colonel Carson," a boy barely seventeen, his face swathed in bandages, said from the next bunk. "Ain't a man among us wants to lose the best officer what ever forked a horse."

Carson sighed heavily, then grinned. A massive load of guilt lifted from his shoulders. "All right, you two," he said. "If you want to risk your hair on my judgment, I guess I won't stand in your way."

He stepped outside the hospital building and drew a deep breath of the crisp autumn air. "Well, Kit Carson, someday you're going to have to learn how to say no," he said to himself. But he found himself whistling as he made his way back to his command post.

A day's ride north of Adobe Walls, the Sioux warrior spat disgustedly, clearing his mouth of the dust kicked up by the freshening wind. *Long Walker is not going to be happy,* he thought for the twentieth time. There would be no help from the Kiowa or Comanche now. The blood of too many warriors had flowed into the river sands to let the two tribes ever field enough fighting men to be more than a minor nuisance. The headstrong Comanche leaders had not listened to reason on how to surround and wipe out the puny little force at the river. The bluecoats had cut them to pieces. So be it.

The Sioux shifted the small pouch over his shoulder to a more comfortable position. In it were the holy medicine bags of his four companions killed on the field of battle so far from home. Of the five braves sent to Comanche country as emissaries seeking new tribal allegiances, only he survived.

But one day, he vowed, *we will return. When Long Walker commands all of the north country, the Comanche will either cooperate or be swept from the earth.*

He pulled his buffalo robe snugly about his shoulders. It was a long and dangerous ride ahead for a lone Sioux warrior. But he should be home before the first snow fell.

Six

Ted Henderson glanced around the semicircle of grim-faced Cheyenne warriors before him. At his side Albert Jonas followed his example by keeping his hand well away from his weapons and making no sudden moves despite the skittish horse on which he sat.

To their practiced eyes, the Indians showed signs of both encouragement and caution. War shields trimmed in scalp locks weighted the arm of each brave, yet no war paint had been applied to either man or horse. Ted instantly read the signs and was relieved. The Cheyenne were prepared to fight, obviously, but not yet ready to ride the warpath.

"Why does Chief of Horse Soldiers ride with but one other into the country of the Cheyenne?" The speaker, at the center of the half-circle, stared expressionlessly into Ted's face.

"Chief of Horse Soldiers has come to seek peace with the war chief Big Nose," Ted replied in his fluent Cheyenne. "He is pleased to find Big Nose well and to wish him success in the buffalo hunt."

Ted involuntarily tensed as a brave at the far left of the semicircle hefted a lance. But a terse command from Big Nose stayed the warrior's hand.

"Chief of Horse Soldiers says he comes in peace, and he is not one who lies," Big Nose said. "This trust shall be repaid. He and black soldier are free to ride the Cheyenne lands of Big Nose." With the warriors so warned, Big Nose turned back to Ted. "You bring promises from the Great Father in Washington?"

Ted noted the ill-concealed contempt in Big Nose's voice at the reference to the "Great Father."

"No, Chief of Horse Soldiers speaks only for himself," Ted

136

replied. "He will not speak false words to a great chief such as Big Nose. All he offers is his own sincere effort to see that the Cheyenne are treated fairly and that no blood be spilled."

"Cheyenne blood already has stained our ground. Why should we not strike back? Are the Cheyenne to sit in the sun and smoke while their women are raped and butchered and babies' heads dashed against rocks?" Big Nose asked angrily.

Ted shook his head sadly. "Chief of Horse Soldiers has heard of such massacres, and the stories leave his heart as heavy as that of Big Nose. Those who have done such cowardly deeds should be punished. But who are they? Chief of Horse Soldiers does not know. His own soldiers do not make war on women and children. He cannot say the same for all white men. As a blood brother to Yellow Crow, and thus to all Cheyenne, your pain is shared. Before more blood is spilled, Big Nose, consider who stands to gain the most if the Cheyenne war against the whites."

The Cheyenne chief did not reply, but Ted knew the same question had repeatedly arisen in the man's mind. Big Nose had not become such a powerful force among his people without using his brain as well as his lance.

Abruptly the Cheyenne slid from the back of his horse and squatted on his heels. Ted followed suit, and the two leaders faced each other in silence for a moment.

"At this instant," Ted said, "Chief of Horse Soldiers' own friend and fellow warrior, Abel Hubbard, is opening a campaign against the Indians to the east, against the followers of the blue-eyed one named Long Walker." He paused and looked directly into the deep brown eyes of the chief. "Chief of Horse Soldiers has no desire to face such a fine warrior as Big Nose on the field of battle. Both our forces would suffer greatly. So Chief of Horse Soldiers has come to ask of Big Nose his wishes, how the bounty of this land might be shared without bloodshed."

Big Nose's eyebrows lifted, the first sign of facial animation since the conference had begun. "You ask a Cheyenne what are his wishes? The spirits must have gone mad from the sun. A white man has never asked—only demanded—of the Indian."

"Chief of Horse Soldiers makes no demands. Just as he makes no promise other than to work for the Cheyenne as well as the whites in councils with the Great Father."

Big Nose plucked a stem of short bunch grass and turned its tip, contemplating the leaf ends burned at the edges by the first frost. For a few minutes, only the noises of the horses shuffling and snorting sounded over the meeting place.

"Big Nose wishes that the white man go back to his former home across the great river and leave the Cheyenne in peace," Big Nose said finally.

Ted shook his head. "That hope cannot be offered. A river, once started, cannot be reversed. It can be stopped by dams of the beaver. Its course can be changed. Yet the river remains. It is our duty to see that it flows in the more just course for both the red man and the white."

The Cheyenne grunted in agreement. "It is so. Too many of these rivers flow into Indian country. One of the worst brings the seekers of metal to the mountains. This river known to the whites as the Bozeman Trail carries many bad fish through our hunting grounds. The seekers of metal attack my people and frighten the game so that bellies once full are now empty. Can you, like the beaver, dam this river?"

Ted selected his words carefully. "The seekers of metal have been banned from traveling the road. Soldiers are stopping many of them. Yet the soldiers are too few at this time, and the miners are many. It will not always be so. Soon the Great War between the whites will end. Then Chief of Horse Soldiers will have many more men. Enough to stop the river of diggers."

Big Nose eyed Ted sharply. The reference to "many more soldiers" was not lost on the Cheyenne chief. He tossed aside the stem of grass, which had crumpled beneath his sturdy fingers. "Let us talk of specific rights," he said.

The council lasted for the better part of a half hour before the two men rose and grasped forearms in the Cheyenne manner of friendship. Big Nose mounted his horse in a single smooth motion and rode away toward his camp, the warriors following in his wake.

Ted heard Albert Jonas sigh heavily with relief. As he slipped a boot in the stirrup and swung aboard his own horse, Ted glanced at the sergeant. Despite the bite of the crisp air, which left breath showing as steam, drops of sweat trickled down Jonas's ebony jaw.

"I swear, Colonel, this black boy's nerves are near shot," he said. "Still haven't got used to ridin' empty-handed into a bunch of Indians. Six bands we've parleyed with on this trip and we've still got our hair, so I reckon you know what you're doin'." Jonas removed his campaign hat and ran a big hand through his tight curls. "Missed most of the talk, Colonel Henderson. My Cheyenne's getting better, but it's still not up to yours. What do you think will happen now with Big Nose?"

Ted pondered the question briefly. It had not been a completely successful parley, nor had it been a loss. "I can't be sure, Albert. I think Big Nose will keep his braves away from the war paint gourd for a while. Provided nobody throws a bobcat into his lodge."

Suddenly Ted doubled his hand into a fist and slammed it into the horn of his saddle in frustration. "Damn it, Albert, the Indians aren't being unreasonable. If the troublemakers on both sides would just get out of the way, we'd have peace on the Plains by spring."

The mention of spring brought a double jolt to the sergeant major. The face of Sally Coker once more leaped into his mind. He had not yet decided which would be the most painful—to give up the military, which he had grown to understand and accept both as a trade and a way of life, or to bury the other half of his heart by letting Sally slip through his fingers. Albert knew he had to make up his mind soon. He and Ted Henderson were to call on two more Indian bands, stop over for a day at Fort Bridger, then return to Laramie. Sally would be waiting. Jonas glanced at the stormy face of his commanding officer and decided now was not the time to bring up his personal problems. Colonel Henderson had troubles enough of his own.

Lieutenant Colonel Abel Hubbard cursed sharply under his breath as he kicked at a charred timber in the remains of Fort Tabor. The outpost, intended to reinforce Forts Sedgwick and Kearny along the beleaguered Overland Trail, had been only half finished when the Indians struck. There was no immediate clue to the fate of the sixty men, all Missouri Volunteers, who had been dispatched to build the fort. The earth breastworks thrown up for protection until a stockade could be erected showed no signs of life or death. It was clear, however, that the defenders had panicked, probably at the first sight of the swarm of red horsemen, and fled in some direction.

Hubbard felt a tug at his sleeve. Corporal Bernie Christian merely pointed. Through the haze of exhaustion, Abel saw the faint movement in the distance, a large flock of big birds soaring in lazy circles.

"I'm afraid, sir, that's where we'll find the Fort Tabor troops. Or what's left of them," Christian said.

Steeled for the worst, Abel and Bernie mounted and spurred toward the circling buzzards.

The sight was one Abel Hubbard had seen before, but still his first reaction was to turn aside in revulsion. The stripped, mutilated bodies of the fleeing volunteer company lay huddled in the center of a shallow depression. In their panic they had raced into the main body of Indians. At least they had had little time to suffer, Abel thought. The signs indicated the battle had lasted less than five minutes.

"Firm up a burial party, Bernie. Better make it a big one," Abel said.

"Yes, sir," Bernie replied sadly. "If only they'd stood and fought, most of them might have made it." The corporal reined his horse about and headed toward the main detachment of soldiers now nearing the Fort Tabor ruins.

The lieutenant colonel eased himself from the saddle and stood for a moment, weak-kneed, leaning against his horse. Four days in the saddle with only a short nap here and there had almost completely drained his endurance. The last forty-eight hours had been the worst: charred ruins of homes, mail coaches, and now an entire fort, bodies stripped of clothing and weapons, some bristling with Sioux and Arapaho and Cheyenne arrows, others hacked to pieces by war axes and knives. And always, it seemed, the Indians were a couple of days, sometimes just a few hours, ahead.

Suddenly Abel stiffened in alarm. The bodies were at least a day and a half old—but the pony tracks he and his troops had been following just an hour ago had been made before dawn! So there had to be at least two large bodies of warriors whose paths had crossed, and one group should be nearby.

He vaulted into the saddle, yanked his horse around, and spurred it toward the troops at the Fort Tabor wreckage. Overtaking Bernie Christian, Abel checked his mount to match the pace of the corporal's horse.

"Forget the burial detail for now, Bernie," Hubbard commanded. "We may be within spitting distance of a couple hundred of Long Walker's braves! My bet is they're headed for Fort Kearny. Any chance of getting a message through to Kearny?"

Bernie shook his head. "All the telegraph lines are down, Colonel. The only chance would be by courier."

Abel grimaced. "That's close to fifty miles through territory swarming with hostiles. I couldn't ask any man to do that."

The slightly built corporal turned to his commander. "Colonel Hubbard, there is no better rider in uniform than me. I've got the best horses in the string. Give me two Shoshone scouts—they can smell a Sioux a mile off, and they're top horsemen—and I'll get your message through."

Abel drew a tattered map from his tunic and studied it as he rode. Finally he looked toward the north, where an ominous line of gray clouds lay near the horizon. "Storm brewing," he said, sniffing the breeze. "It's going to be a cold rain, maybe a touch of sleet." The lieutenant colonel jabbed a finger at a spot on the map.

"Here," he said. "Here is about the only place this band could hole up, Ten Squaw Springs just off the creek that runs into the Platte. Know where it is, Bernie?"

The corporal nodded. "Ted—Colonel Henderson—and I bagged a couple of buffalo there last fall. Unless somebody's moved it, I can find it in the dark."

Abel slapped the refolded map against the back of a wrist. "Bernie, I can't ask you to go—"

"You don't have to, Colonel. I've already volunteered."

"—but if you could get through to Kearny, lead a couple of companies of cavalry to Ten Squaw. There's an outside chance we could nail some of Long Walker's braves." He unfolded the map again and studied the terrain notations. "If our boys set up on the west side and the Kearny boys on the south, we'll have them in a box with no place to go but north. It's a long shot and a terrible risk, Bernie. Are you sure you want to try it?"

The little corporal sighed. "Sir, so far we've been chasing our own tails and not catching up with them, either. I say it's worth a try. At least we can let Long Walker know it's going to get a lot tougher for his people than it has been here lately."

The two men dismounted at the edge of the ruined fort. Ignoring questions from junior officers, Abel started barking commands as Bernie shifted his saddle from his tired sorrel to a fresh, spirited bay. By the time the corporal was ready, two

Shoshone scouts had joined him, and Abel was finishing the message to the commanding officer at Fort Kearny. He handed the paper to Bernie.

"Sir, how do we know the boss at Kearny will play along?" the corporal asked.

"Three reasons, Corporal Christian," Abel replied, smiling. "First, I told him we had to hit the Indians before they burned his fort and fed his remains to the dogs; second, I pulled rank on him; and third, I threatened to tear him to pieces personally if he didn't cooperate."

Bernie folded the message carefully and tucked it in a shirt pocket. "Then, Colonel, I reckon we'll get some help."

Abel held out a hand. "Good luck, Bernie. And keep your hair on. In thirty-six hours we'll be in position and waiting for your signal."

Bernie Christian touched his hat brim in salute, then wheeled his mount, and with the two Shoshone alongside, he set out in a long lope for the distant walls of Fort Kearny.

Abel watched as the trio faded rapidly into the distance, then raised his eyes to the darkening sky. "Lord," he said, "I haven't asked for your help on this campaign, and I don't intend to now. Just, if you can see your way clear, have a word with the Indian spirits and see if they'll step aside, too, just this once. I'm thinking it's time we had a break." Then he began issuing instructions for the upcoming forced march.

Christian and the two Shoshone braves had covered some ten miles before the first drop of chill rain fell from the heavy sky above. The corporal twisted in the saddle, reached for his poncho—and saw six mounted braves racing toward them along a shallow draw a hundred yards away. He yelled a warning to the two scouts, and as one, the three riders dropped lower over the necks of their horses and slammed their heels into the animals' sides.

The horses stretched out in a dead run over the rolling grasslands, gaining slightly on the pursuing Indians. After a hundred yards Bernie risked a glance back over his shoulder. Despite the distance, he could tell they were Sioux, and superbly mounted. Already their fine-boned, fleet, and fresh war ponies had made up the lost ground and were drawing ever closer. Four of the six whooping braves carried rifles.

Bernie turned all his attention to riding for his life,

floating in the saddle, reins slack, giving the big, rawboned bay all the help he could. A rifle bullet whined over a rock a dozen feet away.

Then, just ahead, the corporal found what he was looking for. A gradual slope in the turf gave way to a shallow ravine and its dry creek bed. He waved to the Shoshone scouts and pointed. Their answering nods told him they understood.

Bernie pulled his bay to a sliding stop at the bottom of the ravine, then flung himself from the back of the horse, knowing the well-trained animal would stay close by during the coming battle. Palming his handgun, he huddled against the creek bank, conscious of the pounding hooves approaching. To his left, the pair of Shoshone guides calmly nocked arrows and brought their heavy bows to full draw.

The first Sioux burst over the slight rise before the creek. Bernie's shot caught him high in the chest. Two other Sioux tumbled from their horses, struck by Shoshone arrows. The three remaining braves, surprised by the unexpected stand and unable to check their horses, whipped past the waiting ambushers. Bernie gripped his pistol in both hands and sent a slug hammering into the back of a Sioux. The fifth Indian went down with two Shoshone arrows between his shoulder blades.

The sixth Sioux had almost reached the top of the long grade opposite the creek. Bernie quickly sheathed his pistol and slid his carbine from its scabbard. The sharp rifle blast left the sixth Sioux pony to flee riderless.

Christian reloaded his weapons with trembling fingers. The fight had taken only a few seconds, but six men were dead or dying. He watched without feeling as the Shoshone scouts quickly and efficiently slit the throats of two injured Sioux and scalped them. One of the Shoshone silently pointed to Bernie, then toward the three bodies that had gone down beneath his guns. Bernie shook his head. The scout grinned, then caught up the reins of his own pony and swung aboard.

Within five minutes the three men were riding into the teeth of a chilling, driving rain. Bernie shivered and slipped the poncho over his head, but the Shoshone seemed unaware of the cold.

Thirty-five hours after he had left Abel Hubbard, Corporal Christian crawled, on muddy knees and elbows, to the crest of the slight rise overlooking Ten Squaw Springs. He blinked his eyes, convinced they, and the slight haze of dawn, were playing tricks on him. Then he realized to his horror the scene before him was real.

For once, Abel Hubbard had been wrong. Instead of two hundred Indians, it appeared to Bernie the small army strung out before him was twice as large as the colonel had anticipated.

The clink of metal from the two companies of cavalry a few yards to his rear made Bernie wince. The green volunteers, untested, poorly armed, and poorly mounted, had been dispatched reluctantly by the Fort Kearny commander. Bernie hoped they at least could make some noise at the right time, even if they did not hit anything. Bitterly, Bernie thought he would trade the whole lot of them for two squads of trained and experienced Indian fighters. But the cards had been dealt, and the hand must be played.

The Indian camp below began to stir.

A Shoshone brave suddenly appeared at his side and nodded. Bernie breathed a silent sigh of relief. Abel's forces were in position. Bernie turned and gestured to the lieutenant commanding the Kearny soldiers. The troops moved into a skirmish line. Bernie took a deep breath and cocked his carbine, preparing to fire the signal shot that would begin the attack. Given the odds against them, he decided to make the signal shot count, so he lined the sights on a brave struggling from his blankets fifty yards away. He squeezed the trigger.

The Indian fell heavily. To Bernie's right, a staccato volley of fire raked the Indian camp. The warriors milled about in momentary confusion, grabbing rifles and bows and firing wildly while scrambling for cover. Bernie worked the action of his Spencer and saw the slug kick mud in the face of a Cheyenne scrambling toward cover. A bullet plowed into the ground near Bernie's side, and the battle opened in earnest.

The Indians tried a halfhearted counterattack and were driven back by the accurate rifle fire of Abel's veterans.

Suddenly Bernie cursed. The young volunteer lieutenant had abandoned the plan to dismount and fight on foot. The sight of the Indians retreating was too much for the eager, inexperienced officer, and he sent his two companies of cavalry charging toward the enemy. Bernie groaned as the scene unfolded. The Indians began an apparently confused retreat, pulling the cavalry into the trap, then mounted their own charge. The two companies, almost three hundred yards into the center of the Indian camp, were battered by heavy rifle fire. Sioux reinforcements from the rear of the camp swept in behind the cavalrymen, who were now fighting for their lives.

Only swift action by the Shoshone scout company saved the Kearny troops from complete annihilation. Firing arrows and handguns, the mounted Shoshone cut a path through the mass of hostile Indians, broached the lines closing in on the cavalry, and opened a path to safety. Less than half the green Kearny force managed to follow the Shoshone from the battle-field.

The battle raged for the better part of an hour before the Indians, beleaguered by Abel's sharpshooters and the fierce Shoshone, set up a moving rear guard and retreated toward the north.

Bernie retrieved his own mount and spurred it toward Abel. When he arrived, the lieutenant colonel was surveying the battleground, his face dark with fury.

"Who ordered that cavalry charge?" Abel demanded. "I'll have that man's neck in my hands before this day ends!"

They found the young cavalry lieutenant faceup, eyes staring unseeing at the gray sky. A neat, round bullet hole punctured the middle of his forehead. Almost a hundred of his fellow volunteers had been either killed or wounded in the trap.

Aside from the impulsive volunteer fatalities, casualties to the attacking force were light. Hubbard's group suffered two dead and seven injured, and the Shoshone, despite staying in the middle of battle throughout, lost just five men and had four braves injured. The Sioux, Cheyenne, and Arapaho forces defending the camp had lost more than forty braves with numerous others wounded.

The last rifle shots still echoed above Ten Squaw Springs when a sergeant rode up to Abel and Bernie.

"Pursuit, sir?" the sergeant asked.

"With what?" Abel asked disgustedly. "Those Indians would chew us up like a camp dog on a venison leg before we got five miles. No, Sergeant. We've still got the problem of getting out of here alive. If the Indians realize how few of us there really are and counterattack, we'll all look like porcupines before sundown."

He sighed heavily. "Form up the men, Sergeant. Let's get away from here as quick as we can—if we can."

Five miles from the battleground, Bernie finally felt the muscles between his shoulder blades relax. There had been no sight of Indian pursuit. He kneed his horse alongside Abel's.

"What now, Colonel?"

Hubbard's angry expression slowly dissolved into one of fatigue and disappointment. "What else, Bernie? We keep on trying to do our jobs until we're cutting supplies thin. Then we go back to Laramie and start all over again."

Judy Hubbard leaned against the Laramie Hotel linen closet and gently massaged the muscles along her jawline and temples. She had never realized how difficult it was to smile for hours at a time until she had started waiting on tables.

The hotel had been extremely busy the past few days. All lines of communication to the east had been broken, and Ted Henderson had forbidden travel in that direction except by convoys that included at least a hundred heavily armed men. Consequently, the travelers who came via the Overland Trail found themselves confined in Laramie for days, and the hotel, with its excellent and varied menu, had become a popular gathering place for travelers and natives alike.

Now, with another waitress on duty, Judy could let the strained muscles in her face relax. That did not mean her work was ended, however. Fresh linen had to be distributed on the first floor. But at least she only had to smile when delivering the newly washed sheets to occupied rooms. She found herself admiring the endurance of the full-time waitresses who spent a full shift on their feet, remembering which order went where, carrying heavy platters, and always smiling brightly.

Judy sighed and picked up an armload of linen. At least it was something to do to keep her from brooding about her absent husband. Though she really did not need the money, the tips were good. Abel would be surprised and pleased when she bought his Christmas gift with her own money.

The first few rooms were unoccupied. Judy quickly replaced the soiled linens and remade the beds, then placed a fresh washcloth and towel beside the porcelain pitcher and washing bowl on the bedstand.

Approaching the last room along the narrow hallway, she noticed its door standing slightly ajar. She made a mental note to remind Wilma about the latch, which sometimes failed to drop when the door was closed from the inside. Lifting her hand to rap on the panel, she heard voices from inside the room and paused.

The words were not loud, but they seemed angry. Judy could hear only bits and pieces of the conversation. "Told you . . . never come here."

Instantly she recognized the voice. She had waited on the ore assayer Calvin Winston often enough to recognize his tone and manner of speech. Unwilling to interrupt what seemed to be a quarrel, Judy was about to walk away when she heard an unfamiliar voice reply, "I go where I wish. No man stops me."

"Too important . . . usual meeting?" Winston's broken question piqued Judy's interest. Feeling uneasy and a bit guilty at eavesdropping on a private conversation, she edged closer to the door.

"Whole project . . . at stake." The stranger's voice was obviously one used to command. "The colonel must be dealt with," the strange voice insisted firmly.

Judy suddenly became alarmed. Could they be speaking of Abel? If so, why would an ore assayer be involved? Even as the thought formed, however, she dismissed it as ridiculous. There were more honorary and retired colonels in the West than there were rocks. Still, she hovered just outside the door, hoping to hear a bit more.

"He keeps too many Indians from joining. . . . We will lose advantage . . . stop him soon."

Judy's heart pounded strongly against her ribs. It was obvious now they were talking about a military man. But who?

"So how do we keep . . . out of picture?"

Judy strained to hear more through the tiny opening between the door and its frame, but still Winston's words were broken. Only fragments of sentences reached her. She fought her rising panic; at any moment some guest might enter the hallway and see her with her ear pressed to the door. Suddenly the men in the room dropped their voices even further. Only a few words drifted through: "boy . . . pony . . . canyon . . . hostage . . ."

Try as she might, Judy could make no sense of the few names mentioned: ". . . Nose . . . Cheyenne . . . Crazy Dog . . ."

Finally came the scrape of chairs, as though the conference were finished. She caught a final scrap of sentence: "You know . . . details later. Keep eye . . . need know when . . . best to strike."

Suddenly Judy realized the danger she was in if one of the men opened the door and saw her. She willed herself to remain calm, to think. It seemed very important now that she catch a glimpse of the person in the room with Calvin Winston.

She crept cautiously back along the wall, careful to make no noise. Then, squaring her shoulders and summoning her courage, she walked briskly to the door and rapped on the door frame. "Maid service!" she called brightly.

There was a momentary silence in the room. "One moment, please," she heard Winston call. The sounds of footsteps came through the crack in the door, and Judy heard a window sash whisper in its tracks. A few seconds later, boots walked to the door.

Her pulse racing, she forced a bright, innocent smile onto her face. Beneath the linens, her fingers trembled.

Calvin Winston swung the door open, a scowl marring his boyishly handsome face.

"Good evening, Mr. Winston," Judy said, hoping the words were steady. "It's time for new linens for your bed." She swept past him into the room and immediately glanced at the window. One of the curtains stood slightly askew, marking the apparent exit of the second man who had been in the room.

"Oh, goodness," she said. "Your curtains are in disarray. I'll straighten them for you." She stepped to the window.

"No, thank you, that's—" Winston's voice trailed off as Judy reached the window. Ostensibly straightening the wayward curtain, she stole a quick look toward the back of the hotel. A man wearing the rough clothing of a ranch hand was swinging on the back of a nearby horse. But he settled into the saddle unlike a cowboy, and as he passed the soft square of yellow light from a nearby window, Judy caught a quick glance of high cheekbones and dark skin. Then the rider was gone.

Unwilling to risk tarrying longer at the window, Judy tugged the curtain into place. "There, that's much better," she said. She beamed at Calvin Winston. "We can't have people saying the Laramie Hotel doesn't take care of its guests, can we, Mr. Winston?"

She reached for the linens she had tossed on the bed. "I'll have this fixed for you in just a moment," she said, tossing her long blond hair with a shake of her head.

For a moment Winston stared at her suspiciously, then his face softened. Apparently he had accepted her unexpected presence as merely that of a maid.

"Don't bother making the bed," he said. "I'll take care of that myself."

Judy hesitated. "Are you sure? I mean, it's no trouble, and it *is* part of the hotel's service."

The man suddenly smiled. "No problem," he said kindly. "I expect you're tired anyway. I saw you serve both breakfast and dinner today."

"Oh, I don't mind work," Judy replied. "And Vi Robinson needs the help. Is there anything you need, Mr. Winston? Anything I can get you?"

The sudden leer that flashed in his eyes made her fear she had gone too far. Then he shook his head. "No, thank you," he said. "It's quite comfortable here, really."

"If you're sure, then I'll be on my way. There's still much to do." Judy started for the door.

"Mrs. Hubbard," Winston said, the tone of his voice sending a shudder down Judy's spine, "if you are free some afternoon, would you join me for coffee? I would consider it an honor and a refreshing few minutes. A man gets so bored talking nothing but business all the time."

She nodded politely and flashed him her best smile. "Why, thank you, sir," she said. "Perhaps I will accept your invitation. Now, if you will excuse me, I must be about my work. Have a nice night, Mr. Winston." With that, she swept past him, closed the door firmly behind her, and walked swiftly down the hall.

Judy ducked into a small, cramped cleaning closet and burst into sobs. After a short time she had regained her composure, but her thoughts remained in turmoil.

She did not know the full significance of what she had overheard, but it had been enough to frighten her. She realized she had heard part of a plot directed against the "colonel," and there were only two colonels she knew of who dealt with the Indians: Ted Henderson and Abel Hubbard.

Judy desperately wanted to tell someone—Vi, Abel, anyone—but she knew she did not have enough information to make sense. Fragments of conversation. Names and parts of names. It would probably look like the work of a worried feminine mind, playing games with an innocent bit of idle conversation between two businessmen. Yet her instincts would not listen to reason. She knew her suspicions were justified. She must have more information—and there was only one place to get it.

From Calvin Winston.

The thought made her shudder. To pursue the matter could cost her dearly, perhaps even her life. Not to pursue it could cost even more.

She returned to the hallway, picked up the bundle of soiled linen she had gathered, and started toward the laundry room, determined to finish her day's work. There would be time later to think and to plan.

Judy was halfway to the laundry room when a sudden thought made her stop. She remembered all the discussions she had overheard from both military men and civilians, and Abel's insistence that Confederate agents were not only stirring up the Indians but also supplying them with weapons. She had seen for herself the sleekly lethal repeating rifles in Ted Henderson's gun case.

Could Calvin Winston somehow be involved in this? The thought was staggering. If it was true, the fate of the Plains might depend on her. The military, with all its weapons and sources, had so far been unable to pinpoint the Southern connection. But she possessed resources and weapons the military did not—her beauty and femininity. She had seen the look in Calvin Winston's eyes many times. He wanted her. Now she had an opening—Winston's invitation to coffee.

Judy squared her shoulders, ignoring her churning insides. It would be a dangerous game, dangling herself as bait before Calvin Winston while remaining just out of reach. She knew the danger would be more than just a physical one. Injury or even possible death paled beside her one overriding fear: There would be talk; Abel would hear. In a small community such as Laramie, there was no way that could be avoided. She could only pray that Abel would understand, that their love would overcome any crisis. The thought of losing her husband was almost too much to bear. But Judy felt she could not confide in him before she had some proof and details of the conspiracy.

She dumped the soiled laundry into its proper bin, then stood thinking. She realized she faced a personal mountain that must be climbed whatever the cost, and she must climb it alone, at least until she was more certain of the facts.

The next day dawned bleak and foreboding. It was, Judy thought, a day that fit her own mood perfectly.

She shivered in the cold room despite her heavy flannel

nightgown and waited for the newly started fire to chase the bite in the air. Several times during the night she had reached for Abel, and each time the emptiness inside her deepened as her groping hand felt only the cold pillow on the other side of their bed. It was the touch of nothing but chilled linen next to her that almost led Judy to abandon her plan. The thought of a lifetime of cold pillows, of Abel's not being there, warm and comforting, had shaken her deeply.

But as she slept fitfully in the early hours before dawn, she had seemed to hear a voice. To Judy it was as though her late father, Colonel Wild Bill Robinson, had risen from a cold grave high on a New Mexico mountain to stand unseen beside her bed and repeat the message he had so often spoken to his junior officers.

"Be sure of your objectives, consider the balance between lives lost and lives saved, and once you have analyzed the situation, don't spare the horses until the enemy is yours!"

The half-dream, half-vision had finally solidified Judy's decision. That day she would put the troops in motion, and there would be no retreat. No quarter asked, none given. She hoped and prayed that her marriage would be among the survivors.

Gradually the wood-burning stove prevailed over the Wyoming high-country chill. The first cup of morning coffee, ordinarily such a delight, seemed flavorless. Her fingers trembled as she lifted the cup.

Abruptly she rose from the table and went to her closet. "If I'm going to act the harlot," she muttered, "at least I know how to dress for the part."

She selected a dark brown dress that had always been a bit tight across the bust. The bodice laced from the waist up with a round cotton cord so that the depth of the neckline could be adjusted as desired. The color was a perfect complement to her skin and the gold highlights in her hair. Judy was well aware of the impact her figure made on men— she drew enough stares to have a constant reminder.

Placing her dress on the bed, she wryly recalled another comment from her father. "When you have the weapons available, use them." She took her time dressing, applying the slightest hint of indigo beneath her eyes and brushing her hair until it glistened in the early light.

When the young woman got to the hotel, she realized

with a mixture of satisfaction and dread that her timing was
perfect. She had barely gone on duty when she found herself
smiling at Calvin Winston.

"Good morning, Mr. Winston," she said brightly. "The
same order for you this morning?"

The man's eyes left hers, slowly traveled the length of her
tightly laced bodice, then drifted back to her face.

"Yes, thank you," he said. "Please call me Cal. And
perhaps today you will have that coffee with me?"

"Only if you will call me Judy, Cal. And would you mind
terribly if we made it a drink this evening instead of coffee? I
always need some relaxation after a day's work."

Winston smiled in obvious delight. "I'd be honored,
Judy."

She felt his eyes on her as she made her way to the
kitchen to turn in his breakfast order. It was going to be a long
day, she thought, and the butterflies in her stomach already
were beginning to stir in anticipation of the evening.

Somehow, Judy made it through the day. Shortly before
meeting Cal, she slipped into a storage closet. With shaking
fingers she tugged the bodice tie loose and let the neckline
open daringly. Then, leaning against a wall of the closet, she
tried to steel her nerves for the ordeal ahead.

"Oh, God," she muttered, pushing the door open, "why
do I feel so cheap?"

A few moments later, a sparkling young lady raised her
half-empty glass of sherry to the handsome man across the
table from her. She hoped she would be able to keep the mild
drink down. She had been slightly surprised to discover her
voice did not quaver and her fingers trembled only slightly.
She hoped Calvin Winston would read that tremble as sexual
tension and not as the revulsion and fear she felt toward him.

". . . And that's about it, for my story," Winston said. "A
man just follows the business, and I understand there is a great
deal of ore between here and the West Coast." He paused to
sip his bourbon, but his eyes never left her breasts. "How
about you, Judy? This seems to be a rugged country for such a
lovely woman."

She sighed. "Sometimes, Cal, I simply hate it. And the
army and all this fuss about the Indians. Abel is in the field so
much, and I get so lonely."

Her companion closed one eye in a slow, conspiratorial
wink. "Perhaps there is a way to deal with that loneliness."

Judy flushed at the barely concealed invitation. Her discomfort increased when she saw Vi Robinson's disapproving glance in their direction. "Oh, Cal," she said, her voice low and husky, "I wish—never mind. Laramie is such a gossipy town, full of so many small-minded people. I sometimes wish they would just give it back to the Indians," she added, letting a touch of bitterness creep into her tone.

He made no response. Abruptly she drained the sherry from her glass, then reached out and placed a hand on his. "I must go now, Cal. You know how people talk, and my husband is *so* jealous—and inattentive. Thank you for the sherry. It has been a delight talking with you. Just to spend a few moments with someone not preoccupied with Indians and fighting and tactics has been *so* refreshing."

She removed her hand, pushed back her chair, and stood. Calvin Winston was instantly on his feet. "May I see you home?"

Judy smiled but shook her head. "No, Cal. Not just yet. Perhaps another time. . . ."

"Then could I talk you into having dinner with me one evening?" he asked.

"Why *thank* you. I believe that would be most enjoyable, Cal. We could discuss the cities you've seen, the grand hotels—*so* many things missing from this dreadful frontier." She waved a hand. "Please, finish your drink. I'll let myself out. And thank you again."

She walked quickly away from the table, retrieved her coat, and stepped outside. She knew the sudden sting at the corners of her eyes was not the result of the frigid north wind.

"Please, Abel, wherever you are at this moment, please understand and trust me. I love you, and I miss you so."

Judy set off rapidly for her own cold, empty quarters. The first scene had been played out. Whatever the outcome, she knew she must follow that first step down the risky road.

At the end of the first-floor hallway of the Laramie Hotel, Taylor Elkins eased the travel-worn assayer's field kit back beneath Calvin Winston's bed. There was no doubt in Taylor's mind now. Winston was no ore assayer. The weights were covered with dust, the scales bent and out of balance. It was like a man who claimed to be a gunfighter but did not care for his weapons. A field specialist who produced those tools in a camp full of knowledgeable prospectors would be immediately spotted as a fool and a fraud and probably hanged from the highest tree.

But now that he knew who Calvin Winston was not, Elkins became even more concerned over who the man really was. His first two inquiries to contacts in Washington had yielded nothing concrete. Now, with the Indians rampaging to the east, there was a distinct problem in communications. The mails ran infrequently, and the telegraph only sputtered from time to time.

Taylor glanced around the small room, keenly aware that his time could be running out. He was not sure how long Judy would sit at Winston's table or how long Winston would remain there after she had left. Carefully listening to the hotel's noises, he reached for the traveling bag Winston had carried on his arrival in Laramie. There had to be a clue somewhere; it was simply a matter of finding it—

He froze with his hand on the grip of the travel bag. Bootsteps were coming down the hall. Taylor glanced at the window but immediately discarded it as a possible escape route. The blast of cold air from an opened window would be an immediate tip-off that someone had been in the room. Moving silently, he made his way to the door, the click of heels on the boards growing louder by the moment. He pressed himself against the side of the wall near the door, one hand gripping the butt of his small and deadly derringer beneath his light jacket.

The bootsteps halted at the room next door. The man at the nearby door fumbled for what seemed an interminable time with a key before the latch finally clicked open. The door closed with a solid thud. Taylor could hear shuffling as the occupant moved about. Holding his breath, Elkins cracked the door of Winston's room and quickly glanced down the hallway. It was empty.

Elkins eased the door shut behind him and made his way down the hall, breathing a sigh of relief as he turned the corner toward the hotel dining room. Fingering the thin lock pick in his pocket, he hoped there would be another chance to finish the search.

Vi Robinson stood behind the cash counter of the hotel, scowling as she counted the change for Calvin Winston's drink charges. She handed the coins to the green-eyed Winston with an unusually curt "thank you."

Taylor hesitated, watching the scene curiously. For a moment it appeared Winston was about to try to engage Vi in conversation, but apparently he thought better of it after seeing her expression and made his way from the counter.

Taylor timed his casual approach so that the two men met as if by chance. "Evening, Mr. Winston," Elkins said politely. "How are things in the assaying business?"

Winston shrugged. "Not much prospecting going on at the moment, what with the Indian troubles and the travel ban on the Bozeman Trail."

Taylor shook his head sympathetically. "Perhaps business will improve once the war ends and the Indians are brought under control. I understand the war is not going well for the Confederacy, so we may see a more sudden end to the conflict than we expect."

Anger flared in Winston's eyes. It lasted for only a split second, but Taylor knew he had touched a nerve, perhaps one that could be exploited. Then the expression was gone, and Winston responded with an uninterested shrug. "It's not my war either way, Mr. Elkins. It's merely a business inconvenience no matter which side wins."

Winston ended the conversation by striding toward the hallway leading to his room. Though the meeting had produced little that Taylor could use, other than the hint of anger at the reference to the South's fate, he was satisfied. It had been the most lengthy conversation he had managed to have with the man. Small things had a way of adding up, he thought. The biggest fish sometimes bit the smallest worm.

He walked to the counter where Vi stood, the grim expression still on her face. Unaware of his approach, she started when he stepped to the counter and smiled at her.

"Good evening, Vi," he said. "You appear to be troubled about something. May I be of assistance?"

Vi shook her head, and the stormy look in her eyes subsided somewhat. "It's—a personal thing, Taylor," she said.

He did not press the point. He had seen Judy join Winston earlier in the evening, and he knew Vi was not overly fond of the man. Obviously she was worried about her stepdaughter's potential involvement with the handsome young man.

Taylor very much wanted to reassure Vi. His instincts told him any involvement with a man other than her husband was

totally out of character for Judy. Still, he said nothing. He
knew he might have to use anyone—even Vi or Judy—to
accomplish his mission. But Judy seemed to have some
objective in mind, and Taylor Elkins decided to watch the
young woman closely.

"Vi," he said, "it's almost closing time. Would you
consider joining me, if you aren't too tired, for a drink and a
short walk? I know it's cold outside, but I like the taste of
autumn and could use some fresh air."

Some of the animation seemed to come back to Vi's face.
Her eyes softened. "Thank you, Taylor. I would enjoy a hot
rum and a cold walk. Since I seldom drink and rum is potent,
you may have a tipsy woman on your hands, though."

He laughed in genuine amusement. "Vi Robinson, I very
seriously doubt I will ever see you not in complete control of
yourself." He glanced at the big schoolhouse clock on the wall.
"I'll see you in, say, fifteen minutes?"

As Vi watched him walk away, the flutter began again in
her stomach. *Taylor Elkins,* she thought, *if I don't watch out,
you'll destroy this woman's self-control.*

The warmth of the hot buttered rum settled in Vi's
middle, pleasantly dulling the edge of the crisp night air as
they made their way down the street outside the hotel. She
became conscious of a touch on her hand and allowed her
fingers to rest in the warmth of Elkins's strong palm. His touch
was gentle and reassuring, and Vi felt the stirrings of sensa-
tions that had lain dormant for months.

Conscious only of the warmth and strength in the body
beside her, Vi did not realize immediately that Elkins had led
her down a dimly lit side street. In the deep shadows alongside
the street, Taylor stopped, still holding her hand. She could
barely see his face in the near blackness.

"Vi," he said, his voice tender, "I know what you have
been through, and I won't impose myself on you. But I want
you to know if you are ever distressed or in need, I'll be here."

Instinctively Vi turned and took the man in her arms. She
had not fully realized until then how much she needed the
reassurance, the sharing, of a man's embrace. Elkins's strength
enveloped her, bringing the comfort and warmth she had
almost forgotten. She felt a gentle finger beneath her chin and
let her head tilt up.

"Vi Robinson," Taylor whispered, "you are a beautiful and

sensitive woman. I have a confession to make. I fear I am falling in love with you."

He kissed her gently, almost wistfully. Then the brief contact was broken, leaving Vi breathless with the sweep of emotions she had held in check for so long.

"I've been wanting to do that for a long time," Taylor said, "and I'll make no apologies. I realize how difficult it must be for a woman who has been widowed twice to even consider yet another involvement. I promise I won't press you. All in good time. And even if you turn away for good reason, I'll have had this night."

Too shaken to speak, the woman rested her head against his shoulder. She shivered.

"I'm sorry," Elkins said. "I didn't realize it was so cold out here. I'll get you back to your hotel at once."

Vi dared not tell him the trembling he felt was from something other than the cold.

Arm in arm they made their way back to the hotel.

Taylor Elkins lay awake for a long time that night, savoring the touch of her lips on his. He wanted Vi Robinson. Perhaps, he thought, it was too much to hope for. Perhaps it was not fair to Vi. After all, his was a dangerous business. At least the war seemed to be grinding toward an end, and his mission for the Union would be completed, or would have failed, before too long.

Taylor had waited all his life for the right woman; he supposed he could wait a few more months.

In the meantime, he faced one task above all others: The Confederate connection on the Plains must be ferreted out and eliminated. Too much was at stake for the Union, too many lives were involved, and he had never dodged an assignment for personal reasons, no matter how pressing.

Now, Elkins decided, he had one more reason to succeed.

"The Cheyenne who sits among us and shares our meat talks of living in peace with the white man. Is it possible this Cheyenne fears death and wishes only to live himself?" The Sioux called Bear Killer, leader of the Crazy Dog warrior society, glared hard and long across the council lodge at the visitor.

Yellow Crow stared back impassively at the broad, sneering face. Defying the chill in the lodge, Bear Killer stood with his torso bare. Heavy scars laced his muscular chest and upper arms, in testimony to the encounter years ago when the Sioux, then only a junior warrior, had earned his adult name. Armed with only ax and knife, he had slain a brown bear that had charged from a thicket toward a group of women and children. The hand weapons with which Bear Killer had vanquished his enemy still hung from his belt. The pelt of the bear now lay atop his sleeping pallet.

Yellow Crow had expected a strong stand from Bear Killer. The scarred Indian was the most warlike of the Crazy Dogs, a man with supreme confidence in his considerable fighting ability and the medicine drawn from the blood of the dead bear.

"Yellow Crow of the Cheyenne does not fear death," the visitor finally replied. "The Cheyenne warrior societies spit in the eye of death, as do the Sioux Crazy Dogs. Yet is it not true that among the warrior societies of both tribes there are women and children depending upon the braves for food and protection? There is a time for war and a time for peace. Is it not best to treat for peace with the white man now, while we still have a chance to retain most of our sacred lands and hunting grounds?"

Yellow Crow let his gaze drift from one face to another. The six most powerful leaders of the Sioux warrior societies gave no indication whether they heard his words or not.

"Already the tribes of the Plains have shown the white men their courage and ability as warriors," Yellow Crow continued. "Now, the red man will be able to speak from strength. The whites will listen. There are honorable men among them, men who know that the Indian needs freedom to follow the buffalo. There are also those who would kill all of the red men. If we do not speak now, we will have to speak later with those white men of lesser understanding. The spirits have led Yellow Crow among many tribes to seek peace now."

Bear Killer merely snorted in obvious disgust, eyeing Yellow Crow suspiciously. The Cheyenne sat impassively. He had made his plea, and now the decision rested with the Crazy Dog leaders. Yellow Crow took no personal pride in the fact that it took courage for a Cheyenne brave to ride into the Crazy Dogs' camp. A man simply did what the spirits and common sense willed him to do. The cooperation of the powerful Crazy Dog society would go a long way toward reaching a fair settlement with the white government and, therefore, was worth any personal risk involved.

"There was a time when the words of the Cheyenne warrior Yellow Crow were heard among the Plains tribes. But that was before he became a tame Indian," Bear Killer taunted.

Yellow Crow ignored the deliberate insult. "Men see things differently, Bear Killer. Yellow Crow's time among the white soldiers has opened his eyes to truths as yet unseen by many red men."

Bear Killer glared at the Cheyenne and wondered if a challenge to personal combat might be in order. But at the same time he did not lie to himself; he had heard in detail of the lithe Cheyenne's impressive defeat of Howling Wolf, the best hand-to-hand fighter in the entire Arapaho tribe. There was another way.

"If Yellow Crow remains a warrior and his heart is yet Cheyenne, then his words will be considered," Bear Killer said. "But Yellow Crow must prove his heart is not white."

Yellow Crow's intuition made him apprehensive. "What does Bear Killer propose?"

"That the Cheyenne ride with the Crazy Dogs against the enemy of the Sioux. Even now we prepare to ride the war ponies to the land of the Shoshone, who have gone to the aid of the white soldiers. The Arapaho lack the spirit to punish the Shoshone for their actions. The Crazy Dogs do not. Then while the Shoshone lick their wounds and bury their dead, we will seek out the white soldiers and kill them."

Alarm jolted Yellow Crow's soul. A campaign to punish the Shoshone and a raid against the whites would carry him into a land where he had many friends—into the vicinity of Fort Laramie. "And should Yellow Crow agree to ride with the Crazy Dogs? What then would be gained?" he asked stoically.

Bear Killer's eyes narrowed, and he studied the Cheyenne warrior in silence for several minutes. "Then the entire Sioux nation will know that Yellow Crow remains a strong warrior whose words should be heard in council. He will have proved his spirit as well as his skin has not turned white."

Yellow Crow knew he finally had come face to face with the one thing he most dreaded and feared. Trapped between two cultures in collision, he was being forced from his campaign for diplomacy. If he accepted the challenge, he might be forced to raise his hand against a friend. If he did not, Bear Killer would waste no time in spreading the word that Yellow Crow was but a tool of the white man. His influence among the Plains tribes would be eroded as surely as the stream wears down the boulder until it is but an insignificant pebble.

Yellow Crow knew he had no choice. The leaders of both red and white forces would parley with a warrior. Neither would talk with a coward.

"Yellow Crow will go and prepare his horses and weapons," he said.

Abruptly he turned and walked from the lodge. The spirits sometimes moved in baffling ways, he thought, but never had they failed him. This, then, would be his test of fire.

Yellow Crow's preparations took only a few moments. Then, his heart heavy, he made his way to the crest of a nearby hill to pray to Wise One Above. With the point of his knife, he drew a few drops of blood from his forearm and placed the crimson-tipped blade on a flat rock. Yellow Crow sat for a moment as though in a trance, then lifted both hands toward the sky.

"Wise One Above," he prayed, "Yellow Crow does not ask for success or protective medicine. He asks only that should a white face appear before him in battle, let it be the face of one he does not know. Let the blood upon the knife before you be a symbol of blood unspilled, and guide his hand toward peace in the battles that are to come."

"Dammit, sir, I *will* have peace—even if every one of the bloody savages has to be ground into the face of the earth!" The lieutenant governor of the state of Kansas, angry and frustrated, slammed his fist onto the top of his heavy mahogany desk.

Across the room, a slightly built man with an angular face and darting eyes nodded somberly.

The lieutenant governor stabbed a pudgy finger into a pile of reports on his desk. "I've sent for you, Colonel, because you're regular army, and I like your philosophy of dealing with these redskinned heathens."

Colonel Emery Church shifted his weight in the overstuffed chair. "Only one way to deal with 'em, sir. Kill 'em all."

"My thinking exactly," the government official replied. "I

understand you have had considerable experience as an Indian
fighter?"

"Yes, sir. Served in the Navajo campaign under General
Carleton. We got crossways a bit on how to tame 'em, so I
wound up transferred out of here."

The lieutenant governor rose, approached the army
officer, and offered him a cigar. Church accepted with a
muttered "thanks," and casually lit it.

"Tell me, Church, exactly what would you need in the
way of men and equipment to wipe out these wild animals?
None of our other commanders seems to be having much
luck."

Church puffed at the cigar. "I've been giving that very
thing considerable thought, sir," he said. "I don't see why it
can't be done with maybe a thousand men and a few cannon.
Never met a brave yet who didn't run when it looked like he
was in for a scrap. Wipe out a few villages, stomp a few of the
lice, and they'll be at your front door beggin' for a peace treaty
in a month's time."

The lieutenant governor returned ponderously to his seat.
"And how, Colonel Church, would you reply to those peace
overtures?"

Church glared through the cigar smoke. "With a bunch of
public hangin's, sir. Teach 'em all a lesson."

The man behind the mahogany desk nodded enthusiasti-
cally. "My thinking exactly, Colonel Church. You know the
situation well. Our communication lines are disrupted, our
citizens butchered. Our prospectors can't get to the gold fields.
And all because of a handful of savages. We've whipped the
Rebels out of Kansas, and I see no reason why we can't whip a
few redskins a lot easier." The lieutenant governor lit a cigar
for himself, leaned back in his chair, and stared for a moment
at the high ceiling.

"I can't get any regular army troops for you, Church,
because the Union won't let me have any. But I can raise a
good-sized volunteer army of fine Kansas and Nebraska boys
and give you a blank check for supplies and equipment. And
there's something else I can offer you, Colonel—a place in
history and a major command of your own." The official
abruptly leaned forward, staring at the army officer. "I don't
want you to just clean up Kansas, Church. I want you to sweep
the Plains clear of Indians along every trail between here and

Laramie! And then I want you in command of the frontier. I have friends in high places, Colonel, and I can swing your appointment as commander of the Fort Laramie garrison—the Third, I believe it's called—because, by God, Colonel Ted Henderson sure hasn't produced results!"

Emery Church almost jumped out of his chair at the mention of Henderson's name. Cold hate boiled to the surface, and his mind flashed back to New Mexico Territory when Henderson had gotten the promotion that should have been his and then manhandled him. Since that day when Henderson had ordered him thrown into the stockade just for killing a bunch of Indians, Church had lived for revenge. And now it was being offered to him on a silver platter, with the blessings of the government!

Even more than he wanted to wipe every redskin out of the Plains, Emery Church wanted to make Ted Henderson pay. What better way to get even with the Indian lover than by taking over his command—and then to gain the final measure of retribution by plunking him dead center with a bullet! He had to force himself to pay attention to the lieutenant governor.

". . . Of course, the final plan of attack will be of your choosing, Colonel Church. Follow whatever means are necessary to crush the Indians. Now, how much time will you need to get a force into the field?"

Church shrugged. "Once the army's raised, sir, not long. You don't have to train hard to learn how to shoot Indians. I can be on the move before the winter snows have completely thawed. And there won't be a savage left alive between here and Montana when I'm through."

Less than an hour later, Colonel Emery Church was outside the government building, leaning against the barrel of a cannon and staring off toward the northwest.

Toward Laramie.

"Now, by God, Henderson," he muttered, "we'll settle us up some scores come spring. And I'll show you and that Injun-lover friend of yours Carson how to deal with savages. Then," he added, his voice full of hate, "I'll help myself to a chunk of your skin!"

Seven

Ted Henderson slumped forward on the low dressing stool before the hearth. His exhaustion and tension faded as Wilma massaged his shoulders and neck.

"Woman, you are going to spoil me rotten in my advancing age," he said. "A few days in the field and I'd almost forgotten how good your pot roast is and how it feels to settle into a tub of hot water." He reached back and stroked her hand, luxuriating in her touch. "You should apply for a patent on those massages. You'd make a fortune."

Wilma leaned forward and kissed him lightly on the side of his neck. "You're the only fortune I want, dear. I'm selfish. I think if I can keep these homecomings rewarding enough, it will give you some incentive not to collect any more scars when you're in the field."

He pressed his cheek against hers, drinking in the womanly smells of freshly washed hair, lavender-scented soap, and a lingering hint of the odor of freshly baked bread. "Just your being here is enough incentive for me, darling," he whispered in her ear. "I'm beginning to feel like a young buck again instead of an old, worn-out stag."

Wilma stepped around the stool and knelt before him. She kissed him, long and tenderly. Finally she pulled away, her violet eyes glinting flirtatiously.

"Little William Ted has finally gotten over the excitement of Daddy's coming home," she said huskily. "If we're reasonably quiet, we won't wake him. I want you, Ted Henderson. And there will be no talk of army business or gossip until morning."

She stood, holding his hand in hers, as Ted rose and took

her in his arms. "Would you think me less of a man if I told you that at times like this you almost make me cry?" he asked.

She shook her head and smiled. "That's one of the reasons I'm so much in love with you. You aren't afraid to show your emotions to me." She tightened her grip around his neck. "Enough of this small talk, Colonel. If you would be kind enough to follow me?"

The next morning Ted woke, refreshed and rested for the first time in days, to a bright new dawn and the smell of coffee and bacon from the kitchen. He took his time washing and shaving before slipping into a fresh uniform. At the doorway to the kitchen, he stood for a moment, watching Wilma busy at the stove.

Little Bill was already up and talking, the words somewhat slurred by the hefty chunk of biscuit in his mouth. The boy seemed to have grown even more during Ted's brief absence. Though much of the garrison still debated which of his parents the youngster favored the most, Ted knew he was looking at a mirror image of himself, except for the rich violet eyes he had inherited from his mother. What more could a man ask from life? he wondered.

He stepped into the kitchen. "Morning, folks," he said, pouring himself a cup of coffee. "It seems someone let me oversleep a bit."

Bill bolted from the table and leaped into his father's arms, dribbling soggy pieces of biscuit down his father's shirtfront. "Can you stay home now, Daddy? Can we ride?"

Ted casually ruffled his son's hair and gave him a gentle squeeze. "I hope so, son. For a few days at least." He carried the boy back to the table and plopped him back onto the grown-up type chair with slightly longer legs that Yellow Crow had carved for his godson. Ted remembered the Cheyenne's comment at the time. "Boy sit at table like white man, not strap in silly-looking high chair. He not like other boys. Much good bloodline. Fine godfather. He grow quick to strong young warrior, be man soon."

Ted kissed Wilma good morning. Noting the sparkle in her eyes, he said, "You look especially pert and pretty this morning. Any special occasion?"

"A mail coach managed to get through at dawn," Wilma answered. "The Butterfield Company seems to be one of the few firms determined to deliver regardless of the Indians. Of course, they had a little help, too. Bernie Christian and a squad from Abel's command escorted them in."

"Good," Ted said, pleased that at least part of the communication network was surviving, even sporadically. "How's Bernie?"

"Tired, but in good spirits." Wilma shook her head in disbelief. "I don't understand how he can have such a big heart. He said he planned to catch a quick nap, then report to you at your office." Wilma filled her husband's plate high with scrambled eggs, bacon, biscuits, and fried potatoes.

"What's new around Laramie?" Ted asked between mouthfuls.

"Some good news, some a bit disturbing," his wife replied. "The wagon train got through safely with supplies from Salt Lake City. The Arapaho tried to attack, but young Lieutenant Wills beat them back. It was a sharp, quick fight, but no one was hurt on either side."

Ted nodded, satisfied and pleased to hear that Wills had come out a winner in his first clash. The young man had the promise of developing into a fine officer.

"We managed to get the refugees all settled in for the winter. I'm afraid I may have usurped some of your authority in the process," Wilma continued. "I pointed out to a couple of local merchants they were overcharging for goods. They were reluctant at first, but eventually they came through with some generous donations for the refugee camp."

Ted chuckled softly. His wife could be most persuasive when she set her mind to it. "What's the disturbing news?" he asked.

Wilma glanced at their son. "Perhaps we can discuss it later," she suggested. "It's—something of a rather delicate nature, regarding Judy Hubbard."

Ted knew better than to press the point. Wilma never declined to discuss a problem without good reason, and he trusted her judgment.

"Can we ride now?" William Ted asked eagerly.

His father shook his head reluctantly. "I have some work to do at the office this morning, son. Maybe I'll have some free time this afternoon. How is the pony?"

For the next few minutes, the boy described in considerable detail his experiences with his pony, occasionally using an Indian word when the English equivalent escaped him. Ted was both pleased and surprised at the amount of information his son already had absorbed about horses.

Breakfast completed, Ted said his temporary good-byes to his family and made his way to the commanding officer's post. The fickle weather seemed unable to make up its mind, he thought. The day was beginning bright and unseasonably warm with a touch of late Indian summer. But to the northwest, snows already blanketed most of the mountain range, and the flat color of the sky hinted that when the winter came to stay, it would do so with a vengeance.

Ted exchanged greetings with the officer of the day, then settled down to sort through the messages and letters brought on the welcome Butterfield run.

Midway through the stack of official dispatches, he came across an envelope that grabbed his immediate interest. It carried the official seal of the White House.

He carefully slit the end of the envelope with a penknife, unfolded the single sheet of paper, and began to read:

It was with great interest, Colonel Henderson, that I read in *The Boston Herald* Mr. Taylor Elkins's account of his interview with you and your plan to reach a just settlement with the Indians of the Plains. Your proposals reflect my own feelings in the matter, that the original occupants of this nation be treated in a fair manner. I have instructed my senior cabinet members to draw up recommendations based upon your approach, to be forwarded to Interior and Indian Affairs. As we shall seek no retaliation against the Confederacy, we seek no retribution against the red man. The South once again will be treated as brothers, not as a vanquished enemy, and I strongly feel the same should apply to the Indian. Once again, Colonel Henderson, you have performed a valuable service for your flag and your people, and I am once more in your debt.

> Your obedient servant,
> Abraham Lincoln

Ted carefully refolded the letter and returned it to the envelope, surprised and delighted that the President had thrown his influence behind the drive toward a peaceful settlement. The one-page document from the Great Father in the nation's capitol would be a valuable tool in negotiations with the tribes, since even the Plains Indians held President Lincoln in higher esteem than any other president to date. And from the tone of the letter, the President seemed more than confident of defeating the Confederacy.

Ted made a mental note to personally thank Taylor Elkins. The journalist could well have played a major role in bringing peace to the Plains.

A knock sounded on the door.

"Come in," he called.

Bernie Christian, eyes bloodshot and slender shoulders drooping from fatigue, entered the office. Ted waved off the salute and took the corporal's hand in a sincere handshake.

Bernie's report was characteristically brief, complete, and accurate. Despite early setbacks, Abel Hubbard had posted some successes against the warring tribes to the east of Laramie in long, grinding campaigns. Now, his troops footsore and short of supplies, horses worn out, and ammunition all but gone, Hubbard was leading his command home to Laramie. Losses among the regulars had been light, and while few warriors had been slain or captured, Abel had managed to apply enough pressure on them to keep the Indians from extensive mischief.

"The complete details are here, Colonel," Christian said, producing a packet from beneath his tunic.

"Thanks, Bernie," Ted said, accepting the bundle of reports. "You've earned yourself an extended rest. And my personal appreciation, for whatever that's worth. Go get yourself some barracks time."

Briefly Ted scanned Abel's daily field reports. One note in particular caught his eye:

"It is my sincere belief," Abel wrote, "that any success we may have had, however slight, is in large part due to the diligent efforts of the Shoshone scouts and warriors recruited by Sergeant Major Albert Jonas. They are tireless on the trail and superb fighters. I would rather have twenty Shoshone at my side in a battle than a full company of these so-called volunteers."

Abel's report concluded with what Ted immediately recognized as the most important information gleaned from the entire campaign. It was a listing of names of the various bands and war chiefs encountered in hostilities to the east of Laramie. Ted now knew which Indians were responsible for the raids, or at least a majority of those involved. That knowledge would facilitate punishment of the guilty parties. More important to Ted, it would help assure that innocent bands were not attacked.

He was relieved to find that the names of Big Nose of the Cheyenne and Sitting Bull of the Hunkpapa Sioux were not on the roster for hostiles. Apparently Big Nose was keeping his word to remain on neutral ground, and while Sitting Bull had flatly refused to parley with Ted, the absence of his formidable band of warriors was a reassuring sign.

Like his predecessor at Laramie, Colonel Wild Bill Robinson, Ted hated being in the small office and the paperwork involved in running a military command. Deciding there were no documents that required his immediate attention, especially when he wanted to go riding with his son, he pushed back his chair and walked outside, blinking in the golden wash of the midmorning sun.

Hoping his father would be able to get away from his office, young William Ted stood beside his paint pony, ready to go. He grinned at his father, eyes bright with anticipation.

"Can we ride now?" he asked.

"Just as soon as I saddle the stallion, son," Ted replied, idly scratching the paint pony's chin. "He needs the workout."

Ted soon had his prized mount saddled. He walked the frisky stallion for a few moments to take some of the edge off the animal's antsy disposition before swinging easily into the saddle. The black stallion made one halfhearted effort to pitch, but Ted kept a firm grip on the reins. A sharp word let the black know this was no time for games, and the stallion's ears snapped forward.

Ted kept a close rein on the black as he helped his son mount. The youth rode Cheyenne style, with only a blanket held in place by a single rope on the paint's back and a tight-twisted grass hackamore for control. Bill stretched on tiptoe, slipped a hand through a loop of horsehair braided into the horse's mane, and, with a boost from his father, hauled himself astride his pony.

Ted winked at Wilma, who had come to check on Bill. "Looks like we're going to have to invest in a small saddle one of these days," he said lightly. "Can't have our son spend the rest of his days riding like a wild Indian."

Looking on as her two men put their horses through lazy figure eights to warm them up for more strenuous actions, Wilma felt filled with love. When Ted was riding with his son, his eyes positively sparkled in contentment. Wilma knew how much Ted valued these rare opportunities to be with Bill, to simply relax and enjoy being alive. He made no effort to hide his pride in his son's progress as a horseman. It was equally obvious to anyone who had ever been on horseback that Ted was a superb teacher, quick with a compliment, a gentle suggestion, but never a critical remark.

She continued to watch as the pair rode toward the fort gate at a slow trot, exchanging man talk along the way. Absorbed in the scene, she did not hear Judy Hubbard's approach until the young woman spoke at her side.

"They make quite a sight together, Wilma," Judy said. "You must be very proud of them both."

"Oh, good morning, Judy," Wilma replied. "Yes, I'm proud of them. Two of the finest men in the territory and they're both mine. Are you on your way to the hotel?"

Judy nodded solemnly. "If you don't need me at the refugee center, Vi can use some help. It's awfully busy at the hotel these days."

"Sure, go ahead." The two women watched, fascinated, as Bill suddenly leaned low above the pony's neck and, using only his knees, raced the horse in a tight circle around his father's mount. Wilma sighed. "Look at that, and I was afraid when they first put him on a horse. Now it looks like that boy could put his pony across a canyon without any problem."

A sudden gasp from the attractive woman at her side made Wilma turn. "What's the matter, Judy? You look like you've just seen a ghost."

Judy, her face drained, seemed not to hear. The words still buzzed in her brain. *Boy . . . pony . . . canyon.* The same three words she had overheard outside Calvin Winston's room! She shook her head, dazed. Other scraps of the overheard conversation raced through her memory. *Colonel must be dealt with. Stop him soon. Hostage.* Could it be? Was it possible some evil and twisted mind could have selected a mere child, almost a baby, as a tool in some plan against an army officer? She started at a touch on her arm.

"Judy? Are you all right?"

Wilma's question brought Judy back to the moment.

"What? Oh. I—I'm fine," she stammered. "Just a—twinge of a headache, Wilma." Judy took a deep breath, trying to steady herself. "I'd best hurry on now," she said. "Vi will be waiting."

Wilma watched the young woman move away rapidly toward the hotel. Concerned, she was tempted for a moment to follow Judy and talk to her. Perhaps the rumors floating about Laramie were beginning to take their toll; Judy could not possibly be unaware of the gossip linking her to Calvin Winston. Wilma wanted to reassure Judy, to tell her that she personally put no stock in the malicious gossip. Still, Judy had been spending a lot of time in the company of young Winston. Abel had been in the field a long time, and Winston was handsome.

Berating herself for even acknowledging the existence of such crude gossip, Wilma went back to the house to continue her chores of the day.

Judy leaned against the back door of the Laramie Hotel for a moment. With trembling fingers she brushed aside a wayward lock of blond hair. Her thoughts would not be still. She tried to tell herself the idea was simply preposterous—no one could possibly be so callous as to use a child. Or could they? A face formed in her thoughts, a hauntingly familiar face with green eyes that sometimes flickered with malice. And she could think of no other boy who owned a pony and was the son of a colonel.

No boy other than William Ted Henderson.

Even if her suspicions were true, Judy realized she had no real knowledge or proof of a plot. A few scraps of conversation overheard, a random use of three common words on a fort parade ground, did not prove anything. Most important, they did not answer the questions: Why? How? And when?

Judy knew of only one source for the answer to the questions—Calvin Winston. She shuddered. Even as she battled the desire to cry for help, to confide in someone, Judy knew only one person in all of Laramie could find the answers. It was up to her. Until she had specific details, she was afraid she could confide in no one without jeopardizing the boy's life. If Ted or someone else tried to find out what was going on, Calvin would certainly not tell them and then would be on his guard. If he *was* involved with the Confederacy and stirring up the Indians, and became aware he was under suspicion, a chance to discover the whole network might be missed.

She swung the hotel door open and stepped into the kithen. The scent of baking bread provided no solace as she mechanically prepared for her day's work. The thought sickened her, but Judy knew she must carry on. She must continue to dangle herself before Calvin Winston in hope of finding the truth.

Judy squared her shoulders and approached a table of newly arrived customers. Forcing the bright, welcoming smile onto her face, she breathed a silent prayer: *Lord, I can stand the pain myself, but please give Abel the understanding he will need; I couldn't bear to hurt him deeply again.*

Across the room, Vi Robinson escorted a quartet of customers to a table facing the big bay window offering a view of the busy Laramie street outside. The four were regular visitors, and Vi, anticipating their arrival, already had a tray of pastries and a container of hot coffee waiting for them. After serving them and spending a few moments in small talk, Vi excused herself and made her way toward the cash counter, where Sergeant Major Albert Jonas patiently waited to pay for one of the rare indulgences he enjoyed so much—a cup of the Laramie Hotel's rich, imported hot chocolate.

On the way, she glanced at Judy and felt her mood darken. *If that young woman doesn't start to behave herself soon,* Vi promised herself silently, *I'm going to have a few words with her.*

"How was the chocolate, Sergeant?" she asked, stepping behind the counter.

"Mightly fine, Miss Vi. I'm tempted to have something a bit stronger, though."

Vi looked up, surprised. "Why, Albert Jonas! I know for a fact you seldom drink, and never before supper. What's the occasion, if I might be so bold as to ask?"

Jonas looked very embarrassed. "I'm a bit nervous right now, Miss Vi," he said. "Today's the day. I mean, I'm going to ask Sally. . . ."

Impulsively Vi reached out and placed a hand on Jonas's broad wrist. "Why, Albert, that's wonderful! I don't see how she could refuse. And you two will be my guests this evening to celebrate, on the house, including a bottle of my best champagne!"

"Thank you, Miss Vi, but Sally hasn't said yes yet."

She watched as the man went out the hotel entrance. "Sally Coker," she muttered, "don't you be a darned fool, too."

To Sergeant Major Albert Jonas the hundred or so paces from the Laramie Hotel to Sally's seamstress shop seemed the longest he had ever walked. Conflicting emotions whirled through him. The euphoria of a prospector who had just found the mother lode alternated with the despair of a man on his way to the gallows. The lingering flavor of the rich chocolate had turned to brass in his mouth. Jonas knew that flavor well. It was the taste of fear.

He stood for a moment outside the door, hand on the latch. *I swear,* he thought, *I'd rather face a mess of mad Sioux.* He squared his shoulders, opened the door, and stepped into the small shop.

For once, he did not have to tell Sally to put down her needle. She stood, her back straight and seemingly defiant, at the end of the counter, as he approached within arm's length. Jonas wiped his sweaty palms on the legs of his field uniform and swallowed hard.

"Sally Coker," he said, hoping his voice sounded more self-assured to her ears than it did to his, "I've made up my mind."

Sally merely waited for Jonas to continue, an eyebrow arched in anticipation.

"The army's just about all I know. But there's one other thing I do know—I want you as my wife. Now. Marry me tomorrow an' come spring I'll quit the army. I reckon a man with a wife like you could find some way to make a livin'."

She stared at him for a long moment, and Albert thought he detected a softening in the gold-flecked brown eyes. He was surprised to see the rapid pulsing of an artery in the side of her slender neck; apparently her heart was racing as much as his own.

"Albert," she finally replied, "if this was spring and you wasn't in uniform, I'd marry you quicker'n a squirrel shells a nut. But I ain't sure about this new idea of yours, marryin' right away. I'm gonna give that some study. You know how I feel—weddin' up with a soldier's a quick trip to widow's black, and that ain't my favorite color.

"You give me a spell to think it over. I was ready for a yes or a no, not no maybes. You come back in a couple days, and I'll have an answer—"

The door of the shop suddenly banged open, and the corporal of the guard charged in.

"Sergeant! Report to Colonel Henderson on the double! We got Indian troubles. Sioux war party heading toward the Shoshone camp. Our scout says there's a bunch of them. Colonel wants R Company in the saddle five minutes ago!"

The corporal of the guard spun on his heel and almost sprinted out the door.

Albert looked regretfully at the woman he loved. "I've gotta go now, Sally. You heard the corporal, and the Shoshone are my friends. For now I'm still a soldier. You have an answer ready when I get back, woman—one way or the other."

Sally Coker stood trembling as Jonas left the small shop. A double ache tugged at her heart; she wanted to run after him and yell "yes," but she was also determined to stick by her guns. She wanted that big soldier in her arms, but the thought of losing him afterward was almost too much to bear. Walking to the window she watched the flurry of activity on Laramie's main street as troopers sprinted toward the stables while the bugles sounded Boots and Saddles.

The door opened, and Vi Robinson stalked into the shop. "Well?" The question was as much a challenge as a query.

"I just don't know, Miss Vi," Sally said. "Albert wants a marryin' now, but I want him outta uniform first."

Vi stomped her foot angrily, the unexpected noise jolting Sally. "Sally Coker, I had you figured for an intelligent woman!" Vi's eyes snapped in frustration and a touch of disgust. "It looks like I was wrong!"

The older woman came forward until she was only inches from Sally. "If you want something guaranteed, Miss Coker, you won't find it! What makes you think a farmer wouldn't maybe get kicked in the head by a mule, a miner die in a cave-in, or a rancher freeze to death with a broken leg after a horse falls?"

Vi reached out and placed a hand on Sally's arm. "I had a husband I loved," she said. "He was a soldier. He was killed. It hurt, and it still does. I won't deny that fact at all. But I had him for a time, and it was a beautiful part of my life. I wouldn't trade those few short months for anything.

"There's a fine man out there who loves you deeply. You love him, even if you do try to hide it. If you've got an ounce of courage, Sally Coker, you'll marry that big sergeant just as soon as you can! If you don't, you will regret your selfishness for the rest of your life!"

Stunned at the emotional outburst from the normally composed Vi Robinson, Sally watched silently as the army widow started toward the door. She suddenly realized that Vi's impassioned speech echoed her own unexpressed desires.

"Lawd," she finally muttered, "I been such a fool!" She whipped a shawl from a nearby pile, draped it around her shoulders, and set out almost on the run for the parade ground, where the patrol would be forming.

Cavalrymen from Lieutenant Wills's I Company and the elite R Company led by Albert Jonas already had formed in three-abreast lines as Sally dashed breathless onto the parade ground. Frantically she dodged the hooves of nervous mounts until finally reaching the front ranks and the massive black man on a horse next to Ted Henderson.

Albert Jonas looked down in surprise at the tug on his trouser leg. Tears streamed down the light brown face turned up toward him.

"All right, you stubborn nigger," Sally said. "You got it your way. Just keep that woolly hair on your head till you get back and we find us a preacher!"

The stunned sergeant major could only stare for a few seconds. Then he grinned broadly. As Ted Henderson raised a hand to signal the patrol afield, Albert Jonas leaned down and planted a quick kiss on the lips of his bride-to-be.

Sally stood in the whirling dust of the parade ground while the two companies moved out at a quick trot. "If you don't get yourself back, Albert Jonas, I'm gonna be awful mad at you," she called.

At the head of the column, Ted twisted in the saddle and studied the grinning face of his sergeant major.

"What was that all about, Albert?"

Jonas's grin widened even more. "Nothing special, sir. Reckon you could see your way clear to stand beside a big black non-com all nervous in front of a preacher?"

Despite the urgency of their mission, Ted felt his own spirits lift. "Congratulations, Sergeant," he said. "I'd consider it a high honor. How did you manage to wear her down, anyway?"

Jonas shook his head, still bewildered. "Don't reckon I know, Colonel. Must've had some help from a higher authority."

* * *

The crack of rifle fire and a swirling dust cloud clearly showed the location of the threatened Shoshone village a scant half-mile away in a shallow canyon along a tributary of the Green River. Despite the urgency of the battle, Ted Henderson kept his cavalry column spread, and they approached the village at a walk to minimize a dust trail that would alert the attacking Indians that additional forces were on the way.

Carl Keller, one of Ted's most trusted scouts, rode slowly back toward the approaching column and reined his horse alongside Ted's. "Looks about like we guessed," Keller said. "The Shoshone are dug in pretty good and givin' 'em fits. Turned back the first charge handy enough. Facin' about a hundred, little more maybe."

Ted nodded. "At least for once we'll have the edge in numbers."

Keller spat in the dust. "Don't know as I'd say that, Colonel. Them Sioux up there are Crazy Dogs, and a few Cheyenne, too. As Injuns go, ain't none tougher. And half our troops are green as grass. Wills and the I Company boys got a nasty fight comin'. Reckon they can handle it?"

"We'll know soon enough, Carl," Henderson said. "They have to get their feet wet sometime. If they can hold their own against Crazy Dogs, they'll be a welcome addition to this man's army."

Ted ran over the battle plan once more in his mind and decided he was satisfied with it. The Crazy Dogs were attacking from the east up the shallow canyon. The Shoshone would have to hold until I Company slid down to reinforce them, then Wills and his troops were to drive the Sioux back. At the proper time, R Company would link up with Wills's right flank, putting the Sioux under fire from west and south. The boulder-strewn hillsides sorely limited the mobility of R Company, and Ted knew this was likely to shape up as a rock-to-rock, hand-to-hand fight before it was over.

He deployed his troops along the ridge, taking the left point for his own position. Should something go awry with Wills's push against the Sioux, he would be in position to take over I Company command; the crack R Company worked together so well it needed little if any field leadership.

Below, the Sioux milled about, preparing another assault on the entrenched Shoshone. So far, Ted realized with satisfaction, the Sioux were unaware of the presence of soldiers. He glanced at the sun. "Come on, Wills," he muttered, "it's time—"

As if Wills had heard, I Company raced from a draw, spurring their horses toward the Shoshone forward position. The sudden appearance of the blue-clad cavalrymen caught the Sioux completely by surprise. The charge they had been forming faltered, and Wills's men, advancing from brush to boulder on foot, opened fire. A couple of braves went down in the initial volley; then the Indians regrouped for a counterattack. Their effort faded into retreat after a brief, intense clash. I Company, with Lieutenant Wills in front, kept up the forward pressure, forcing the Sioux toward the trap set by Ted's R Company.

Ted turned to the man at his side. "Keep your head down and your hair on, Albert," he said. "You have something to come home to now. Here we go."

On the battlefield below, a Sioux glanced up toward the ridge, then turned and yelled to his companions. R Company's sharpshooters on the crest of the rocky slope opened fire, sending the attacking Indians scurrying for cover. A slug whined from a rock near Ted's ear as he darted from boulder to boulder, intent on linking up with the end of Wills's line. Albert Jonas's carbine barked, and a brave tumbled from behind a patch of scrub brush.

Ted reached the side of a white-faced young soldier grimly firing a handgun toward the enemy.

"Brace yourself!" Ted yelled above the crackle of gunfire. "They'll be coming at us now! Crazy Dog Sioux don't like to back up!"

He swung his Henry carbine to his shoulder and fired in one smooth motion. A painted brave dropped his rifle and turned, clutching his side.

Ted heard a dull *click* as the young soldier's handgun hammer fell on an empty chamber. He whipped his spare Dragoon from his belt and handed it to the soldier. "No time to reload. Just don't forget where you got it!"

The Sioux conterattack did not come in waves, as it would have if the Indians had been on horseback, but in a hail of covering gunfire and arrows as they sprinted from rock to rock. The quick, dashing movements left scant time for aimed fire, and only the best marksmen among the soldiers were able to score hits. Smoke from black powder weapons hung over the foward lines like a fog, with no wind to blow it from the scene.

Thumbing cartridges into his Henry, Ted crouched behind a fallen tree trunk, his lungs aching from the bite of powder smoke. A Sioux arrow thumped into the log before him, and then the braves poured from the jumble of boulders just ahead.

Ted had chosen his defensive position well, his rifle dominating a small area clear of boulders. To his left, Albert Jonas and the young soldier with Ted's spare handgun crouched on opposite sides of the base of a V-shaped rock formation. A half-dozen painted warriors suddenly appeared, charging toward Jonas. Ted's rifle cracked, sending the lead warrior to his knees, and another fell before the blast of the young soldier's borrowed handgun.

All at once Ted found himself fighting for his life. A rifle ball tore his campaign hat from his head, leaving a stinging track alongside his scalp. Ted fired by instinct, levering the Henry as fast as he could. One Sioux tumbled heavily in the small clearing. Another staggered, apparently hit in the rapid-fire barrage, then limped toward the safety of the rocks.

Through the din of gunfire and the war whoops of the Sioux attackers, Ted sensed a new danger, a fleeting movement at the corner of his vision. He whirled, shouldering the Henry and bringing the sights level—and froze in shock and dismay.

A half-dozen steps away, a familiar face peered down the sights of a Spencer .56 lined on Ted's chest.

It was Yellow Crow.

The Cheyenne warrior stood against a backdrop of drifting gray smoke. War paint streaked his cheekbones and forehead. Ted could even see with startling clarity the fingers he had so often grasped in friendship and brotherhood curled about the stock and trigger of the Spencer.

Recognition flashed in the Cheyenne's face. For a long moment the two men stood, sights lined on each other's breast, the shock and tension becoming almost a physical presence between them.

Then, as one, the two blood brothers lowered their weapons. As suddenly as he had appeared, Yellow Crow was gone, a wraith dissolving among the swirl of smoke. Yet the expression in the dark eyes of the Cheyenne remained etched in Ted's brain, a reflection of his own dismay and pain at the near tragedy.

Ted let his body sag against the rock. He released his grip

on the receiver of the Henry and wiped the sweat from his brow with trembling fingers. "Ride in peace, my brother," he whispered. "And may the spirits forever spare us as they have this day."

Gradually Ted realized the firing had begun to die down. The attacking Indians were beginning an orderly withdrawal in the face of superior firepower and numbers. Though the Crazy Dogs were perhaps the fiercest warriors on the Plains, they were not stupid. They would retreat, to fight another day.

A sudden gust of wind punched a hole in the swirling smoke and dust before Ted. A short distance away, a Sioux, heavy scars crisscrossing his chest, stumbled and fell. From a nearby clump of shurb brush, Yellow Crow instantly sprinted toward the downed Indian. Ignoring the slugs that whined close by, kicking dirt at his feet, the swift Cheyenne scooped the much heavier Sioux from the earth, tossed him easily over a shoulder, and dashed through the storm of lead to the safety of a shallow creek bank that meandered away toward the east.

As the echoes of the fusillade died away, Ted heard Lieutenant Wills cry, "Stand your positions! Don't try to follow! The fight is ended!"

By the time the smoke and dust had settled, Ted could see a line of Indians—many riding double—on horseback, urging their mounts away from the battleground. A sense of relief surged through him when he saw a familiar palomino gelding racing away, two braves on its sturdy back.

Still badly shaken by the encounter with Yellow Crow, Ted slid to a sitting position alongside the boulder. Finally he became aware of a huge black hand on his shoulder.

"Ted—are you all right? You've been hit—"

"What?—Oh. Nothing serious, Sergeant Jonas. Not on the outside, anyway." Ted struggled to his feet. He made no effort to explain the strange remark, and Albert Jonas knew better than to press his commanding officer.

"Tell Lieutenant Wills his men performed admirably," Ted said, "and ask him to report casualties as soon as possible. I'll be up there"—Ted pointed toward a lone piñon tree atop the ridge—"when I'm needed."

An hour later, Lieutenant David Wills approached the solitary figure leaning against the tree. His salute went unreturned as his colonel stared blankly into space.

"Sir?"

Ted blinked a couple of times, forcing himself back to the moment. "Yes, Lieutenant?"

"Casualties fairly light on both sides, sir. We lost two privates, with five injured, one seriously. As near as Sergeant Jonas and I can calculate, the Sioux lost perhaps twenty warriors either injured or dead. The Shoshone were harder hit than we were, sir. Eight dead, six wounded." The young lieutenant shook his head in amazement. "You'd think, sir, with all the shooting there would be more casualties."

"That's the way it is with Indian fighting, Lieutenant," Ted replied. "A lot of noise and smoke and, fortunately, not too much blood. On either side."

"Yes, sir. I see now where you are right. Colonel, the Shoshone expended a lot of their lead and powder defending their village. I've asked my men to spare all the ammunition they can for distribution to the Shoshone."

Ted finally stirred, moving away from the lone tree against which he had been leaning. "Good thinking, David," he said, unaware he had used the young officer's Christian name for the first time. "You have the makings of a good field officer."

"Thank you, sir. Do we form up a pursuit party?"

Ted shook his head. "No. We're going home. And, David, do me a favor?"

"Certainly, sir."

"You and Sergeant Major Jonas lead the troops back home. I have some heavy thinking to do. I'll be along shortly."

The lieutenant hesitated. "But, sir, isn't it dangerous for you to be out here alone—and wounded as well?"

Ted absently stuck a finger through the hole in his hat where the slug had gone through. "I'll be all right, David. You just get the wounded back to Laramie for treatment. I'll catch up to you later."

Lieutenant Wills studied the brooding face for a moment, then nodded and moved away.

A short time later, the long column of cavalrymen filed past a few yards from the tree where a solitary figure stood, staring into the distance.

"Any idea what's wrong with Colonel Henderson?" Wills asked the scout riding beside him.

Carl Keller gnawed a fresh chew from his diminished plug of tobacco. "Yep. He ran into some bad medicine." The scout spurred his horse forward without further explanation.

* * *

A wisp of smoke rose from the herb leaves and sliver of dried meat smoldering atop a flat rock on a low hill outside the camp of the Sioux Crazy Dog leader Bear Killer. Far into the night, Yellow Crow fed fresh leaves into the tiny flame, then again crossed his arms over his chest. He did not feel the bite of the wind or notice the frost as it formed on the short grass and stones of the hilltop. Finally, his tormented spirit stilled, he rose and made his way to the small trail lodge in the center of the camp.

Bear Killer was awake and alert, his stoic eyes reflecting no pain despite the ragged wound in his side. The Crazy Dog leader beckoned Yellow Crow to sit, and the two faced each other in silence for several minutes.

"Yellow Crow has talked with the spirits?" Bear Killer asked.

Yellow Crow nodded. "Wise One Above has given a sign in the heat of battle. For a time Yellow Crow was confused, his spirit restless. Now he understands. Wise One Above wishes Yellow Crow to carry forward the plea for peace."

Bear Killer pondered the Cheyenne's words briefly. "Then it shall be," he said. "The Sioux recognize the wishes of the Cheyenne's Wise One Above. Yellow Crow has proven his courage and that he is an able warrior. Wakan-Tanka placed Yellow Crow near so that Bear Killer might live when the white man's gun broke his medicine. Yellow Crow's words will be heard in council."

Yellow Crow rose to his feet, satisfied. Bear Killer was a fierce warrior, a man who would choose his spot to die rather than give up his freedom to ride the trails of the holy mountains, the treasured streams, the waving grasslands of the buffalo. He also was a man whose words were his bond. Yellow Crow knew that wherever the Crazy Dogs or other Sioux met in Bear Killer's presence, his plea for peace would be repeated by the scarred warrior. The words would not be impassioned, merely stated. It was enough.

"The time has come that our trails part," Yellow Crow said. "Perhaps we will one day meet again. In the meantime, may the spirits ride with Bear Killer and bring him many sons."

Bear Killer raised a hand. "May Yellow Crow's medicine be strong, and his sons both wise and brave."

Yellow Crow stepped from the lodge into the sharp predawn air. He saddled his palomino, mounted, and reined the animal toward the east.

At the crest of a ridge a mile from the Crazy Dog camp, he checked his mount and sat staring in the direction of Fort Laramie. A face formed in his mind, the gentle features of a young Blackfoot maiden.

"When the spring thaws come," he murmured aloud, "Wise One Above will have spoken through me among the tribes. Then, Talking Bird, I shall come for your answer."

Biting sleet knifed across the ridges and badlands of the Black Hills into the trio of horsemen. Long Walker blinked into the stinging pellets at the broad and expressionless face a few feet away. The blue-eyed Indian battled a seething rage. Already, Sitting Bull had stolen some of his thunder by the mere fact of placing his guests facing into the biting wind. It was a constant struggle to keep the horses facing into the storm as the animals tried to turn their tails to the cold.

At Long Walker's side the Santee Sioux known as Antelope, who had just returned from an aborted attempt to gain allegiance from the Kiowa and Comanche, settled the buffalo robe more tightly about his shoulders. Antelope was content to listen. His rank among the braves was considerably less than that of Sitting Bull or even the newcomer Long Walker.

"Sitting Bull has not changed his mind?"

"There has been no reason," the chief of the Hunkpapa band replied. "Sitting Bull has had no visions, no signs, that would lead him to reconsider."

"And what of our success against the whites to the east?" Long Walker asked, trying to keep the testiness from his tone. "Did Long Walker's braves not stop the wagons, the talking wires, the soldiers? Were not many scalps taken, many guns and blankets captured?"

"Perhaps," Sitting Bull replied laconically. "But what of the cost to Long Walker's band? Did the Long Knives under the subchief of Fort Laramie not also count coups? Is it not true that Long Walker's braves have been walking the path of war too long, without taking time to hunt?"

Sitting Bull's powerful hand appeared from beneath the blanket draped about his shoulders. "Feel the wind, Long Walker. Already it brings the small ice. Soon it brings the snow. Already it is time for winter camp. Sitting Bull's people shall wait out the snows. When the grass again turns green and brings strength to the ponies, then a decision will be made."

"Yet Sitting Bull refused to talk with the soldier chief of peace," Long Walker said.

"This is true. As Sitting Bull's people do not join with Long Walker's, they do not join the whites." The blanket moved in the suggestion of a shrug. "Many others talk to Ted Henderson. Among them, numbers choose to follow the soldier chief's advice. It is for each chief, each band, to decide."

"Does Sitting Bull trust this Henderson?"

"Sitting Bull has no reason to trust or not trust him. He is a man whose word is good; of this Sitting Bull has heard many speak. It is said that he plans to ride the winter out, talking peace among the tribes. Who is to say he will not succeed? A man views peace in more favorable terms when the great snows howl outside his lodge, his ponies weaken from hunger, and his women have little for the pot."

Long Walker fought his urge to curse, white-man style. "And does Sitting Bull plan to parley when the soldier chief comes to the land of the Hunkpapa?"

The broad head moved slowly from side to side. "No. Sitting Bull makes no declaration of peace or war until the new flowers and grass shall come. This he has said before, he says now, and will say again."

With that, Sitting Bull abruptly wheeled his horse, kicked the animal into a trot, and headed deep into the Black Hills and the Hunkpapa winter encampment.

Long Walker snorted in disgust as the broad back of the Sioux chief disappeared beyond a veil of slanting sleet. "Sitting Bull," he said sarcastically, "is a squaw."

Antelope glanced sharply at the blue-eyed Indian. "It would not be wise to repeat that in his presence, Long Walker. Sitting Bull's medicine is strong. And in war his lance bites deep." The Indian sighed. "Antelope thinks it best that Long Walker plan to move against the whites next spring without Sitting Bull's help."

Angrily Long Walker yanked his horse about, tail to the wind, and glared at Antelope.

"Sometimes Long Walker wonders at Antelope's advice," he said caustically. "First he brings word that no help will come from the Kiowa or Comanche—"

"Take that up with Kit Carson, Long Walker." The challenge in Antelope's tone was clear, and Long Walker decided on a more prudent course of directing his anger elsewhere. He needed Antelope, and all the other allies he could muster. Long Walker feared no man, but he admitted to himself that the powerfully built Santee might prove to be a tough steak to chew. He raised a hand, as near as Long Walker could ever get to issuing an apology.

"Long Walker does not blame Antelope. He finds no reason to think Antelope spoke other than the truth, that the southern tribes acted foolishly in the attack on Carson at the river. Long Walker is angry at the loss of their help and at the reluctance of Sitting Bull and Big Nose to join the fight. Most of all he is angry with those who talk of peace with the soldier chief." Long Walker sighed, and the frost of his breath whipped away on the growing wind.

"For now, Antelope and Long Walker part company. Go to the winter camp of your people. Long Walker has a small but important mountain to climb. Antelope and Long Walker shall speak again soon."

With no further word of parting, Long Walker kicked his pony into a slow lope toward the south and Fort Laramie. Along the way there would be a small detour, to pick up a certain outlaw Ute with whom he had worked before—a man with no conscience, no tribal allegiance, and therefore one who was expendable.

Long Walker was pleased with his plan. What one did not gain by war or diplomacy one gained by stealth. He could see no flaws in the bold stroke that would take the peace talker Ted Henderson from the field, one way or another.

Each man had a weakness, and Long Walker, with the help of his Confederate contact in Laramie, Calvin Winston, had found Ted Henderson's soft spot. It was an overriding love for a small boy on a paint pony.

When Ted Henderson learned that a knife rested at his son's throat, he would not be quite so anxious to continue these talks of peace. Already he had been too successful; it was time to put an end to the man's interference. Even now Calvin Winston would be studying the patterns of the Henderson family's daily routine and choosing the proper time and place to strike.

As for Calvin Winston's soft spot, that had been easy

enough for Long Walker to locate. Though both the Indian and the Southerner were working for the Confederacy, Winston had agreed to carry out Long Walker's scheme only because of the gold the half-breed had offered him. Long Walker had given Winston half the gold already; he would pay him the balance after the plan was carried out.

Soon the child would be his. The boy would live until his usefulness was at an end. Then a simple word to the Ute, a quick slash of the knife, and Long Walker would have secured his power base from which to build his empire. With Ted Henderson paralyzed, the man who rode from winter camp to winter camp would be an Indian with blue eyes. The talk would not be of peace, and by spring he would be prepared to strike with an army of red men unlike anything ever seen on the Plains.

And just in case, there already had been drawn up a secondary plan. As he and the Ute grabbed the child from beneath the colonel's very nose, the renegade band of Sioux Crazy Dogs already would be encamped in the canyon above the hideout. Any rescue attempt would end in a short, quick, and bloody surprise.

Many snares were out for the rabbits. The abduction itself would appear to be the work of the Cheyenne, the one tribe with the strongest ties to Ted Henderson. The demands would be delivered by Winston, who then would have outlived his usefulness as well. There would be nothing left to tie Long Walker to the scheme.

He felt no remorse over the pending death of a young boy. What, after all, was the significance of a single little candle burning before a prairie fire?

Long Walker checked his animal, reducing its speed to a steady, ground-covering trot. He saw no need to hurry. "The white man taught Long Walker well the many faces of treachery," he muttered aloud. "Now the whites will know their words were heard. The seeds they planted so long ago will bear strong fruit. The harvest will be mine, and its flavor will be sweet."

Luxuriating in his own cleverness, the blue-eyed Indian fell silent. *Soon,* he thought, *my power will be greater than that of the stubborn Sitting Bull, greater than that of the soldiers; from Canada to Mexico, one voice will be heard— Long Walker's.*

The wind no longer felt so cold.

* * *

The freezing rain hammered at Laramie's back doors, turning windows into solid sheets of ice that reflected the flames from the open hearths of fireplaces. The north wind probed for the tiniest chinks between boards and sent its chilling tendrils to wrap about the ankles of those who strayed from the comfort of their fires.

Abel Hubbard sat by the dying fire in his quarters, unaware of the cold seeping into the room. His fingers trembled, not from the touch of winter, but from pent-up rage, frustration, and pain as he once more crumpled the small piece of paper and then opened his clenched fist again. He spread the message on the wide arm of his overstuffed chair and smoothed it as best he could.

He read the words as a man compelled. Each one drove a stake deeper into his heart. The letters that had torn his world apart were printed, all in capitals.

YOUR WIFE IS SEEING ANOTHER MAN—A FRIEND.

The paper had somehow appeared near the top of the stack of morning reports. Abel had stared at it in shock and dismay. Then, ignoring the startled comment from the officer of the day, he bolted from the commanding officer's quarters. Skidding on the treacherous ice underfoot, he had hurried home—only to find the quarters deserted. Impatient, Abel had slammed the door behind him and had gone searching for Judy. Several hours later he had returned and had been sitting in the overstuffed chair ever since.

The door swung open as he sat there, and Judy swept into the room, brushing the ice from the collar of her coat and shivering.

"Oh, Abel—what a nice surprise! I thought you would be on duty all day!" She moved quickly to him, kissed him on the cheek, then turned to the fire. "It's cold in here, dear. I'll stoke up the fire, and we'll have some nice, hot—"

"Forget the chatter, Judy!" The sharp, commanding tone in Abel's voice stopped her in midreach toward the woodpile by the fireplace. Her heart shrank in her chest as she slowly stood and turned to face her husband. His expression was as bleak and angry as the leaden sky outside.

"What—what is it, dear?" Judy heard the tremor in her

own voice. Still seated, Abel roughly thrust a scrap of paper toward her. Tears welled in her eyes as she read the words.

"Abel, I—"

"Shut up, Judy! I've heard all the rumors. I've tried to ignore them. But this"—he waved toward the oft-crumpled message—"just about closed the lid. Then, when I found out you weren't here, I went looking. I saw you, Judy. I saw you through the doorway of the hotel—with that man, Calvin Winston! And don't try to deny it!"

The scrap of paper fluttered to the floor. Judy had tried to steel herself for this moment, but all her resolve faded before the agony in her husband's eyes. She tried to match his unblinking stare but was forced to drop her eyes.

"Abel, please—it isn't what—"

"If you have an explanation, Judy, tell me! Tell me now, or you'll be talking to the wall!"

Judy raised her shaking hand and wiped the tears from her cheeks. "Abel, please—it isn't the way it seems. I—can't tell you now." Her voice broke into sobs, and she dropped her face into her hands. "Please, Abel—please—just trust me and—love me." She heard Abel get out of his chair, then his hand twisted her hair painfully, forcing her face up.

"Trust, Judy? Love?" He spit out the words bitterly. "Blind, forgiving acceptance?" Abel's face was contorted in pain and barely controlled violence. "While I'm out in the field, you're playing house with some stranger, and you have the nerve to ask for *trust*?" Abruptly he pushed her away.

"Abel, please listen—it was nothing. Nothing happened!" she pleaded.

"Then, for God's sake, Judy, tell me! Give me some reason to believe you! Give me back a reason to love you!" Abel suddenly turned his back on her. "If you had reason to act like some hussy, speak now!"

Gasping for breath between sobs, Judy looked at the sloping shoulders and narrow hips of the only man she had ever loved. She felt her whole world begin to crack and crumble. Now Judy understood the expression in the eyes of a trapped animal as it dashed itself against one side of the cage and then the other.

She ran to her husband, throwing her arms around him from behind. "Abel, please—"

Her hands were roughly torn from their grip on his

uniform. "All right, Judy. If you won't tell me, I'll go ask Winston himself!"

"No, Abel. No! You mustn't—there's so much at stake—"

Abel slowly turned to face her. "One Colin Dibley in your life wasn't enough, was it? Or do you just hate the thought of an empty bed?" All the spirit, all the fight drained from his face.

Judy thought frantically. She *had* to tell Abel; at least tell him enough to convince him she was not breaking her marriage vows. "Abel, please! It's not what you think. I was in his room to find out—"

"Oh! So you were in his room!" Abel's eyes flashed furiously once again. "You admit it, do you? Was anyone else in the room with the two of you?"

Judy shook her head, desperately trying to find the proper words to let her husband know Calvin Winston might well be the elusive Confederate spy. "No, you don't understand, it wasn't what you think. It was an accid—"

Livid, Abel cut her off. "Oh, I understand all right. I understand only too well. Me and the rest of Laramie! And I suppose while you and your new lover were all alone in his bedroom, Vi Robinson thought you were busy working for her. I'll bet she had no idea you were really working for yourself. Or do you charge pretty men like Calvin Winston for your time?"

Tears poured down Judy's cheeks, and she was sobbing so hard she could hardly speak. Desperately she fell to her knees and clutched Abel's right leg as fiercely as she could. She had to make him understand, she *had* to. Her mind whirled, refusing to cooperate. All she could do was stammer, "Boy . . . pony . . . canyon—danger—Little Bill."

Abel kicked himself free and roared, "How *dare* you try to involve Ted's child in your filthy plans! Have you no shame at all?"

He stood looking at his wife, who was now lying on the floor, sobbing hysterically. "It won't work, Judy. You fooled me once. I thought you had changed, but I suppose once a whore, always a whore. Don't worry about your boyfriend. I'm not going to kill him, even though it's what I want to do. I'll leave him alive—for you. Just don't let the bastard into my bed. He can have you and good riddance, but I'll be damned if you'll ply your filthy trade in my house as long as I'm around!"

"Abel, please! I love you—" But Judy's words were lost in the slam of the heavy hardwood door.

After a long time, emotions totally exhausted, she raised her eyes toward the door. "Oh, Abel, someday. . . . Without you my life has no meaning. But there is a young boy out there, barely more than a baby . . ." Overcome by despair, her voice trailed away, and Judy sat unmoving as the fire died away and the night chill crept unnoticed through her.

The next day, Wilma Henderson tucked an extra blanket over the small form shivering on the hospital cot. She dabbed the sweat from the child's fevered brow with a clean cloth and helplessly heard the rattle in the tortured chest as the youngster battled for air.

Wilma felt a gentle hand on her shoulder. She looked up into the drawn face of the camp's chief surgeon, Dr. Mason.

"There's nothing more we can do for them, Mrs. Henderson, except wait. You've been working harder than anyone here since this outbreak began. Go on home and get some rest. You have a husband who needs you, also."

Wilma straightened and massaged the small muscles in her aching back. She shivered slightly.

"Can we add some more wood to the fires?" she asked. "It seems awfully chilly in here, especially with the children so sick."

Dr. Mason shook his head. "Not without burning part of the post, ma'am. We're running low on firewood."

"Perhaps I can help with that, at least," Wilma said.

She let herself out the door of the infirmary. The storm had eased, but a half-inch coating of ice left footing hazardous as she struggled toward her husband's office. Slipping and skidding, she finally made it. She managed to tug the heavy door open and step into the welcome warmth from the blazing fire at the hearth.

Wilma noticed that the fire's warmth was not reflected in her husband as he sat staring at an unfinished report. Her heart went out to him as he glanced up. She knew the reason for his depression, since he had told her of his battlefield encounter with Yellow Crow. Wilma felt a deep pang of sorrow for them both, the white soldier and the Cheyenne warrior, whose bonds went much deeper than the blood brother ceremony. It must have been as devastating to Yellow Crow as it had been to Ted, she thought.

"Oh, hello, dear," Ted said absently. "How are things at the refugee center?"

Wilma neither exaggerated nor downplayed conditions, simply reporting the scarcity of firewood and the growing number of cases of lung fever among the refugee children.

"I'll double the wood details," Ted promised. "That should help some. Dr. Mason, of course, can have any medical supplies the army can spare."

Wilma smiled her thanks, but in the back of her mind she could think of only one thing: What her husband needed was a surgeon of the spirit. She had tried without success to boost his morale by reminding him of his many positive accomplishments as a peacemaker with the Indians. The size of the village of Black Kettle on the South Platte was increasing almost daily as Ted's converts to peace filtered in for the winter, and the camp along the Niobrara River was growing almost as rapidly.

Wilma massaged the last of the chill from her fingers, approached her husband, and embraced him from behind.

"Are you still troubled by the episode with Yellow Crow, dear?" she asked softly.

"Yes. I relived it again last night in a dream." He reached up, stroked her arms, and leaned his head back against her. "I was only a trigger squeeze away from killing my blood brother, Wilma—a man who ranks as high in my heart as my own family." Ted sighed heavily.

"It's as though some force, some spirit, were determined to drive a wedge between me and the red man. Not just Yellow Crow. All Indians. You know what they said about me, dear, that I am as much Indian at heart as any warrior whose skin is red? There is some truth to that. Like Yellow Crow, both my cultures are under attack. And I cannot choose both sides."

Wilma released Ted from her embrace, stepped beside him, and took both his hands as he turned to face her. "I know what you're going through, Ted. You can't change the whole world. But you can help change our small corner of it. You must return to the field, darling. Continue pleading for peace. Do what you can to avoid bloodshed. I'll worry about you during your winter trips, and it will be lonely here while you're away. But I'll be busy with the refugees, and our son is beginning to make his own world."

She leaned forward and kissed him lightly, then smiled. "I refuse to be selfish, Ted Henderson. You are a man too valuable to this country to waste your time moping about Laramie when there is work to be done elsewhere."

Ted stood and gathered his wife into his arms. "Oh, Wilma, how I found such a woman as you forever escapes me. Thank you for understanding and for your love." He kissed the top of her head. "I know at times I'm not the easiest man in the world to live with. . . ."

The door opened, letting in a blast of frigid air and interrupting their embrace. A slightly sheepish Abel Hubbard entered the room.

"Oh," Abel said. "Sorry—I should have knocked."

Wilma laughed brightly. "Don't worry about it, Abel," she said. "Regardless of appearances at the moment, this is a military office, not a bordello, and I think your rank is sufficient that you needn't knock."

Abel smiled and inclined his head in a silent "thank you," then turned to Ted. "I want to apologize for last night," he said.

Ted waved a hand casually. "No harm done, Abel. I suppose every man is entitled to a small drunk now and then, especially when he has been under pressure."

All three people knew full well what Ted's reference to "pressure" really meant. It was his way of offering to lend an ear if Abel wanted to unload his feelings on a friend.

"Ted, I didn't come on personal business," Abel said. "It's an army matter."

Wilma tucked her heavy scarf securely around her neck. "If you two men are going to talk soldier talk, I'll excuse myself and go rescue Anna Keller from the clutches of one active boy. Anna's a marvelous baby-sitter and a fine second mother, but even her Old World composure can stand just so much of Wild Bill and little Ellen together." With a brief wave, Wilma let herself out the door.

A couple of blocks down the street, she saw a figure bundled in an expensive, stylish coat and standing idly on an icy sidewalk, apparently looking in her direction. She shuddered as she recognized Calvin Winston. Picking her way gingerly toward the Keller home, she muttered under her breath, "I hope you catch pneumonia, you home wrecker! It would serve you right."

She paused at the Kellers' door and glanced back down the street. Winston had turned and was starting back toward the Laramie Hotel. Wilma wondered why Calvin Winston was displaying a sudden interest in her comings and goings. She had spotted him watching her on several occasions, which made her nervous as well as angry. She shrugged the feelings off and went inside.

In the second-floor corner room of the Laramie Hotel, Taylor Elkins peered through the small hole in the window ice he had thawed by repeatedly and painfully applying his palm to the inside of the glass. He watched as Calvin Winston disappeared from view. The fake ore assayer had been keeping a close watch over Wilma Henderson's movements the last few days, and Taylor found that fact disconcerting as well as puzzling. Winston did not seem the type to venture outside in the ice and cold unless the trips were of some importance.

What they were, Taylor did not know. But Judy Hubbard might—or at least she might have some thoughts about the motives behind Winston's actions. The increasingly frequent drinks or dinner meetings between the beautiful, young blonde and Winston had intrigued Taylor from the start. He felt a pang of pity for the young woman. Unlike other members of the Laramie community, Taylor did not buy the rumors of infatuation, the broad hints, and sometimes outright accusations that Judy was having an affair with Winston.

Taylor Elkins knew Judy Hubbard's personal history almost as well as he knew his own. Once, young and impetuous, she might have been guilty of innocent indiscretions. But not now. She had fought too hard to regain what she had almost lost. Judy Hubbard's attraction to Winston had to be something other than physical. It was a relationship that demanded further observation.

A light tap sounded on the door. With his hand inside his coat gripping the butt of the derringer in its shoulder holster, Taylor moved soundlessly to the door and cracked it open. A bright, sparkling eye peered back through the small opening.

"Mr. Taylor Elkins, mail call!" The buoyancy in Vi Robinson's voice seemed to be forced.

He swung the door open wide. "Good morning, Vi," he said, "won't you come in? You look so gorgeous today, though, it could be hazardous territory."

This time her laugh was obviously genuine. "Thank you for the invitation, sir, and the compliment. However, it is quite busy downstairs. A dispatch rider just came through with a fresh mail pouch. It's so impersonal just to stick letters into little pigeonholes that I make it a practice to deliver them by hand. The guests love the extra touch."

She handed him a letter, the penciled address somewhat smudged and the envelope the worse for wear, but Taylor needed all his experience not to let his excitement show. The return address was State Street, Boston.

"Letter from home?" Vi asked, then quickly added. "I'm sorry. It's none of my business."

"No problem, and yes," Taylor replied. "It is a letter from home, so to speak. One I've been awaiting for a long time."

"I trust it contains nothing but good news," Vi said. "Now, sir, I must go on about my duties. Coffee this evening? My turn to buy."

"Delighted, Vi. And thank you." Taylor waited until the door had closed and the light footsteps faded down the hallway. Then, after double-checking the door bolt, he quickly carried the letter to his small table alongside the bed and slit it open with a penknife.

On the surface it appeared to be no more than a chatty letter from home, full of names and details of crops and weather. But in the second line, Taylor found his key.

"Janice had her baby yesterday," the sentence read. "It was some fine birthday present for Charlie. He was 26 when the baby boy was born."

The code was a difficult one for the author to work with, but almost impossible to break. The age reference, "26," told Taylor which code was being used. He popped open the side panel of his suitcase and from the papers in the concealed compartment pulled a slim book. He added the numbers in the age reference and turned to page eight in the small book.

For almost an hour, Elkins carefully transcribed the coded letter onto a piece of scratch paper. Then he smiled and reread the decoded message.

> Operative in Mobile spotted gun shipment headed your way listed manifest as wagon parts. Followed and intercepted at Fort Leavenworth. Weapons and wagon crew captured. Buyer fits your description Calvin Winston according wagonmaster. Boston office confirms true identification subject

Winston as Calvin Dibley, cousin previously assigned
Confederate operative your area. Baker.

The message committed to memory, Taylor crumpled the
paper and tossed it into the small stove in the corner of his
room. It flared briefly, then crumbled to ashes.

Now, Taylor thought, *I have a name and a connection. But
I still don't know what's ahead.* He returned the code book to
its hiding place. Then, his mind probing numerous possibilities, he turned to stare out the window.

He did not notice the small scrap of paper poking from the
top of the secret compartment.

Wind Flower took a deep breath of the fresh, sharp winter
air. Somehow it seemed to hold the smell of two homes both
dear to her heart, the old life of wintertime in the Canyon de
Chelly and a similar flavor of her new life amid the beauty of
towering peaks the white man called the Rocky Mountains.

The clouds had gone for the moment. The low sun bathed
the isolated Wyoming valley in a golden wash, bringing more
color than warmth, and the crisp north wind promised the
approach of bitterly cold nights. She did not mind. A rich elk
stew bubbled in the cooking pot, and when the coals of the fire
died down in the night, the arms of her big Irish husband
provided all the warmth she needed.

At her heels the large mongrel dog suddenly growled, a
low and ominous rumble. The thick hair along the animal's
muscular neck and shoulders was standing erect.

"Quiet, Toby," she said in Navajo. "Wind Flower sees
them."

In the near distance a wagon pulled by two powerful
Morgan-bred horses rounded a bend in the twisting road
through the low hills edging the west side of the ranch. Wind
Flower recognized the rig immediately and wondered why
Earl and Dot Newkirk were coming to call. The O'Reilly ranch
was a good three miles out of the way from any destination
their neighbors normally would be bound for.

The Indian woman felt the dog press against her leg,
prepared to defend his mistress if need be. She knew Toby
sensed the dislike that Dot Newkirk had for her. The Navajo
woman was no stranger to prejudice, but she felt a sense of
personal loss that her previous attempts at cultivating Dot

Newkirk's friendship in their rare meetings had been so abruptly spurned. Still, Wind Flower resolved she would continue to try. Dot Newkirk would seem to need a female friend in such a sparsely settled land.

A girl of perhaps twelve shared the hard wagon seat with her mother, who held a baby, bundled against the cold, in her lap.

Wind Flower heard her husband come around the corner of their house. Kevin stepped to her side and called a greeting as the wagon pulled to a stop in the hard-packed area that served as a yard.

"Hello, Earl—Dot," Kevin said. "What brings you to this place? No trouble afoot, I hope."

Earl Newkirk pushed a boot against the brake of the wagon, then slacked the reins. "Could be trouble ahead, Kevin," he replied. "Durin' the ice storm we had us some wolf trouble. Lost three head. Deer and elk has moved out, and the pack's got nothin' to live on but rabbits and stock."

Wind Flower stepped to the side of the wagon and smiled at Dot Newkirk. All she received in return was a contemptuous, icy glare from the thin woman.

"Please come inside and warm yourselves," Wind Flower said. "I have something to eat and coffee, or tea if you prefer."

Dot Newkirk shook her head. "Ain't stayin' that long." Wind Flower glanced at the young girl and was dismayed to see the hate in the mother's eyes reflected in the daughter's face.

"How is the baby?" Wind Flower asked, still trying to engage the woman in conversation.

"Fine." The single word was terse, abrupt.

"May I hold him?"

"No." Dot Kewkirk made no effort to explain the denial.

"Heard some wolves howling a couple of nights ago," Kevin was saying. "Sounded like a fair-sized pack."

"Also saw signs of a big cat," Earl Newkirk said. "Looked like he'd got his foot hurt. Might do well to keep an eye on your stock, Kevin."

"I'll do that, and thanks for the warning. Won't you all come in the house for a minute? We don't get that many visitors out here."

Newkirk glanced at his wife, who sat stiff, staring straight ahead. He shook his head. "Reckon not, Kevin. We best get movin' on."

Kevin did not press the point. Dot Newkirk's animosity toward Wind Flower was obvious. He also knew the stubborn woman would sit through a blizzard before she would share a fire with an Indian, even his wife. It angered Kevin, but he controlled his emotions. Earl Newkirk was a good neighbor and a hard worker, and Kevin could not blame Earl for his wife's prejudice.

Newkirk kicked the brake loose and swung the team about. Wind Flower and Kevin watched as the wagon carrying their nearest neighbors moved back along the road and disappeared around the bend.

Wind Flower stooped and retrieved the firewood she had placed on the porch when the wagon first came into view. Kevin held the door open for her, and Toby followed along at her heels. The dog plopped down on the hearth, relaxing in the warmth from the fire, but his ears remained erect and alert.

Wind Flower brushed the bits of bark from her hands into the tinderbox beside the fireplace. She stood for a moment, pensive, then turned to her husband.

"Kevin, how can a person hate so much? I have done nothing to Dot except try to be her friend."

Kevin shrugged. "I wish I knew, darling," he said, taking her in his arms. "I don't know how anyone could help but love you, little Medicine Woman. Lord knows I do." He kissed the top of her head lightly. "You keep a rifle and a shotgun loaded and handy, Wind Flower, just in case the wolves drift into our valley."

"I have dealt with wolves," she said confidently. "They were frequent visitors to the Navajo sheep herds in the winter months when snows were deep and game scarce."

Kevin released her and stepped to the window. Wind Flower could read his concern in the set of his shoulders.

"It's shaping up to be a nasty winter," Kevin said over his shoulder. "Thanks to your 'Black Spirit' routine earlier, we won't have any trouble with the Ute raiding our herds. But we could have problems with other tribes—as well as that wolf pack. I must admit I'm more worried about that crippled cat. An injured mountain lion can easily become a stock killer. If it's cornered or hungry enough, it's likely to turn on humans. A healthy cougar is bad medicine, but a hurt one is a major threat. It looks like I'm going to be doing more riding than I expected. I just hope you'll be safe here."

Wind Flower knelt by the fire and scratched Toby's ears. "With a big strong dog, a gun, and a solid house, I will be safe enough. And when you are here, Kevin, the nights will not be cold, no matter how deep the snows."

Colonel Emery Church squinted through the glare of the winter sun on new-fallen snow, cursing steadily and bitterly as he watched the melee unfold in the broad plain just outside Fort Leavenworth.

The center of the ragged skirmish line wavered and then collapsed as a horse lost its footing and went down hard, slamming its rider to the half-frozen turf beneath the powdery snow. The practice charge instantly forgotten, two men dismounted and rushed to aid their fallen comrade.

Church's own sorrel tossed its head and danced sideways nervously. Church yanked back hard on the reins and ripped a sharp spur into the sorrel's side. The horse stopped fidgeting and stood, cowed and fearful. Flecks of bloody foam dripped from the animal's mouth, severely cut by the cruel high-port spade bit.

"Want to throw another fit, you buzzard-bait sonofabitch?" Church snarled at his horse. He reached inside a tunic pocket and produced a thin Mexican cigar. He nipped the end and spat it into the snow. Scratching a kitchen match on the pommel of his saddle, he lit the cigar, waiting impatiently as the young volunteer lieutenant rode toward him.

"Lieutenant Slaker," Church snapped as the rider pulled up, "that was the sorriest excuse for a flank-wheel charge I've ever seen! Damn good thing this outfit's gonna fight nothing but Injuns! One good squad of Confederate infantry would chew the Fourth Kansas Volunteers up like a Ute squaw gnawing on a fresh-cooked dog leg! Now do it again—and see if you can't get something right this time for a change!"

Slaker shifted uncomfortably in his saddle. Despite the below-freezing temperature, the lieutenant's horse was sweating heavily. Wisps of steamlike condensation drifted from the animal's body, and puffs of thin smoke came from the horse's nostrils.

"Sir," Slaker began hesitantly, "the men are just about worn out, and I don't think the horses will last through another run. We've been at this since dawn. . . ." The lieutenant's voice faded on a pleading note. His eyes dropped under Church's piercing stare.

"For somebody who bought his commission, Slaker, you're awful concerned about the troops all of a sudden. You don't want to follow orders, I'll give your two hundred back—and you can be a private in an infantry company!" Abruptly Church's tone changed. "Ah, what the hell. Sorry as they are, this bunch could still go through the whole Cheyenne nation. Just lope 'em through it once more, easylike, Slaker."

The lieutenant nodded and turned his tired horse toward the waiting soldiers. Fifty yards away he paused to confer with a non-com, then went back to Church.

"Kellog twisted a knee pretty bad when his horse went down, Colonel. He's hurting considerable. Horse is okay, though."

Church took a deep drag on the Mexican cigar and studied its glowing tip for a moment. "Tell Kellog to play like that knee's got a Cheyenne arrow in it—and go on and do his job," Church said icily. "Those two men who quit to help him—tell them they're on extra guard duty for a week! A man in this outfit goes down in action, he's on his own! I won't let one louse-hide redskin get away because a bunch of troopers are out nursemaidin' each other!"

Slaker turned to go. "Slaker!" Church called. The lieutenant looked over his shoulder. "Tell the men I've just upped the bounty on every Injun scalp from here to Laramie by two dollars apiece! That ought to put a little 'sic-em' in those boys."

"Officers, too?" Slaker asked with a crooked grin.

"Sure enough," Church replied. "And that's for any Injun scalp, man, woman, or kid."

Colonel Emery Church puffed, satisfied, at his cigar as Slaker made his way back toward the troops. The Fourth Kansas Volunteers would be ready enough come spring. Ready enough to wipe out that ragtag bunch of redskins on the South Platte—Ted Henderson's pet Indians. *Then, Henderson, I'm going to to rub your nose in those scalps—and put your own on my belt,* Church thought to himself gleefully.

Eight

Colonel Ted Henderson stood relaxed and slightly amused at the side of the big black man in front of the altar of the post chapel. Beads of nervous perspiration speckled Albert Jonas's upper lip as he awaited the arrival of his bride-to-be. Remembering his own nervousness at the ceremony when he and Wilma were wed, Ted felt an even closer kinship with the burly sergeant major.

"What's the matter, Albert?" a grinning Bernie Christian asked from his assigned post at Jonas's other shoulder. "It ain't like you were riding into some hostile camp, you know. I swear, you even look pale."

The sergeant major, looking rather uncomfortable in the hand-tailored dress uniform Sally Coker had made for him, shuffled his feet.

"I've rode into hostile camps, Bernie," he said, "but I never got married before. Seems a little scary." He waved a big hand toward the packed pews of the chapel. "It's supposed to be a small, quiet wedding, and there's not room enough in here for a field mouse."

Ted surveyed the chapel. Every member of Jonas's R Company who was not on special duty had reported in "off detail" to attend, along with a substantial number of soldiers from other companies. Ted was pleased at the turnout, which was a testimony both to Albert Jonas's personal popularity and the devotion of the troops he commanded.

A number of women from the community also were in attendance, some sitting at their husbands' sides. Ted tightened his lips when he saw Abel and Judy Hubbard. Abel had neither looked at nor spoken to Judy since their arrival.

The diminutive Christian, whose sleeve chevrons barely

reached Albert's belt, peeked around the sergeant and winked at Ted. "Reckon for once I've got the same rank as the commander of the fort."

Ted returned the grin. "I certainly don't object to sharing the honor, Bernie, if you don't."

Their brief exchange was interrupted by the arrival of the bride. Sally Coker, flanked by her honor court of Vi Robinson and Wilma Henderson, generated more than a few admiring comments from the packed pews. She was one of the most serenely beautiful women Ted had ever seen, her creamed-coffee skin glowing richly against a plain white dress un-adorned by lace or other traditional trappings.

Sally stepped to the altar. An instant later, responding as if in a trance to a gentle push from Bernie Christian, Jonas stepped to her side.

"Dearly beloved," the chaplain intoned, "we are gathered here for the purpose . . ."

The ceremony was brief yet deeply touching, and the chapel erupted in whistles and cheers as Albert kissed his new bride bashfully and the couple turned to walk together from the chapel. The reception, hosted by Vi at the Laramie Hotel, promised to be a lively affair.

Ted and Bernie joined forces to give the initial toast to the newlyweds, Bernie hoisting a cup of spiked punch and Ted more than content with his glass of soft cider.

He had just completed offering his personal congratulations to the couple and reminding Albert he had two weeks' leave when Ted felt a hand on his arm.

"Can you spare a few minutes, Ted? There's something I want to go over with you in the office," Abel Hubbard said. The two excused themselves from the lighthearted atmosphere of the reception and returned to the serious world of the professional soldier.

Abel settled into a rawhide-covered chair and stretched his long legs. "Ted, I wanted to wait until after the wedding to bring this up. I have a plan that could save us some problems come spring."

Ted cocked a curious eyebrow.

"I want to lead a winter campaign against the Indians involved in last fall's uprising," Abel said. "The warring bands are in winter camp now. A small, mobile strike force, properly equipped, could make it a difficult winter for the Indians.

Pressure them, keep them on the move, but avoid any direct, all-out warfare. Push them from their permanent camps, keep them from their hunting grounds, even destroy lodges and equipment when possible. It would serve notice to every band and tribe that the Third Cavalry means business. And when springtime comes, what ponies survive will be so weak, the Indians won't be capable of mounting any major offensive."

Perched on the edge of his desk, Ted picked up a stone paperweight and casually tossed it from hand to hand as he balanced the military advantages against the probable cost. His instinct was to quash the idea out of hand, since previous winter campaigns by other commanders had proven disastrous to the army. But they had been amateurs, and Abel was no military greenhorn.

"It's a bold plan, Abel, and it will be hazardous. These Plains winters can be brutal," Ted reminded him.

"I'm not exactly a pilgrim when it comes to winters out here," Abel countered. He rose and paced the floor. "With proper and sufficient equipment, we can pull it off." He strode to a map tacked to the wall and briefly outlined his route of march. The expedition, some sixty men using pack animals instead of wagons to carry supplies, would sweep up the Powder River, drive almost to the northern Dakota Territory border, then move against the warring bands along the Missouri. The campaign would resupply at various forts along the way and conclude the mission by arriving at Fort Kearny in late winter or early spring.

"What losses do you anticipate?" Ted asked.

"Probably fifty percent of the animals, perhaps ten percent of the men," Abel replied grimly. "It's a heavy toll, I know. But the cost to the Indians, who will be unable to sit and wait out the winter, would be far greater."

Gradually the details of the campaign were hammered out, and as the planning continued, Ted became more and more convinced the daring gamble might pay off.

"Of course," Abel concluded, "we will be completely out of touch until spring. I won't be able to spare any couriers, and there are no mail or stage lines where we'll be going. Where we go will be in the hands of the Shoshone scouts as much as mine."

Ted continued to study the map, his mind leaping from one objection and problem to the next. With Abel's campaign limited to those tribes known to have participated in the raids of the fall, he would remain free to follow his own winter plan of campaigning for peace among the uncommitted tribes. The winter campaign and the letter from President Lincoln could add some strong ammunition to his arguments for peace. Still, there was one major doubt nagging at Ted's mind.

"Abel," he said, "I hate to ask this, but I have to know. Is this winter campaign a purely military move, or does it have something to do with your personal problems at home?"

Abel's eyes turned icy. "My personal problems, Colonel, are none of your business as long as they don't interfere with my efficiency as a soldier and field commander. If you think that's the only reason for this plan, then tell me now!"

Ted raised a hand. "All right, Abel. I have nothing but confidence in your ability afield. But I had to ask. If the situation were reversed, you'd want to know the same thing."

Abel's attitude softened a bit. "I apologize. I should know you better by now."

"No apology needed. Start recruiting your volunteers and equipping for the campaign. But I would like to keep R Company intact here, Abel—just in case. We'll be short of men and supplies, and R Company can handle situations that might be beyond the reach of any two other companies on the frontier.

A surprising number of spectators braved the fresh, ankle-deep snow and a biting wind to watch, and occasionally wave to a friend, as Abel Hubbard led his sixty-man cavalry detail toward the gates of Fort Laramie.

Most of the grim-faced troopers, heavily bundled against the cold and with packs bulging with additional clothing and supplies, stared straight ahead, painfully aware of the suffering and danger awaiting them on the frozen Plains.

Passing the spot where Wilma and Ted stood, Abel snapped a crisp salute. Ted returned the gesture, as much as a signal for good fortune as it was a military courtesy. In a few days he himself would go out on his peace mission to the Indians.

A few paces away Judy Hubbard stood alone, head bared to the icy wind and snow flurries, her blond hair whipping about her face on each fresh gust. Wilma saw that Abel never so much as glanced at his wife. It was, Wilma thought, as if he really did not care if he returned from the field or ever saw Judy again. She realized then just how deep the rift had become between the two. Even while Abel was in the fort for the few days involved in planning his winter campaign, Judy had made no apparent effort to resolve the deteriorating relationship; in fact, she had continued to be seen in Calvin Winston's presence.

Wilma squared her shoulders against the nip of the wind and made up her mind. If no one else would try and talk some sense into that blond head, she would!

Watching her husband ride by without a glance in her direction, Judy fought a losing battle against tears. Every nerve in her body screamed at her to dash to his stirrup and beg to be heard. But she remained in place. Winston was among the group watching from the far side of the street. Even though Judy had managed to learn little about the suspected plot, she had a feeling she was very near a breakthrough. She needed only two more answers—when and how—and then she would be free to warn Ted and Wilma of the danger to their son.

She also would be free to win back her husband.

Judy shuddered in the growing chill as the long line of pack animals moved by. She remained standing long after the last animal in the cavalcade had passed through the gates. Finally, she turned and began a slow, resigned trek through the new-fallen snow toward the Laramie Hotel.

Vi Robinson paused for a moment in the overheated kitchen of the hotel. She dabbed the perspiration from her brow with a clean handkerchief and stepped through the door into the subdued babble of conversations in the crowded dining room.

Business had been brisk lately, leaving Vi with mixed emotions.

On the one hand, the twelve- and fourteen-hour days had helped her keep her mind from the increasing distress she felt over Judy's conduct toward Calvin Winston. Since Abel had ridden out of town only a few days earlier, the situation had bordered on outright scandal.

The disturbing part of being so busy was that work cut into her time with Taylor Elkins. The thought almost made Vi blush. She knew herself well enough to recognize the slide from friendship to infatuation and now to the anxious warmth of a growing love for the dapper journalist. He had been increasingly in her thoughts and her dreams as she lay alone in her cold and empty bed.

She moved from one table to another, smiling and stopping from time to time to chat with regular customers and friends. Then she frowned as she saw Judy place a plate before Calvin Winston, leaning close to speak quietly to him in the process.

The frown faded as Taylor Elkins entered through the main door, shaking the snowflakes from his derby. Vi moved toward him, intercepting Taylor as he stopped for a moment at Winston's table.

"Latest word from Boston is that the war may be near an end," Taylor was saying. He seemed to be studying Winston as if awaiting a reaction, Vi thought. Winston merely shrugged, as though the news were of little importance. "The Confederacy appears to be in trouble, and the indications are President Lincoln has already begun laying plans for the future of the South," the journalist continued.

Sensing Vi's presence, Taylor looked up with a bright smile. "Good morning, Vi," he said. "You heard the news just now?"

Vi nodded. "I certainly hope the end of that awful war is near. It has been such a horrible waste of young lives on both sides. Would you like a table?"

Elkins, still gripping the brim of his derby, shook his head. "There is something, though. Vi, is there a place we can talk privately?"

She led him to her small, cramped office. He declined the offer of a chair. "What I have to say won't take long, Vi. I'm asking you to marry me."

Vi studied the gentle face before her for a long moment. "There can be only one answer to that, Taylor," she said solemnly. "The answer is—yes."

She saw the joy dance in his eyes and was afraid, for a moment, he was going to whoop aloud in delight. Instead, he pulled her to him silently. Their kiss was long and tender. Finally Vi pulled away.

"You know, of course," she said, "that you're getting used merchandise."

Taylor grinned. "I always heard it was best to buy a filly

already broke to bit and saddle if you plan to keep her forever. Now, woman—when?"

"There are so many things to plan, Taylor. And some personal business to be set straight. Would you mind waiting a bit?"

"Vi, I've waited all my life for a woman like you," he said. "A while longer I can handle. Now, if you will forgive the setting and the brusque proposal, I must be about my news-hounding. When the telegraph is in operation, my editors expect stories from the frontier." He kissed her once more, then left the small office whistling.

A glow seemed to remain behind in the room, and Vi stood for a long moment, basking in the sensation, before returning to her work. Stopping to check on progress in the laundry, Vi noticed a pile of freshly cleaned shirts in the niche reserved for Taylor Elkins's room. She picked up the clothing and informed the laundress she would made the delivery in person. Making her way up the stairs to Taylor's corner room, she wondered if her voice had reflected the singing of her heart.

She let herself in with the hotel master key, crossed the room to the low chest of drawers, and placed the shirts in a neat row. Turning to leave, she noticed the suitcase standing open on the bed. "Might as well get used to picking up after a man again," she said aloud, reaching for the travel bag.

Something out of place caught her eye—a yellowed scrap of paper apparently stuck to the end of the suitcase. She picked it up. Thinking it was perhaps a favorite story of Taylor's that he had saved, she smoothed a wrinkle from the paper and glanced at it.

Seconds later, Vi Robinson's new life was shattered. Tears of shock and anger poured down her cheeks.

According to the clipping, Taylor Elkins was a fugitive from justice!

The detailed account in the aging story from *The Baltimore Sun* drew a stark and crushing picture in Vi's mind: an illegal duel on a fog-shrouded morning four years ago in a secluded patch of woods outside the city, the crack of a pistol and a man falling, shot through the heart. The description of the killer matched that of Taylor Elkins, down to the most minute detail. And a reward of one thousand dollars had been posted for information leading to the killer's arrest!

Weak-kneed, Vi sat down on Taylor's bed, her mind whirling. The quarrel that had led to the duel, the newspaper clipping said, had begun over a woman in a house of prostitution on the seedy side of Baltimore.

"You really can pick them, Vi Robinson," she said aloud. "You fall in love with three men. Two of them are killed—and the third is a killer!" Suddenly she realized she had tried and convicted the man she loved on the basis of a single yellowed piece of newspaper. Perhaps there was some mistake, although that seemed impossible. When he returned, she would confront him and demand an explanation.

If the story was true, she would personally eject Taylor Elkins from the premises—no establishment of hers would knowingly harbor a murderer. She folded the hated newspaper story carefully, tucked it into a pocket on her apron, and made her way back downstairs.

The crowd had thinned considerably from the dining room, with only a couple of tables now occupied. Vi felt a new flash of anger as she saw Judy and the green-eyed Calvin Winston in earnest conversation. She choked back the impulse to break up the two and give Judy the good, sound spanking she deserved. In her present state of mind, Vi knew, however, she would be lashing out at her own frustration as much as at Judy. She turned away from the scene and entered her small office, closing the door behind her.

Calvin Winston reached across the small table and took Judy's hand in his own. Judy felt her muscles tense at his touch and hid her instinctive attempt to withdraw her hand. Instead, squeezed his gently. His hand was soft, damp, the fingers well manicured, and for an instant Judy could not help but remember the firm, work- and weather-marked grip of her husband. The memory only rekindled her ache.

"Judy," Winston said, "I may not be able to keep our dinner date this evening. I have some business to attend to. And within a few days I'll be leaving Laramie."

Judy was suddenly alarmed. Whatever was in store, then, was about to unfold. She looked into Winston's eyes, hoping he would read the obvious dismay in her own as a reflection of losing his company.

"Oh, Cal—must you? We—we've hardly begun to know each other. . . ." She saw the glint of lust in his eyes. "And it's been so lonely here, except for you."

"I want you, Judy. I have ever since I first met you. We could go to my room right now," he said hopefully.

She shook her head vigorously. "No, Cal. We can't—not in Laramie. There are—too many eyes and ears about." She almost gagged on the words but managed to say, "Perhaps later, when your business is done. I want you, too, Cal. But I'm confused. I need some time. Perhaps you might consider taking me along when you leave. I've grown to hate this wretched frontier so, and it's been so long since I've had a man—but we mustn't talk this way, not here."

Winston squeezed her hand, eased his grip, and squeezed again, as though massaging her breast. Judy inwardly cringed at the not-so-subtle gesture.

"Where will you be going for this—business meeting?" She tried to keep her voice light despite her growing sense of urgency and fear.

"Away from the fort. But I should return by nightfall." Judy read his final comment as both a question and an invitation. She knew she had pushed Winston almost to the limit. Very soon the bait would either have to be yanked away or be swallowed by the prey.

She took a deep breath. "We'll talk later," she said, "when your business is completed. That will give me time to reach my decision, Cal."

He released her hand, the disappointment obvious in his expression. But he recovered as his eyes swept her full breasts. He nodded silently.

Judy pushed her chair back and stood. "I must go now, Cal," she said, aware of the tremble in her voice. "I promised Wilma Henderson I would help her work with the refugees today." The comment was a bald lie, but it was the only thing Judy could think of to give her the excuse she needed to saddle her mare and be ready to follow when Winston rode out of Laramie. Judy strode toward the cloakroom by the front door, deliberately exaggerating the sway of her hips as she felt Winston's eyes follow her.

Outside, she blinked against the white of the new snowfall and quickened her steps, knowing she had little time to reach ~~r own quarters, change into riding clothes, and be prepared ~~w when Calvin left Laramie. She sensed his "business ~~ as of major importance, that it was crucial she know ~~nts of that meeting.

She had just passed the Henderson quarters, moving rapidly, when a call sent her heart skidding.

"Judy!" It was Wilma Henderson. "Come in here a moment, please!"

Judy turned to face the stern features of her friend. "Please, Wilma," she said, aware of the desperate tone of her voice, "I'm in a terrible hurry!"

"Not such a hurry you cannot spare a few minutes." Wilma's tone left no doubt that she meant what she said. Judy fought her growing panic and glanced toward the stable. "Please, Wilma, can we make this quick?"

"Come on in, Judy!"

The door closed solidly. At one side of the room, young William Ted carefully went about one of his chores, separating wood chips for starting fires into different sizes, his cheeks rosy from the warmth of the nearby fireplace. The child glanced up.

"Hello, Aunt Judy," he said brightly. He crossed the room as Judy knelt. His small arms went around her neck, and the warmth of the brief embrace went through Judy's heart like a stake. She managed only a choked "hi."

"Sit down, Judy," Wilma said, indicating a nearby chair. Judy forced herself into the chair, feeling the passing of precious time in each beat of her heart.

"There is something I want to discuss with you. It's long overdue." Wilma turned to the child busy at the wood box. "William Ted, will you please play in your room for a few moments?"

The boy looked quizzically from his mother to Judy but did not question his banishment; there was little of interest in woman talk, anyway. The door closed behind the boy, but to Judy it seemed his presence remained. Their brief embrace had shaken her more deeply than she had realized.

"All right, Judy Hubbard," Wilma said sharply, "if you're going to act like some lovesick schoolgirl, I'm going to talk to you like one. Your conduct has been absolutely shocking! I demand an explanation for your obvious infatuation with this Calvin Winston, and I want it now!"

Judy had to grasp the lapels of her coat to hide the anxious trembling of her hands. "Wilma—I can't tell you—not yet," she said in a halting voice. "Please—give me a few days, and I'm sure you'll understand."

"A few days, Judy? Why not now? There's still time to

send a courier to catch up with Abel—if you want to send a message to him. If you don't, I suppose that means you're too involved with that man to care about your own husband!"

Judy shook her head vigorously. She could not tell Wilma yet about her fears. "I can't, Wilma. But you must believe me—I love Abel with all my heart and soul!"

"Don't tell me, Judy—tell Abel. If you act now, perhaps you can save your marriage. If not, Abel deserves to know that, too!"

Wilma slowly approached the young woman, took Judy's hands in hers, and stared into her eyes.

"You are throwing away a marriage to one of the finest men in the world, Judy Hubbard! If any other couple on this post were involved, I'd keep my distance and my nose out of their business. But you and Abel are as much family to me as Ted and little Bill, and I won't stand idly by and see Abel—and you—destroyed! Is a tumble with Calvin Winston worth it, Judy? Do you know what pain you've caused your husband, and Vi as well?

"For God's sake, Judy, tell me!" Wilma's voice had changed from anger to pleading. "All I want to do is help."

Judy glanced over Wilma's shoulder at the clock on the mantel just in time to see another precious minute lost in the jerk of the long hand. The panic in her breast fueled her resolve. Dry-eyed, she abruptly yanked her hands free of Wilma's grip.

"If you really want to help," Judy said desperately, "you can simply trust me. In a few days, you will understand. Now, I'm leaving. I'm late for an appointment."

Judy strode to the door and yanked it open.

"Late for a tryst with your lover, Judy?"

Judy spun on a heel and for an instant stared icily at Wilma. "Think what you want!" she snapped. "This isn't what it appears to be—and there is more at stake than a marriage!"

Judy slammed the door behind her and stepped into the freshening storm. Almost running, she hurried toward the stable, ignoring the wet, swirling snowflakes. At the corner of the stockade, she scrambled up to a lookout station and glanced toward the northeast.

In the distance a familiar shape on horseback was a dim blur through the blowing snow.

Judy hammered a fist into the top of a stockade post in

frustration and fury. Now she would never be able to track Calvin through the storm. By the time she had saddled her mare, the wind would have covered any signs of Calvin's passing, and, besides, she was no expert tracker.

The horseman faded beyond a veil of drifting white. Judy lowered her head in dismay, the picture of a small boy's face forming in her mind. Wilma Henderson's well-meaning intervention at just the wrong time had cost Judy her best chance of finding something solid on which to build her case. Now she had only two options. She could wait until Ted returned from his one-man peace mission and confide in him alone, or she could regroup her emotions and make yet another effort to pry some information from Calvin Winston. Both choices could be wrong. Ted Henderson, she knew, was like a wounded bear when his family was threatened. He likely would go after Winston with fatal consequences to one or the other, which would solve nothing, for she was convinced that Winston had accomplices in the scheme and his death or arrest would not deter the others. To resume her apparent affair with Winston would almost certainly destroy her marriage and possibly place her in physical danger as well.

Dejected, Judy descended the ladder from the lookout post. Her own fate now seemed secondary, almost of no importance. She started the long, cold walk back toward the Laramie Hotel, feeling more alone than she had ever felt in her life. With a sickening sensation, she knew she had no real choice. She must once more play the hazardous cat-and-mouse game with Calvin Winston. Perhaps that night after his return to Laramie, he might rise to the bait she had held tantalizingly just out of his reach for so long.

"All right, Taylor—I'm waiting." Vi Robinson stood with her arms folded across her chest in the center of the room. "All you have to do is tell me it's some mistake."

Taylor Elkins folded the clipping from *The Baltimore Sun*. The yellowing paper seemed heavy as a stone in his fingers. The woman he loved believed him to be a criminal on the run.

For a long time, the only sounds were the windows rattling under the blast of a storm. A single oil lamp cast its feeble glow against the turbulent night. Taylor felt as if a trap had just slammed shut, slicing him in two. He was sworn to absolute secrecy. He could not tell Vi the truth, or even hint that perhaps hope lay ahead. From the set of her jaw and the challenge in her eyes, Taylor also knew that he could not ask for time before explaining.

Only his rigorous training and his dedication to his mission kept dismay from his face. To confide in Vi would not only breach his vows of secrecy, it might well place her life in danger. She must not know that he was closing in on Calvin Winston, that all he needed now was proof the man was in fact working for the Confederate cause among the Indians. When he had the final names, dates, and points of contact, then he would be free to file his report and tell Vi the truth behind the yellowed newspaper clipping. Until then, he had no choice.

"I can't deny it, Vi," he said calmly. "I am the man described in the newspaper article."

The last glimmer of hope faded from Vi's face, and tears came to her eyes.

"I'm sorry it has to be this way, Vi, for I truly love you," he said.

Vi struggled to regain her composure. "Only the fact that I feel something for you, Taylor, stops me from reporting your whereabouts to the authorities this instant," she said. "You have until the end of this snowstorm, then get out of my hotel and out of my life!"

Vi spun around and slammed the door behind her. Taylor sat heavily on the edge of his bed, still holding the newspaper clipping. "Someday soon, Vi, I'll be able to tell you the whole story," he said sadly. "Until then, maybe ignorance will keep you alive and unharmed. I won't let you go this easily."

Ignoring the ache in his heart as best he could, Taylor returned to the job at hand. The message he had to send was simple, but transcribing it to code would take most of the night.

"Expecting break soon," the message read. "Subject Winston showing signs of tension. Latest ride Winston brief; believe contact made with fellow conspirators near fort. Action near, possibly within forty-eight hours. End message. Stoner."

In a secluded corner of the almost-empty bar portion of the dining room, Judy Hubbard winced inside when Calvin Winston touched her knee. She sensed the clammy dampness of his palm even through the heavy wool cloth of her skirt and the layers of camisole and cold-weather long stockings. She glanced at the clock, grateful that in a minute or two it would be closing time, and she would be free of his disturbing touch. She had a growing feeling of helplessness as she realized Cal Winston was not inclined to disclose anything of importance. She knew no more about his "business trip" now than she had known earlier.

With his free hand Winston picked up the oil lantern and puffed life into the end of a foul-smelling small cigar. Between puffs he asked, "Well, Judy—how about it?" His hand crept farther up her leg. "My room will still be nice and warm."

She shook her head slowly, as though declining even while tempted by his offer. "No, Cal," she said, keeping her voice low. "I've decided it just—can't be, not in Laramie. But when we've ridden away from this horrid place . . ." She let the implication grow in Winston's mind for a moment. Then, as though on impulse, she leaned forward and looked deep into his eyes. "When do you think we might leave?"

Judy thought she saw a warning flare in his green eyes, but the expression quickly faded. Winston merely smiled in a noncommittal way. "Soon, Judy. It might be well if you kept a bag packed. We might be leaving on short notice, depending on the weather and traveling conditions."

She forced a bright smile. "I'll do that, Cal. And I'll be dreaming of you until then." She waved a hand toward the clock above the bar. "It's almost closing time, and I have a big day ahead of me tomorrow. I'd best run on home now and get some rest—after I pack that bag." Judy reached beneath the table, patted the back of his groping hand, and stood.

"I'll see you tomorrow, Cal. Thanks for the evening. I'm glad your business meeting went well. It's such dreadful weather to be out in and still accomplish nothing." She walked toward the cloakroom, trying not to show her haste to be away from him.

Winston watched her go, his eyes locked to the feminine and promising sway of her hips. He thought, *It's coming sooner than you think, my naive little maiden. . . .* He puffed at the cigar and sipped from his glass of bourbon. *And after I'm through with you, my dear, I'm sure the outlaw Ute would love to have you warm his vermin-infested lodge until he tires of you and sells that young, white body to the highest bidder. I trust you will be happy as an Indian slave.* He smiled.

Rumors around the post said Ted Henderson would be

home by week's end with two more bands of "tamed Indians" in tow.

"So the eagle is about to return," Calvin Winston muttered, "to an empty nest. . . ."

The snow had changed, Anna Keller thought, as she watched it fall from the kitchen window of their cramped but pleasant quarters, which now rang with the laughter of two young children.

The snowfall was no longer sticky and wet; tiny, dry flakes, little more than specks of ice, drifted on the wind. She doubted that even an accomplished tracker and experienced scout such as her husband, Carl, could follow many trails in weather like this.

A sudden howl of girlish glee drew her attention. Little Ellen swept up the last of the red-tipped twigs before her, leaving William Ted stuck with two blue twigs in their made-up game.

The boy grinned, seemingly unaffected at having lost. "Ellen pulled a trick," he said. "I'll remember next time."

Anna felt a glow of contentment as she watched the two at play, the little Arapaho girl adopted by Anna and Carl and the energetic young son of Ted and Wilma Henderson. In many ways they were closer than most brothers and sisters. Anna found it increasingly difficult to follow their conversations, a strange mixture of three or four different languages depending upon which word best described what they wanted to say. Both were growing rapidly, though Ellen, being two years older, remained a head taller than William Ted.

Anna's love for Little Bill had grown until she considered him as much a part of the family as Ellen was. She looked forward to the times when he came to visit, as today, when his mother was occupied at the refugee camps.

Ellen suddenly looked up, an ear cocked toward the door. "I hear a sound outside," she told her mother. "Like a foot on snow."

Anna motioned for silence. She sometimes worried because their quarters were at a spot in the compound near the gates and set apart from the other homes of officers and scouts. She listened intently for a moment, then shook her head.

"Probably just a dog rummaging for food," she said. "Or maybe one of your friends coming to call—"

Anna gasped as the door suddenly burst inward. Two figures wrapped in heavy robes dashed into the room. The faces were Indian, one with shockingly blue eyes. Each man held a war club at his side.

"Now, see here!" Anna protested. "What is the meaning of this intrusion—" Her voice froze as the blue-eyed Indian closed the door and pointed toward the children standing startled beside the fireplace.

"Take both," the blue-eyed one said. "Red one is daughter of white scout."

The smaller of the two Indians took a step toward the children. The motion sent fresh fear through Anna. "Run, children! Get away!" she called. She whirled toward the cabinet drawer nearby where Carl kept a spare pistol loaded and capped.

A powerful hand closed on her wrist. Anna was spun around, and a fist crashed into her temple, sending her sprawling. Through a crazily tilted world, she saw the second Indian reach for William Ted, only to yelp in surprise and suddenly leap back when the boy bit the man's hand and aimed a swift kick at his captor.

"Ellen! Run!" William Ted's cry in Arapaho sent the girl into action, darting beneath an outstretched arm toward the door. The blue-eyed Indian jumped forward, roughly grabbing Ellen's shoulder.

Anna staggered upright, her head still reeling from the blow, and grasped the handle of a heavy cooking pot on the stove. The blue-eyed Indian grunted in pain as Ellen suddenly sank her teeth into his thumb. Anna swung the heavy pot with all the fury of a lioness protecting her young cubs.

The pot caught the Indian on the side of the head, momentarily staggering him. But the intruder did not go down. Instead, he fell sideways against the door, cutting off the children's best chance to escape. Anna swung the pot once more, slamming the weapon into the Indian's shoulder. Then—too late to duck—she saw the war club descending. The hard wood cracked into her temple, and the world spun into blackness.

Long Walker, still feeling the sting of the wild swings of the pot, finally managed to get the young Indian girl under control. He turned to see how the outlaw Ute was making out in his attempts to capture the white boy.

If it had not been for the urgency of their situation, Long Walker would have laughed as the Ute lunged, grasped only empty air, and was caught by a wicked whack on the instep from the little boy's kick.

Angered and humiliated, the Ute raised his war club to smash the boy's skull.

"No!" Long Walker's command stayed the enraged Ute's hand. "He is of no value to us dead—for now!" The Ute, his hand on William Ted's neck, grudgingly lowered the club.

Within moments, both children were wrapped tightly in blankets stripped from the bed, their cries of protest silenced by gags of washcloths.

Long Walker tossed the boy's trussed body over his shoulder and waited for the Ute to do the same with the girl. "Young ones put up good fight," Long Walker said. "Come on! Let's get out of here before someone comes by!"

At the door Long Walker paused and dropped a small object on the floor.

No one saw the two figures with their strange bundles slip from the Keller home and move quickly through the swirling snow toward the stockade wall and the rawhide-braided rope hanging from the top of the post.

A mile from Fort Laramie, the two Indians eased their tiring mounts to a stop in the cover of a small clump of trees. Long Walker removed the gags from the children's mouths. He was secretly pleased that neither child cried nor pleaded. Instead, both of them stared at their captors defiantly.

Leading his horse, Calvin Winston stepped into the clearing. He handed the reins to the Ute, then moved alongside Long Walker's mount.

"Any problems?" Winston asked.

Long Walker shook his head. "None."

"The woman?"

"Dead. I crushed her skull with a war club." There was no hint of either satisfaction or remorse in the Indian's tone. It was a simple statement of fact. Long Walker glanced at the captive girl and saw pain and loss in her large brown eyes, but she refused to cry.

"Fine," Winston said. "Now I will deliver the message for

you." He removed his hat, baring his head to the blue-eyed Indian. "Make it look good, Long Walker."

"It will be my pleasure—as one gentleman to another," the Indian replied solemnly. Then in one smooth motion he swung his war club against Winston's cheekbone. The green-eyed man dropped to his knees, half-conscious. "You will have no trouble convincing those at the fort you were attacked while trying to stop the abduction," Long Walker said.

Groggily Calvin Winston staggered to his feet. One eye was already beginning to swell shut. A redness, which would become a spectacular bruise, spread across his cheek. Without a word, Winston took the reins of his horse from the Ute and after two tries managed to struggle into the saddle and rein the horse through the swirling snow.

The two Indians and their captives watched until Winston had passed from view. Then Long Walker and the Ute kneed their ponies toward the camp in the canyon a dozen miles distant.

Wilma quickened her pace as she neared the Keller home. It had been a tiring but satisfying day among the refugees. The lung disease appeared to have run its course. Many of the stricken children had been able to leave their beds and eat solid food for the first time in days. Now she was anxious to get home to the warmth of her own fire and the arms of her healthy son about her neck.

As was her custom, Wilma rapped twice on the door and then swung it open. What she saw left her stunned, unable to move. The interior of the Keller home was a shambles. A dented cooking pot lay near the outstretched body of Anna Keller—and the children were nowhere to be seen!

Dazed by fear and dread, Wilma moved to Anna's side and shook the woman's shoulder. "Anna—please—where are the children? What happened?"

There was no response.

Wilma touched Anna's neck. Her skin was cool and clammy, and only the faintest of irregular heartbeats pulsed beneath Wilma's fingertips. One side of Anna's face was covered with hair matted by blood. Wilma staggered to the door.

"Help, someone! Please!" she called frantically.

A young soldier passing a few yards away sprinted to the doorway. "What is it, ma'am? What happened?"

Wilma grasped the trooper's arm. "Get Dr. Mason—quickly! Anna Keller's been hurt, and the children are gone! Find one of the scouts—we must get word to her husband!"

The soldier sprinted toward the post hospital. Dr. Mason arrived, winded, a few minutes later. He pushed past Wilma into the room and knelt at Anna's side.

The surgeon was still at work when Pappy Lehman reached the door where Wilma still stood in shock. He grasped her shoulders and shook her gently. "Wilma—what's going on here?" he asked.

The touch and a familiar voice seemed to jar Wilma from her trance. "Pappy, you must find Carl Keller. His wife is badly hurt. And the children are missing. And Ted—must know, too. He shouldn't be far, somewhere along the Sweetwater. Hurry, please!"

The veteran scout merely nodded, then hurried toward the stable, forcing his way through a stream of people headed for the Keller quarters. Wilma watched him go without truly seeing him. Her world—and Ted's—was suddenly in shambles. Her son was missing, perhaps lying still in the snow somewhere, perhaps calling for her. . . .

That long night was a jumble of reality and nightmare in Wilma Henderson's mind. Friends of both couples crowded the room in the infirmary next to the surgery where Dr. Mason worked feverishly over Anna Keller, capably assisted by Vi Robinson and a young private with obvious talents as a nurse.

Wilma tried to keep up a strong appearance as she thanked friends for their weak-sounding assurance that all would be well in the end. She found real comfort only in the strong, silent embrace of Sergeant Major Albert Jonas and the quiet voice of his new bride.

Shortly after dawn, Corporal Bernie Christian suddenly appeared at Wilma's side and touched her arm. "The colonel's coming," he said quietly, leading her toward the door.

Ted Henderson, his face reflecting the agonies that churned inside him, swung down from the lathered mount and gathered his wife into his arms. Christian silently picked up the reins and led the exhausted, half-dead horse toward the stable.

For a long moment, Ted and Wilma merely embraced,

each drawing strength from the other, from the power that only love can give in a crisis. Finally Ted pulled back. "Pappy told me some of it," he said. "Anything you can add?" The pain in his eyes was almost too much for Wilma to bear. She lowered her face to his chest and, voice breaking, related the events of the previous afternoon.

"I rode the night out," Ted said. "Is Carl here yet?"

"Yes. He got here a little before you did."

"And Anna?"

Wilma shook her head. "The surgeon doesn't know yet. She's still unconscious. Oh, Ted—" Her voice broke. "I feel—so guilty, and so helpless. If only—I'd stayed home—"

He pulled her close again. "Don't blame yourself, dear. What's done is done, and now we've—"

He was interrupted by a commotion in the street. Calvin Winston, one eye closed and a badly bruised cheek severely swollen and discolored, leaned against a blue-clad soldier and shuffled toward Ted and Wilma.

"Colonel," he said, his voice slurred because of his swollen face, "I have word of the children—your son."

Ted eyed the man suspiciously for a couple of seconds, then stepped to his side. "What happened?"

"Was out—exercising my horse," Winston said. "Two Cheyenne jumped me—said to take a message to you. One hit me with a club, must have knocked me cold for some time."

"The message, man!"

Winston's one good eye blinked rapidly. "They said if you—ever wanted to see your son—and the girl alive—you would stay out of the field. Stop the peace talks. In—two weeks you'll get—more instructions—"

Wilma, her hand on her husband's arm, felt his muscles tense and knew he was about to lash out at the man. "Ted!" she said.

That single word seemed to penetrate the haze around her husband's mind. Gradually the muscles relaxed.

"All right," Ted said, his words lifeless. "You've delivered the message, Winston. Now, go and get a doctor to check out that damage."

The couple watched Winston leave; then Wilma embraced Ted. "What do we do now?" she whispered.

"I—don't know, darling. We need more information if we're to save the children. We don't know where they are"—

Wilma became aware of the quaver in her husband's normally strong voice—"and if I just go charging off in any direction, I could get them killed." He pulled her even more tightly to him. "For now, we wait—no matter how much it hurts. . . ."

Down the street, in the civilian telegraph office, Taylor Elkins took over the key himself, tapping out the story as it formed in his mind.

LARAMIE—This small settlement on the Western frontier stood in silent shock today as the war between red man and white reached out to touch two innocent young lives.

As this reporter has pieced the story together, two children—one the white son of Colonel Ted Henderson, commander of this post, the other the adopted Indian daughter of a white scout, were kidnapped by two men, allegedly Indian, and are being held for ransom. The wife of the scout lies unconscious, battling for her own life after putting up a valiant struggle to save the two children.

The abductors are demanding confinement to the post of Colonel Henderson, who long has been one of the most active spokesmen for peace among the tribes. His views have been reported in prior issues of this journal.

Clues as to the identity of the guilty parties remain scarce. A Cheyenne medicine pouch was found at the scene, and a Laramie resident reportedly confronted the two Indians shortly after the abduction. He was beaten after being told to deliver apparent ransom demands to the colonel. The resident identified the two braves as being Cheyenne, but positive identification of the tribe involved has not been made.

Even the most experienced scouts have been unable to pick up the trail of the abducted children— and in the meantime, all the stunned citizens of Laramie can do is stand by, wait for some word as to the fate of the youngsters—and pray.

Elkins added a few more paragraphs, including details of the almost brother-sister relationship between William Ted

Henderson and Ellen Keller, and background material on Colonel Henderson's legendary exploits as a Pony Express rider, Indian fighter with Kit Carson, army officer, and devoted husband and father. Less was known about the scout Carl Keller and his European-born wife, Anna. Elkins included all the details he knew to be fact, then signed off.

He sat for a moment, staring at the shining brass key before him. He had not added to the story that he had seen Calvin Winston ride from the fort only moments after the apparent time of the abduction—not before, as Winston claimed. Elkins struggled with his alternatives. His status in the secret government circles gave him authorization to kill when circumstances seemed to warrant. Yet, as much as he wanted to line the sights of his short-barrel revolver on the head of the Confederate agent, he knew he could not. Not now. He was convinced beyond any doubt that only one person in Laramie knew where the children were being held.

That man was Calvin Winston.

And for the next few days, Taylor vowed, wherever the Confederate operative went, he himself would not be far behind.

Judy Hubbard sat despondent on the edge of her unmade bed. She did not feel the growing chill in the room as the fire dwindled to tiny specks of embers. She had cried herself out in the last few days. Since the abduction of the children, she had gone through the most agonizing time in her life.

If only, she had told herself time and again, she had tried harder to make her husband believe her, if only she had spoken to him before he received that horrid note, the two youngsters might be playing happily at home. She had gambled—and lost.

From beneath the edge of the bed, the corner of a packed bag protruded. To Judy it was a symbol of her failure. At the same time, however, the small bag contained her only hope to rescue the children, no matter what the personal cost.

Judy tugged at the waistband of her heavy wool riding skirt. Such garments had become her daily costume since Calvin Winston had told her to be ready to leave Laramie by horseback on a moment's notice. She did not trust Winston; she knew she must remain near him or face the possibility of being left behind and lose her final chance at redemption in the eyes of her husband and the Laramie community. Even worse, she knew, that could doom the children. She would not let that happen.

Judy had aided the people of Laramie in their deliberate ostracism of her. Part of her isolation was planned. She had to stay near Calvin Winston. And part, she admitted, was her own reluctance to face the haggard, drawn features of the tormented Ted Henderson or the agony in Wilma's violet eyes.

She tucked a wayward strand of blond hair into place beneath her fur cap. Her world had crumbled, but her newly found resolve did not weaken. If she must trade her body for information that could save two young lives, so be it. Winston was not about to get one without the other.

She slid her hand down her leg to the top of her fur-lined boots and touched the handle of the thin-bladed, razor-sharp skinning knife. Once she knew where the children were, she still faced the problem of escape. The knife was her final way out. And she knew she would use it if necessary.

Judy toed the travel bag back out of sight beneath the bed. She slipped into a heavy coat, and forcing herself to keep her head held high, she stepped into the street in search of Calvin Winston. At least the snow had stopped, she thought, striding toward the Laramie Hotel.

Colonel Ted Henderson slumped wearily over his desk, the grit of sleepless nights raking his eyes with each blink of the lids. The telegraph wires had been humming since Taylor Elkins's story of the kidnapping had appeared in major newspapers throughout the nation.

The national sense of outrage at the incident had left Ted with his hands full preventing overeager volunteers from forming groups and scouring the countryside. Ted knew that such an action would result in the death of his son and Carl's daughter—if the children were still alive. He also had been hard pressed to fend off potential reprisals against the Cheyenne since most residents of Laramie and the surrounding territories truly believed the tribe responsible.

Ted did not buy that theory. He was as much a Cheyenne as any white man, and to use children to reach a military goal would never enter the mind of even the most devious warrior of the tribe.

Ted knew he could not keep the lid on much longer. Even

the seasoned veterans of R Company were growing restless at the lack of any attempt to rescue the children. Yet he had considered and rejected scores of plans in his own mind and almost as many suggestions from others. He knew he must do something soon. But one telegram among the huge pile on his desk did offer some hope.

"Don't get reckless," the brief message said. "On my way. Kit."

If any man could locate the spot the children were being held, it would be Kit Carson, Ted thought for the hundredth time.

A sudden commotion from the parade ground outside drew Ted to the door. Flanked by a half-dozen armed soldiers of R Company, a lean Indian on a palomino gelding rode slowly toward the office.

Yellow Crow had returned!

Ted greeted his Cheyenne blood brother solemnly and escorted the Indian into his office. Yellow Crow shed his blankets, draping them on hooks near the fire to dry, then turned to Ted.

"Yellow Crow's heart is heavy," the Cheyenne said. "The fate of his godson is unknown. He does not know how the spirits will guide his hand, but he has come to help his brother."

"It is good to have such brothers at times like this," Ted replied. "Perhaps the eyes of Yellow Crow will see something all others have missed. There is hope yet, my friend. And if the children are killed, together we shall ride the path of vengeance and lift many scalps. Those responsible shall pay a heavy price."

The Indian nodded. "So it shall be. The Cheyenne did not take the small ones, as the whites say. The Cheyenne would never leave his medicine pouch behind, even if returning for it meant certain death."

Ted nodded. "The Cheyenne are without blame in my eyes and in those of all thinking men."

"And thinking men are what we need at the moment," a familiar voice from the doorway said.

"Kit!" Ted was at the side of the small frontiersman in two quick strides, pumping his hand. "I only received your wire four days ago. You certainly wasted no time getting here."

Kit Carson merely shrugged, as though a solitary ride

through snowstorms and hostile Indian territory was but a brief Sunday afternoon excursion. He stripped off his riding gloves and held his hands toward the fire. "The high passes were a might ouchy at times," he said, "and it's a long ride from Fort Garland. I'll be needing the use of a horse for a few days. I'm not sure even Bernie Christian can save mine after that ride."

Carson stepped away from the fire, greeted Yellow Crow as an old friend, then settled into a chair. He studied Ted for a moment.

"You look terrible, friend. And with good reason. I came not only as a former comrade in arms and as a friend, but to offer my services in planning a rescue. Ted, a man under a strain like yours may not be exercising the best judgment. That isn't a criticism, just a fact. Now, let's get our heads together and see what the three of us can come up with."

Judy Hubbard clutched the handle of her carpet bag with cold-stiffened fingers and tried to ignore the growing numbness in her cheeks. She had to keep kicking the dun mare to maintain the steady, ground-covering pace set by the man in front of her.

Judy did not know why he had chosen this particular day; it was enough that she was riding with him through a snow-covered wilderness toward, she fervently hoped, two young children. She could only pray that they were still alive.

Judy carefully studied each landmark along the way. A certain rock or lightning-struck tree was committed to memory, and as they rode past, she twisted in the saddle to mentally record what the feature looked like from different angles. She had no doubt in her own ability to retrace their trail.

Once, glancing back at a particular rock formation, she thought she saw a movement along the back trail. She fervently hoped they were being followed, just in case her efforts should fail. At least then the Hendersons and the Kellers would know how to find their children. She studied the back of the man before her. He had seemed extremely nervous at first, but with each step the horses took away from Laramie, he seemed to be regaining his composure. She wondered what was going through his mind.

Calvin Winston gradually felt the tension drain from

between his shoulder blades as they passed the halfway point in the journey. The pressure had been mounting by the day. The constant presence of the newspaper reporter Taylor Elkins had not helped. But what really disturbed him was the unexpected arrival in Laramie of Kit Carson and the Cheyenne brave named Yellow Crow. That told Winston a move would soon be made to try to free the captives, and he wanted a lot of ground between himself and Laramie before that happened.

He would not tell Long Walker. Let the cocky bastard find out for himself, Winston thought. Soon he would no longer need the Indian or the woman tagging along behind. If Long Walker did not have to make his final payment, a hefty sack of gold, Winston would not have bothered with this ride. The Confederacy was rapidly becoming a lost cause, and that last sack of gold was his ticket to Europe and the good life. It did not matter that his cousin's death would remain unavenged. He had never liked Colin Dibley that much, anyway.

Freedom lay only a few miles and a day or so away. He was glad now he had not slit Judy Hubbard's throat when she appeared in his room as he was packing. Reason, plus desire, had stayed his hand; her death would have been immediately linked to him in Laramie. This way, suspicions would be confirmed; she had simply ridden away with him and would never be seen again.

Winston felt a stirring in his loins as he mentally pictured her naked in the trapper's cabin near Long Walker's hideout. There he would take that body he so wanted, and afterward, the look of shock on Judy Hubbard's face as he handed her over to the outlaw Ute's pleasure would be the final touch of satisfaction.

"How much longer, Cal?"

He turned in the saddle and stared at her for an instant. "In terms of distance, Judy, not far. In terms of your future, forever—unless you choose to turn back now."

"Cal, why would I even want to turn back? I'll have you as my future," she insisted with as much sincerity as she could.

"You'll have more than that," the man said. "You will be an accomplice. You see, I'm the one who arranged the abduction of the children."

Judy gasped and feigned a look of complete surprise and shock. "But—but why?" she finally stammered.

"I have my reasons. At any rate it doesn't matter now.

You're in it to stay, Judy, like it or not." Abruptly he turned away from her, looking down the trail ahead. Judy let the silence hang for several moments, then called his name. "It doesn't matter—not to us. But . . ."

"But what?" he asked curtly.

"I was just thinking, could I see the children? I mean, wouldn't it be to everyone's advantage if later on, when we reach civilization, I could notify Ted Henderson his son was still alive?"

Winston merely shrugged without turning in the saddle. "Sure. Why not?" He did not see any harm in the reassurance. There would be no survivors anyway, after a short time. . . .

He reined his horse toward a cluster of rocks. Just beyond the jumble of boulders, the trail fell away sharply into a winding canyon. Past a narrow neck in the canyon wall farther on, his fortune and then his pleasure waited.

The two entered Long Walker's camp unchallenged, although several pairs of curious eyes followed the woman. A blue-eyed Indian stepped from a tipi and spoke earnestly with Calvin in a language Judy did not understand. She waited patiently until the Indian produced a heavy pouch and handed it to Winston. Then, almost offhandedly, Winston waved toward a tipi at the edge of a frozen stream.

"The kids are in there," he said. "You have only a couple of minutes. Then we'll move back upstream to the old trapper's cabin—for the night."

Judy, her heart pounding, pulled back the flap of the tipi and squinted in the near-darkness. She was almost knocked over when she stepped inside as a small body flew at her.

"Aunt Judy!" William Ted's voice was bright with hope. "Will we go home now?"

Judy hugged the boy to her. "Keep your voice down," she cautioned. "I can't take you home right now. There are too many Indians outside. But now I know where you are, and I will escape and tell your father. He will take you from this awful place." She reached out a hand and felt Ellen's dainty fingers slide into her palm. "I have to go now," Judy whispered. "You children must be strong and brave—and very quiet—for just a while longer.'

With a final loving squeeze for both children, Judy reluctantly left the tipi. She was extremely relieved the children seemed all right and furious that such innocent beings should be put through so much stress.

She forced a smile onto her face as she faced Winston. "I'm ready, Cal," she said. "It's nearing sundown—and the night is ours." She mounted her horse and pretended to adjust a stirrup, brushing her fingers against her fur-lined boot. The touch of the knife handle beneath her trembling fingers was reassuring.

From his hideout high on the canyon wall, Taylor Elkins committed the layout of the village and surrounding terrain to memory. He was reasonably sure he had not been spotted as he carefully followed Judy and Calvin from Laramie.

Taylor silently cursed as three horsemen, not two, made their way up the canyon toward the cabin in the distance. The third rider appeared to be an Indian. A complication. The Indian would have to be removed, and silently, before Judy could be pulled from the clutches of the Confederate agent.

Now Taylor knew why Judy had appeared so eager to keep Calvin Winston's company. He had seen her enter the tipi and emerge a moment later. Obviously that was where the children were being kept. Judy would have no other reason to go there. He felt a genuine admiration for the young woman. Despite all the abuse she had been subjected to in Laramie, she had persevered.

Her life was in grave danger, however. By now Elkins knew his prey well enough to realize that no one, not the two children nor Judy Hubbard, would ever leave this canyon alive—unless he lent a hand.

As nightfall began to descend, the spy left his perch and cautiously approached the cabin. A yellow glow from the single window served as a beacon for his stalk through the deepening blackness.

When he was only a few yards from the cabin, he saw the door suddenly swing open. Taylor ducked into the protective cover of a pile of boulders. A figure wrapped in blankets emerged from the cabin and squatted near the door. Apparently Winston had told the Indian to stand guard outside.

Taylor slid the stiletto from its spring sheath in his boot. Now, he thought, the odds could be reduced much more simply. He dropped to his belly and, inch by careful inch, began to close the distance between himself and the lone figure outside the cabin.

Inside the cabin Judy Hubbard fed another small log into

the blaze in the rock fireplace. The knot of desperation and growing fear tightened in her stomach as she felt the almost physical caress of Winston's eyes on her. *Stay calm*, she told herself. *You're only going to get one chance.*

Somehow Judy forced a smile onto her lips as she turned to face Winston. Her façade almost crumbled, however, when she saw the man before her. The normally handsome face was twisted in an ugly grin, the green eyes bright with lust. Winston stood in the center of the small single room, leaning against a table.

Judy removed her fur cap and shook her head, letting her rich blond hair fall about her shoulders.

"Well, Cal," she said, hoping the shakiness in her voice would be heard by Winston as excitement rather than raw fear, "here we are at last—and I've waited so long."

She walked over to him and pressed her body against his, lifting her face for his kiss. It was bruising and violent. Judy tasted her own blood beneath his cold, demanding lips. Steeling herself, she raised her right thigh slowly against the outside of Winston's leg. She felt his hips thrust forward in response.

She forced a sigh of false passion and let one arm fall casually to her side. Her fingers groped for the handle of the thin skinning knife. Slowly she began easing the weapon from her boot, poised to strike upward beneath the ribs—and screamed as a hand clamped painfully on the wrist that gripped the knife!

Calvin Winston took a half-step back, his eyes blazing. Keeping her trapped in his paralyzing grip, he slapped her savagely with his free hand. The impact whipped Judy's head to one side, but she did not feel the blow. Panicked, she struggled frantically to break away from his grasp, but her strength was no match for his. Her knife was twisted from her fingers, and Calvin slowly raised it to her throat.

"Tricky bitch, aren't you?" Winston asked icily. "All right—you want to play rough, we'll play!"

The knife point flicked down. Judy felt a tiny, cold track where it grazed her breastbone. Its razor edge slowly sliced through the cloth of her shirt. Winston's hand ripped away the material, leaving her breasts exposed and heaving as she struggled in vain to break free.

"Maybe I'll cut you up a little first," Winston said, his

voice growing even more excited. Paralyzed with terror, Judy watched as the sharp point of the knife touched her left breast—

The door of the cabin suddenly swung open. Taylor Elkins burst into the room, training the short-barreled revolver toward Winston's back. But Winston quickly whirled Judy about, placing her body in front of his own, and held the knife to her neck.

"Put the gun down, Elkins, or she's dead!" he demanded.

Taylor took one look at the wild-eyed Confederate agent and knew he meant what he said. With a sinking sensation, Taylor placed the five-shot pistol on the table.

"Step back!" Winston ordered.

Taylor did as he was told. Winston, knife still held at Judy's throat, edged to the end of the table and reached for the revolver.

His split-second distraction with the gun gave Judy her chance. She lunged against him, slamming both palms against the forearm of his knife hand. The sudden jolt caught the man by surprise. As the knife wavered, Judy ducked under his arm and dropped to the floor.

Instantly Taylor Elkins reached beneath his armpit and launched himself toward Calvin Winston. The two shots from the .41 derringer were muffled, the barrels rammed against Winston's body.

Winston's face melted, sagging into slack-jawed surprise and shock. Then a small trickle of blood appeared at the corner of his mouth, and he slumped forward, a dead weight against Taylor.

Elkins lowered the lifeless form to the floor and instantly went to Judy's side.

"The—the Indian," she whispered, her face white with fear.

"He's dead," Taylor said. "It's all right, Judy. You're safe now."

With the derringer still clutched in one hand, Judy's rescuer gathered her to his breast. He waited until her shaking had subsided and her tears of relief had soaked his shirtfront. Slowly she began to regain her composure. He led her to the fire, examining the shallow cut between her breasts.

"Are you hurt anywhere else?" he asked.

Still speechless, Judy shook her head. Elkins rummaged

in a pack nearby and produced a new shirt. "Hope you don't mind wearing one of Winston's," he said.

Judy stripped off the tattered remains of her own shirt and donned the dead man's clothing. She tried not to look at the huddled form on the floor. Death was never pretty, no matter how despicable the victim.

"Taylor, how—did you know?" she finally managed to ask.

"It wasn't that difficult," he said, reloading the derringer. "I knew Winston was up to something and that you weren't after him for his body." He dropped the pistol back into his belt holster.

"You were very brave, Judy," he said. "You'll have to keep that courage going a while longer. We still have to escape and get back to Laramie. We can't rescue the children ourselves. I'm going to leave you alone for a moment. We must not leave any traces of what happened here tonight. The Indians might come to the cabin later, and they must think the three of you have merely ridden on." He turned toward the body at his feet.

"Taylor—what are you going to do?" she asked.

"Dispose of the bodies where they will never be found." Taylor hoisted the lifeless form of Calvin Winston to a shoulder and moved toward the door.

"Can I help?" Judy asked, her composure rapidly returning.

Taylor shook his head. "I'll take care of the Indian, too. It's a bit messy. I had to cut his throat."

Judy could not help shuddering at the matter-of-fact statement.

"While I'm busy at this, you might want to get set to travel. When the fire has been out for two hours or so, we'll gather the horses and set out for Laramie."

He smiled at the young woman. "It's going to be a long, cold ride to Laramie," he said, "but I'll lay odds you get a warm welcome there for a change."

Nine

"Ted, we have to look this bear straight in the jaws," Kit Carson said, studying the drawn features of the man behind the desk. "No matter how many demands are made and met, the children will die if we don't find them—and soon."

Carson walked past his friend to the map on the wall. "There are a thousand places out there where they could be," the ex-frontiersman said over his shoulder. "We aren't going to find them sitting around this office. Who are your best scouts?"

Part of the weariness and worry slipped from Ted at the hint of pending action. Forced inactivity and recurring nightmares of a small body lying in the snow had taken a heavy toll on his strength. He knew he was near the breaking point and that Kit Carson was right. Regardless of the outcome, they had to do something.

Ted was running the roster of Henderson's Scouts through his mind when the door suddenly burst open. An excited Bernie Christian escorted Judy Hubbard and Taylor Elkins into the office.

"They've found the children, Colonel!" Bernie exclaimed.

Ted was on his feet instantly, grasping Judy's chilled fingers. "Judy—are they—all right?"

"They were last night when we left them," Elkins answered. Briefly, the newsman recounted Judy's determined and successful trek, brushing off his own part in the escapade as incidental.

"My God, Judy! Why didn't you tell us?" Ted exclaimed, leading her to a nearby chair. "And all this time we thought—"

She brushed off his comments with a wave of a hand. "Just find them, Ted, and bring them back safely. That's all that matters now."

Kit Carson draped a blanket over the woman's shaking shoulders and turned to Taylor Elkins, gripping his hand firmly. "Mr. Elkins, you and Judy can never be repaid for what you've done. I know you must be cold, tired, and hungry, but we need your services for a short time yet. Speed is of the essence now."

"Of course, Colonel Carson," Taylor replied.

Ted called Bernie Christian to his side. "I must tell Wilma," he said. "In the meantime, I want you to find Yellow Crow. He will be a great help in planning the rescue." Ted added the names of three other scouts to be summoned, then glanced at Taylor Elkins. "How about you, Taylor? You've certainly earned the right to go along."

Elkins shook his head. "I'm no Indian fighter, Colonel," he said. "I'm a short-gun specialist, not a rifleman. Besides, perhaps it would be best if I stay here and watch over the women—just in case."

"That might not be a bad idea," Ted conceded. He turned to leave.

"I'm going along, Colonel," Bernie Christian said, gripping Ted's arm. "The only way you can stop me is to shoot me. The Third's the only home I've ever really had, and that boy of yours is part of my family, too!" Before Ted could reply, the wiry corporal was out the door.

Moments later Ted was at home, and Wilma was in his arms, tears streaking her cheeks. Ted understood what was going through her mind—joy that the children were safe warred with the horrifying possibility that the rescue party now assembling might not succeed.

Finally Ted eased Wilma's arms from around his neck. "I must go back to the office now. Kit and Yellow Crow will be narrowing down the options."

"Ted—suppose something goes wrong—" Wilma asked anxiously.

He placed a finger on her lips, cutting her short. "Don't let yourself think of it, Wilma. I know it will be more difficult for you than for me because waiting is harder to endure than action. But we *will* get them back. In the meantime, you can help. Fix up a spare pack, with one of Bill's heavy coats and as much ammunition for the Henry forty-four as you can stuff in it. Then you might tell Vi of the circumstances. I'm sure she'll be delighted to learn of Judy's role in the whole incident."

Leaving Wilma bustling about, Ted stepped onto the parade ground and headed back to the office. He had covered only a few steps when he felt a presence nearby.

Sergeant Major Albert Jonas fell into step with his commander. "How's it look, Colonel?"

"We have a good chance to get them back, Sergeant. We'll be sending a top crew out."

Jonas nodded. "Good. I'll fetch my equipment."

Ted stopped in his tracks. "Albert, I can't let you go. You have a new wife at home."

"Colonel Henderson, until next spring at least, I'm still in this man's army," Jonas replied firmly. "Don't make me disobey no order this late in my career." A grin flashed across the sergeant's face. "Besides, it's the first time Sally's agreed with me an' made no fuss about it. I'm dealin' myself in, sir."

Moved by the loyalty, Ted merely nodded and continued toward the office.

Inside, he glanced over the gathering. Christian was already there, along with the grizzled Pappy Lehman, the young but efficiently deadly Jack Grant, and the gray-bearded, wily Dick Dunn from the scout troop. Carl Keller, his eyes red with sleeplessness and worry, glanced up as Ted entered.

"That little Arapaho girl out there's as much mine and Anna's as if we'd birthed her ourselves, and I'm a-goin," he announced.

Ted placed a hand on the scout's shoulder. "I suppose you have as much right as I do, Carl. And frankly, there are few people I'd rather have at my side under these conditions."

In a far corner, Yellow Crow and Kit Carson were in deep discussion with Taylor Elkins. Kit looked up, caught Ted's eye, and motioned him to join the group.

"No doubt now," Yellow Crow said in English. "Judy see blue-eyed Indian. Elkins describe paintings on lodges and shields outside. Long Walker's camp. Crazy Dogs there." The Cheyenne glanced around the room. "No matter. This bunch handle Crazy Dogs all right."

Ted could find no fault with the simple and direct plan Carson outlined to the rescue party. After a night ride, they would strike before dawn. Yellow Crow would have the most dangerous job, rescuing the children from the tipi where they were being held. Then the group would hurry back to Laramie. Any armed clash was to be avoided if at all possible, but each man would carry spare ammunition and weapons just in case.

"Any questions?" Kit concluded. There were none. "All right. We've talked the hair off this buffalo," the ex-scout said. "Now it's time to go steal his horns. We move out at midafternoon."

Ted crouched in the frigid predawn darkness that was broken only by a gray smudge along the eastern rim of the canyon. Kit Carson knelt at his side, intently watching the progress of a shadow flitting from brush to rock below. Jack Grant had silently and efficiently dispatched the lone sentry, and now Yellow Crow was nearing his objective—the tipi where the two young children were being held.

Ted held his breath as the shadow that was his blood brother reached the side of the tipi away from the main circle of lodges.

"Try to relax, Ted," Carson whispered. "All we can do now is wait and hope."

Ted glanced about nervously, knowing the positions of other members of the rescue team but unable to spot them. In the canyon two hundred yards back, Bernie Christian would be waiting with the horses. Ted tightened his grip on the receiver of the Henry repeating rifle, knowing each member of the group would be doing the same. At least, he thought, they would have plenty of firepower if it was needed. Every man had either a Spencer or a Henry, a couple of spare handguns, and enough ammunition to fight a war.

On the canyon floor below, Yellow Crow knelt in the shadows behind the captives' tipi. With his voice barely a whisper, he called in Cheyenne, "Little ones—we have come to take you home. You must remain very quiet and brave."

The razor edge of his skinning knife deftly sliced a hole in the side of the buffalo-hide tipi. A small head of tousled hair quickly appeared at the opening, eyes wide with fright. Yellow Crow helped William Ted through the opening, and little Ellen scrambled out quickly. Both children were coatless and shivered in the bitter morning air. William Ted threw his hands around his godfather's neck in an emotional but silent greeting.

"Now, little ones," Yellow Crow whispered, "it is time to leave. You must be as silent as the bobcat that stalks the rabbit." Then, with the two youngsters at his side, Yellow Crow began the long, careful walk away from Long Walker's camp toward the waiting men in the canyon above.

His heart in his throat, Ted Henderson watched intently as the trio of shadowy figures moved gingerly from one spot of cover to another.

Yellow Crow and the children were only a few yards from safety when a sudden cry rang out from the camp. Instantly lodge flaps were flung open.

Ted watched in shock as the Crazy Dog Sioux scooped up their shields and shouldered their weapons. One brave pointed up-canyon to Yellow Crow and the fleeing children. The camp boiled to life with the shrill pursuit cries of the Sioux warriors.

"Run for it, Yellow Crow—now!" Ted said aloud. As if the Cheyenne had heard, Yellow Crow suddenly scooped up both children and sprinted toward the waiting rescue squad.

A wild shot from below nicked a boulder almost at Yellow Crow's shoulder and ricocheted with a nasty buzz over Ted's head. He lined the muzzle of the Henry at the charging braves below.

"Not yet, Ted!" Kit Carson's urgent voice said in his ear. "Wait until the kids are out of the line of fire! We still have surprise on our side!"

Time froze for Ted until, suddenly, Yellow Crow dashed between two boulders and a small boy flung himself into his father's arms.

"Daddy!" Little Bill cried.

Part of the word was drowned in the blast of Kit Carson's rifle. A running brave plunged forward into the snow. Other rifles cracked, the shots measured and deliberate. Two more Crazy Dogs went down under the accurate fire from the canyon walls. The remaining braves dashed for cover.

Ted untangled himself from his son's firm embrace. "Stay behind me, Bill! We aren't out of this yet!" He snapped a shot at a dodging Indian but saw the slug kick snow at the brave's feet. Working the action of the Henry, he aimed with more care and squeezed the trigger. The Indian stumbled and fell only inches from a tumble of dead trees.

Arrows and answering rifle shots from below plowed into the snow nearby as the Crazy Dogs began to isolate targets, firing at the muzzle flashes from the rescue party's weapons.

Kit Carson called "Retreat!" and the scouts began a desperate rock-to-rock scramble back toward their horses, pausing only long enough to fire one or two shots from each patch of cover. Kit and Ted fought side by side, bringing down another Indian each. Reloading, Ted glanced to one side and saw Carl Keller drop behind a boulder, his adopted daughter held tightly against his side. Keller's Spencer cracked, and the slug found its mark.

There was a sudden silence as the Crazy Dogs ceased firing. Then, from the canyon floor, came a cry that turned Ted's blood to ice—the high-pitched "yip" of the Sioux war cry!

Abruptly the canyon filled with mounted Indians, all charging hard toward the rescue party's position. Ted muttered a sharp curse. *There must be a hundred of them,* he thought, *and we're still a long way from the horses!*

"Looks like old Long Walker had him an ace in the hole," Kit Carson said calmly, sighting along the barrel of his carbine. "If we don't break their first charge, we'll never get out of here!" Cool and collected, the veteran Indian fighter waited, then squeezed the trigger, sending a pony thrashing into the snow.

Atop the echoes of Carson's shot, a hail of bullets ripped through the Indian ranks. The braves leading the charge paid the highest price; a half-dozen Sioux went down in the first blast of rifle fire. The charge stalled for a moment, but Ted found little hope in that since the Crazy Dogs knew little of retreating when facing a smaller force. He twisted around to face his son.

"Bill," he said, "if it looks like we're going to be overrun, hide!" Despite the terror in his eyes, the boy nodded, blinking back tears.

Ted pulled the extra pack from his shoulder, reached inside, and handed the wide-eyed, shivering boy the spare coat Wilma had packed. "Hide well! Don't let the Indians find you!" Ted instructed as his son quickly slipped into the heavy coat.

A yell from behind him grabbed Ted's attention. He blinked in disbelief.

Bernie Christian had brought the horses!

Ignoring the bullets and arrows that zinged about him, the young corporal spurred his mount from post to post, delivering horses to the embattled rescue troop. He yanked his own horse to a stop beside Ted and leaned from the saddle.

"Get back to the pass behind us!" Christian yelled above the din of gunfire. "We can hold them off from there!"

Ted swung his son into the saddle and vaulted up behind him. From the corner of his eye, he saw a Sioux brave stand and loose an arrow. Ted yanked his horse about brutally and immediately felt the heavy blow of the arrow against his left shoulder. He braced himself for the pain he knew would come. At least, he thought, he had managed to wheel his horse in time to take the arrow that otherwise would have struck his son.

As the strength drained from his left arm, Ted transferred the reins to his right hand and spurred the horse hard. The animal lunged through the snow.

One by one, other members of the rescue squad wheeled their horses toward the relative safety of the canyon's narrow neck. Trusting his mount to keep its footing on the hazardous terrain, Ted glanced around. His quick look was just in time to see the bewhiskered Dick Dunn stiffen in his saddle, grasp at the small of his back, and then topple to the ground.

Pappy Lehman shouted an obscenity. "Trying to flank us!" Lehman yelled, pointing toward a bench along the canyon wall. A half-dozen braves were quirting their horses along the narrow shelf of the canyon.

Before Ted could react, Lehman dropped his carbine back into its sling, wrapped the reins around his saddle horn, and a pistol in each hand, kneed his horse toward the Indians on the shelf.

Ted tried to call out, but the shock of his shoulder wound left him barely able to open his mouth.

"Damn Injuns!" Lehman shouted. "Let's see jist how tough you Crazy Dogs really are!" One of his handguns barked. A Sioux pony stumbled. Then Lehman's horse raced up the slope. Two warriors dropped under Pappy's guns before a Crazy Dog bullet straightened the aging scout in the saddle. Still he rode on, firing by instinct, and another warrior dropped before Pappy Lehman finally slid from his saddle.

The flanking attempt was broken, shattered by a tough old scout's final, heroic charge.

A slug snapped by Ted's ear, jarring him back to reality. Hunching his body over his son, and with his rifle and reins both gripped in his right hand, Ted settled in to riding for their lives.

It seemed to take an eternity to cover the final few yards to the safety of the narrow neck of the canyon. But finally Ted's horse reached the boulders. He reined the animal to a stop and had begun to dismount, preparing to make a final and expensive stand, when a shout from Bernie Christian stopped him.

The corporal already had reached the boulders and dismounted, shouldering his way alongside the massive bulk of Sergeant Major Albert Jonas.

"Stay up, Ted! You and the boy have to get clear! Carl's already gone ahead with the girl!"

Yellow Crow, Kit Carson, and young Jack Grant reached the rocks and pulled their mounts to a stop in a shower of snow. Their rearguard action had only momentarily checked the Indian pursuit.

Christian glanced over his shoulder at the scores of approaching Indians. "Albert and me have decided," he said. "We can stand them off from here for a while—give you a chance to get away!"

"Bernie, I can't—" Henderson began.

"Shut up, Colonel," the corporal snapped. "This is the only chance we've got, and you know it! Just leave us every gun and every bullet you can spare."

"Albert—" Ted's protest was halted by the huge sergeant major, who stared at Ted with great determination. "Bernie's right, Colonel. They'll be on us quick. Leave us somethin' to fight with and get the hell outta here!"

"They're right, Ted," Kit Carson said quietly. "Two men can hold this pass for quite a while. It will give us time to buy some distance. It's the only chance we have."

Carson handed his carbine to Bernie Christian and stripped a cartridge belt from around his middle. Ted surrendered his Henry to Albert Jonas.

"Tell Sally—I hope she has better luck next time," Jonas said. "She'll understand."

Four rifles and a half-dozen handguns, with spare ammunition for each, were rapidly arranged among the rocks. Yellow Crow silently handed over his own treasured Spencer and ammunition belt.

Bernie Christian reached into the pocket of his shirt, then

held out a hand to Ted. In his palm were several military decorations.

"I don't want any Indian wearing Frank Armbrister's medal of honor, sir," Christian said. "Take these. I'll have no further use for them. A couple are mine. I'd like you to have them, too."

"Bernie—I—"

"You're running out of time, Colonel Henderson! Now, light a shuck out of here!" the corporal urged.

Suddenly Kit Carson leaned forward and pulled the reins from Ted's numb fingers. Leading the horse carrying Ted and his son, Kit kneed his own mount in the direction of Laramie.

The ache in Ted's shoulder seemed little more than a pinprick compared to the pain in his heart. For a moment he did not understand why he could not see clearly. Then he realized that for the first time in many years, he was crying openly.

The survivors of the rescue party, plus two precious bundles snuggled firmly against their fathers' bodies, had covered a valuable hundred yards before the first rifle shot sounded from the rocks in the pass.

Wilma Henderson anxiously paced the floor of her crowded living room, walking first to the window to peer into the swirling snow, then retracing her steps to stare at the mantel clock above the fireplace. She knew very well that no military action could be tied to a time schedule, but still, the clock moved with agonizing slowness.

She turned at a touch on her arm. "Don't you worry none, Miz Wilma," Sally Jonas said, her voice firm and confident. "We know they's overdue and the storm's worse, but walkin' a hole in the floor won't hurry nothin'. They gets back when they gets back, not before."

The new bride steered the veteran soldier's wife to the nearby sofa. "I'll fetch you some spiced tea," Sally said.

Wilma sat on the comfortable horsehair-stuffed cushions and looked into the soft brown eyes before her. "I don't know where you get your strength, Sally. Your husband is out there, too."

Sally smiled. "You gotta have faith, Miz Wilma. Faith in your man and faith in the Lawd." She turned to the kitchen, where a tea kettle was steaming on the wood stove.

It's supposed to work the other way around, Wilma thought; *I'm the one supposed to be comforting her.*

Across the room, Vi Robinson once more squeezed her stepdaughter's hand. "Judy," Vi said, blinking hard, "can you ever forgive me—all of us—for not trusting you? I should have known from the start; the only love in your life is Abel—and the children. That was a very brave and unselfish thing you did, and we treated you so badly."

Judy Hubbard, still showing the exhaustion and horror of her journey, patted Vi's arm with her free hand. "Don't be so hard on yourself. There's no need to apologize. Had the circumstances been reversed, I would have thought as you did. I only wish we could somehow get word to Abel."

Vi glanced up at Taylor Elkins, who was standing at the end of the love seat where the two women sat. "As for you, Mr. Elkins, please forget what I said earlier about your having to leave. You have my undying gratitude for your actions in saving Judy's life."

Elkins merely shrugged. "Anyone would have done the same. It was special only because a young woman and two children dear to all our hearts were involved." He desperately wanted to blurt out the entire story, but the time and place were not yet right.

The door swung open, admitting Dr. Mason. "Good news," he said, brushing snow from his hat. "Anna Keller has come out of it. She's awake now."

Wilma jumped from the sofa. "Is she—?"

The surgeon smiled. "She's in full control of her senses, Wilma. There are no signs of any brain impairment. Except for a splitting headache, she's still Anna and—"

"Here they come!" The cry from the parade ground cut off any further conversation.

The people in the room raced through the door, coats and wraps forgotten in their haste.

The figures of horsemen materialized at the fort's gate, partially obscured by the freshening blizzard. Nine had left. Only five were returning.

Suddenly Wilma screamed and began to run toward a familiar figure slumped in the saddle. Her heart soared when she saw a small, round face peeking from her husband's heavy coat. Grasping her son in her arms once again, she stood in the snow, sobbing. Little Bill's grip around her neck was fierce.

"Daddy and Yellow Crow saved us," the boy said, his words muffled against his mother's shoulder. "Aunt Judy found us."

Through the blur of her tears, Wilma looked at the pale, drawn face of her husband as she walked alongside his horse.

Carl Keller leaned down, spoke briefly with Dr. Mason, then kneed his horse toward the hospital where Anna lay. Young Ellen sat silently erect on the saddle in front of her father.

The parade ground erupted in bedlam as word of the rescue party's return swept through the fort. The horsemen made their way through the crowd, then stopped at the Hendersons' door.

Wilma finally found her voice. "Welcome—home, dear. Come inside where it's warm."

"Not sure I can climb down from this horse, Wilma," Ted said, his voice barely audible. "I'm afraid I picked up a little souvenir back there."

Dr. Mason was at Ted's side instantly, shouldering Wilma roughly out of the way. She watched as Kit Carson, Yellow Crow, and the physician eased Ted gingerly from the saddle and helped him inside. For the first time she saw the feathered shaft of the arrow angling across her husband's back.

Just outside the door, Ted pulled away from the helping hands and stood wavering on his feet. All alone at the edge of the crowd was a stricken face.

"I—I'm sorry, Sally," Ted managed to say before the darkness closed in..

The next day Ted struggled back to consciousness, aware first of the fiery pain behind his left shoulder, then of a subdued murmur that became conversations as his senses returned. He realized that he was lying on a hospital cot, but in his own living room. Then, as his eyes began to focus, he became aware of yet another pain.

Dry eyed, Sally Jonas sat on the couch, quietly talking with Wilma and Vi.

"You was right, Vi," Sally was saying. "At least I had him for a spell, and if it wasn't for you a-chewin' me out, I wouldn't of had that much. It was worth it."

"Sally," Ted said from his cot, his voice hoarse, "I—don't know what to say."

The young widow rose and went to Ted's side. "Colonel, Albert done what he wanted to do. Livin' without him ain't gonna be easy, but I can handle it. And I ain't gonna stand for you wearin' no heavy load like it was your fault. He was a soldier. Besides, that big nigger loved you and that young'un of yours, too."

She placed a firm hand on Ted's free arm. "We talked it over, and me and Albert agreed. If he hadn't of gone, he wouldn't of been the same stubborn man I married. Now you get some rest."

"The surgeon said you were lucky, darling," Wilma added quietly. "The arrow hit your shoulder blade at an angle and deflected. Any other way, it could have gone straight in." She shuddered at the thought. "Is there anything I can get you, dear?"

"Just a drink of cold water and my son."

Wilma smiled lovingly at her husband. "You can have the drink, but Bill's asleep. You're going to be staying home for a while, and you can spoil him all you want the whole time."

Ted cocked an eyebrow. "Staying home? How long?"

"Dr. Mason says you should be laid up for two months. But since you're a fast healer and a downright stubborn man, he thinks it likely you'll be in the saddle in half that time."

Ted motioned Wilma closer and whispered, "When is the memorial service for Albert and Bernie and the others?"

Wilma glanced at Sally Jonas. "This afternoon. You'll have to miss it, Ted. The doctor insists you stay in bed."

"Did the patrol get back with their bodies already?" Ted asked softly.

Wilma shook her head sadly. "The patrol couldn't find any bodies. The Indians must have taken them for some kind of medicine ceremony." Seeing the shocked look on her husband's face, she quickly added, "You get some rest, darling. Try to sleep now."

For a moment Ted listened to the wind rattle the window frames; then he looked up into Wilma's red-streaked eyes. "Like hell I will," he declared. "They were friends of mine as well as soldiers in my command. I'll be there if someone has to carry me."

Concern showed in Wilma's face. "Ted, you shouldn't. You're still weak, and we don't know what the strain might do to you in your condition. You'll be in extreme pain—"

"Wilma," Ted interrupted quietly, "I couldn't be hurting worse inside than I am now. I'm going." He rose onto his good elbow, wincing at the pain from the movement, and sipped at the glass of water Wilma held to his lips. Then he settled back on the cot.

A few hours later, with Kit Carson on one side and Wilma on the other, Ted walked slowly down the aisle of the packed chapel. In the silence Ted noticed there were few dry eyes, even among the hardened veterans of R Company. He settled into the hard pew and glanced at Sally Jonas. She sat, outwardly calm and serene, a handkerchief held in her crossed hands.

The post chaplain stood behind the black-draped altar. From a small stanchion at his right, the battle-torn guidon of the Third Cavalry Regiment drooped, apparently lifeless in the still chapel.

His voice raised above the howl of the wind outside, the chaplain began: "Greater love hath no man, the Scriptures tell us. We need no further proof of the truth in those words than the memory of four strong and brave men who died willingly and with courage in the faith that others might live."

Ted felt a sting in the corners of his eyes as the roster of the dead was read. Only one, Sergeant Major Albert Jonas, had any known survivors.

"Our hearts and our deepest sympathies go out on this day to Sally Jonas," the chaplain continued, "and each of us who knew Albert shares her grief. But our world has been made better by his touch, by the simple act of his being here. No less can be said of Pappy Lehman or of Dick Dunn, two men who left their mark on the land as well as its people. And of Corporal Bernie Christian, whose courage was an inspiration to us all, even to the last—"

Ted looked at Wilma sitting beside him. Tears were streaming down her cheeks. He swallowed painfully as the words of the chaplain triggered the familiar faces and memories in his mind.

"Let us not grieve forever, but let us never forget—" Suddenly the chaplain stopped speaking. Astonished, he stared openmouthed toward the rear of the chapel.

All at once Ted felt a cold breeze on the back of his neck.

In the silence he heard the barely audible words. "Always figured—I'd be late—for my own funeral."

Ignoring the pain in his shoulder, Ted twisted, unbelieving, to stare at the huge bulk leaning against the open door, a rifle clutched in one big black hand. Without realizing he had moved, Ted found himself at Albert Jonas's side, his free hand slipping around the blood-soaked waist in an instinctive attempt to lend support.

Sally Jonas, barely a half-step behind Ted, reached out and touched the stubble on her husband's cheek as if in a trance.

"Albert—how—?" Ted began.

Jonas's eyes were glazed with exhaustion and pain, but a spark of pride gleamed brightly. "We held out—'til near dark, Colonel. Bernie—won't be—coming back. I snuck past the Sioux. Waited—till full dark an' headed home."

Dr. Mason shouldered his way through the crowd, followed by Yellow Crow. The physician glanced at the big sergeant major and immediately called for a litter.

"Reckon we—killed us a mess of Sioux, Colonel. Couldn't bring Bernie home. Sioux standin' all around him. They—didn't scalp him or—nothin', near as I could tell. Just put a lance—in ground beside his head—like a tribute to one of their own."

With Ted and Sally flanking the wounded sergeant, Dr. Mason began working on Albert before the litter arrived.

Tears of joy streaming down her face, Sally brushed the ice from the woolly hair on Albert's head. "You big nigger," she said. "I knew you wouldn't let me outta this marriage that easy!"

"Reckon not, woman." Jonas smiled weakly as the litter bearers hurried to the door. Slowly and painfully he raised a hand toward Yellow Crow, the receiver of the Spencer .56 still clutched in his half-frozen fingers. "Brought your rifle back, Yellow Crow," Jonas muttered.

The Cheyenne gently removed the weapon from Albert's hand. "There's one round left." Jonas winced as he was eased onto the litter. Yellow Crow worked the action of the Spencer, ejecting the last short, pointed cartridge into his palm.

"Big gun once more bring strong medicine," he said, holding the single cartridge aloft. "This bullet one day tear the heart from blue-eyed Indian named Long Walker."

Four burly soldiers knelt alongside the litter, gripping the sturdy support poles. Ted stepped back, leaving room for Sally

Jonas to grasp her husband's hand. "Looks like you'll be needin' a new sergeant for a spell," Albert said to Ted. "Reckon I'll be laid up awhile—couple good-sized holes in me, Colonel."

"Be quiet now, Albert," Ted said firmly. "Don't waste your strength talking any more."

Jonas ignored the order. "God, Colonel—I'm gonna miss that stubborn little ex-Reb of a corporal." Then Albert Jonas's eyes closed as the soldiers hoisted the litter and moved through the door.

Ted felt a hand on his free arm. "Go with him," Kit Carson said. "I'll represent the Third for the dead, you watch over the living. Besides, you've opened up that shoulder again and need a doctor yourself."

The chaplain's voice carried above the murmur of the crowd. "Let us rejoice. For as He rose from the dead, so He has returned to the fold one of His sheep believed lost."

As Ted, supported by his wife, walked through the storm behind the litter bearers, he knew there was much to rejoice over.

A pair of wood-burning stoves blazed red hot at each end of Leavenworth's Buffalo Saloon, trying to hold at bay the blizzard outside. Cries of "Shut that damn door!" sounded with each arrival and departure, and there were many.

The combination of weather, Saturday night, and payday filled the popular south-side watering hole to near capacity. The two bartenders found themselves hard pressed to keep up with the demands, as did the girls in the small upstairs bedrooms, who supplied a different type of warmth to the saloon's more affluent clientele.

Colonel Emery Church made his way unsteadily down the steep staircase. His glowering descent quieted the few who had been good-naturedly taunting previous upstairs customers. Those among the crowd who knew the colonel were well aware that his vicious temper was even worse when he was drinking.

Except for the brief trip up and down the stairs, drinking had been Emery Church's sole occupation for most of the afternoon, through suppertime, and into the evening. He shouldered his way to the bar and thumped a fist on the well-worn pine.

"Barkeep! Gimme a double whiskey!" Church barked the order as if he were on a parade ground. The man behind the counter gave Church a long look but reached for a jug; it was not his job to be friends with the customers—just to serve them and take their money.

Lieutenant Slaker, leaning against the bar at Church's side, put a hand on his commanding officer's shoulder. A sour glare from Church caused him to remove the hand quickly.

"Sir," Slaker said, "it's not my business, but don't you think you've had enough?" The lieutenant's speech was, itself, slightly slurred.

"Mind your own damn business, Slaker," Church snapped. "I'll let everybody know when I've had enough." As if to prove his point, Church lifted the glass placed in front of him and drained half its contents.

"Know what I saw up there, Slaker? One of them girls is a damn *Injun*! And there was a soldier in the room with that squaw!" Church's voice was loud and accusing. "Damn good thing he wasn't one of my boys! I'd have him cashiered for sure! Rather bed a nigger, myself!"

Slaker glanced over his shoulder toward a nearby table. A stocky black soldier had come half out of his chair but reluctantly settled back as his white drinking partner put a restraining hand on his arm.

"Ah, Colonel, don't get yourself all riled up," Slaker said nervously.

Church glared morosely into his drink, then hefted the glass and emptied the remaining liquor. He waved to the barkeep for a refill. "What kinda place you runnin' here, anyway—trottin' out some louse-bit squaw for *white men*?"

The bartender glowered at Church. "You don't like it here, Colonel, the Coach Lamp's just down the street."

"Pour, dammit! I'll drink where I please, and I'll say what I want!"

The barkeep shrugged and tilted the bottle. "Your head— and was I you, I'd watch my tongue to save my teeth." The bartender moved away.

Church took a hefty slug of the new drink. "Damn me if Kansas ain't goin' to hell in a handbasket. Know what, Slaker?" Church suddenly cackled mirthlessly. "I bet you ol' Ted Henderson owns this place—the Injun-lovin' bastard!"

A slender, slope-shouldered man in civilian clothes and a

stocky mountaineer in buckskins pushed back from a nearby table and walked to the bar. The slender one muttered something to the two men at Church's left, and the pair promptly surrendered their spots at the bar. The slender man placed his half-empty beer stein on the bar and turned to face Church. Slaker, looking past the colonel, felt a sudden twinge of alarm. He did not like the look in the new man's eyes.

"Henderson!" Church fairly spat the name. "Him and that half-assed bunch of his! I wish he was here now. We'd see just how much of a stud hoss he really is! Hadn't been for that damn coward, I'd have cleaned the whole damn country plumb out of redskins!"

"Colonel," the slender man at Church's side said quietly, "if Ted Henderson was here, you'd most likely wind up chewin' on a knuckle. And if you don't shut up right now, it could happen anyway."

Church turned to face the speaker, blinking as he tried to focus his eyes. "Yeah? Who's gonna do that?"

"Me, maybe," the man replied. "Name's Jud Stewart. I served with Colonel Henderson's Third Cavalry Regiment in the New Mexico campaign against the Confederates and then against the Navajo. I'd be with him yet except I caught a rifle ball in the hip in the Canyon de Chelly. My friend here is Dutch Gordon. Formerly one of Henderson's Scouts."

Gordon casually downed his drink and stepped away from the bar. An expectant hush settled over the nearby tables. Drinkers at the bar gingerly stepped back.

Dutch Gordon spoke quietly. "I reckon you best take back them things you said about Colonel Henderson. Never was a finer officer in my book, or a better man."

Church glared at the stocky ex-scout. "Well, now," he said loudly, "looks like we got us a couple more Injun-lovers here, Slaker. Brownnosers from Henderson's outfit to boot."

Jud Stewart sighed in resignation. "Okay, Colonel," he said softly, "you're on the pot—now piss or get off!"

"Damn you—" Church launched a wild swing at Stewart. The thin man clamped Church's fist in a solid grip with his left hand and slugged the colonel in the jaw with his right. Church's knees buckled under the combination of whiskey and the solid clout from Stewart. He would have gone down, but Stewart yanked him back upright and slammed a fist into Church's midsection.

Lieutenant Slaker's hand made a stab for the cavalry pistol at his side. He never made it. Dutch Gordon's heavy fist caught him in the temple, almost knocking the lieutenant over the bar. Gordon expertly plucked the handgun from its holster, cocked the weapon, and stuck the barrel under Slaker's chin. "Reckon as to how you best stay out of this," he said menacingly, "unless you want to see your brains on the ceiling of this here saloon."

Stewart continued to pound the now-helpless Church, short punches that in moments reduced the colonel's face to a bleeding mess. Then the ex-soldier spun Church about, grabbed his collar and the seat of his pants, and lifted the colonel into the air. He walked to the door and tossed the almost-senseless colonel out into the snow.

In a moment Stewart returned, massaging a bruised right hand. He calmly ordered a beer, then turned to Slaker and Gordon. Slaker's head was bent far back over the bar, his eyes wide in pure terror. The muzzle of the handgun bored into the soft underside of his chin.

"What you think, Stewart? Reckon I oughta kill this 'un?" Gordon asked.

Jed Stewart shrugged. "Nah. Like Ted would say, he's not worth the effort. Just toss him in the snowbank on top of his colonel. Keep the handgun, though. Looks like a good one. No sense wasting a nice weapon."

Slaker felt himself spun around, one arm twisted painfully behind his back. Then he was suddenly outside, his face in the snow. At his side Emery Church struggled to his knees. Blood dripped from his face onto the snowbank.

"Bastards," Church muttered through split lips. He spat out a tooth. "If I'd been sober—" The battered face twisted into a glare of pure hatred. "That's just—one more—thing to settle up with Henderson," Church gasped. "He'll by God— pay for this. . . ."

Lieutenant Slaker heaved himself to his feet and watched his commanding officer trudge away toward the fort, stumbling in the knee-deep snow. Somehow, commanding a cavalry company in the Fourth Kansas Volunteers had lost some of its glamour, Slaker thought. He shivered, coatless in the bitter cold. "Come spring, Colonel," he said to the departing figure, "I'm gonna be somewhere else."

* * *

Abel Hubbard struggled stiffly from his thin blankets. The intense cold of the high Yellowstone River country air burned his lungs. For a moment he was confused by something in the half-frozen camp. Then he realized it was the absence of sound that had tricked his senses.

The wind no longer howled. The shelter halves housing himself and his patrol no longer flapped and popped in the gale. The blizzard had finally run its course.

He crawled from his cramped shelter and stood blinking in the bright light of a low sun. Blue specks seemed to dance across the sweeping vista of snow broken only by pine trees and jagged rocks.

A heavily bundled figure struggled through knee-deep snow, skirting drifts taller than a man's head, and approached the lean field officer.

"Looks like we weathered the storm in better shape than we'd hoped, Colonel," the veteran sergeant said. "We had three horses freeze to death on the picket line, but the only casualty in the troops is Adams. His feet froze on guard duty last night."

Abel nodded. "Follow standard procedure on the dead horses, Kirk. Carve off what meat can be saved. Horse meat may leave a bad taste in a cavalry trooper's mouth, but at least it's something to eat in an emergency." Abel waved his arms vigorously, trying to restore the circulation. "God knows the meat won't spoil in this weather. Get a fire going and see what you can do for Adams. If we're lucky maybe we can save his legs, maybe even a toe or two."

Abel ran a hand across his bearded chin; each man in the company had been instructed to let his whiskers grow for some protection from the cold. He felt sorry for some of the men, too young to grow beards, who felt the full bite of the subzero weather.

Hubbard started his morning rounds, adding a word of encouragement here, a greeting there. Across the camp, troopers struggled to clear frozen actions on their carbines. At least, Abel thought with a small measure of satisfaction, the blizzard would have swept some snow from the higher ridges; that would make travel a bit easier.

His morning rounds were interrupted by the approach of a dark-skinned horseman. Abel raised a hand in greeting to Tosh-ko-nay, the Crow who had joined the Shoshone scout team and knew every campsite, valley, spring, and tree in this inhospitable northern Dakota Territory. Tosh-ko-nay returned the greeting and swung down from his horse. Abel wondered how the Crow could survive such bitter weather with apparent ease.

"They are there," the Crow said simply.

"Our scouts do magic," Abel replied, "and Tosh-ko-nay is the strongest of the medicine. Whose tribe is camped below Killdeer Mountain?"

The Crow scout removed his heavy furred cap and slapped it against a leg. Ice crystals flew from the headgear. "It is the tribe of Antelope, the Santee Sioux whose people rode with the blue-eyed one called Long Walker against the whites at the last turning of the leaves."

Abel nodded in satisfaction. "Good," he said. "Another push or two and Antelope may have second thoughts about Long Walker's plans. We've pushed him a good hundred miles. A few more just might turn his thoughts in the right direction."

He called for Sergeant Robert Kirk. "Pass the word to the boys, Sergeant, Boots and Saddles. It's time to give old Antelope another bump in the backside. And remind the younger troops to put bear grease on their faces. Even a weak sun on this snow can cause sunburn in the high country."

Sergeant Kirk nodded. "Hell of a place, Colonel. Ride into the shade of a tree and you freeze; ride out of the shade and you fry without even knowing it. Same routine?"

"Same song, Kirk. Tosh-ko-nay will take us to the camp on the best tactical route. No firing unless fired upon. Capture the pony herd if possible. Hit them quick and stop pursuit as soon as they form a rear guard. No women and children are to be hurt in any way."

The sergeant grinned wryly. "Bet old Antelope's getting tired of you nipping his rear end."

"Hope so," Abel replied. "Maybe this time we'll get lucky and can then move on to another tribe or camp."

"How many does Antelope make now, Colonel?" Kirk asked.

Abel shrugged. "I've lost count, Sergeant. But I think we've put a dent in some pride and emptied a few bellies along the way. Antelope's the biggest yet, though. He'd whip our tails in an all-out fight, so we play his game—hit and run."

Abel waited patiently until the column had formed up.

Each day it seemed to take longer; horses and men grew weaker from the continual exposure to the elements. Fodder for the horses and mules was nearly exhausted, and not a man among the company had even smelled coffee or bacon for weeks. He swung aboard his own rail-thin mount and chewed at a chunk of dried meat, his belly growling in protest at the faint memory of ham and eggs. But one more strike at Antelope, and the company would be able to turn toward Fort Berthold and fresh supplies. That was enough motivation to turn a hungry soldier into a force to be reckoned with.

He kicked his tired mount into motion behind Tosh-ko-nay.

Late that afternoon, Abel Hubbard poked his head over a low cedar and regarded Antelope's camp in the shallow valley below. Their dogged pursuit was about to pay its biggest and perhaps final haul. The pony herd, lightly guarded, had drifted downstream as the bony animals pawed away snow for a few mouthfuls of dried grass. It would be a simple matter to cut them off and capture the entire herd, a job for the stealthy and competent Shoshone. At the same time, a mounted rush by the troopers should take care of the village.

Before the sun had dipped noticeably, a column of soldiers had crept undetected to the mouth of a small dry wash opening onto the valley. At its head Abel cocked his carbine and waved.

The whooping Shoshone whipped their mounts toward the Indian pony herd, and the cavalry wheeled from the wash into a skirmish line, pushing their tired mounts into a semblance of a charge.

The sudden apparition rising from the snow threw the Sioux camp into confusion. Women dropped pots, grabbed children, and dashed from lodges, fleeing back up-canyon to the north. A few braves put up a determined defense, buying time for the band to escape, but were forced to withdraw or be overrun by the advancing soldiers.

In only a few moments, the Indian camp lay abandoned, lodges, cooking utensils, and personal possessions lying as they had been dropped in the Sioux flight. Abel moved quickly to establish his own defense of the camp in case of counter-attack, trusting in Sergeant Kirk and his squad to engage the rear guard briefly and then fall back.

A few sporadic shots sounded in the distance as Abel walked through the abandoned rubble. Each stride increased his sense of victory. A cry from Tosh-ko-nay drew him to a large tipi in the center of the camp. Tossing the tent flap aside, Abel gasped. There in the semigloom lay the greatest prize of all— almost the entire winter food supply of Antelope's band! It was the most crushing defeat ever handed a Sioux war leader.

Abel emerged from the lodge as Robert Kirk and his squad trotted back into camp. To the south, the Shoshone, having promptly dispatched the horse guards, kept the ponies milling about in the center of the valley.

Sergeant Kirk swung down from his horse. "Looks like we kicked him a good one this time, Colonel," he said. "Every man, woman, and child had to bolt north to the higher ground, and there's only one place the rear guard could set up. Old Antelope's in for a cold night for sure."

Abel issued instructions rapidly, and soon the soldiers were moving into recently abandoned lodges. Everything the troops could not use—metal pots, lodge poles, extra tipis— became fuel for a raging fire in the middle of the camp.

Sure the activities of the soldiers were being watched from above, Abel made a great show of having half the food taken from the storage lodge and added to the flames.

As evening fell, the smell of bubbling stew drifted over the former Indian camp as the troops helped themselves to the first solid food they had enjoyed in days. The men laughed and joked as they warmed themselves by numerous small fires. In the center of the camp, the huge conflagration continued to blaze, consuming most of the worldly goods of Antelope's Santee Sioux band.

Hungrily digging a spoon into the rich dried-meat stew, Abel stared toward the north. He could almost feel the despair from the hills above. "I wouldn't be surprised if we had a visit from Antelope himself come dawn," he said to Kirk between bites. "That is one worried Sioux out there right now."

After a cozy night in Antelope's own lodge, warmed by the chief's robes and blankets, Abel stepped into the dawn of the new day refreshed. Despite the destruction of the previous evening, Abel was mildly astonished at the amount of food, robes, and clothing that remained. He was halfway through a rough inventory when Robert Kirk rode into camp, escorting a squat, solidly built Indian wearing the symbolic robe of a war chief.

"You figured right, Colonel," Kirk said. "He wants to parley."

Abel studied the outwardly calm features of the Santee Sioux. The nearly black eyes, however, showed a deep concern.

"Welcome," Abel said in the chief's own tongue. "If Antelope comes in peace, no harm will befall him. Come. We will talk."

The colonel did not wish to add further insult to Antelope by conducting the talks in the chief's own lodge. He led him instead to the nearly depleted food storage tipi. A small, smoky fire guttered in the dim light of the lodge. For a long time, neither man spoke. Finally Antelope broke the silence.

"The white soldier chief is like the wolf on the trail," Antelope said. "It seems Antelope has underestimated him. Perhaps he will tell why the people of Antelope's band have been touched by his anger?"

"Antelope and his warriors rode against the whites when the leaves last turned," Abel replied. "Now the hunter has become the hunted. The rabbit of autumn has turned to the mountain lion of winter."

"Does the lion of winter think the way to peace is to starve women and children?" Antelope asked.

Abel answered the challenge bluntly. "Does Antelope deny that while at the side of the blue-eyed one called Long Walker, his warriors lifted the scalps of many white women and children?"

Antelope could not deny the charge. "What has been has been," he said. "Now we must look to the future. Our women and children, our old ones will die for lack of food. There are few ponies for the hunt, only such blankets as were on our backs when the white soldiers struck."

The Santee paused for a moment. A quick flash of despair and defeat darkened the chief's face. "What is that which the white soldier chief seeks? What are his terms of surrender?"

Abel shook his head. "There will be no surrender, Antelope. However, the white man—unlike Long Walker—does not wish to make war on women and children. To the white man, a small life is a precious thing. His hearts are heavy that the Santee will starve before the spring grass comes."

Abel deliberately plucked a strip of dried meat from the

pile on a nearby rack, bit into it, and chewed thoughtfully. He tossed the strip of meat casually back onto the pile.

"There is a way for the Santee led by Antelope to survive," Abel said. "Not all the food, blankets, and lodges have been destroyed. Enough remains so that, with care, Antelope can keep his people alive long enough to reach the camp on the Niobrara River. There he can obtain supplies from the soldier chief at Fort Laramie."

"So it is surrender the white man seeks, then?" the Sioux asked.

Abel shook his head. "It is Antelope's choice to join those at peace or to ride out the winter and return to the warpath with Long Walker."

Antelope's shoulders slumped.

"Should Antelope choose the path of peace, he must first give his word he will not again raise the lance against the white m ," Abel said. "In exchange for this vow, one of every three ponies will be returned to him along with such food and blankets and lodges as remain in this camp.

"Antelope will show his intent to keep this pledge by having his braves surrender their rifles and pistols," Abel added. "One of every six braves will be allowed to keep his weapons for hunting purposes. Bows, arrows, and lances may be retained for protection. All the tribe's medicine symbols and holy objects will remain in the hands of the Santee."

Antelope pondered the terms; under the circumstances, they were more generous than he himself would have given, had he walked in the white chief's boots. "Agreed," he said.

Abel stood. "Then we welcome Antelope and his band in peace. Bring your people in from the hills."

A little later, sullen braves filed past one by one and dropped their weapons onto a growing stack at the edge of the camp. With more than passing interest, Abel noted that many of the rifles were new Henry .44 repeaters. Ammunition for them seemed plentiful among the Santee band. Now, Abel told himself, his own troops would be equipped with the deadly, rapid-fire weapons. The irony was not lost on him that the guns used such a short time ago against the whites now would be turned in the direction of warring bands of red men.

A long line of women and children filed by after the last of the braves. Some still showed the effects of the bitterly cold night they had just gone through. Abel was relieved that, while the nights ahead would be no picnic for them, they would not suffer as much.

Suddenly he cried out. With two quick strides he reached the Indian line and grasped the arm of a young girl.

Blond hair cascaded about her shoulders, her blue eyes were fearful. What stunned Abel was the captive girl's appearance.

He was looking at a twelve-year-old miniature of Judy!

Conflicting emotions tore Abel's heart. One part of him wanted to pull the girl to him, to hug her close. The other part wanted to strike her. Slowly it dawned on Abel that his reaction toward the girl was exactly his feeling toward Judy. He wanted to hit her, to punish her for the agonies she had caused him. And yet . . .

Abruptly he released the captive girl and turned his back. He heard her scurry back into line.

He muttered a sharp curse. "Let her go, Abel," he said to himself through clenched teeth. "She made her choice!" He could not bring himself to admit that, despite her infidelity and all that had happened, he still loved his wife very much.

Abel was unaware of Sergeant Kirk standing at his side until the non-com cleared his throat.

"Several captives in the band, Colonel. I see you just met one of them," Kirk said. "Do we take them with us?"

Abel shook his head. "They will be better off with Antelope than with us," he replied. "We have too many miles to cover, and we will likely be hurting worse from the cold than Antelope's band will be. Ted Henderson can sort out the captives once Antelope reaches the Niobrara."

"Yes, sir. Incidentally, Colonel, I've just finished an inventory of the captured weapons. Quite a haul. We came up with a couple dozen Henry rifles and more than six hundred rounds of ammunition for them."

"Distribute them to our best marksmen," Abel instructed. "Tell the troops to carry both the Spencers and the Henrys. If we run into a dogfight down the road, at least we'll have a little firepower to work with."

With a nod of agreement, the sergeant walked away to tend to the duties. He stopped at Abel's call.

"How long have we been in the field, Kirk?"

The sergeant's brows knit in thought for a moment. "I make it sixty-one, maybe sixty-two days."

Despite the brutal demands being made on both men and animals during the winter campaign, Abel sighed with relief that it would continue for several weeks. It was just that much longer before he had to return and face Judy—provided he did not catch an Indian arrow or bullet in the meantime. And so far he had been lucky. From a military standpoint the campaign was a success, and his own losses had been few.

"Sergeant," he said, "tell the men they have done a tremendous job—and to hang on a few weeks longer. With luck we should reach Fort Kearny by first grass, and then home to Laramie."

Ted Henderson carefully eased his left arm from its sling and tested the movement of his fingers. He was pleased with his physical progress. Just a few more days, he calculated, and he could once more be in the saddle for days at a time and carrying the case for peace to the Indians.

He pushed his chair away from the cluttered desk and wandered to the window. For a moment he imagined himself in the mountains, hearing the *crack* of tree limbs as they shattered in the bitter cold. Winter in the high country was a man's world, where survival was in his own hands and one lived with the land or died in it.

Sighing, Ted turned from the window and wondered if he would ever be free to ride the high country again. He settled back into his chair and attacked the pile of paperwork. It had become a constant struggle to keep people, both red and white, alive as the winter deepened. Yellow Crow, a single Spencer cartridge tucked into a pocket of his buckskin shirt as he had ridden from the fort, already had succeeded in convincing three more bands to settle on the Niobrara. The Cheyenne warrior had redoubled his own efforts after Ted's injury, and his work was paying off. Abel Hubbard also had contributed a substantial number of new mouths to feed.

Between the growing number of peaceful Indians and an increase in the flow of refugees into Fort Laramie—whites defeated not by Indians but by the Plains winter—Ted found himself hard pressed to keep adequate supplies flowing into the fort.

He had been forced to call repeatedly on his friendship with William Hepburn Russell. The Pony Express founder had responded with enthusiasm, and freight wagons from Russell, Majors and Waddell battled the elements to keep Laramie's demands at least partially satisfied. The War Department fussed about the expense, but with prodding they paid up.

A knock on the door interrupted Ted. He replaced his pen in the inkwell, welcoming a break from the endless stack of paperwork even if it meant trouble.

Taylor Elkins entered the office, grinning as he stripped off his gloves and blew on chilled fingers. "Sorry to interrupt, Colonel, but I just received some news I thought you should know firsthand."

Ted waved toward a chair by the fire. "Warm yourself, Taylor, and thanks for giving me a break from the desk. I think I was about to get what you newsmen call writer's cramp."

Taylor hitched the chair a few inches closer to the fire. "Good news from the war front," he said. "Sherman's punishing Georgia, and Grant's putting pressure on General Lee. My editors believe the war may be at an end in late winter or early spring."

Ted nodded in agreement; the military dispatches he had received indicated much the same. "It will be a relief to see it end," Ted said. "Too many good men on both sides have died."

Taylor produced a letter from a shirt pocket. "Closer to the home front," he said, "the Eastern press is becoming more and more vocal toward just settlements with the Indians. The interview I had with Colonel Carson during his stay here had quite an impact. I think people are beginning to see the man and his ideas, not some legend pulling the teeth out of a grizzly bear."

"That's good news, Taylor. Of course it's easier to be generous toward the red man when you've already pushed him far from your own front porch," Ted said wryly.

"True. Sympathy tends to build as the distance between reader and danger increases," Taylor agreed. "Also, there is quite a movement afoot to honor the memories of the men killed in the raid to free the children. Bernie Christian, in particular, seems to have captured everyone's imagination. *The Boston Herald* not only played the story on page one but also started a fund to erect a monument to his memory."

"Bernie was his own monument, Taylor," Ted said sadly. "But I'm glad to hear he won't be forgotten as so many fine men, soldier and civilian, have been."

Elkins sighed. "I just wish there was some way we could get word to Abel Hubbard about his wife's actions. Poor Judy has gone through a lifetime of torment, not knowing if her husband will ever know or understand why she acted as she did."

Ted gestured helplessly. "I've examined the possibilities and keep coming up with nothing. I don't even know where Abel's patrol is at the moment. According to the Indians who have come in as a result of his campaign, he seems to be everywhere at once. For the time being, I suppose all we can do is wait."

Elkins stood, tugging on his gloves. "There is one more thing I want to discuss with you, Ted, but I must inform someone else first."

Ted raised a quizzical eyebrow but did not press the point. As far as he was concerned, the man had earned the right to be as secretive as he wished. "Taylor, I've said it before, and I'll repeat it now. I'm in your debt, deeply. I can't place a value on my son's life, but if there is ever anything I can do for you, all you need do is ask."

Taylor merely smiled and, touching the brim of his derby in salute, let himself out the door. Shivering in the icy air, he patted the message tucked into his pocket and set out for the Laramie Hotel.

Vi Robinson was in the kitchen, testing the contents of a pot on the stove with a long wooden spoon. Her nose wrinkled in distaste. "No, no," Vi hastened to reassure the cook, who was crying in dismay, "the seasoning is fine. I just can't stand the taste of turnips."

"Then we should get along well, Vi," a voice behind her said.

Vi turned to face Taylor Elkins. "Good afternoon, Mr. Elkins," she said, her voice cool. "I'm sure you are aware that the kitchen is off limits to guests."

"I didn't come to sample the turnips, Vi," Taylor replied. "I came to see you—on a matter of considerable importance to both of us."

"Very well," Vi said with a sigh. "I suppose I can spare a few minutes. Come into my office, please."

Vi entered the tiny cubicle, then turned to face the journalist defiantly. "Well, what is it?"

"Vi, my work here is almost done—" he began.

"Good," she interrupted. "As soon as you move on, I'll feel better about having harbored a fugitive—"

"Shut up, Vi Robinson, and listen to me!" The sharp tone of Taylor's voice caught her by surprise.

"Things are not always as they seem," he said, his voice softening a bit. "I am no fugitive from justice, Vi. I never have been. That newspaper story you found in my suitcase was a deliberate falsification."

"But—what—?"

Taylor raised a hand. "Hear me out, and then I'll answer any questions you might have. I couldn't tell you before, no matter how much it hurt us both. From the start, I knew Judy was on to something, and she was the best lead I had. Now that my complete report has been received and confirmed in Washington, my previous restraints are lifted."

He plucked the message from his pocket, the first hint of a smile touching his lips. He tapped the paper against the palm of a hand. "Vi, I am—was, I should say—an operative, a spy if you wish, for the Union. Until this morning." He flipped open the paper and read from it. ". . . Your resignation is accepted with regret and with gratitude for long and meritorious service." Taylor handed her the paper. "Read it for yourself if you wish, Vi."

She took the paper in trembling fingers but did not look at the document. "But, Taylor—the newspaper story—"

"A simple plant," he said casually. "The whole thing was made up, staged, for the benefit of the Confederate agents in Baltimore. Somehow they stumbled upon the identity of one of our best operatives in the Baltimore area. More than just the agent's life was in danger; he knew intricate details of the network it took us so long to set up. We could not afford to let him fall into Confederate hands."

Taylor reached out and placed a hand on Vi's arm. "I was working the Boston docks at the time," he said. "As far as we could determine, the Confederate spies had no line on me. So it was a simple, and effective, matter for me to pick a pretend quarrel with our own agent over a girl in a house of ill repute. We suspected she was one of the Southern connections and discovered later we were correct. That's why our man was there in the first place.

"The 'duel' was, of course, rigged from the start. The man who 'fell dead' is now safely abroad. In France, I believe. But the Confederates saw the duel. They saw the 'victim' in a casket, and they saw a casket buried—with a hundred-sixty pounds of sand nailed tightly inside. A skipper on a French schooner hired a new able seaman and hoisted canvas the following day."

"But, Taylor—if they had seen, then why the story?"

"Ah, my sweet little Vi," Taylor said, smiling, "not a suspicious bone in your body—which, incidentally, is a rather nice one. At any rate, the story was planted to confirm what the agents had seen. Dueling is quite illegal in Baltimore. Even murder is frowned upon there. Very staid city." Taylor sighed. "Had something not appeared in the local press about the incident, the Reb operatives would certainly have noticed the omission and become suspicious."

Taylor steered a visibly shaken Vi to the chair behind the desk and stood at her side, a hand resting affectionately on her shoulder. "Obviously," he continued, "I had to be sent from the East immediately or risk being lost as an operative to prison."

Vi looked up at him, mist beginning to form in her eyes. "So they sent you here."

Taylor nodded. "We knew the Confederacy had an operative—perhaps more than one—in the Plains, keeping the Indians supplied with arms and stirred up by the scent of war. With Judy's help, I found the major connection. Calvin Winston and the blue-eyed Indian, Long Walker."

Vi was sure the pounding of her heart was audible throughout the room. She handed the unread message back to Taylor, her fingers still trembling. "But—but why keep the clipping? Isn't it a danger to you?"

Taylor smiled gently. "It was my final escape route. Had my identity been discovered, I would have simply produced the clipping and 'confessed.'"

"And spent the remainder of the war safely behind bars," Vi concluded, the final piece of the puzzle dropping into place. Then the emotional dam finally burst, and Vi threw herself into Taylor's arms. "Oh, Taylor," she gasped between sobs of joy, "I should never have doubted you—"

He patted her reassuringly as he tightened their embrace. "You had every reason, Vi," he said quietly. "You've been hurt twice by the loss of a loved one and twice more over the last few months by Judy and by me. I'm only sorry you had to suffer. I wanted to tell you sooner, but circumstances wouldn't permit it."

Taylor placed a gentle finger under her chin and lifted her tearstained face. "The only thing I'm guilty of, Vi Robinson, is love—for my cause, my country, and you." He kissed her softly. "Now," he said, breaking their embrace and holding her at arm's length, "will you reconsider my proposal of marriage? We wouldn't even have to leave Laramie. I can write from here as well as from anywhere."

Vi hurled herself back into his arms. "Yes, Taylor. My God, yes!"

Her tears were soaking his shirt, but Taylor Elkins did not mind in the least. "In the spring, as originally planned?" He felt her nod against his chest. He sighed. "It's going to be a long few weeks," Taylor said quietly.

Wind Flower gently kneed her big horse around the deeper snowdrifts, tightening her grip on the shotgun that rested across the crook of an elbow as she glanced from time to time at the freshening sign. The big cat's tracks were unmistakable, one front paw dragging, rather than stepping, through the new-fallen snow.

The blizzard had broken shortly after dawn, and the wind had dropped. Wind Flower no longer felt its bite through her tightly woven blankets. Not even the great stealth of the mountain lion could conceal its passage through the fresh snow. Twice the beast had successfully claimed a new calf from the O'Reilly ranch. But this morning its luck had failed before the sharp, upturned horns of a determined mother cow.

Wind Flower called out in Navajo, and Toby, the mongrel dog, stopped and waited for her to ride alongside. The tracks of the cat, and Toby's raised hackles, left no doubt in Wind Flower's mind that the mountain lion was nearby. She checked her mount and studied the terrain ahead with care. At the horse's side the dog growled, an eager, throaty rumble.

Despite the chill of the air, Wind Flower slipped the blankets from her shoulders and draped them across the horse's withers. When the encounter came, the colorful blankets would not interfere with her movements. For an instant she glanced back toward the south, wishing Kevin were with her. But the two had ridden in opposite directions, Kevin to the south and Wind Flower to the north.

Wind Flower knew she had ridden past their northern boundary onto Newkirk property, but she could not abandon the trail. The cat had taken more than its share.

She kicked the horse back into motion. The gelding snorted nervously, and Wind Flower knew the scent of the lion was strong in the horse's sensitive nostrils. The dog's teeth were bared, sinewy muscles rippling under its short hair. "Quiet, Toby," she said in her native tongue. The dog stopped growling, but its muscles continued to quiver in the excitement of the hunt.

The gelding picked its way through a tangle of fallen trees into a wide clearing and suddenly snorted, fidgeting nervously. In the center of the clearing, a small figure crouched on hands and knees, frozen in terror. Wind Flower immediately recognized the small figure—Dot and Earl Newkirk's daughter. Somehow she had strayed almost a mile, alone, from the safety of the Newkirk house.

On the far side of the clearing, a tawny hide suddenly flashed in the underbrush. The big cat! And the young girl was its prey!

Wind Flower was wise to the ways of the great cats and knew that only an agonizing hunger would drive the beast beyond its ingrained fear of the smell of a human. She also knew that any sudden movement would send the cat into flight—or into attack.

Slowly and deliberately, Wind Flower dismounted and ground-hitched the horse, then cocked both barrels of her shotgun.

She spoke quietly to the dog, hoping to calm his instinct to attack. Toby was a powerful animal, but one swipe from the cat's deadly claws would kill him. Still, Wind Flower knew she would not hesitate to order Toby forward if the choice came down to the young girl or the dog.

Carefully placing her feet, Wind Flower started making her way toward the small form in the middle of the clearing. She felt rather than saw the yellow eyes of the big cat in the underbrush beyond. A dozen strides from the girl she stopped.

"Do not fear, child," she said in English, her tone soothing.

The girl looked around sharply, startled at the sound of a human voice.

"Do not move, child!" Wind Flower called. "Stay perfectly still!"

Shuffling through the snow, Wind Flower placed her body

between the girl and the spot where she had glimpsed the mountain lion. Six feet away, Toby crept forward, belly on the snow, teeth bared once more. Wind Flower could almost sense the turmoil in the great beast across the clearing—the drive of starvation battling against its natural fear of man and dog.

Then the brush parted, and the huge cat stepped into the clearing. Its ribs showed tight against the shrunken skin, the yellow eyes were glazed, its tail twitched ominously.

"Oh, great cat of the mountain, hear me," Wind Flower called in Navajo. "Your heart is strong, your courage great. Wind Flower shares your suffering, the pain in your belly. Once you were a great hunter, ruler of mountains. Now your medicine has left you. Old and crippled and tired, your reign as king has ended."

The cat's big head swung from side to side, looking first at the woman, then at the dog crouched near her.

"Perhaps the spirit of Wind Flower's father guides you toward an end to your misery, for his bones now lie in the cave of your brother in a far distant place."

The mountain lion lowered itself almost onto its belly. Soon, Wind Flower knew, it would spring.

She swung the shotgun into line and called above the barrels: "Do not fear death, great one, for your offspring bear your blood—the blood of kings."

The mountain lion seemed to gather itself, then it soared in the air, leaping toward Wind Flower. She fired, and the big cat tumbled to the snow. It struggled to its feet and snapped at its own ribs where the buckshot had hit it.

The wounded cat collected itself as if to spring once more. Wind Flower pulled the second trigger—and heard only a flat *click* as the hammer fell. Her heart skipped a beat when she glanced down at the weapon. The cap had somehow fallen from its nipple above the deadly powder charge.

"Toby! Now!" Wind Flower yelled. The mongrel dog's charge was a blur in the corner of her eye as Wind Flower's fingers probed her pocket for a spare cap. The injured cat twisted to meet its new assailant, slapped with a front paw, and missed. Toby's solid body rammed into the cougar, his powerful jaws ripping at the cat's shoulder. The attack sent the cat onto its side, spilling Toby free of the thrashing claws. The dog whirled and crouched on his belly, waiting for another opening to attack.

After what seemed forever, Wind Flower finally found the cap, eased back the shotgun hammer, and dropped the new ignition primer into place. She swung the weapon against her shoulder and yelled, "Toby! Back!"

For a split second the dog paused, torn between his desire for battle and the sound of his mistress's voice. Then he whirled away from the crouched lion.

Wind Flower squeezed the trigger. The big cat leaped into the air as its muscles convulsed, then fell heavily into the snow.

The cat raised its head and looked at Wind Flower with eyes beginning to glaze in death. "May you find peace in the otherworld, spirit brother," the Navajo woman intoned. The cougar's head dropped.

Wind Flower quickly reloaded the shotgun, then turned to the wide-eyed girl behind her.

"It is all right now, little one," she said, gathering the girl to her in a reassuring embrace. "You are safe. The great cat is dead."

Tears tumbled down the young girl's cheeks. "I—went out to—get wood. Got lost—in snow," she sobbed. "Couldn't—see—house."

Wind Flower lifted the girl and carried her to the nervously stomping horse nearby. She calmed the gelding, then wrapped the girl snugly in one of the blankets before placing her on the horse.

"Come, Toby!" she called.

The dog abandoned its watchful post near the dead cougar and trotted obediently to Wind Flower. She was relieved to find Toby was uninjured except for one small scratch along a hip, which had stopped bleeding already. She grasped the dog's ears and shook his head affectionately from side to side. "You are a brave one," she said in Navajo before mounting her horse.

"Come, child. It is time you went home to your mother and father and a warm fire. It is over now. Do you have a name by which I might call you?"

The girl's sobs of terror and relief had subsided into an occasional hiccup. "I'm Nancy."

"It is a nice name," Wind Flower said, kicking the gelding into motion toward the Newkirk ranch.

They were still twenty yards from the front door when

Dot Newkirk, tears streaming down her thin face, reached up to take Nancy from Wind Flower's arms. Earl Newkirk arrived moments later, having spotted the two figures on horseback as he topped a nearby hill in a fruitless search for his missing daughter.

Finally Dot looked up into Wind Flower's eyes. "It—it's a miracle, no less," she stammered. "We thought—we'd never see her alive again." Dot placed a trembling hand on Wind Flower's knee. "Is there—any way we can ever—repay you?"

Wind Flower smiled gently. "It is enough that the child is safe." Nancy solemnly removed the Navajo blanket and returned it to Wind Flower. Wind Flower shook her head. "You keep it, Nancy," she said. "It is your medicine blanket now. It will keep you safe in the nighttime, and one day it will protect your children as well. It also will remind you not to stray too far from safety in a snowstorm."

Dot Newkirk, touched by Wind Flower's gesture, nodded to her daughter it was all right to accept the gift. To Wind Flower she said, "In the past I treated you real bad. You didn't deserve that. I see it now. Wind Flower, if you'll forgive me for my mistakes, I'd be honored to call you my friend."

The Navajo woman smiled. "It is good," she said, "for I have always considered you a friend." She refused an invitation to come inside. "It is late, and I must be returning soon, for Kevin will worry. Perhaps another time I might visit—and hold the baby?"

Too full of emotion to speak, Dot could only nod. "Our house is open to you and Kevin at any time," Earl Newkirk said.

Wind Flower reined her horse back toward home, with Toby trotting alongside. Dot and Earl Newkirk, standing on either side of Nancy and hugging her tightly, watched until Wind Flower had passed from sight.

"I reckon I was wrong," Dot Newkirk said quietly. "Looks like they's some good Injuns after all."

Long Walker sat disgusted in his solitary overnight camp on the downwind side of a ragged bluff. The half-cooked prairie hen that had been his supper sat heavily in his stomach.

He cursed bitterly in the white man's tongue. He had found English to be the most expressive of languages when it came to giving vent to darker emotions. And Long Walker had reason to be displeased.

Since the failed kidnap attempt, the blue-eyed Indian had found himself in a difficult round of diplomatic talks in an effort simply to hang on to what support he had. The Sioux Crazy Dogs, badly battered in the encounter with the scouts, had almost revolted against his leadership. They had lost fifty warriors in the clash in the canyon, an unacceptable figure for even their militant warrior society.

And now this latest round of failures, Long Walker thought, rage glowing in his face. Six camps he had visited; five times he had failed to recruit more warriors. Always it was the same story. The Cheyenne Yellow Crow had been there first, an eloquent spokesman for peace. Even Ted Henderson had returned to the field, only three weeks after catching an arrow in the battle at the pass. It seemed to Long Walker that where Yellow Crow had not been lately, Ted Henderson had.

The peace movement adherents were becoming more vocal, and Long Walker knew a great deal of that enthusiasm came from the constant pressure of the Laramie subchief Abel Hubbard and his handful of bluecoats. Their latest strike had cost him Antelope, one of his most valued lieutenants.

Long Walker picked up a stone and hurled it angrily. "Let Antelope turn into a tame Indian if he wants to be a squaw. No squaws ride with Long Walker," he growled.

Privately he admitted the courage of the soldier chiefs Henderson and Hubbard and the Cheyenne Yellow Crow. While the Indians huddled about campfires and waited for first grass, those three were in the saddle. Long Walker had managed to incite one band of Arapaho into a string of winter raids, but the string snapped under a surprise attack by Henderson's crack troops known as R Company. Since then, not one band—even the Cheyenne Dog Soldiers—would talk of winter raids.

Perhaps, Long Walker thought with distaste, that was one reason the white tide was so difficult to turn. The red man still saw war as a game to be played on warm and sunny days. The white man did not care about the weather. He simply waged war.

Long Walker sighed deeply. He had known it would not be easy and had anticipated complications along the way. He had gained little ground during the winter, but on the whole he had not lost that much, either. Sitting Bull and Big Nose still were uncommitted, waiting to see how the winds of springtime blew. Other, less powerful, chiefs followed their example. Long Walker pulled his buffalo robe tighter against the growing cold. At least, he thought, a few things were working in his favor.

The fall of the Confederacy, which he saw as inevitable, was one such thing. The white man always took a long time to shift his armies from one battlefield to another. Even without the warriors of Sitting Bull and Big Nose, Long Walker had enough braves to gain his foothold on the empire of the Plains before the Eastern bluecoats drifted west.

Secondly, signs of spring were pushing against the grip of winter. Already where the snows had receded, tender young grass showed green in the lower meadows. Soon the Plains would once more nourish the weakened ponies of the Indians. Then he would loose his braves on the outnumbered soldiers and settlers.

And finally, if he had learned nothing else about the white man, he had discovered one thing—given enough time, someone would do something stupid. And all he needed to unite the Plains tribes was one simple act of stupidity by the white man.

The coming of spring brought an almost festive spirit to the community of Laramie. Isolated patches of snow still nestled in shaded areas, but spring became a fact on a sunwashed morning in early April. Little Ellen Keller, returning from a pony ride with William Ted under the watchful eyes of Carl Keller and Ted Henderson, proudly clutched the first wildflower of the season she had plucked from a nearby meadow.

Wilma Henderson's spirits lifted as she sniffed the mild fragrance of the bloom. She fell into step with the horsemen as they headed for the stables. The two children, she thought with relief, continued to show no ill effects from their ordeal at the Indian camp or their traumatic rescue.

She saw Ted wince as he pulled the saddle from his horse. Certain movements still strained his shoulder, though the wound was knitting nicely.

As the riders cared for their animals and equipment, Wilma waved to the couple across the street. Sergeant Major Albert Jonas, on Sally's arm, walked slowly and stiffly. From a distance, the giant soldier seemed but a shadow of his former self. His severe wounds and the slow, painful recuperation would have drained the spirit of a lesser man. Even though Jonas could not function as an active soldier, Ted had extended his enlistment for six months to keep the sergeant major on the army payroll during his recovery.

Ted emerged from the stable and took Wilma's arm in his as the two youngsters raced off to play with friends nearby. Strolling leisurely down the bustling Laramie street, Wilma studied her husband's face. There seemed to be a growing tension in Ted, she thought.

On impulse, Wilma hugged her husband's arm. "Spring is such a wonderful time of the year, darling," she said. "It's like the earth is coming out of hibernation and is ready to burst into new life."

Ted sighed. "I only wish I could share your enthusiasm, dear," he said. "I certainly don't want to dampen your spirits, but I'm worried. This could turn out to be a nasty season—a soldier's spring. It won't be long until the grass has grown enough to put the Indian ponies back into shape, and I'm afraid we haven't seen the last of Long Walker and his bunch."

"I know," Wilma said solemnly. "It's just so difficult to think of war on such a lovely day. And you and Yellow Crow have worked so hard for peace. . . ."

"And we still have much to do," Ted added as Wilma's voice trailed off. "I'll be riding out again in a few days."

Vi Robinson and Judy almost bumped into the Hendersons as they emerged from a store, each with wrapped bundles.

Once more Wilma was struck by the contrast between Vi and her stepdaughter. Vi seemed almost bouncy, younger than her years. The normally lively Judy looked subdued and pale, a haunted, anxious look in her eyes.

"Good morning, Vi—Judy," Ted said, touching his hat brim. "How's the soon-to-be bride?" he asked, smiling at Vi.

"Getting more nervous by the day," she replied, her cheeks slightly flushed. "You would think after going through this twice, I'd be a bit more organized."

"Ted, is there any more word of Abel?" Judy asked anxiously.

Ted shook his head slowly. "I'm sorry, Judy. We still don't know where he is. All we know is where he's been, and that information comes rather late, from Indians who have come to plead for peace. I'm sure he's all right," Ted added, trying to sound reassuring. "Abel can handle himself in the wilderness."

Not wishing to compound Judy's heavy burden of worry, Ted refrained from mentioning his own concern. When hostilities began, as they surely must, Abel could be caught afield and unaware with only a sixty-man force. Ted could only hope that Abel and his patrol might reach the safety of a fort somewhere along their line of march before the Indians could strike.

"Would you two join us for coffee?" Wilma asked hopefully.

Vi shook her head. "We still have a lot to do before the wedding. I'm afraid I've let my wardrobe slide badly. One moth-eaten flannel nightgown doesn't seem to be adequate to start a new life with."

Ted grinned at Vi's blush. "I'm sure Taylor wouldn't mind one bit, Vi. Another time, perhaps, for coffee?"

With a brisk nod, Vi led Judy on down the street.

"I certainly hope this marriage works out better for Vi; she's suffered so much in the past," Wilma said, watching the retreating figures. She tugged at Ted's arm. "Come on, Colonel, let's enjoy your rare day off duty."

Ted's day off came to an abrupt end at midafternoon with a knock on their door. A grinning Lieutenant David Wills stood in the doorway, a piece of paper trembling in his excited fingers.

"This just came in by telegraph, sir," Wills said. "General Lee has surrendered to General Grant at Appomattox! The Confederacy has fallen! The war is over!"

Wilma gasped in astonishment. "Is it true, David? Really true? The terrrible thing is finally finished?"

"Yes, ma'am," Wills said. "It's finally over." He handed the message to Ted. The news came as no real surprise to Ted, who had been kept informed daily on the war's progress by Taylor Elkins. Yet the final reality still came as something of a shock. For a moment he stared silently at the dispatch, then sighed. "America's biggest mistake has finally been resolved," he said quietly. "Inform the troops, David, and spread the word in the civilian sector. I expect there will be a wild celebration in Laramie today."

"Yes, Colonel. It will be my pleasure." Wills turned toward the door.

"David?"

The lieutenant paused and looked back. "Yes, sir?"

"I'm afraid you and I won't be celebrating with the rest. Will you please report to me in an hour at my office?"

"Certainly, sir," he said, closing the door behind him.

Wilma was instantly in Ted's arms. "Ted, I can hardly believe it!" she said. "It seemed that dreadful war would last forever!"

"It did, Wilma. For thousands of people, civilians and soldiers, it literally has been an eternity. My God, so many needless deaths . . ." he said sadly.

Outside, a rifle discharged, and a soldier whooped in joy. Within minutes, Laramie was in bedlam. As Wilma left in search of their son, Ted changed into his uniform and made his way through the yelling throng to his office.

The lieutenant already was there, awaiting Ted's arrival. Wills's smile faded as he greeted his commanding officer.

"Sir," Wills said, "you don't seem very pleased that we've won."

"Nobody won this war, David," Ted replied sharply. "The wounds will last for generations and may never heal. But now we have problems of our own, I'm afraid."

"Sir?"

"Unless I'm a failure as a student of human nature, we are looking at some big Indian troubles soon. The majority of our troops, at Laramie and other frontier forts, are volunteers. I expect many of them will want to go home and pick up the pieces of their interrupted lives."

Wills began to understand. "That means—"

"That we will be undermanned for quite some time. For the moment, the War Department and the nation as a whole will have forgotten the frontier. We can't expect regular troop reinforcements for some time. In short, Lieutenant, we're on our own against some of the finest fighters the world has ever seen."

A knock at the door cut through the shouts and gunshots outside. A young private entered and saluted nervously.

"Lieutenant Wills," the private said, "my enlistment was up last week—and, well, sir, I'd like to go home now."

The lieutenant glanced at Ted, who merely nodded.

"Very well," the lieutenant said. "Report to the quarter-master and draw your pay."

"Yes, sir," the private said, twisting his campaign hat in

nervous hands. "I—I'm sorry, sir, but I have a farm and a family—"

"No need to apologize," Wills said. "We have no intention of holding you hostage. I assume there are others who want to go home?"

"Yes, sir. Quite a few, Lieutenant."

"Then," Ted said, his voice even and matter-of-fact, "I would recommend that those who intend to leave band together and travel as a group. There may be Indian trouble ahead. Anyone who does not have private weapons may draw from the quartermaster's excess of old Springfields. I would hate to see men who have fought well die on the way home from lack of protection."

"Yes, sir," the private said. "Thank you. May I be dismissed now?"

Ted looked at Wills as the door closed behind the ex-soldier. "He was just the first. There will be many more, probably even a number of regular army enlistees." Ted sank into the chair behind his cluttered desk. "How about you, David? You're regular army and a Point graduate, but as you told the private, I'll hold no hostages."

The young man shook his head firmly. "I'm staying, Colonel, until you kick me bodily off the post or I get orders to report elsewhere."

The next few days were hectic ones for Laramie. Ted's pessimistic forecast proved to be uncomfortably accurate as the ranks of blue at Fort Laramie dwindled daily. Ted was pleased that only two men from R Company requested discharge, both with good reason and great reluctance.

Finally the last tally was in. Laramie's active force had been reduced by more than a third. And, Ted grumbled to himself, it had been too small a force to begin with. He signed the last of the discharge papers on his desk, flexed the aching muscles in his writing hand, and dug his knuckles into his tired eyes. As he prepared to go home, he glanced at the calendar tacked to the wall. It was April 15, 1865.

Stepping through the office door, Ted heard a metallic chatter from the small dispatch office next door. At least the telegraph was not out for long this time, he thought.

Wilma brushed a bit of soil from her skirt, her muscles protesting the day's work in the refugee's community garden plot, and pushed open the door of their home.

She was alarmed at the sight that greeted her. Ted leaned against the fireplace, his head bowed, one hand resting on the bronze statue of the Pony Express rider beside the framed letter from President Lincoln saluting Ted's service to the Pony Express and the nation. His shoulders were slumped in defeat, a scrap of paper clutched in his free hand.

Wilma raced across the room. "Ted—what is it? What's wrong?"

Slowly he turned to face her, tears in his eyes. He weakly waved the scrap of paper.

"President Lincoln is dead," he said, his voice choked with emotion. "He was shot by a crazed actor at a theater last night. He died this morning."

"Oh, my God," Wilma whispered, gathering Ted in her arms. She knew of her husband's deep affection for the tall, bearded man who despite his hectic schedule had managed to find the time to write personal letters. Ted was banking heavily on the President's lenient attitude toward a peaceful settlement with the Indians as outlined in his latest letter.

"Darling—I'm so sorry," she said through her own tears. "We've lost—a good friend."

Finally Ted regained his composure. "The South, and possibly the Indians, have lost a friend as well," he said. "Andrew Johnson is now President. Who knows what his Indian policy will be?"

The news of Lincoln's assassination plunged Laramie into a state of mourning. Ted made his way to his office the next morning, his mood as black as the bunting draped over many of the settlement's buildings.

Sorting through the messages that had come in during the night, he found that telegraphs did not always bring bad news. The military authorities had approved his recommendation that David Wills be promoted from lieutenant to captain, with brevet rank elevation to major. At least now, in Abel's absence, he had a competent field officer of substantial rank.

"I wish the news could have come at a happier time for us all, David," Ted said, after informing the officer of his sudden, two-rank jump.

Wills, still somewhat stunned at the news of Lincoln's death, solemnly agreed. "I'll try to wear the rank well, Colonel," he said as Ted pinned the new insignia on his uniform.

Ted clapped him lightly on the shoulder. "There's no doubt in my mind that you will, Major," he said.

Ted's mood brightened in midafternoon as he saw a familiar figure on a big palomino gelding enter the fort gate. He hurried to greet Yellow Crow warmly. "It is good to see you again, brother," Ted said, grasping the Cheyenne's forearm. "Come. Wilma and your godson have been pestering me to death about when you would return."

Yellow Crow was almost knocked over by the enthusiastic greeting from Wild Bill. After a few moments of small talk in several different tongues, Yellow Crow shook his head at a question from William Ted.

"Not have time to ride pony today," he told the boy in English. "Need big medicine tonight. Maybe tomorrow Yellow Crow have own squaw, not need kidnap Henderson woman."

Grinning, Yellow Crow teased, "Wilma need close mouth or catch many flies." Briefly he recounted the proposal he had made to the young Blackfoot captive. "Tonight Yellow Crow get answer," he added. "Little worry, much nervous."

Riding once more toward the fort gates, Yellow Crow twisted in the saddle to wave at the Hendersons, then settled in for the tense trip to Black Kettle's village and Talking Bird's answer.

The evening fires had been banked in the village when Yellow Crow paused to pay his respects to the Cheyenne chief. As quickly as possible, he was standing before the dark-eyed Blackfoot woman. "The time has come to choose, Talking Bird," he said calmly.

Talking Bird's eyes sparkled as she let the silence drag on for several heartbeats. Yellow Crow felt a growing sense of dismay when she did not speak. Then she smiled.

"While Yellow Crow was gone from Black Kettle's camp, Talking Bird gave him much thought," she said. "Talking Bird then put hands to work. At edge of Black Kettle's camp stands new lodge." She knelt and picked up a bundle from beside the flap of the tipi. "We go there now. Yellow Crow and Talking Bird have long life together, many sons, if spirits so will."

Suddenly feeling nine feet tall, Yellow Crow followed his bride to their new lodge.

Two miles south of the Overland Stage Route, a lean man in the buckskins of a scout reined his horse to a stop at the front of a long column of armed men.

"Colonel Church," the scout said, "'bout nine miles north of Fort Kearny there must be near onto a thousand Injuns. They's painted for war. Sioux, Cheyenne, handful of Arapaho, and Ute. You wanta fight Injuns, here's a chance to come out a hero fer sure." The scout nodded toward the artillery unit nearby. "Them four big guns can handle a mess of redskins, and I reckon as to how the commander at Kearny could use a hero pretty quick."

Colonel Emery Church tongued his stub of a cigar from one side of his mouth to the other and fixed the scout with an icy stare. "Weaver," he said, "I don't give a tinker's damn about Fort Kearny. Let the commander there stomp his own snakes. You just find us a way to get through without getting jumped by some renegade Indians. It's Laramie I want!"

"Hell, Colonel, the only Injuns close to Laramie is Black Kettle's bunch. Tame Injuns," Weaver explained.

Church spat the cigar stub at the scout's feet. "Don't you know by now, there are no tame Indians? One redskin's no different than any other. You get me safely to Black Kettle's camp, and I'll show those pompous asses in Washington how to handle Indians!"

Weaver snorted in disgust. "I hired on with this outfit to find Injuns, not run from 'em. Reckon you best find yourself another scout, Colonel."

"I don't suppose a thousand-dollar bonus would change your mind?" Church asked, his face darkening.

The scout eyed the fox-faced officer for a long moment. Then he sighed. "I reckon it might," he said. "You want Laramie, by God, you'll get Laramie!"

"That's what I want, Weaver. Lock, stock, and scalp."

As the scout yanked his horse about, Emery Church fingered the letter in his jacket pocket. The big shots would not go along with the lieutenant governor's request to relieve Henderson, he thought, but it was not that hard to forge a set of orders.

Church stared hard toward the northwest. "By damn," he muttered. "Henderson, I'll have you out on your butt within a week—and a pile of scalps stirrup-high to boot."

Ten

Yellow Crow awoke refreshed and relaxed in the predawn darkness. He lay for a long moment, wide awake and luxuriating in the warmth from the body beside him. Talking Bird's delicate hand rested lightly on Yellow Crow's hip, the gentle touch a sharp contrast to the intensity of their lovemaking the previous evening.

The Cheyenne warrior smiled in the darkness of his new lodge. It was said, he thought, that the Blackfoot tribe boasted the most beautiful women of all the Indians, and that reputation was certainly not endangered by the young woman at his side. Over the past few days as they had grown to know each other, Yellow Crow felt his heart grow warmer by the hour. For the first time in years, he felt complete. And he knew now what had been missing from his life. The love of a woman.

Gently, so as not to disturb her even, deep breathing, he lifted her hand from his hip and slid from beneath the blankets. He pulled on his lightweight buckskins and slipped silently from the lodge.

Black Kettle's village had not yet begun to stir. Almost seven hundred Indians, sheltered in more than a hundred lodges, dozed in the comforting sands of the South Platte river bend. Yellow Crow breathed the cool springtime air deeply, then strode toward the nearby grassy meadow where his palomino gelding had been tethered for the night. The horse greeted him with a soft snuffle.

Slipping the rope hackamore about the animal's head, Yellow Crow glanced toward the lightening eastern sky. Above the horse's withers he glimpsed something, a movement in the shadows of a low bluff overlooking the Indian camp. Curiosity quickly gave way to alarm as individual figures began to take shape in the distant darkness.

Mounted men were approaching the camp. Soldiers! Yellow Crow knew this was no unit from Fort Laramie, for Ted Henderson had left orders the camp was to be approached only in daytime to avoid frightening the women and children. And the approaching force was too large to have been dispatched from Laramie. With a growing sense of urgency, he swung aboard the palomino's broad back and kneed the horse toward Black Kettle's lodge.

Glancing once more toward the east, Yellow Crow caught his breath. In the growing dawn a single shadow detached itself from the main body—a cannon!

Yellow Crow suddenly kicked the palomino into a run and after covering a couple of hundred yards yanked the animal to a sliding stop before Black Kettle's lodge.

"Black Kettle!" Yellow Crow called, dismounting and dashing into the chief's lodge with no other greeting. "Soldiers come. They have cannon! They are going to attack!"

The broad-faced chief climbed from his blankets, smiling and unconcerned. "They do not attack, Yellow Crow," Black Kettle said. "We are peaceful. The soldiers know this."

"These are not soldiers from Laramie," Yellow Crow emphasized. "They are going to fire on this camp!"

Black Kettle sighed. "Yellow Crow is seeing demons in the night," he said heavily, "yet Black Kettle will take precautions. He will raise the American flag above his lodge, with a white flag beneath it. Then they will know the village is friendly."

Yellow Crow glared at the chief in increasing anger and frustration. "Black Kettle trusts too much," he said. "If the chief will take no other action, Yellow Crow will." He spun on a heel and sprinted from the lodge.

"Soldiers come!" he called, mounting and yanking the palomino toward his own lodge. "Take up your weapons! Prepare to fight!"

Cheyenne warriors emerged from lodges, some clutching bows or rifles, others milling about in confusion. At Yellow Crow's shouted instructions, a number of the braves began racing toward the eastern edge of the camp to set up a defensive line. Yellow Crow raced toward his own tipi, calling Talking Bird's name. "Run, woman!" he barked as he scooped up his Spencer rifle and ammunition pouch. "Run back upstream! Take nothing with you! Quickly!"

Talking Bird did not stop to argue or ask questions. She leaped from the comfort of her blankets, threw on a buffalo skin robe, and dashed away, pausing only long enough to scoop a bewildered and crying child into her arms.

At that instant the first cannon shell burst in the center of Black Kettle's camp. Bodies were tossed into the air like small dolls. A grape canister shell spewed its deadly contents through one edge of the Indian camp. Cries of shock and pain erupted beneath the barrage as stunned women and children began to dash about aimlessly, their screams adding to the confusion.

Yellow Crow heard Talking Bird's voice shouting instructions as she attempted to organize the flight of the women and children to safety. He forced back the almost overpowering urge to go protect her. The defense of the camp came first.

As hooves thundered toward the village, Yellow Crow and a score of Cheyenne braves dug in to meet the charge. Yellow Crow's rifle slammed against his shoulder, and a rider tumbled over the rump of his horse. Then the other Cheyenne were firing, fighting with the determination of men who would die if their deaths bought time for the women and children to escape.

Something slammed into Yellow Crow's side, the impact half turning him and knocking his breath away. He glanced down and saw a spreading stain beneath his left arm. Yellow Crow braced himself for the pain he knew was to come. Next to him a warrior grunted and pitched forward into the sand. Yellow Crow became aware that fewer and fewer shots were being fired from the Cheyenne defensive line, yet the cavalry rush faltered. The braves had bought a few precious moments. But Yellow Crow knew the charge would resume and their position would be overwhelmed.

He shouted above the rattle of gunfire, "Retreat! Fall back to the sand pits on the river!"

Of the twenty braves who had rushed to defend the camp, only six remained to scramble back toward the village. The cannon continued to roar, their muzzles shifted from the camp itself toward the mass of Indians fleeing up the riverbed. The lance of pain in his side was but a mosquito bite compared to the ache in Yellow Crow's heart as he kneed his palomino through the wrecked camp. Bodies of men, women, and children lay tossed about. The cries of the wounded came from all directions.

Yellow Crow slammed his heels into the gelding trying to blot from his mind the destruction of what had been a village of peaceful Indians slumbering in a spring dawn.

The cannon fire abruptly ceased as Yellow Crow broke free of the west side of the decimated camp. The absence of the big guns' roar added an even more ominous note to the battle—when the cannon stopped, soldiers could not be far behind. Slugs cracked the air about Yellow Crow's head, and once the palomino stumbled, sending a flash of dread through the Cheyenne. But the animal had not been hit; it regained its footing and settled into a run, opening the distance between Yellow Crow and the pursuing soldiers.

He pulled the horse to a stop and dismounted at the first row of rifle pits dug into the sands of the South Platte. Crooked Stick, from whom he had purchased his new bride, was in the front of the rearguard unit, squinting down the barrel of an ancient muzzle-loader. Blood streamed from a gash alongside Crooked Stick's head.

"Talking Bird! Have you seen her?" Yellow Crow asked as he thumbed fresh cartridges into the Spencer.

Crooked Stick numbly shook his head.

Then the first of the soldiers, most on foot, poured into the riverbed. Crooked Stick's old rifle belched smoke, and a soldier fell. It was the opening shot of the last desperate stand of some forty braves determined to hold the attackers at bay until the women and children reached the relative safety of the hills to the northwest. Only a few of the Cheyenne had firearms, but the accuracy of the bowmen blunted the initial assault. Yellow Crow grunted in pain and shock as a rifle ball dug a vicious furrow along his thigh.

Crooked Stick tamped home a fresh powder charge and ball, then calmly dribbled a few grains of powder into the flash pan of his old rifle. As he cocked the heavy hammer, he turned to Yellow Crow.

"These are not soldiers from Fort Laramie," he said. "Crooked Stick's blood will feed the sands of this river. Here, today, he will die. But Yellow Crow must escape. Those who survive will be in need of a leader, and the camp on the Niobrara must be warned." He squinted down the barrel and fired, then reached for the powder flask. "You are more valuable alive than dead, my friend," Crooked Stick said. "Go quickly—even now the soldiers move to surround us."

Yellow Crow started to protest, then admitted the logic in Crooked Stick's words. Also, Ted Henderson must be warned and the butchers of Black Kettle's people punished. He clasped Crooked Stick's shoulder in a gesture of farewell and, his strength fading from his wounds, struggled back aboard the palomino.

Yellow Crow did not turn to look back until he had reached the first of the low hills. The scene below wavered before his eyes, drifting in and out of focus like a dream. The Cheyenne rear guard, heavily outnumbered, vanished beneath a swarm of soldiers.

Yellow Crow rode among the fleeing Cheyenne, and at last, one cloud lifted from his spirit as he spotted a familiar figure. Within moments, Talking Bird was mounted behind her husband as the two led the dazed and unbelieving survivors of the South Platte massacre deeper into the hills toward safety.

At the bend of the South Platte River, Colonel Emery Church surveyed the ruins of Black Kettle's camp. He smiled broadly as he moved from one red body to another. "Sergeant!"

The volunteer non-com appeared at Church's side. "Yes, Colonel?"

Church rammed a toe into the ribs of a dead Cheyenne. "I want every one of these damn redskins stripped, scalped, and cut up like suckling pigs," Church snarled. "Burn the camp. I said there would be no survivors, no captives, and I meant it."

The sergeant leered at Church. "Found one fair-lookin' red wench in one of the lodges. What you think, Colonel?"

Church shrugged. "Help yourself, then cut her throat. Bring me one of her tits. I need a new cigar pouch."

"Yes, sir." The sergeant moved rapidly toward a nearby tipi, tugging at his belt.

"Colonel Church?"

The officer turned at the voice behind him. "Yes, private?"

The young soldier held a small girl, barely six years old, firmly by the arm. "What do we do with this one, Colonel?"

Church stared at the wide-eyed girl for a moment, then

casually pulled his pistol and shot the child in the head. "Stopped one whole generation of redskins with one slug," he said. He glanced at the horrified young private. "What's the problem, son? It ain't like they was human. To control coyotes you gotta get rid of the breeding stock."

Emery Church turned his back on the scene and heard retching sounds behind him. He grinned. "Scalp her and skin her, Private," he ordered. "Maybe that'll help you develop some guts. Can't have any squeamish soldiers in my outfit."

The incident immediately forgotten, Church resumed his tour of the devastated camp. The sound of approaching hoofbeats made him glance up. The lean scout named Weaver stared at Church for a couple of heartbeats, his face drawn and tight. "Satisfied, Colonel?" he asked bitterly.

"Couldn't be happier, Weaver. We showed the rest of the world how to handle Indians here today, by damn!"

Weaver spat a stream of tobacco juice near Church's boot. "I didn't sign up for this, Church," he said contemptuously. "They's more than two hundred dead Injuns out there—"

"Good!" Church interrupted.

"—And six outta ten are women and kids," the scout said. "I snuck you past a bunch of real warriors on the way. I got you to Black Kettle's camp. Laramie's just a couple days' ride thataway," the scout said, waving a hand toward the northwest, "and I'm drawin' my pay. This country'll be swarmin' with mad Injuns mighty quick, Church. Real Injuns, not old men, squaws, and little kids. I'm gettin' my tail outta here while there's still time. Just hand over my thousand bonus, and I'll be on my way."

"You'll get your bonus, Weaver," Church said, easing a hand toward his holstered pistol—and abruptly stopped the movement. The muzzle of Weaver's long gun pointed dead on Church's belly.

"Go ahead and reach, Church," Weaver snarled, "but you better come up with a sack of gold when you do!"

Church held his sudden fury in check; he knew the lanky scout was serious. Church reached into a pocket of his tunic and tossed a small but heavy sack toward Weaver. The scout caught it deftly with his free hand.

"Adios, Church," Weaver said. "I ain't gonna wish you luck. Wouldn't do any good. If the Sioux, Cheyenne, Arapaho, Ute, or Shoshone don't get you, Ted Henderson will." Weaver spurred his horse past the colonel, heading east at a swift trot.

"That's where you're wrong, Weaver!" Church shouted at the departing figure. He tapped the forged orders inside his tunic. "In a couple of days I'll own Laramie and the Third Cavalry. No louse-bitten Indian's gonna whip Emery Church—and Ted Henderson's as good as dead right now."

A half-day's ride south of the Indian camp on the Niobrara River, Ted Henderson watched, first in curiosity and then in growing concern, as the lone rider approached through the rolling, tall-grass prairie.

Even from a considerable distance Ted thought he recognized the horseman. And the man was in a hurry.

Scout Carl Keller checked his lathered mount alongside Ted's horse. "Trouble at home," Keller said without further greeting, then outlined the massacre on the South Platte. As the story unfolded, Ted felt only a hard knot of rage.

"Who's responsible?" Ted interrupted.

Keller slumped forward a bit in the saddle, staring at Ted. "Afraid you won't like the answer to that question much," the scout growled. "Fourth Kansas Volunteers. Colonel Emery Church commanding."

At that announcement the Laramie commander's self-control snapped. For a man who did not cuss much, Keller thought wryly, Ted Henderson was pretty darn fluent in four languages. Ted's eyes were hard, icy, and reckless, and Carl Keller knew he was seeing a new side of Ted Henderson—a man obsessed with a drive to kill from passion and not from military necessity.

"I'll tear that little fox-faced sonofabitch to pieces with my bare hands," Ted concluded in a voice made even more ominous by its soft tone, "and I'll feed the pieces to the coyotes. That butcher . . ." Ted's words trailed away as he once again remembered a scene etched into his soul: Kit Carson's office in Navajo country, a pile of Indian scalps tossed defiantly to the floor, his own handgun resting beneath Church's pointed chin. "God," Ted said to himself, "why didn't I kill him then?" He recalled Church's final remark as he was led away, banished from the Navajo campaign for brutality and the massacre of peaceful Indians: "The next time I see you, Henderson, it will be over the sights of a gun." *You were dead right, Church,* Ted thought, *and you're going to make good on that challenge.*

"Colonel," Keller said, "I hate to keep slugging a man who already has a headache. Yellow Crow was hit twice in the fight at South Platte."

Ted glanced back at the scout, startled. "Is he—?"

"Not bad," Keller rushed to reassure. "He'll be out of action for a time, but he'll make it. Tough Indian, that one. Some talk already among the Cheyenne about making him new peace chief.

"There's something I don't have to tell you, sir," Keller continued, his brows bunched in concern. "The lid's going to blow off this country now. Every Indian old enough to be carrying a bow is going to be smoking the war pipe."

Ted nodded somberly. "Thanks to Church, we're right back where we started. Only worse off. All the bands that were neutral before won't be now."

Keller nodded in the direction of the camp on the Niobrara. "I'll get word of what happened to Antelope and the others over there. They'll hear soon enough. Might be best if we told 'em ourselves, and you'll be wanting to get back to Laramie."

The scout noticed that Ted's hand had unconsciously dropped to the worn butt of the Colt Dragoon strapped around his waist. "You'll find Church and his bunch camped outside Laramie. He brought some papers supposed to give him command at Fort Laramie. Major Wills didn't buy. Said he had to have verification, and David's taking his own sweet time about it."

The scout smiled in grim satisfaction. "Didn't set well with Church when a mere major tossed him and his troops out of Laramie."

Ted nodded. "Keep your hair on, Carl." Abruptly Ted reined his horse toward Laramie, spurring the animal into a long lope.

Keller watched the departing figure for a long moment. "Colonel Church," he said to himself, "I think you stepped in it this time. Problem is, the rest of us will get splattered, too. This country's gonna be hock deep in mad Indians pretty quick."

Abel Hubbard knelt in the center of a wide swath of tramped-down grass and probed the earth with his index finger. After a moment he stood and brushed bits of soil from his hands.

"Two days ahead of us, Sergeant," he said, knowing that the lines of worry on Kirk's weathered and weary face were reflected in his own. "Same bunch we cut sign on yesterday. I make it mostly Sioux, some Cheyenne and Arapaho. Headed straight as an arrow for Fort Kearny. Probably there by now."

"What do we do if we catch up with them, Colonel?" Kirk asked wryly. "Tell them to surrender because we're surrounded?"

Abel turned to survey the remnants of his comand: fifty men, their uniforms in tatters, exhausted from months on patrol and almost endless skirmishes. Down to fifteen rounds per man for the repeating rifles. Fifty men against maybe eight hundred well-armed and well-mounted Indians. Yet they had only one chance to survive.

"Somehow, Kirk, we've got to get through to Kearny. We can't go home. You heard the Shoshone scouts' reports. We've got Indians in any direction we ride, and they're looking for scalps. If we don't reach Kearny, where we can get ammunition and supplies, we've bought the farm."

Sergeant Kirk stared for a moment in the direction of Fort Kearny. "This bunch don't act like any Indians I've ever run across," he said. "Kearny's a tough nut to crack, and most hostiles I know don't cotton to the idea of trying to take a major fort."

Abel tossed the reins around his horse's neck and prepared to mount. "This isn't any ordinary war party," he said. "I'd bet a month's pay or more we're behind a blue-eyed Indian named Long Walker."

Kirk lifted an eyebrow. "Better behind that one than in front of him," he said. "Fights too much like a white man. Nine miles of bad road, he is." Kirk heaved himself into the saddle. "Reckon you're right, though, Colonel. In another week a shirttail Ute kid could whip this outfit. I'll tell the troops there's tobacco and coffee in Kearny. If that don't make them fight harder, nothing will. What the hell's happened to this country, anyway? It's like every Indian from Kansas to Oregon all at once got a mad on. Never saw so many smokes in my life."

Abel shook his head. "I don't know, Sergeant. If we manage to stay alive, maybe we can find out." Abel touched knees to his horse, and the gelding moved out at an easy trot. *At least*, he thought, *the horses are beginning to recover,*

*getting stronger by the day as the grass grows taller and
greener.* And up ahead lay the biggest military challenge of his
career. Despite the odds, Fort Kearny must not fall; it was the
key post along the telegraph lines and the Overland Trail. But
it was manned by volunteers. Fifty tired men might not make
that much of a difference in numbers, but they would in
leadership—if they were able to break through.

The column was still three miles from Kearny, but the
distant sound of rifle fire drifting on the south breeze
confirmed Abel's fear.

Fort Kearny was under attack!

Along the line, veteran soldiers quietly checked the loads
in their weapons and counted the few remaining rounds as
they geared for what could be their final battle. Even if they
reached the walls of Fort Kearny, Abel conceded, they still
would be in a trap. But at least they would have a fighting
chance.

From the south a horseman appeared, riding fast toward
Abel. Abel spurred his own mount out to meet the Shoshone
scout and conferred at length with the Indian as the column
moved up.

"It's as bad as we thought it might be, Kirk," he said as the
sergeant reined in. "Long Walker has Kearny surrounded and
is giving them fits. But our scout has found a weak spot in their
lines. We should be able to break through with a surprise
charge at night."

Kirk grinned. At Abel's questioning look, the sergeant
said, "It really isn't all that funny, Colonel. But I was just
thinking about that handful of men down Texas way some years
back who shot their way into a fort under siege. Looks like we
got another Alamo out here in the prairie."

The desperate charge began two hours before daybreak,
with the efficient Shoshone leading the way in the faint
starlight. Most of the few Sioux defending the spot were asleep
when the first pounding of hooves and the initial pistol shot
shattered the morning air. The fifty-man column and a half-
dozen Shoshone rode in close formation, whipping through
the halfhearted Sioux defenses and leaving a number of bodies
in their wake.

Breaching the Indian lines, Abel urged his men faster
toward the dimly black bulk of the walls of Fort Kearny,
silently praying the soldiers inside would not fire on them by
mistake. A handful of Sioux ran for their ponies and opened

pursuit—and rode straight toward the muzzles of the Shoshone rifles as the scouts wheeled to form a rear guard. With almost every muzzle flash, a Sioux pony went down or raced away riderless.

Ahead, Abel heard a shout from the sentry on duty. Then, with a sigh of relief, he saw the fort gates swing open. Abel yanked his horse to a skidding stop on the parade ground as lights flared and soldiers, many clad only in trousers, sprinted for firing positions on the walls above.

Abel twisted in the saddle and watched in disbelief as the last of the Shoshone rear guard reached the gates. They had not lost a single man!

"Who's in command here?" Abel demanded as he dismounted before a youthful-looking corporal. The startled noncom silently pointed toward a building nearby.

Inside, a lieutenant struggled with his suspenders as Abel strode into the room and saluted. "Are you in charge?"

The officer nodded mutely, confused. "Colonel Abel Hubbard, Third Cavalry," Abel said, extending a hand.

"Lieutenant Kenley, Seventh Nebraska Volunteers," the young officer stammered. "We certainly weren't expecting any reinforcement, sir."

Abel smiled wryly. "I don't know that I would call fifty men and some Shoshone scouts reinforcements, Lieutenant Kenley. Where are your superior officers?"

"Dead, sir. I'm the ranking officer now. And I'll freely admit I'm happy to see you—your name is not exactly unknown, and we can use an experienced commander."

Abel nodded. "As you wish, Lieutenant. I'll check on my men now, and in an hour or so I would like a briefing on your situation here."

The situation Kenley outlined was not reassuring, Abel reflected while sipping a cup of strong coffee as the sun climbed above the horizon. Casualties had been heavy in the initial attack; there had been no communications with Laramie for over a week because of downed telegraph wires; and fewer than two hundred men remained to defend Fort Kearny. Food supplies were adequate, however, and the post had its own deep well of pure water. There was adequate grain for the horses, although the hay supply was dangerously low.

"Here they come!"

At the call from the lookout tower, both officers sprinted

from the command quarters. Abel scrambled up a rough wood ladder to a firing station and peered over the wall. A half-circle of perhaps a hundred braves fanned out across the prairie to the north, walking their horses toward the fort.

"Sergeant!"

Abel's yell brought Kirk on the run.

"The Sioux are going to attack from the south!" Abel yelled. "Put every available man on the south wall! Make every shot count!"

The sergeant nodded and sprinted away. At Abel's side Lieutenant Kenley asked, "Sir, how do you know that?"

Abel pointed toward the mounted Indians to the north. "Cheyenne," he said. "They aren't carrying shields. No Cheyenne rides into battle without his war shield. Bad medicine. This is just a feint, to get us to split our defenses."

Abel had barely finished his explanation when hoofbeats thundered outside—to the south. The war whoops of the Sioux mingled with rifle shots as the Indians charged. Kirk's marksmen waited until the lead Indian was almost within pistol range before opening fire. The deadly volley ripped into the Indian ranks, shattering the charge as if the Sioux had hit a stone barrier. The Indian force withdrew, leaving the battlefield littered with bodies.

"They'll return to retrieve the dead and wounded, Lieutenant," Abel said. "Let them. But let's keep men on watch; they might try to sneak a few members of the retrieval party in to fire on the fort. I doubt there will be another attack soon. The Indians will be confused by our arrival and unsure of how many reinforcements came through. Let them stew for a time while we figure what to do next."

From his vantage point atop the wall, Abel suddenly snapped, "Why aren't those cannon in position, Lieutenant!"

Kenley stammered a nervous reply. "Th-There's—no ball for them, sir. Plenty of powder but the army sent the wrong size ball."

Abel snorted in disgust. "That figures. Perhaps you had best show me the rest of the fort, including the ammunition dump!"

Abel stared in disbelief as the lieutenant opened the door of a wooden shed that stood near the center of the parade ground. Inside was the post's entire supply of powder and ball.

"Dammit!" Abel shouted. "Who was the idiot responsible for putting this ammunnition in a wooden building?"

"I'm afraid my late husband issued those orders, Colonel."

The woman's voice startled Abel. He spun around. Standing in the sunlight was a remarkable-looking young woman. Short auburn hair barely touched her shoulders, which were more square than most women's, and framed a gentle-looking face highlighted by wide eyes of a surprisingly deep green. She wore a simple housedress, which did nothing to hide the ample curves of her body.

Feeling very embarrassed, Abel swept his campaign hat from his head. "Sorry, ma'am," he said. "I had no idea there was a woman about the post. I apologize for my language."

"No apologies are needed, Colonel," she replied calmly. "I'm afraid my husband wasn't much of a military man."

Abel suddenly became aware of his own appearance—uniform ripped and soiled, beard untrimmed, and he knew he was at least two weeks on the other side of bathwater. "You said—your late husband, ma'am. What happened?"

"He was killed on a patrol shortly after we arrived here a couple of months ago. He went off in pursuit of a small band of Indians and into an ambush. None of the party survived."

Abel nodded solemnly. "I'm sorry to hear that, ma'am. My condolences."

She nodded, the motion sending ripples of light dancing through her auburn hair. "Perhaps you might join me for dinner this evening, Colonel, if you aren't too tired." She smiled softly.

"Thank you very much, ma'am, but with a fort to defend, I don't think there'll be much time for leisurely meals. Alas," Abel added quickly.

"Commanding officers who are rested are always more effective than those who are exhausted," she said. "I quite understand your concerns; after all, I am in this fort, too. But surely your troops can spare you for thirty minutes."

Knowing she was right, Abel bowed slightly. "I would be honored, ma'am."

She extended a hand that was surprisingly strong. "My name is Victoria Coulter."

"Abel Hubbard. I'm pleased to make your acquaintance, Mrs. Coulter, and I'd be delighted to have dinner with you, if I can find a pair of scissors and a bathtub first."

Her laugh was throaty and genuine. "I'm sure the post has

all the items you might need. And please call me Victoria. Lieutenant Kenley can point out my quarters for you. About six, shall we say?"

Abel agreed and watched her walk away. Her strides were long and self-assured without the pronounced hip sway of most well-developed women.

"Kenley, I want all the ammunition inventoried and moved to one of the sod buildings," Abel finally said. "A stray fire arrow on that wood shack and we wouldn't have enough powder to dust a skunk. I want the move made and the inventory list within the hour."

Stepping from the ammunition shed, Abel motioned Sergeant Kirk to his side. "Sergeant, I want those cannon moved into position and charged. Strip every piece of metal, especially chains, from the wagons in the storage shed. Scrap makes as good a defensive charge as explosive ball, even if the range is cut down. When the lieutenant finishes his inventory, we'll have a better idea of where we stand with munitions. Then have the men get what rest they can."

Kirk nodded, then said, "Looks to me like you've got something in mind besides defense, Colonel."

"Could be, Sergeant. If things break our way, we have a chance to blow a hole in Long Walker's medicine that can't be patched." Abel's voice trailed off, his eyes seeming to focus on a spot far distant. Sergeant Kirk did not press his commanding officer for details of any potential plan; he had worked with Hubbard long enough to know that when the time was right, every man in the group would be told what was up.

Already Abel Hubbard had pulled off a couple of solid miracles. Kirk would not be surprised if the colonel had another in mind, and from the expression in those eyes, it would be a big one. He watched Hubbard walk away, preoccupied, and muttered aloud, "I wonder if he can walk on water, too?"

The sun was still well above the western horizon when Abel, freshly bathed and now clean shaven except for an impressive, trimmed mustache, tapped lightly on Victoria Coulter's door.

Despite the exhaustion that nagged at his bones, Abel felt his spirits lift as Victoria opened the door. She had changed from the simple housedress into a more formal gown of rich green that enhanced the color and depth of her eyes.

The high-necked, floor-length gown was almost austere,

but it seemed only to emphasize the womanliness that drifted like perfume around Victoria Coulter.

Her welcoming smile was warm. "Come in, Abel. I'm glad you could make it," she said. "I hope you enjoy plain cooking. I limit my meals to the same food available to the soldiers."

The rich smell of a hearty roast sent a rumble through Abel's stomach. "I'm sure it will be better than anything they serve in Saint Louis, Victoria," he said, pleased to discover she did her own cooking.

Victoria laughed softly. "A hungry man will find anything palatable," she said. "I'm sorry I can't offer you a drink or some wine. My husband had a tendency to drink far more than was necessary or desirable, and when he died I gave all the liquor we had to the post surgeon. It seemed like a much more appropriate use."

She led him toward a table, already set with plain, sturdy dishes and utensils. She smiled as she studied his face. "If I'm not being too bold," she said, "I suspected there was a handsome man behind that scruffy beard." Abel felt the color rise in his cheeks at the unexpected compliment. "Keep the mustache," she added. "It seems so natural."

Abel soon discovered that Victoria Coulter was a fine conversationalist as well as a marvelous cook. She seemed to have read everything that had been written since the invention of the quill pen, and she was incisive in her analysis of national political events. Only once did she mention military matters.

"Abel, tell me the truth. Will we leave here alive?"

He studied her for a moment and found no fear there, only a calm anticipation of his verdict. "Yes," he said with a sigh, "with luck."

She nodded solemnly. "I think you make your own luck, Abel Hubbard."

As the meal progressed, Abel relaxed more than he had for months. He had forgotten what a wonderful thing it could be to share a good meal with an attractive woman. And Victoria Coulter *was* an attractive woman.

They both reached for the salt at the same time, and their hands accidentally brushed.

"Sorry," Abel said. "After you."

Startled by the brief physical contact, Abel dropped his eyes and speared another piece of the roast, intensely aware of

the auburn-haired woman across from him. Her physical presence suddenly seemed overwhelming. It had been a long time since he had been alone with an attractive woman. Not since Judy.

Judy! At the thought of his wife, Abel almost choked with rage.

"Is anything wrong, Colonel?" Victoria asked with great concern.

Abel took a quick sip of water to help wash down the meat in his throat. "No. Thank you. I'm fine now."

As their eyes locked, Abel felt an unavoidable stirring in his loins. His long dormant desires for a woman refused to go away during the rest of the meal, and when Abel left Victoria's quarters to check on his men, he felt almost relieved to go.

"Gunpowder and fire," he muttered to himself four hours later as he finally made his way toward the barracks where he would catch a few hours' sleep. Another attack at dawn seemed more than likely, then a swift and unexpected strike by the soldiers. Abel tapped the arms inventory list in his pocket and paused, listening to the sounds of blacksmith tools echoing across the parade ground. Satisfied with his plan, he strode to the barracks and his waiting blankets.

Abel's dreams were restless even in his extreme fatigue: wave upon wave of mounted Indians; a blue-eyed Sioux lining a rifle on Abel's chest; fresh scalps dangling from lodge poles and lances. Most disturbing of all, he saw himself in the middle of a quiet clearing, the only sounds those of birdcalls and the rush of water in a small brook. Before him stood two women, one an auburn-haired figure in sharp relief, arms open. Another wavered, outlines blurred, blond hair fluttering in the breeze, also with arms opened toward him.

In his night visions, Abel Hubbard stood rooted to the spot, unable to move toward either woman.

Sitting Bull of the Hunkpapa Sioux calmed his nervous war pony with the reasurring pressure of a strong hand on the animal's neck. The broad-faced chief grunted in satisfaction as he looked over the battleground. Victory cries rang from brave to brave as warriors moved among the dead bodies of the bluecoats. Soon the buzzards would be feeding on the stripped and scalped remains of another sixty soldiers, and the bowl of the war pipe had barely cooled.

An inner rage still burned in Sitting Bull at the white

man's treachery in the massacre on the South Platte. News of Black Kettle's fate had swept the Indian nations, and for the first time in the memory of the eldest grandfather, Sioux, Cheyenne, Arapaho, and Ute had united in an outburst of fury.

Sitting Bull admitted to himself that he felt some regrets at smoking the war pipe with the blue-eyed Indian called Long Walker; that one, he still did not trust. And even in his initial rage at the war council, Sitting Bull had made it a point to sit where the war pipe would pass from his lips to those of Long Walker and not the other way around. The snub was lost on the onetime Seminole, and Sitting Bull could not miss the quick flash of anger in Long Walker's eyes.

Sitting Bull turned at the approach of the Mexican who had risen from the rank of captive to that of senior warrior through sheer courage and determination. In war paint, Iron Shield looked as much Sioux as was his heart.

"Another day of strong medicine, Sitting Bull," Iron Shield said with satisfaction. "Perhaps Long Walker was right. The blue soldiers flee before the Sioux. Those who remain die. Soon this land will be free of white faces."

Sitting Bull snorted in disgust. "Do not begin the celebration too soon, brother," he said. "Long Walker reads the signs wrong. Those Long Knives who fled the Sioux lands were not of this soil; those who died here today were of no experience as fighters. It is a different matter when one faces the peace chief who is a warrior, the one named Ted Henderson. Or his subchief Hubbard, the one who stalks as the wolf in the snow."

The Hunkpapa chief frowned. "Soon more soldiers will come. In a vision Sitting Bull saw a sea of blue sweeping across an island of red. What must be done, Iron Shield, is to regain as much Sioux land as possible before that sea of blue reaches the Indian shore. Then perhaps the red man can save—for a time at least—part of his traditional hunting grounds. The red man has friends among the whites, Iron Shield. At some time they must be trusted."

Iron Shield spat in contempt. "Iron Shield will never trust the white eyes." He yanked his horse about sharply and rode away.

Sitting Bull remained calmly astride his pony and watched the warriors below conclude their business with the bodies and begin to re-form into loose ranks, ready to continue the push southward. In the next few moons, Sitting Bull thought, the red man would have the upper hand. His legions of warriors would sweep south, pushing the whites back; and to the east, Long Walker would begin the battle to take Fort Kearny. Big Nose's powerful band would even now be moving toward Fort Laramie itself, to punish those who had killed Black Kettle's women and children.

Sitting Bull sighed deeply, then reined his mount toward the waiting lines of braves. The job ahead, he thought, would not be easy.

Colonel Emery Church lounged on his cot in the Fourth Kansas Volunteers' temporary camp outside the walls of Fort Laramie, a packet of cigars and a bottle of brandy within easy reach. *That pipsqueak of a major will pay for this,* he thought bitterly. And Henderson would not find any refuge when he returned from wherever the hell he was.

The canvas of his tent rustled as the flap let in a cool evening breeze. The oil lamp on the table beside the cot fluttered in the gust.

"Dammit, I left orders not to be disturbed—" Church abruptly stopped talking and stared in shock at the figure standing just inside his tent. Instinctively he reached for the handgun at his side.

"Try it, Church! I'd like nothing more than to blow your head off here and now!" Ted Henderson's voice was tight with fury. Church's reach for a weapon stopped as he stared down the barrel of a Colt Dragoon. Even in the pale yellow wash of the oil lamp, Church saw the icy determination in Henderson's eyes. He knew Henderson would not hesitate to pull the trigger.

"So, you murdering little bastard," Henderson said quietly, "we meet again. I should have killed you in the Navajo campaign, you butcher of women and children."

Church opened his mouth. "Don't try calling for the officer of the guard," Ted warned. "He won't be hearing anyone for a while yet." Ted's eyes narrowed until they were mere slits, and only the greatest effort of his life could stop him from putting that final bit of pressure on the trigger.

"What's the matter, Church? You like the deck stacked in your favor?" he taunted.

"Damn you, Henderson! You give me one chance and I'll put a hole in you—"

Ted shook his head grimly. "You'll have your chance,

Church—at full moon tonight in the old pueblo ruins along the river. It's a short ride. Come alone. The last time we met, you said the next time you'd see me over the barrel of a gun. Now, Church, is the next time," Ted added ominously. "Let's see if you're as tough against a man as you are against women and kids."

Church's fear checked the surge of rage and hate as he stared at his longtime enemy. For the first time, Church noticed that Ted Henderson was clad in the buckskins of a scout.

"You're out of uniform, Henderson," Church said.

Ted nodded. "I told you once I wouldn't soil the uniform on the likes of you. I meant it then, and I still do. My official resignation is on Major Wills's desk at Fort Laramie. So you see, Church, it's not a military matter any longer. It's just you and me—when the full moon is straight overhead. And, Church," Ted added, "I've always hated killing. Until now."

As suddenly as he had appeared, Ted Henderson was gone from the tent, only the gentle movement of the canvas flap marking his passage.

Church sat on the cot for several long moments, more shaken than he cared to admit. Deep down, he knew he feared Ted Henderson as much as he hated him. He wanted nothing more than to look on the dead face of the man in buckskins. And there was one sure way to see that happen. He stepped from the tent, and minutes later he jabbed a toe into a sleeping form.

"Get up, Snider. Fetch that fancy double shotgun of yours. I've got a job for you."

The full moon was well above his left shoulder as Carl Keller of Henderson's Scouts waited patiently in a clump of scrub brush overlooking the ancient Indian pueblo ruins below. The white wash of moonlight clearly defined the crumbling walls of the long-ago civilization and washed across the main plaza between multistory buildings. The shadows were black as ink, but Keller knew one of them concealed a buckskin-clad man with whom he had shared the joys and heartbreaks of many years. Keller had no intention of interfering unless Ted Henderson went against a stacked deck. In that case . . .

Two horsemen suddenly broke into the soft flood of moonlight, approaching the ruins from below. One of them, larger than the other, carried what appeared to be a long gun. Keller watched as the pair neared the walls, and when only one man emerged on the other side, the scout moved silently toward the spot where the other rider had vanished.

Carl eased his way along the blackness of an outside wall. From only a few yards away came the voices of two men.

"All right, Church," he heard Ted Henderson say in a deadly tone, "it's down to just what you and I have both wanted for a long time. What'll it be? Handguns, knives, or fists?"

There was silence for a couple of heartbeats, broken by the sound of creaking leather. In his mind's eye Keller could visualize the smaller of the two men dismounting.

"Don't matter to me, Henderson," a thin voice said. "You're a dead man anyhow."

Keller saw a form rise from the shadows almost within arm's length. The moonlight glinted from the twin tubes of a shotgun that began to take aim.

"Take him, Snider!"

At the shout from the clearing, Carl Keller took one step and swung an Arapaho war club. The fire-tempered, hard wood thumped solidly against the concealed gunman's temple. The man dropped like a pole-axed steer. Keller caught the shotgun before it reached the ground.

"Snider ain't helpin' now, Ted!" Keller yelled. "Go get the little sonofabitch!"

The cry from outside the wall took Church by surprise, and he turned to glance in that direction. Ted took advantage of Church's momentary confusion to close to within six feet. Then, as Church recovered and started to swing his already-drawn handgun toward Ted, Ted launched himself in a low dive. His shoulder cracked into Church's shins. The handgun blasted above his head, the flash of burning powder scorching Ted's buckskins across one hip. The handgun was jarred from Church's grip as the impact of Ted's solid body flung him backward.

Church frantically yanked a leg free of Ted's grasp and scrambled to his feet, glancing around in a futile attempt to locate the fallen revolver. Icy fear built behind his belt buckle as he turned to face Ted.

"Like I said, Church," Ted growled, "it's just you and me now." Slowly and deliberately Ted unbuckled his own pistol belt and tossed it aside. "Hand to hand and eye to eye," he said. "Think you can take me, Church?"

Church's hand whipped to his belt and came up grasping a heavy skinning knife. Ted leaned forward, putting his weight over the balls of his feet as he drew his own thick-bladed steel. The two men circled each other warily, their breathing the only sound in the moon-drenched plaza.

Suddenly Church lashed out, his knife's edge aimed at Ted's ribs. Steel clanged on steel as Ted parried the blow outward. He flipped his own wrist and neatly sliced a chunk of flesh from Church's forearm. The smaller man screamed in surprise and pain.

"What's the matter, Church? Finding it harder to use a blade on a grown man than on a pregnant squaw or a baby?" Ted's taunting was purposeful and deadly.

The sudden realization that he was alone against a quick and powerful enemy sent a push against Church's bladder. His own quick gasps for breath contrasted with Ted's measured breathing as the pair again circled, half-crouched and ready to spring.

Church feinted with his knife, then spun on a heel, whipping into a full circle to slam the blade toward Ted's neck. Ted raised an arm, blocking the thrust. In the same motion he hooked his instep behind Church's forward foot and yanked. The smaller man tumbled to the ground but came back to his feet in a roll as Ted's blade ripped the air by his shoulder.

"Cute, Church," Ted said, his features plainly twisted in hate in the moonlight, "but not cute enough." He flicked out his own knife, the keen edge of the blade almost severing Church's right ear.

With a cry of pain and desperation, Church spun away, then whirled and threw his knife. Ted calmly turned aside, the spinning blade humming harmlessly past his body. "Might as well keep it even," he said, tossing his own knife aside. Suddenly he stepped forward and jabbed a straight left into Church's nose, then a right fist to the midsection. Church folded, but Ted straightened him immediately with a knee to the face. Church staggered backward, blood streaming from his battered features, but Ted—now consumed by a fury beyond his control—ripped rights and lefts pummeling Church with a vengeance.

Ted felt teeth crumple beneath his left fist. A rib popped beneath a roundhouse right that carried all of Ted's solid

weight behind it. Ted slammed a knee into Church's groin. As
Church started down, Ted raised his arm high and cracked his
elbow into the back of Church's neck. Then he was astride the
smaller man, his hand entwined in Church's hair, hammering
the foxlike face again and again into the dirt.

With a snort of disgust, Ted tossed Church's face down
once more and stood, rubbing lacerated and bruised knuckles.
He stared down at the unconscious man for a moment, then
glanced up at the sound of a footstep.

Carl Keller stepped to Ted's side and eyed the senseless
form in the dust. "Thought you might have killed him a couple
times, Ted. How come you didn't?"

Ted gasped air back into his heaving chest. "Finally got—
enough mad out of my system—to think straight. This—this
thing has—caused too many atrocities—not to pay some of
them back."

"Ted, are you thinkin' what I'm thinkin'?" Keller asked
quietly.

Ted nodded. "I think the Cheyenne need a present. A gift
to prove the white man isn't all bad. Maybe," Ted added as the
huddled form began to twitch and moan, "Big Nose is due
some justice for what happened to Black Kettle."

"Couldn't hurt," Keller said. "Little bastard deserves it.
I'll help you strap him on his horse." Keller bent, scooped up
the half-conscious Church, and tossed him into the saddle of
the skittish sorrel Church had left at the edge of the plaza. Ted
tugged at one end of a rope securing Church's feet into the
stirrups and winced at the flare of pain. "Shouldn't have hit
him so hard," he said. "Cut my knuckles all to pieces."

Keller laughed in genuine enjoyment. "It was a mighty
good scrap, if a bit one-sided."

Ted leaned against the sorrel's neck and studied the scout
as Keller finished wrapping Church up like a Virginia ham.
"Carl, I'm not complaining, but how did you happen to be
here, anyway?"

Keller shrugged. "Major Wills is a funny duck," he said.
"Come got me up from the supper table to do some thinkin'
out loud. Said to himself it weren't no military matter, but he
sure wished he knew a good friend of a fellow named
Henderson. Hell, son. I taught you a bunch of what you know
about readin' sign and trackin'. Don't take no mental whiz to
figure what was happenin'."

"Well, I guess I owe you another one, friend. And the

major, too. How about that one you cold-cocked back there? I saw the shotgun muzzle over the wall."

"He ain't goin' nowhere. Arapaho make good war clubs. I poured a pint of rotgut whiskey on him. If he gets back to camp, nobody'd believe him anyway."

Ted pulled a clean kerchief from a pocket and dabbed at his torn and bleeding knuckles. "Carl," he said, "there could be some trouble over this. . . ."

Keller grinned. "Over what? I know for sure I told Church not to go prowlin' around by himself—not with all the mad Injuns about. Reckon Wills told him the same thing."

Ted stuck a bruised hand toward his scout. "Thanks, Carl. And if you'd do one more thing for me—"

"Sure. Be glad to tell Wilma you're alive and healthy. Just be sure you get back in the same shape. Old Big Nose might lift your hair before you can get a sideways word in. See you back at the fort, Ted."

Ted watched as the scout ambled away toward a horse concealed somewhere beyond the walls of the pueblo ruins. Then he retrieved his own mount, wrapped the reins of Church's bridle around his saddle horn, and put his horse into a swift trot toward Cheyenne country.

Two hours after sunrise, Ted found what he was looking for, a veteran Cheyenne brave on a scouting tour. Church, still dazed from the beating but conscious enough to realize what was in store, could only make incoherent mumbles of protest through his broken teeth. Ted and the Cheyenne spoke briefly, and the Indian pointed toward the northwest, where a group of Indians on horseback were gathered.

Ted could feel the hostility in the air as he rode toward Big Nose, here and there greeting a warrior by name. They were painted and carried shields. Partly as a precaution and partly because he was tired of hearing Church whimper, Ted had stuffed a rag in the colonel's mouth. Church could still wheeze air in through one nostril that was not quite swollen shut.

Ted pulled his horse to a stop in front of Big Nose. "I come to speak with the great war chief Big Nose," Ted said to the stoic man on horseback. Big Nose stared hard for a moment, then nodded, the motion rippling the feathers in his war-bonnet.

"I come bearing a gift for the Cheyenne," Ted said, twisting in the saddle and gesturing toward the wide-eyed Church, now sweating profusely in pure terror. "This is the white soldier who led the attack on Black Kettle's people. I give him to you."

The Cheyenne war chief leveled a glare of pure hatred toward the cowering Church. "Why do you bring him here?" he asked. "Is it not said that among the white man there is no crime in killing Indians, therefore, no need for justice?"

"I cannot deny that is the feeling of some white men, Big Nose," Ted replied. "It is not the feeling of all. His crime was against the Cheyenne; his punishment should be at the hands of the Cheyenne."

Big Nose kneed his horse closer and stared at Church. "It is true. This is the one who led the soldiers against Black Kettle. What is your price for him?"

"Only this," Ted said earnestly. "That when the time comes, as it must soon, to talk peace, then Big Nose will remember this gift from the white man to the Cheyenne."

Big Nose nodded. "It shall be so. Other chiefs as well will hear of this, that some white men know of justice." The war chief reached for the reins to lead Church's horse away.

Somehow Church had managed to spit out the gag. "Henderson—for God's sake—you can't do this—to a white man—"

Ted pinned Church with a bitter stare. "You've forfeited any claim you might have ever had to being a man—red, white, or any other color. Count your blessings, Church. Cheyenne justice is relatively quick. It could be worse—they could be Comanche, and then you'd be in a big chunk of trouble."

Ted turned back to Big Nose. "He is yours now. My job is done. Big Nose, I am no longer a chief of horse soldiers. I have left the army. I will be no part of an organization that breeds vermin such as this." He gestured toward Church. "In the future I shall work only as a peace chief. Perhaps in this manner I may better serve both white man and red."

Big Nose grunted in satisfaction. "It is good. Ted Henderson has proved he is a great warrior chief and that he is a great peace chief as well. It is known that he thinks as an Indian and understands the ways of the red man. His voice will be heard when the time comes. Until then, he may ride freely and without fear through the lands of the Cheyenne. This Big Nose shall declare."

With that the Cheyenne war chief wheeled his pony and

set off toward the main Indian encampment a short distance away. Ted watched them go, the bound officer in blue led to justice by a prominent war chief of a powerful nation. He felt no remorse, only a grim satisfaction.

Ted turned his horse back toward Laramie. It had been a long time since he had been home. And with the frontier riddled with smoke, he knew he faced many more days in the saddle before his work was done.

Major David Wills tossed the reins of his lathered mount to a waiting corporal and dismounted stiffly, feeling twice as old as his twenty-five years.

"How'd it go, Major?" a junior officer asked.

"Same as usual, Corporal," Wills said, sighing heavily. "A lot of miles and always late." He brushed at the heavy accumulation of dust on his uniform. "Sometimes I wonder if I'm in way over my head." The new acting commander of Fort Laramie—at least until Abel Hubbard's return—watched the corporal lead the horse away, then trudged wearily into his office.

Despite Ted Henderson's parting advice before he took to the peace-talk trail once more, David found himself constantly wondering if he was making the right moves. He knew he would be forever grateful to Ted Henderson for convincing the crack soldiers of R Company to stay in uniform. And his original command, I Company, rapidly was gaining a reputation as a group to be taken seriously in Indian camps.

Wills glanced at the papers on his desk and found no new telegraph transmissions. He sighed and turned to peer at the map. It was the sense of isolation, a feeling of being an island in an ocean of warriors, that was so frustrating. Communications to the west were sporadic; to the east they were nonexistent. Not even a courier could be expected to survive a run through the prairies, which now teemed with Indian warriors.

David Wills knew one thing, though: There would be no help or supplies coming through on the Overland Trail. It was firmly under Indian control.

The only information on which he could rely were the reports from his scouts, and they were not reassuring. A small town had been sacked twice by Indians, under the noses of the undermanned force at Fort Sedgwick. Sitting Bull's warriors held the territory from the Republican River northward.

Surprisingly, Big Nose had stopped his swarm of warriors a few miles north of Fort Laramie itself, just when it seemed he planned to attack. Big Nose appeared content merely to keep control of all roads and trails leading into the Laramie area.

Sharp battles with heavy losses to both sides had raged along the Platte River, until finally the thin line of bluecoats had pulled back to the questionable safety of nearby forts or been wiped out to the man.

Commanders at Fort Halleck and Fort Bridger had been hard pressed to contain the Arapaho and Ute, and ranchers were forced to band together for defense. Wills had convinced the Shoshone to aid the ranchers, and so far losses in the civilian sectors had been light; the Arapaho and Ute had little stomach for an all-out war with the dangerous Shoshone.

Even at his front door, Wills had problems. With the "disappearance" of Emery Church, the population of Laramie had been divided. Some of the more vocal residents hailed Church as a hero, while others viewed Church as a butcher. Wills wondered how much he had contributed to the uproar. His first act as commanding officer had been to place the entire Fourth Kansas Volunteers under "house arrest," confining them to Fort Laramie and assigning them fatigue duties to free experienced Indian fighters for field campaigns. At least, he thought wryly, they could not do any more harm.

A heavy influx of civilians fleeing the Indian uprising sorely taxed Fort Laramie's supplies. Wills picked up a pen and scribbled in a journal for a moment.

"Four weeks," he muttered to himself, "and we'll be out of everything, even on half-rations for everyone." He tossed the pen to the desk and turned once more to the map.

The only hope was that somehow Fort Kearny could hold out. That lonely outpost was the key—the only spot from which support could be fielded in numbers large enough to relieve the crisis along the Platte and at Fort Laramie.

A light tap sounded on the door. A young blond woman entered. Judy Hubbard had lost too much weight, he thought. Her eyes still reflected her pain and worry.

"I'm sorry, Judy," he said softly. "There's still no word of Abel."

She nodded in anticipated disappointment and left the office.

"Abel Hubbard," Wills grumbled, "wherever you are, you'd best be bringing yourself home soon. There's two of us here who need you desperately. The difference is that I need your experience—and your wife needs all of you."

"All set, sir," Sergeant Kirk reported. "Cannon are in position, charged, and ready."

"Very good, Kirk," Abel Hubbard said from his vantage point atop the fort wall. "The men have their instructions?"

"Yes, sir. Rifles only on the first charge, save the ammunition for the repeaters."

Abel nodded, lowering his field glasses. Long Walker was playing it by the book—the white man's book. The first wave would once more be a probing assault, a search for the fort's prime weakness. If only minimum resistance was encountered, then the main body of his warriors would be unleashed. And that group was in for a little surprise. The Indian who followed the white man's style of war was in for a taste of redskin-type ambush.

"Here they come!" a sentry shouted.

The call from the north, or front, wall sent men scrambling for firing notches between the logs. Abel watched through his glasses as the first assault wave drew closer and closer. He shifted his glasses toward a distant knoll. A lone figure sat there on horseback, watching the drama unfold. "Enjoy yourself while it lasts, Long Walker," Abel said softly to the distant figure. "By dawn tomorrow one of us will have broken the other's medicine."

The first crack of rifle fire cut through the air. For the first time, Abel Hubbard was not among the riflemen. Now he was in the role of observer, armed with a Shoshone scout's report of the strength of Long Walker's forces and even a rough sketch of the layout of his village. It was showdown time in this poker game, with both sides feeling the pinch for ammunition and patience—and the defenders of Fort Kearny holding a couple of solid hole cards.

Abel smiled as scattered rifle fire sounded along the walls. If he were in Long Walker's moccasins, he would read the gunfire as a sign of growing weakness. A rifle ball from the Indians below sent a splinter of wood whirling past his cheek, and a Sioux arrow struck and quivered just below his post. The Indian charge appeared to break and fall back, leaving only a few scattered bodies behind.

Then, from the ridge before the fort, a seemingly endless line of warriors quirted painted war ponies toward the fort.

Long Walker had taken the bait. "Easy, men," Abel called. "Don't touch anything off too soon."

The howling mob of Indians was within fifty yards of the fort and closing fast when Abel shouted, "Now!" Even as he spoke, the heavy blast of a cannon shook the wall of the fort.

Whirling chains and bits of scrap metal slashed a bloody hole in the Indian ranks, downing warriors and ponies in screaming, squealing piles. A second muzzle blast shook the fort, then a third, and all the while marksmen on the wall selected individual targets with care. Abel was sickened at the carnage the scrap-loaded cannon left on the battlefield.

The confused and stunned Indians milled about for an instant; then a warrior in the rear of the ranks spun his mount and drove hard for the safety of the nearby ridge. His flight triggered a wild stampede; the Indians had had enough. In their wake, Long Walker's braves left what appeared to be at least a hundred dead, another fifty wounded. The pitiful screams of wounded ponies filled the air.

Veteran soldiers stared in shock at the devastation left by the cannon. Even Sergeant Kirk, at Abel's side, stood in silence for a long moment. "God, Colonel," the sergeant finally said, "I've never seen anything like that before."

Abel sighed heavily. "Neither have those Indians out there, Kirk. There should be some long arguments in Long Walker's lodge tonight. Bad medicine has hit this bunch hard. And tonight we make it even worse."

Slowly Abel climbed down the ladder from his observation deck. In the west, thunderheads towered high into the sky. Secretly Abel prayed for a heavy thunderstorm that would keep the Indians in their camp.

A pale-faced Lieutenant Kenley fell into step with Abel. "Sir, I—I never thought about using scrap for cannon fodder—" The young soldier shuddered at the havoc the chains and bits of iron had created.

"Lieutenant," Abel said firmly, "if you're going to be a soldier in this man's army, with no supply lines and quartermaster corps backing you up, you learn to make do with what's at hand. It isn't pretty, mind you, but, by God, it's effective."

Abel abruptly turned aside. The young lieutenant's education might leave his gut churning, all right, but it beat the daylights out of losing one's hair to some bear-greased and painted warrior. He stepped into a large shed, where a sweating private who had been a wheelwright in civilian life hammered a wooden peg into a strange-looking wheeled platform.

"About ready, Private?" Abel asked.

"Yes, sir—be ready to go in an hour."

Abel clapped the man's shoulder. "Private, you may have just invented a brand-new weapon for Indian fighting."

"Maybe so, Colonel. Who would have thought a swivel gun—a navy weapon—could be made into a howitzer?"

"A little one, at least," Abel said. "And when we charge this baby with horseshoe nails, it's going to be like a whole company of shotgunners cut loose on old Long Walker."

Abel walked back onto the parade ground, glancing at the sky. The storm clouds were building higher and turning an ominous green. Bolts of lightning danced between the clouds. "Looks good," Abel said to himself.

Next he located a short and slightly built soldier, who was busily oiling a saddle. He waved off the man's attempted salute.

"Private Peoples, you can still back out and no questions asked," Abel said. "I can find another volunteer, and this could be a short ride if you're unlucky."

Jim Peoples grinned up at Abel. "Colonel, I don't want to sound too cocky, but if any rider on this post can get through to Omaha, I can. Besides, it's only a couple hundred miles and probably not more than twenty, thirty Indians to the mile."

"Victoria—Mrs. Coulter—has offered you the use of her own horse. I've checked him over. He's well fed and in top condition, looks like he has plenty of speed and a lot of bottom. It's the blood bay in the end stall."

"At least if I don't make it, the horse's color is right," Peoples said with a wry smile. He finished rubbing down the lightweight saddle and dropped a stirrup to the floor. "Don't worry, Colonel. I'll get us some reinforcements, if I have to bring them back at gunpoint."

Abel offered his hand. The wiry little private's grip was calloused and strong. "If you do, Private, you'll be a legend on the Plains. If you don't, we're all likely to be dead in a few days. Take one of the Henry rifles and twenty extra rounds of ammunition—and a slicker. Looks like a storm blowing in. You know when to leave?"

Peoples turned to packing a few lightweight items in a slim saddlebag. "Yes, sir. And, Colonel, give my regards to those Indians out there tonight."

"We'll try, Private. We'll try."

The storm broke at sunset, hurrying the dark. A dozen men, led by Lieutenant Colonel Abel Hubbard, surrounded the awkward-looking carriage bearing the little swivel gun and slipped through the front gates of Fort Kearny. Each of the riders carried a repeating rifle and a pair of handguns beneath his poncho. Their horses' hooves had been wrapped with rags, even those of the draft animal pulling the makeshift cannon carriage. All bits of metal had been wrapped or removed for silence.

Turning his face from the driving rain, Abel briefly thought of Victoria, then turned his attention to negotiating the tortured trail they must follow to come up behind a specific lodge in the Indian camp beyond the ridge. Uncomfortable though it was, the rain would drive Long Walker's sentries to cover. Abel's primary concern was the lightning; if one of those bolts happened to strike the carriage and the swivel gun, the horseshoe nails intended for an Indian village would wind up in the flesh of a small band of horsemen instead.

Long Walker's lodge was jammed with war chiefs and senior warriors, all arguing in loud voices.

"Silence!" Long Walker shouted.

For a moment the only sound in the lodge was the deep roll of thunder and the drumbeat of raindrops on the buffalo hide covering the shelter.

"Bear Killer!" Long Walker jabbed a finger at the scarred torso of the Sioux warrior. "What is this talk of bad medicine, of white man's magic?"

Bear Killer glowered at the blue-eyed Indian. He had no fear of Long Walker—especially not now. "Bear Killer speaks for his band when he says that Long Walker's medicine is bad. Long Walker said we could take the fort with ease. Instead, we lose many men. Then the soldiers come and break through our lines. The fort sprouts cannon by magic, and many warriors lie dead. The soldier chief who harried our people through the deep snows is in that fort now. Bear Killer saw him during the charge when the big guns bellowed. His medicine is strong. Bear Killer's warriors leave this place of death, to fight no more for a pile of logs. We return to the old ways of war."

A babble of voices rose in support of Bear Killer's stand. Long Walker fought a growing sense of failure. He knew he must do something, and quickly, or the alliance he had so carefully forged with the finest warriors of the Plains would shatter.

Bear Killer pulled the flap aside, preparing to step from the tent, when a lightning bolt shattered the darkness. Only a few yards away there were figures crouched behind a strange machine.

"Soldiers!" Bear Killer cried.

At that instant another flash split the night, another boom sounded—but this was not of nature's doing.

The horseshoe nails from Abel's swivel gun blast ripped through Long Walker's lodge. Bear Killer tumbled backward, riddled by a dozen small holes. Other warriors cried out and fell to the floor. Long Walker felt a streak of fire across his own belly as he dived for cover behind a dead warrior. In the light of what had been a council fire, Long Walker looked down in disbelief. A tiny puncture wound dribbled blood onto his breechclout. His left arm would not move, the flesh having been torn in several places. Once more he heard the boom of the small cannon. The walls of the lodge suddenly shredded as if the claws of a great mountain cat were pulling at them. Fear gripping his heart, Long Walker tugged at the bottom of the lodge skins and wormed his way through the opening. As rapidly as he could, he dragged his wounded body through the mud toward the safety of a small, water-filled pit.

Just before the pain sent him into unconsciousness, Long Walker saw the little cannon roar, spouting flame and iron through a body of warriors who had dashed forward to see what had happened. They fell like straw before the wind. Then the blackness came, and Long Walker's face dropped onto the mud of the edge of the pit.

At Abel's call the cavalrymen abandoned the swivel gun, its work done, and spurred through the main encampment, rifles and pistols spitting fire and death. Then they were in the clear, pounding through the mud toward the fort. Abel turned in the saddle and grinned. Once more he had been lucky; not a soldier had fallen.

The following day dawned clear and bright, sparkles of light rippling over the surface of water holes freshened by the storm. And brightest of all to Abel Hubbard's eye was what he did not see. There were no columns of smoke rising from behind the ridge, from Long Walker's camp. Through his field glasses he could see a thin, dark line snaking through the rolling hills to the north. The Indians were retreating, the siege of Fort Kearny broken.

Abel felt no sense of elation, only the heavy weight of many lives lost. Yet he knew he had done his best, and a temporary reprieve had been won.

A solitary figure suddenly appeared on the ridge crest. Abel swung his field glass in that direction. An Indian, seemingly slumped in pain, pulled his pony to a halt and stared at Fort Kearny for a long moment. Then, straightening in the saddle, the figure raised a hand gripping the receiver of a rifle high overhead and shook the weapon toward the fort.

Abel realized Long Walker was sending a message: He would defy the white man in the face of defeat. Perhaps he would even return. But Abel knew Long Walker's medicine had been badly bent, maybe even broken, and many moons would pass before the blue-eyed Indian could raise another army.

On impulse, Abel stepped to the top rung of the observation post ladder. Sure that the Indian on horseback could see him as well, he raised his own rifle and shook it toward Long Walker. The challenge, he knew, would not go unnoticed. Someday, if the fates willed, they would meet again.

He watched in silence as Long Walker kneed his pony from the crest of the ridge and faded from sight.

Word of Long Walker's defeat at Fort Kearny spread like wildfire among the Indian tribes. It was, they said, an omen, like sighting an owl before battle.

The news reached Ted within an hour after he arrived at Yellow Crow's lodge on the banks of the Niobrara River. Ted glanced at his Cheyenne blood brother as the runner spread the word.

When they were alone again, Yellow Crow nodded to Ted. "It is coming, my brother," the Cheyenne said solemnly. He struggled to his feet, still heavily bandaged and obviously weak from the wounds suffered at the hands of Emery Church in the attack on Black Kettle's village. "Now we must use all our powers of persuasion in our search for peace."

Ted got to his feet, alarmed. "Yellow Crow, you aren't well enough yet to travel. The effort could kill you."

Yellow Crow's eyes were calm, his words serene. "What better cause to die for than peace, if the spirits so decide?"

Yellow Crow limped to Ted, grasped his forearm in the Cheyenne symbol of friendship, and looked deep into his blood brother's eyes. "This war is not yet at an end," he said softly. "Many chiefs will fight on until more white soldiers come. Some will fight in the mistaken belief they will win. Others, like Sitting Bull of the Sioux and Big Nose of the Cheyenne, will fight to establish and hold hunting grounds, to retain a position of strength from which to bargain."

Yellow Crow glanced up as Talking Bird entered the lodge, a brimming water pot cradled in a slender arm. She moved to Yellow Crow, kissed him on the lips, then turned to wink at Ted. "Not all the white man's customs are bad," she said with a smile.

Ted could not resist a brief grin.

"It is our fate, Ted Henderson, to be caught between two worlds. The spirits have willed that it be so," Yellow Crow continued. "We understand the wishes of both sides. Thus we are able to serve as spokesmen for both red and white, to search for the proper words of an agreement fair to both. Once more we ride together on the hunt, for the largest and most prized game of all."

The Cheyenne warrior turned at the sound of rustlings at the side of the lodge. Talking Bird already was putting items into traveling pouches and bundles. She glanced up at Yellow Crow. "Where you go, Talking Bird goes," she said. "When first we met, Talking Bird was but a captive. Now she is a wife. In spirit we are one. The white man has a word for this," she said, a note of finality in her voice. "The word is love."

Ted smiled at Yellow Crow. "It seems," he told the Cheyenne, "that your woman has adopted other ideas from the whites—like, how to handle a husband."

Victoria Coulter's deep green eyes were soft as she looked across the small table. In the last few days, with Long Walker's defeat, Abel's military operations had been limited to brief patrols. He was beginning to feel a bit rested after the grueling winter ordeal. Dinner with the attractive widow had become a daily event, and that day they were having lunch together as well.

"Abel," Victoria said after the meal, "it is time I said something I think, perhaps, we've both been avoiding. You may be bad medicine as an Indian fighter, but I sense a great gentleness in you, and . . . and more."

She stood and walked to the fireplace, her back to her guest. "I am going to be rather bold, perhaps even forward, Colonel Hubbard," she said. "I have seen the way you sometimes look at me—"

"Victoria," Abel interrupted quickly, "the last thing I want to do is hurt you. It's true that I am very aware you are a woman. Any healthy man in his right mind could not escape that fact. But it would be unfair—to both of us, and to another—for us to go any further, to be more than friends."

When she turned, he saw the pain in her eyes and wished desperately he could somehow soothe it. "You see, Victoria," he said, "you are a wonderful woman—but the wrong woman—for me. I've just realized something I've tried to deny for many months. I still love my wife. Can you understand, Victoria, that in my mind it would not be you but Judy? Despite all she has done, I would do anything to win her back."

A single tear sparkled in the corner of each green eye before him. Then Victoria walked to him and kissed him lightly.

"I suspected that all along, Abel," she said, leaning against him for a moment. "But I had to know—and to make you admit it aloud, for your benefit as well as my own. And Judy's. You're a good man, Abel. I hope someday to find one like you for myself."

"Thank you, Victoria," Abel said. "I hope you find what you want in life." He started for the door, then paused, his hand on the knob, and turned to her. He was surprised to see a gentle smile lifting the corners of her full lips.

"I'm pleased that you finally came to your senses," Victoria said.

"I owe you more than can ever be repaid," Abel said softly as he closed the door and began to walk across the Fort Kearny parade ground.

"Company coming, Colonel!" a lookout called from his post in the watchtower.

"Can you make out who it is?" Abel asked.

"No, sir!" the lookout replied. "Just a big dust cloud. If it's Indians, we're in big trouble."

Abel scrambled up the ladder as soldiers scurried into position for a possible attack. They waited with growing tension as the dust cloud neared the crest of the slope to the east. Then a line of riders, three abreast, came into view—and at the front of the column, a red, white, and blue flag fluttered in the wind.

"Soldiers!" Abel called. "We have help, men!"

The announcement triggered whoops of celebration and relief, and a pair of burly troopers heaved the heavy fort gates open. Through his glasses Abel could make out the small figure on the blood bay riding at the flag bearer's side. Young Jim Peoples had somehow made it through two hundred miles of hostile Indians—a ride Abel was sure would become an instant legend on the Plains.

An hour later, Abel and Colonel Maxwell Marshall sat and compared notes on the planned campaign against the Indians. Marshall's regiment was but the vanguard of a massive army that even now would be moving out down the Overland Trail with orders to clear the route all the way to Laramie. The troops were equipped witht repeating rifles or metallic cartridge breechloaders and backed by an enormous supply effort and an impressive number of cannon.

From Marshall, Abel heard for the first time of the massacre at the South Platte. Now he understood the suddenness and violence of the Indian outbreak. He also learned that a newsman named Taylor Elkins had filed a complete story from Laramie, an accurate description of the massacre of peaceful Indians. The story had received prominent and outraged play in the Eastern press and had, in fact, set in motion the drive to field an army on the Plains. In addition, a peace commmision was now forming in Kansas City, empowered to hammer out a peace treaty with the warring tribes.

"We will be spearheading the drive toward Laramie," Marshall said. "Would you be interested in tagging along, Abel? I could use an experienced Indian fighter's help and advice."

Abel sighed. "I wouldn't miss it, Colonel. For the first time in months, I have a chance to make it home."

Both commanding officers were Victoria Coulter's guests for dinner that night. Abel, at first a bit uncomfortable, gradually regained his self-composure in Victoria's presence. The meal turned more to news from the East than to the worn topic of Indian campaigns, and Abel saw the delight in Victoria's eyes as Colonel Marshall described at length new fashions, new books, and new plays in Washington, Baltimore, and New York.

After voicing their appreciation for the meal, the officers rose to take their leave. Abel held back for a moment.

"Victoria," he said, "before much longer the way will be clear for safe travel. Will I be seeing you again?"

She nodded. "Yes, Abel. I've decided to continue on to Fort Laramie and perhaps beyond. I've grown to love the West. I think I'll stay. Perhaps here I can find the thing that has been missing from my life."

Mile by mile and step by step, the fresh army troops led by Marshall and Hubbard wrested control of the Overland Trail from the Indians. It was not an easy task, and both sides suffered heavy casualties. But the pressure of the unending wave of blue proved too great for the Indians.

It was not a pitched battle that eventually ended the conflict, but an almost insignificant encounter a few miles north and east of Chimney Rock in the Wyoming Territory. There, a handful of soldiers equipped with repeating rifles dealt a bloody blow to a band of elite Sioux Crazy Dogs.

Watching from a nearby hill as brave after brave fell before the repeating rifles of the troops, Sitting Bull sighed in despair. The day he knew would eventually come had dawned.

He turned to the subchief at his side. "It is time," Sitting Bull said, "to talk of peace. Break off the attack."

A lean, solitary man in buckskins rode toward the long line of soldiers. Abel Hubbard recognized the rider immediately and slammed spurs to his mount. When they reached each other, they dismounted. Abel saw his own relief and joy reflected in Ted Henderson's eyes as they embraced. After a few moments in which each recapped his adventures for the other, Ted suddenly raised a hand.

"Abel, I've been looking for you for a week, ever since I heard rumors among the Indians that you were in the area. There's something I must tell you, something about Judy. . . ."

Ted spelled out in detail Judy's role in discovering the plot against his son and in the rescue that followed.

At the end of his friend's monologue, Abel stood stunned for a long time. Then life began to sparkle once more in his eyes. "You mean—?"

Ted nodded. "She was never unfaithful to you, Abel. She was faithful also to a cause and to her friends, and my son is alive today because of her."

"My God! And—after what I put her through—how could I have doubted her?" Abel's shoulders slumped. "Is there any chance I can win her back?"

Ted smiled as he swung back into the saddle. "You never lost her, Abel. Just misplaced her for a spell. She's waiting for you in Laramie, worried almost to the sickbed that you won't return."

He leaned down and clapped Abel on the shoulder. "Keep your hair on until you make it back to Laramie. You've got a lot to live for now."

Abel watched his friend ride back toward the north, knowing full well why the diminishing figure seemed blurred.

Abel Hubbard was crying, and he didn't give a damn who knew it.

Laramie sat poised on the edge of yet another celebration. The first had come with the appearance of the column of soldiers led by Colonels Marshall and Hubbard. Its focal point had been the long and tender kiss between Abel and Judy, who were oblivious to the swirl of soldiers and elated pedestrians in the center of the parade ground. The second, smaller celebration followed a brief and simple wedding ceremony as Vi Robinson became Mrs. Taylor Elkins, much to the confusion of a young ring bearer named William Ted Henderson and the delight of the flower girl, Ellen Keller. Judy Hubbard, her eyes dancing with joy, stood with her stepmother as the vows were exchanged.

Now, in a big tent just south of the settlement itself, the final stages of a historic moment were unfolding. The peace commissioners had listened with sincere faces as Ted Henderson outlined the requests of the Indians, followed by impassioned speeches from Yellow Crow, Big Nose, and other leaders of the Indian nations.

At last terms were agreed upon: The Indian tribes each were to be granted a substantial region as an inviolate reservation, with hunting rights to huge sections of the Great Plains "as long as the buffalo graze"; the hated Bozeman Trail would be officially declared closed to civilian traffic; and the United States government would supply such food, clothing, medicine, and other essentials required by the tribes.

The peace commissioners signed the document. Then one by one, the Indian chiefs approached the table and made their mark upon the paper—except for one.

"Sitting Bull will not sign," the broad-chested Sioux declared. "My people will abide by the terms of the treaty as long as the white man does the same. But Sitting Bull's mark will not appear on the paper."

One of the peace commissioners glanced at Ted, and at his nod said, "Sitting Bull's word is sufficient. I hereby declare this document to be in effect."

The chiefs began to leave the tent, carrying word of the agreement back to their respective bands. Ted and Yellow Crow were among the last to leave, heading toward Fort Laramie where the first sounds of the wild celebration already were rising. The two shouldered their way through cheering throngs of civilians and soldiers, the crackle of gunshots fired skyward an almost constant roar.

In the relative quiet of the Henderson's home, Wilma and Talking Bird were engrossed in conversation when Ted and Yellow Crow entered.

Wilma immediately rose and embraced Yellow Crow, who stood with his free hand resting lightly on Little Bill's shoulder. "Your wife is a fascinating and gentle person, Yellow Crow," Wilma said. "I congratulate you. May the future bring you many children of good health."

Yellow Crow winked at Ted. "Good thing Talking Bird work out to be good squaw. Now Wilma safe from savage Cheyenne. One good woman enough for Yellow Crow."

A knock on the door interrupted everyone's laugh. Ted swung the door open and found himself staring at the throat of a huge form that almost blocked out the light.

"May we come in?" Kevin O'Reilly asked.

Ted's hand disappeared in Kevin's hamlike fist. "Around here, Kevin, you need never ask."

The big Irishman stepped over the threshold, followed by the shy Wind Flower. Ted took her hands and smiled at her. "You get more beautiful by the day, Wind Flower," he said.

Kevin's laugh was hearty. "Many women look best when they're expecting," he said, grinning broadly. "There'll be another O'Reilly on the ground by first grass."

Ted added his own voice to the babble of congratulations, then waited until the women had settled down to their own conversations.

"What brings you to town, Kevin?" Ted finally asked.

"Came in for supplies, along with our neighbors, Dot and Earl Newkirk. Thanks to Wind Flower, they're now among our best friends." Kevin briefly told about Wind Flower rescuing the young girl from the mountain lion, which had broken the ice and allowed a strong friendship to bloom.

Ted shook his head in amazement. "That woman never ceases to amaze me, Kevin."

"Also," Kevin said, "I came to pay you. We made a profit this year." Grinning, O'Reilly dropped a double eagle gold piece into Ted's palm. "Maybe it's not much," he said, "but it's a start." O'Reilly turned solemn. "Ted, since you've left the army, you'll be wanting something to do. The ranch is yours, you know."

Ted shook his head emphatically. "Our agreement was for a minimum of three years, and it stands," he said. "Besides, why should I break my back trying to run a ranch when I've got a big, stout Irish friend to do it for me? Don't worry, Kevin. We're not exactly poor, and I'm ready for a rest. A short one, anyway. I have a son who needs more attention than I've given him of late."

Outside, a band started tuning up. "Looks like we're in for a street dance," Ted said, looking out a window. "At least the new supply of soldiers has some musicians with more talent than the Third." At the edge of the street, he saw Abel and Judy Hubbard standing arm in arm alongside a strikingly attractive auburn-haired woman, who seemed to be getting a lot of attention from Major David Wills.

The band struck up a lively tune. Abel and Judy were among the first to move into the street, closely followed by Wills and Victoria Coulter.

"Good luck, David," Ted said to himself. "Looks like a fine catch from here." The hard-packed street soon filled with dancers. Ted caught a quick glimpse of Albert Jonas, whirling Sally in a gentle embrace. Idly Ted wondered what the big sergeant major would do when his extended enlistment ran out and he was fully recovered.

A touch on his arm pulled his attention from the street dance.

"We go now," Yellow Crow said. Wilma started to protest, but the Cheyenne raised a hand. "Yellow Crow's place is with his people," he said. "A peace chief is not as free to roam as he was as a warrior."

A few minutes later, Ted and his son stood beside Yellow Crow as the Indian tugged the cinch tight on the palomino and then boosted his wife aboard her own pony.

Yellow Crow turned to face Ted, his expression solemn. "I do not know, brother, how long this peace will last. In my blankets this morning, the dream of the crow and the red-and-white grains came once more. And again the bird was uncertain." Yellow Crow tapped the pocket of his buckskin shirt. "The Dream Woman was confused about the crow and the corn. She thought perhaps the corn kernel that is both red and white represents neither of us. Perhaps it is the symbol of the white Indian Long Walker. I still carry the bullet intended for his heart. It could be the bird in the dream was pointing this out to Yellow Crow."

The Cheyenne reached out, grasped Ted's forearm, then repeated the gesture with William Ted. "When the leaves turn, godson," he said, "your father and his blood brother the Cheyenne will take you into the high country. It is time you learned the ways of the hunt."

Yellow Crow suddenly turned away, mounted his palomino, and, with Talking Bird alongside on her pony, headed toward the Cheyenne encampment nearby.

After a hundred yards or so, Yellow Crow twisted in the saddle and raised an arm in salute. Feeling the sadness of separation once more in his heart, Ted returned the gesture. He and his son stood quietly until the two riders had passed from view.

"You will miss him, Daddy?" Little Bill asked.

"Yes, son," Ted replied, and sighed. "I will miss him a great deal."

"But there is peace now. We can go visit sometime."

Ted nodded. "Yes, son. There is peace now." He stared toward the east, seeing in his mind's eye two shining rails piercing the Plains—the beginning of the railroad to the west. Yes, he thought, there was peace for the moment. A costly peace, measured in more than bleeding bodies. He could only wish his own spirit were at peace. But a slice of his heart rode with the Cheyenne, an ache for a way of life lost now, *lost forever*. The wall between himself and the red man had grown still higher, many of the bricks placed there by his own hand.

"Come, son," he said quietly. "Your mother is waiting."